# THE BUCCANEERS

EDITH WHARTON

---

# THE BUCCANEERS

Edith Wharton died before her manuscript for
*The Buccaneers* was completed. Books IV and V of this
edition are written by **Angela Mackworth-Young**,
based on the screenplays for the television
serialization of *The Buccaneers*
written by **Maggie Wadey**.

VIKING

VIKING
Published by the Penguin Group
Penguin Books USA Inc., 375 Hudson Street,
New York, New York 10014, U.S.A.
Penguin Books Ltd, 27 Wrights Lane,
London W8 5TZ, England
Penguin Books Australia Ltd, Ringwood,
Victoria, Australia
Penguin Books Canada Ltd, 10 Alcorn Avenue,
Toronto, Ontario, Canada M4V 3B2
Penguin Books (N.Z.) Ltd, 182–190 Wairau Road,
Auckland 10, New Zealand

Penguin Books Ltd, Registered Offices:
Harmondsworth, Middlesex, England

This edition published in the United States of America
in 1995 by Viking Penguin, a division of Penguin Books USA Inc.
Originally published in Great Britain by Penguin Books/BBC Books.

1 3 5 7 9 10 8 6 4 2

ISBN 0-670-86645-8

This book is printed on acid-free paper.

Printed in the United States of America

# CONTENTS

# INTRODUCTION

In most of her novels and short stories Edith Wharton wrote about the way the rich and leisured classes lived, in both Europe and America, at the turn of the nineteenth century and beyond. Although her novellas, for instance *Ethan Frome* and *Summer*, are set in small, impoverished New England communities, her prevailing concern throughout her long writing career was with those privileged by wealth or by birth, those struggling to join them at the top of the ladder and those who lose their footing and fall from social grace.

It is, therefore, quite surprising that the only novel she set amongst the aristocracy of England is her last and incomplete *The Buccaneers*. Here Wharton writes about the socially ambitious, not the socially secure. She puts those who are issuing a challenge to the establishment, her brash American girls, at the heart of the story. Distinguished neither by birth nor breeding, these adventurous young ladies – or 'buccaneers' – take England's aristocracy by storm and capture the most eligible men of the age in marriage.

Edith Wharton knew a good deal about life in the upper classes of both America and Europe. Edith

Newbold Jones was born in 1862 into one of the 'first' families of New York. Her mother, Lucretia Jones, was reputed to be the best-dressed woman in New York and her father, like other men of his background, had no occupation other than that of 'gentleman'. They were in the social group known as the 'Four Hundred' – the number that would fit comfortably into the ballroom belonging to the Astors, the famous banking family. They divided their time, when in the United States, between New York and Newport, Rhode Island, the holiday resort of the rich.

The Jones family often travelled abroad and in the period following the American civil war, like many affluent Americans, they felt that they could live more luxuriously in Europe than at home. As a result Wharton spent five or six of her childhood years travelling throughout France, Italy, Germany and Spain. This was the beginning of a wanderlust that never faded. Edith Wharton was equally at home in Europe as in America and settled permanently in France from 1907 until her death in 1937. She also travelled frequently to England and Italy where she had many friends.

After their European expeditions of the 1860s the Jones family returned to live in America and Wharton's important teenage years were spent in her native land. She was educated at home by governesses and was allowed to roam freely in her father's library as long as she never read a novel without her mother's permission. It was in New York that Edith made her own début into society and met and married her husband, Edward (Teddy) Wharton, a Bostonian who was a friend of Edith's brother, Harry. The courtship of Edith Jones by the much older

Teddy was conducted at some speed, Edith being considered by her mother and society at large to be almost beyond the age at which girls could still marry without seeming desperate. Edith Jones apparently had a reputation as a bluestocking and her dangerous interest in reading and even in writing was held responsible for the absence of suitors for her hand. Just as for the American girls in *The Buccaneers*, marriage was the only occupation then considered suitable for a woman. Whilst men had the chance to change their minds about their profession, the majority of the women Edith Wharton wrote about would have to risk all – reputation, social position, security – in order to change their minds about their commitment to their husbands. Nan St George, Edith's heroine in *The Buccaneers*, is a good example of a girl whose life has been blighted by an immature and ill-considered acceptance of an offer of marriage.

Edith Wharton's own marriage was a failure and ended in divorce in 1913. Although Teddy Wharton was amiable enough and shared some of his wife's interests, in dogs and travel, for instance, he never felt at home with Edith's aspirations as a writer nor with her literary friends. She and Teddy were incompatible physically as well as intellectually and the marriage caused both of them a good deal of pain and suffering. Wharton's biographer, R.W.B. Lewis, tells how she locked Teddy out of her bedroom for the first three weeks of their marriage, chiefly because of her ignorance of what was expected of her. This fear of the unknown, and in particular what might happen to her on her wedding night, drove the young Edith to approach her mother, reputedly an extremely cold and formal woman, for information. In her unpub-

lished memoirs, *Life and I*, probably written around
1922, Wharton describes her mother's response and
the effect that it had upon her afterwards:

. . . a few days before my marriage, I was seized
with such a dread of the whole dark mystery, that I
summoned up courage to approach my mother, and
begged her with a heart beating to suffocation, to tell
me 'what being married was like'. Her handsome face
at once took on the look of icy disapproval which I
most dreaded. 'I never heard such a ridiculous question!' she said impatiently; and I felt at once how vulgar she thought me. But in the extremity of my need I
persisted. 'I'm afraid, Mamma – I want to know what
will happen to me!' The coldness of her expression
deepened to disgust. She was silent for a dreadful
moment, then with an effort, and the expression of a
person whose nose is assailed by a disagreeable smell,
she said with an effort: 'You've seen enough pictures
and statues in your life. Haven't you noticed that men
are – made differently from women?'

'Yes,' I faltered blankly.

'Well, then –?'

I was silent, from sheer inability to follow, and she
brought out sharply: 'Then for heaven's sake don't ask
me any more silly questions. You can't be as stupid as
you pretend!'

The dreadful moment was over, and the only result
was that I had been convicted of stupidity for not
knowing what I had been expressly forbidden to ask
about or even to think of! . . . I record this brief conversation, because the training of which it was the
beautiful and logical conclusion did more than anything to falsify and misdirect my whole life.'

This lengthy extract from *Life and I*, whilst illustrating some of the difficulties in the relationship which existed between mother and daughter, also demonstrates the close links between the experience of Edith Wharton and the story of Nan St George. The disastrous outcome of the marriage of Edith and Teddy Wharton was partly the result of the awful ignorance in which the young girl of the nineteenth century was kept. Maggie Wadey, who wrote the screenplay for *The Buccaneers*, makes explicit Nan's lack of understanding of the sexual side of marriage. In doing so, she is true to the spirit of the age which deemed that a young girl must be kept in ignorance of the nature of physical relations between men and women. Nan is seen to be only faintly confused by the difference between what her sister told her would be her uncomfortable fate on her honeymoon and what actually happens, Virginia's innuendo being her only source of information. In the case of Nan, her ignorance is prolonged because the Duke, uneasy with the physical side of marriage himself, is happy to take advantage of her naïvety in order to keep his distance. Thus, in her unnatural innocence, Nan becomes isolated from her friends as well as from her husband.

Nan St George is portrayed as no more wordly-wise than Edith Wharton herself and the language and images of imprisonment and suffocation which Wharton uses in *Life and I* and elsewhere to describe her own feelings of loneliness and confusion are also characteristic of her depiction of Nan St George. Although Edith Wharton did not live to complete *The Buccaneers* she did leave a plan of how the novel was to end and the projected scenario is unique in her fiction in terms of the ultimate fulfilment of the central character in a relationship of both intellectual and emotional understanding. The relationship which Wharton herself never had and which she constantly denied to her characters is consummated finally between Nan and Guy Thwarte. This is in spite of the social rules and taboos which they must break in the process of achieving their perfect love. As already mentioned, Wharton's own marriage was a disaster; she and her husband had an extremely negative effect on each other's mental and physical health and as their marriage went on they could find no common ground on which to base their relationship.

When she was twenty-one Edith had met a young man called Walter Berry who might have provided her with the kind of complete love she craved, but he went away and she did not see him again until she was in her mid-thirties which was when their friendship really flourished. He was the man with whom she could imagine 'having it all'; as she says in her autobiography, A Backward Glance, published in 1934. Meeting him had given her 'a fleeting hint of what the communion of kindred intelligences might be'. Berry, unfortunately for Wharton, had a taste for the frivolous in his women, he preferred the female company he met in the Ritz to those he could meet in Edith's drawing-room and despite constant rumours during their lifetime that they were lovers it seems unlikely that their relationship ever took this turn.

Wharton paid moving tribute to Berry after his death in her autobiography: 'I cannot picture what the life of the spirit would have been to me without him. He found me when my mind and soul were hungry and thirsty, and he fed them till our last hour together. It is such comradeships, made of seeing and dreaming, and thinking and laughing together, that make one feel that for those who have shared them there can be no parting'. The neediness which Wharton makes so important a part of the character of Nan St George, her expressed desire to penetrate to 'events or emotions below the surface of life', is a good indication of Wharton's deep affection for her creation as it comes very close to her own, often stated, need to make sense of the relationship between the internal and external worlds of her own life. The perfect understanding which springs up between Nan and Guy when they first meet is articulated as their mutual sense of a truth deeper than language, of a shared intuitiveness which goes beyond words into the realm of the spirit. In allowing Nan St George to elope with Guy Thwarte, Wharton endows her last heroine with the chance to love and live with the same man. In her other novels Wharton denies her heroines the chance to fulfil themselves in marriage. Ellen Olenska will never live with Newland Archer in *The Age of Innocence*, he will adhere to his duty and stay with his wife. Lily Bart dies of an overdose on the very day that Lawrence Selden has made up his mind that their love is more important than society's approval or a large bank balance in *The House of Mirth*. Ethan Frome and Mattie Silver are terribly maimed, sentenced to a life of pain and torment instead of the shared beautiful death they promised each other as the only way to be together in Wharton's bleak novella *Ethan Frome*. Justine Brent in *The Fruit of the Tree* is ultimately disappointed in the ability of her husband to transcend the prejudices of his age towards the role of women in either domestic or professional life. The list of the failed and the disillusioned is as long as the list of Wharton's novels and stories.

It is tempting to look upon the 'happy ending' for Nan St George and Guy Thwarte as the product of the writer's benign old age, but, of course, alongside Nan's happiness is the destruction of Laura Testvalley's hopes for a real relationship based on interests and intellect as well as attraction. At the end the woman who most closely approximates to Wharton herself in her role as cross-cultural mediator, is left alone. It is Laura Testvalley who introduces the Americans to Europe, who arbitrates their passage into society and who rescues her dearest pupil, Nan, from the misery and confinement of an unhappy marriage. But she remains, at the last, an outsider, doomed to be an observer of other people's happiness.

Edith Wharton did not live entirely without experience and understanding of what it was like to feel sexual attraction and desire and to have those feelings reciprocated and gratified. When she was in her mid-forties she had an affair, which lasted for about three years, with an American journalist based in Paris called Morton Fullerton. Fullerton was utterly charming, clever, handsome and very experienced as a lover. She marked the period of their relationship with all kinds of written tributes to the sexual and emotional awakening which her involvement with him provided. She kept a diary of the affair entitled *L'Ame Close* or *The Life Apart* in which she described both what they did together and her feelings. The all-consuming nature of the passion she felt for her lover is communicated very powerfully in the diary and it forms a vivid testament to her awareness of how exceptional and fragile each emotion was in her life and yet how ordinary it was in the lives of others: '. . . at the theatre, when you came into the box – that little, dim beignore (No 13, I shall always remember!) – I felt for the first time that indescribable current of communication flowing between myself and some one else – felt it, I mean, uninterruptedly, securely, so that it penetrated every sense and every thought . . . and said to myself: "This must be what happy women feel."'

Unfortunately for Wharton the relationship did not endure and although it seems to have been the case that Fullerton managed to remain on good terms with his ex-lovers Wharton was under no illusions as to the adequacy of a relationship that remained outside the accepted social mores. Despite having had this affair and being forced, when his mental illness became finally unendurable for her, to divorce her husband, Wharton was a deeply conventional person who believed in romantic love and in the institution of marriage. She is recorded as having said to her friend, Charles du Bos: 'Ah, the poverty, the miserable poverty, of any love that lies outside of marriage, of any love that is not a living together, a sharing of all.' The tragedy for Wharton, as for Laura Testvalley in *The Buccaneers*, is that she never met the man who was and could remain equal to the power of her imagination, who was adequate to all her parts, to all her talents.

Edith Wharton made an enormous amount of money from her writing, her books were bestsellers and in the 1920s they were sometimes made into films soon after publication, the film rights generating even more money. Her income and her expenditure were always equal, however, and she used what she earned to support her chosen lifestyle. After the First World War, which she spent in Paris, working for the relief of refugees and those made homeless and destitute by the conflict, she moved out of Paris to a village north of the city, St Brice-sous-Fôret, where she bought a large house called the Pavillon Colombe. She also leased a château in the Riviera town of Hyères, the Château Ste Claire, as her winter residence and divided the majority of her time between these two houses, maintaining quite a large staff and usually entertaining a number of guests. Wharton always wrote in the mornings, in bed, surfacing at lunch-time to fulfil domestic responsibilities – gardening was her passion – and to be with her guests. *The Age of Innocence*, published in 1920, was one of the first fruits of this settled life in France, and this novel was followed by a series of novellas entitled *Old New York* (1924) which, like *The Age of Innocence*, was concerned with recreating the society of her youth, 'the tight little citadel of New York' as she called it.

Wharton was drawn to the historical novel at particular points in her life for very specific reasons. Whilst all her fiction is concerned with the effects of change – for the individual as well as for society in general – her historical novels mark periods during which Edith Wharton wanted to lay hold of the past and demonstrate not only its difference but also its relationship to the present. *The Buccaneers* is no exception to this. Only in this her last, unfinished novel, she writes from the outside looking in rather than as an insider. Her heroines are intruders in their own country, refused access to the social circle to which they or their parents aspire, and also intruders in England, the country to which their ambition leads them. Like Laura Testvalley, the 'little brown governess' who initiates the girls' invasion of England, in this story Wharton throws in her lot with the outsiders. Edith Wharton spent most of her life away from her native land. Laura is also an exile and understands all too well both the exciting and the destructive effects of expatriation, effects which, in the novel, are played out through the emotional heights and depths of Nan St George's journey from girl to womanhood.

Edith Wharton was by no means a reactionary but she was a conservative person and subscribed, in general, to the majority of the social conventions of her day. This is not to say that she did not question those conventions or portray those whose lives were distorted or even ruined by adherence to a particular code of conduct: as a novelist of manners she naturally found her subject in the conflict between the individual and the social world she or he inhabits. Wharton's own friends tended to be, like herself, affluent and involved in the arts whether as creators or as patrons; their households were variously organized to accommodate their chosen lifestyles and a substantial number of the men with whom she formed long and lasting friendships were homosexual. Morton Fullerton, the man with whom she had an affair, was bi-sexual and had had a number of affairs with men as well as women.

Although Wharton would not have expected her publishers to have accepted descriptions of explicit sexual encounters between men and women or between partners of the same sex, even if she wanted to write them, she did not shy away from the controversial in her work. Her novel of 1927, *Twilight Sleep*, for instance, touches upon issues as controversial as incest, sexual exploitation of the young by the promoters of alternative religions, and murder. A fragment of a story or of the idea behind a story called 'Beatrice Palmato' was found among Wharton's papers when they were opened in the late 1960s. Like many of the other oddments of stories or novels in the Wharton archives at Yale University this piece is unfinished and although the narrative is planned in detail only one section of the story is fully written. This piece, called by Wharton the 'unpublishable fragment', concerns a sexual encounter involving oral and penetrative sex, which is conducted between a father and daughter. Whilst incest is at the heart of the tragedy plotted for the story it is never mentioned directly in the scenario, it is, if you like, the mystery at the heart of the tale which readers would have had to find for themselves. The description of the sexual encounter would most certainly never have found its way into the finished text. It was written to remain unpublished, its place is outside or even beneath the story that would have been presented to the reading public. The 'Beatrice Palmato' fragment is evidence of an extraordinary imagination; it is explicit and controversial in itself but perhaps the most interesting thing about it is that Wharton left it amongst her literary papers for future biographers or critics to find. She wanted us to know that she had insights into the variousness of sexual energy and the toils into which sexual attraction or dissatisfaction can lead people.

Maggie Wadey, the dramatist of *The Buccaneers*, has taken the hints, the clues and details in Wharton's portrait of the young Duke of Tintagel and she has given him an explicit sexuality as a homosexual. This does two things for the audience of *The Buccaneers*: it makes Ushant's fears and reticence more understandable and also translates them into dramatic action or plot. Wadey has given Ushant, or Julius as he is called in the televized version, a definite sexuality and in so doing modernizes the story of the marriage of the Duke and Duchess. Wharton's sketchy characterization of the young Duke of Tintagel is probably one of the things that she would have worked on had she lived to revise the whole book. As it stands, the dominant note of her portrayal of Ushant is his dullness and his mild terror of the outside world and its gaze. Wharton describes him as being frightened of women, especially pretty ones, and as shrinking from any emotional or physical demands that might be made upon him; he lives in constant fear of being 'hunted'. In revealing his sexuality Wadey also makes Ushant into a much more sympathetic character; with his inherited obligations he is shown to be a prisoner, like the women of his age, of the class and social system which says that he must marry and produce male heirs. Despite his apparent adherence to every one of his inherited obligations he is as much a victim as his wife of the marriage plot. Just as the description of the encounter between Beatrice Palmato and her father would have explained why her mother and her elder sister kill themselves in the full story, so the revelation of Ushant's sexuality gives the television audience the opportunity to understand why certain things happen. We are able to sympathize with him in a much more fully developed way and can also understand how his own and Nan's ignorance of their own physicality is one of the grounds for the tragic turn of events. However, it would not suit Wharton's original intent or Wadey's dramatic purpose to remove our sympathies too far from Nan. So, a new development in the plot—Ushant's unfeeling rejection of his sister's suitor—is introduced to remind us of his inflexibility and coldness. We are prevented from having too much sympathy for him at the time when Nan needs the audience to understand her feelings.

This is a good example of a dramatic device not plotted by Edith Wharton in her plan for the novel but one which in the hands of both the contemporary dramatist and novelist makes the character of Ushant more fully rounded. The assignment of a specific sexuality to Ushant by Maggie Wadey is not replicated by Angela Mackworth-Young in the novel. Quite properly, it terms of consistency with a novel written in 1937, Mackworth-Young treats the whole matter obliquely, as Wharton would have done. Whatever it is Nan sees when she goes to Ushant's room late at night we are not directly told but its significance is plain in terms of the story. It is, perhaps, helpful to think of the television version as serving the purpose of explicating the book just as the 'unpublishable fragment' of 'Beatrice Palmato' might explain the tragedy of the Palmato family. The violent desperation which marks both the consummated and unconsummated sexual encounters between Ushant and Nan goes some way towards revealing the reasons behind the failure of their marriage.

As well as making characters like the Duke of Tintagel more complicated Wharton would, in revising the book, have paid a good deal of attention to further substantiating the characters of those who have significant parts to play in the action of the novel. So effectively does Lizzy Elmsworth's strength of character blaze out in her confrontation with Lady Churt at Runnymede that it shows how much work there was to do in order to put flesh on the bones of Lizzy's other appearances in *The Buccaneers*. The scene at Runnymede was one of the few that Wharton had revised and it is significant that its dramatic power is such that Maggie Wadey could transplant it almost untouched into her script. Whilst such well-written scenes can be translated onto the screen quite straightforwardly, the undeveloped and unfinished scenes and characters also offer positive opportunities to the dramatist. The under-developed aspects of plot and character provide an unusually open text for the dramatist to work on. It is not only the character of the Duke of Tintagel which is made more complex. There are all sorts of other points in the dramatization at which the relative simplicity of Wharton's plot is complicated and intensified in order to make the story more compelling for the television audience. A good example of this is to be found in the encounters between Sir Helmsley Thwarte and his son, Guy. The groundwork has been done by Wharton in suggesting the complex tangle of resentments and disappointments – both financial and emotional – which determines the course of their relationship. Their feelings are more fully developed by Maggie Wadey in her dramatization of the rivalries between them and the sheer immensity of the love and pride which both divides and unites them. The struggle here for the dramatist was not in discovering ways to omit huge portions of the action or to find ways in which to render into dialogue long passages of description or particular forms of figurative language but to give more detail and to quicken the pace of the drama, both in terms of characterization and plot.

It was plain from the direction in which the story of *The Buccaneers* was leading that Laura Testvalley was taking up more space in the novel than Wharton seemed to have intended in her original plan. Although there are a few working women in Wharton's fiction, usually they are at work because a reversal in their fortunes has led them to seek employment. The life of the governess as a compelling subject for fiction, although well-established in English letters of the nineteenth century, was not especially Wharton's sphere of interest. Her purpose was generally to communicate a picture of the lives of the privileged members of New York's élite and she would not have been able to penetrate to the heart of the social scene had she focused on a working rather than a leisure-class woman. The story of *The Buccaneers*, however, requires the services of a person with a very particular set of attributes; an understanding of the conditions of exile, of wage-slavery and an active aesthetic sensitivity, all of which Wharton happily and convincingly combined in the person of the 'great-souled' Laura, as she calls her in the novel plan.

The character of the governess is cited by Edith Wharton in *A Backward Glance* as having walked fully formed into her imagination:

'Laura Testvalley. How I should like to change that name! But it has been attached for some time now to a strongly outlined material form, the form of a character figuring largely in an adventure I know all about, and have long wanted to relate. Several times I have tried to give Miss Testvalley another name, since the one she bears, should it appear ever in print, will be more troublesome to my readers than to me. But she is strong-willed, and even obstinate, and turns sulky and unmanageable whenever I hint at the advantages of a change.'

The names Wharton gives to her characters in *The Buccaneers* can often seem 'troublesome', and indeed the obscurity of some of the names led Maggie Wadey to change them in the dramatic version. However, in any description of the way in which stories and characters presented themselves to her Wharton always talks about the fact that her 'characters always appear with their names' and if 'unchristened' die instantly. On their arrival Wharton usually had no idea of the relative importance of her characters or indeed what would happen to them as the story in which they were participating grew. In his afterword to the first, posthumously published, edition of *The Buccaneers* Wharton's friend and literary executor, Gaillard Lapsley, in discussing the necessity for more to be made of the part of Nan St George if she was ever to dominate and compel our attention in the way that Wharton originally planned, talks about the hi-jacking of the novel by Laura Testvalley. Lapsley, in fact, suggests that Wharton might eventually have found herself in conflict with her own creation if Laura seemed to demand, at the last, the kind of fulfilment which is promised in a relationship with Sir Helmsley Thwarte. In the event, however, Laura loses, as Lapsley puts it: 'the great prize, the chance in October of what had been denied to her in May, ease, rank and the companionship of a cultivated man who was also her lover.' Nevertheless, the figure of Laura Testvalley is one of the features of *The Buccaneers* which makes it most compelling; in this novel Wharton shifts our attention not only from her usual class position but from the charms of beauty, wealth and youth to the tolerance and wisdom of a penniless governess.

At the end of her life Wharton wrote of a love which she allowed to transcend the constraints of its time and place. In 1920, in *The Age of Innocence*, when Ellen Olenska gently chides Newland Archer for having proposed that they run away together to a place where they can be alone and unknown, she says: "'Oh, my dear – where is that country? Have you ever been there? . . . I know so many who've tried to find it; and, believe me, they all got out by mistake at wayside stations: at places like Boulogne, or Pisa, or Monte Carlo – and it wasn't at all different from the old world they'd left, but only rather smaller and dingier and more promiscuous.'" The South Africa to which Nan and Guy journey in the completed version of the novel offered to you here is not a real place; we do not know how society there will react to the lovers, and we as readers have no business with it except to know that they will be together there. The only real place at the close of *The Buccaneers* is the place where Laura Testvalley will dwell in 'old age and poverty', known, as she says, as 'the governess who facilitates elopements'. Someone always has to pay for the happiness achieved in Wharton's novels and whilst duty and decency prevail in *The Age of Innocence* at the expense of a great passion, the triumph of love here means that 'the great old adventuress', as Wharton calls her in the novel plan, remains, at the last, an exile and alone.

*Janet Beer Goodwyn*

# TELEVISION CAST LIST OF PRINCIPAL CHARACTERS

| | |
|---|---|
| Laura Testvalley | Cherie Lunghi |
| Nan St George | Carla Gugino |
| Virginia St George | Alison Elliott |
| Conchita Closson | Mira Sorvino |
| Lizzy Elmsworth | Rya Kihlstedt |
| Lord Seadown | Mark Tandy |
| Lord Richard Marable | Ronan Vibert |
| Julius *Ushant, Duke of Tintagel* | James Frain |
| Lord Brightlingsea | Dinsdale Landen |
| Lady Brightlingsea | Rosemary Leach |
| Sir Hemlsley Thwaite *Sir Helmsley Thwarte* | |
| | Michael Kitchen |
| Guy Thwaite *Guy Thwarte* | Greg Wise |
| Idina Hatton *Lady Idina Churt* | Jenny Agutter |
| Lady Honoria Marable | Sophie Dix |
| Lady Felicia Marable | Sienna Guillory |
| Lady Georgina Marable | Emily Hamilton |
| Miss March | Connie Booth |

| | |
|---|---|
| Mrs Parmore | E. Katherine Kerr |
| Mrs Elmsworth | Conchata Ferrell |
| Mrs St George | Gwen Humble |
| Colonel St George | Peter Michael Goetz |
| Mrs Closson | Elizabeth Ashley |
| Dowager Duchess | Sheila Hancock |

The names in italics represent Edith Wharton's original choice of characters' names. They are preceded where appropriate by the names used in the BBC Television adaptation of *The Buccaneers*.

BOOK

 I

# ONE

IT WAS THE HEIGHT OF THE RACING-SEASON AT SARATOGA.

The thermometer stood over ninety, and a haze of sun-powdered dust hung in the elms along the street facing the Grand Union Hotel, and over the scant triangular lawns planted with young firs, and protected by a low white rail from the depredations of dogs and children.

Mrs St George, whose husband was one of the gentlemen most interested in the racing, sat on the wide hotel veran-dah, a jug of iced lemonade at her elbow and a palmetto fan in one small hand, and looked out between the immensely tall white columns of the portico, which so often reminded cultured travellers of the Parthenon at Athens (Greece). On Sunday afternoons this verandah was crowded with gentle-men in tall hats and frock-coats, enjoying cool drinks and Havana cigars, and surveying the long country street planted with spindling elms; but today the gentlemen were racing, and the rows of chairs were occupied by ladies and young girls listlessly awaiting their return, in a drowsy atmosphere of swayed fans and iced refreshments.

Mrs St George eyed most of these ladies with a melan-choly disfavour, and sighed to think how times had changed since she had first – some ten years earlier – trailed her crino-lined skirts up and down that same verandah.

Mrs St George's vacant hours, which were many, were filled by such wistful reflections. Life had never been easy, but it had certainly been easier when Colonel St George devoted less time to poker, and to Wall Street; when the children were little, crinolines were still worn, and Newport had not yet eclipsed all rival watering-places. What, for instance, could be prettier, or more suitable for a lady, than a black alpaca skirt looped up like a window-drapery above a scarlet serge underskirt, the whole surmounted by a wide-sleeved black poplin jacket with ruffled muslin undersleeves, and a flat 'pork-pie' hat like the one the Empress Eugénie was represented as wearing on the beach at Biarritz? But now there seemed to be no definite fashions. Everybody wore what they pleased, and it was as difficult to look like a lady in those tight perpendicular polonaises bunched up at the back that the Paris dress-makers were sending over as in the outrageously low square-cut evening gowns which Mrs St George had viewed with disapproval at the Opera in New York. The fact was, you could hardly tell a lady now from an actress, or – er – the other kind of woman; and society at Saratoga, now that all the best people were going to Newport, had grown as mixed and confusing as the fashions.

Everything was changed since crinolines had gone out and bustles come in. Who, for instance, was that new woman, a Mrs Closson, or some such name, who had such a dusky skin for her auburn hair, such a fat body for her small uncertain feet, and who, when she wasn't strumming on the hotel piano, was credibly reported by the domestics to lie for hours on her bedroom sofa smoking – yes, *smoking* big Havana cigars? The gentlemen, Mrs St George believed, treated the story as a good joke; to a woman of refinement it could be only a subject for painful meditation.

Mrs St George had always been rather distant in her manner to the big and exuberant Mrs Elmsworth who was seated at this moment near by on the verandah. (Mrs Elmsworth was always 'edging up'.) Mrs St George was instinctively distrustful of the advances of ladies who had daughters of the age of her own, and Lizzy Elmsworth, the eldest of her neighbour's family, was just about the age of Virginia St George, and might by some (those who preferred the brunette to the very blond type) be thought as handsome. And besides, where did the Elmsworths come from, as Mrs St George had often asked her husband, an irreverent jovial man who invariably replied: 'If you were to begin by telling me where we do!' . . . so absurd on the part of a gentleman as well known as Colonel St George in some unspecified district of what Mrs St George called the Sa-outh.

But at the thought of that new dusky Closson woman with the queer-looking girl who was so ugly now, but might suddenly turn into a beauty (Mrs St George had seen such cases), the instinct of organized defence awoke in her vague bosom, and she felt herself drawn to Mrs Elmsworth, and to the two Elmsworth girls, as to whom one already knew just how good-looking they were going to be.

A good many hours of Mrs St George's days were spent in mentally cataloguing and appraising the physical attributes of the young ladies in whose company her daughters trailed up and down the verandahs, and waltzed and polka-ed for hours every night in the long bare hotel parlours, so conveniently divided by sliding doors which slipped into the wall and made the two rooms into one. Mrs St George remembered the day when she had been agreeably awestruck by this vista, with its expectant lines of bentwood chairs against the walls, and its row of windows draped in crimson brocatelle heavily festooned from overhanging gilt cornices. In those days the hotel ball-room had been her idea of a throne-room in a palace; but since her husband had taken her to a ball at the Seventh Regiment Armoury in New York her standards had changed, and she regarded the splendours of the Grand Union almost as contemptuously as the arrogant Mrs

Eglinton of New York, who had arrived there the previous summer on her way to Lake George, and after being shown into the yellow damask 'bridal suite' by the obsequious landlord, had said she supposed it would do well enough for one night.

Mrs St George, in those earlier years, had even been fluttered by an introduction to Mrs Elmsworth, who was an older habituée of Saratoga than herself, and had a big showy affable husband with lustrous black whiskers, who was reported to have made a handsome fortune on the New York Stock Exchange. But that was in the days when Mrs Elmsworth drove daily to the races in a high barouche sent from New York, which attracted perhaps too much attention. Since then Mr Elmsworth's losses in Wall Street had obliged his wife to put down her barouche, and stay at home on the hotel verandah with the other ladies, and she now no longer inspired Mrs St George with awe or envy. Indeed, had it not been for this new Closson danger Mrs Elmsworth in her present situation would have been negligible; but now that Virginia St George and Lizzy Elmsworth were 'out' (as Mrs St George persisted in calling it, though the girls could not see much difference in their lives) – now that Lizzy Elmsworth's looks seemed to Mrs St George at once more to be admired and less to be feared, and Mabel, the second Elmsworth girl, who was a year older than her own youngest, to be too bony and lantern-jawed for future danger, Mrs St George began to wonder whether she and her neighbour might not organize some sort of joint defence against new women with daughters. Later it would not so much matter, for Mrs St George's youngest, Nan, though certainly not a beauty like Virginia, was going to be what was called fascinating, and by the time her hair was put up the St George girls need fear no rivalry.

Week after week, day after day, the anxious mother had gone over Miss Elmsworth's points, comparing them one by one with Virginia's. As regards hair and complexion, there could be no doubt; Virginia, all rose and pearl, with sheaves of full fair hair heaped above her low forehead, was as pure and luminous as an apple-blossom. But Lizzy's waist was certainly at least an inch smaller (some said two), Lizzy's dark eyebrows had a bolder curve, and Lizzy's foot – ah, where in the world did an upstart Elmsworth get that arrogant instep? Yes; but it was some comfort to note that Lizzy's complexion was opaque and lifeless compared to Virginia's, and that her fine eyes showed temper, and would be likely to frighten the young men away. Still, she had to an alarming degree what was called 'style', and Mrs St George suspected that in the circles to which she longed to introduce her daughters style was valued even more highly than beauty.

These were the problems among which her thoughts moved during the endless sweltering afternoon hours, like torpid fish turning about between the weary walls of a too-small aquarium. But now a new presence had invaded that sluggish element. Mrs St George no longer compared her eldest daughter and Lizzy Elmsworth with each other; she began to compare them both with the newcomer, the daughter of the unknown Mrs Closson. It was small comfort to Mrs St George (though she repeated it to herself so often) that the Clossons were utterly unknown, that though Colonel St George played poker with Mr Closson, and had what the family called 'business connections' with him, they were nowhere near the stage when it becomes a pleasing duty for a man to introduce a colleague to his family. Neither did it matter that Mrs Closson's own past was if anything obscurer than her husband's, and that those who said she was a poor Brazilian widow when Closson had picked her up on a business trip to Rio were smiled at and corrected by others, presumably better informed, who suggested that divorcée was the word, and not widow. Even the fact that the Closson girl (so-called) was known not to be Closson's daughter, but to bear some queer exotic name like Santos-Dios ('the Colonel says that's not swearing, it's the language,' Mrs St George explained to Mrs Elmsworth when they talked the newcomers over) – even this was not enough to calm Mrs St George. The girl, whatever her real name, was known as Conchita Closson; she addressed as 'Father' the non-committal pepper-and-salt-looking man who joined his family over Sundays at the Grand Union; and it was of no use for Mrs St George to say to herself that Conchita was plain and therefore negligible, for she had the precise kind of plainness which, as mothers of rival daughters know, may suddenly blaze into irresistible beauty. At present Miss Closson's head was too small, her neck was too long, she was too tall and thin, and her hair – well, her hair (oh, horror!) was nearly red. And her skin was dark, under the powder which (yes, my dear – at eighteen!) Mrs St George was sure she applied to it; and the combination of red hair and sallow complexion would have put off anybody who had heard a description of them, instead of seeing them triumphantly embodied in Conchita Closson. Mrs St George shivered under her dotted muslin ruffled with Valenciennes, and drew a tippet edged with swansdown over her shoulders. At that moment her own daughters, Virginia and Nan, wandered by, one after the other; and the sight somehow increased Mrs St George's irritation.

'Virginia!' she called. Virginia halted, seemed to hesitate as to whether the summons were worth heeding, and then sauntered across the verandah towards her mother.

'Virginia, I don't want you should go round any more with that strange girl,' Mrs St George began.

Virginia's sapphire eyes rested with a remote indifferent gaze on the speaker's tightly buttoned bronze kid boots; and Mrs St George suddenly wondered if she had burst a button-hole.

'What girl?' Virginia drawled.

'How do I know? Goodness knows who they are. Your pa says she was a widow from one of those South American countries when she married Mr Closson – the mother was, I mean.'

'Well, if he says so, I suppose she was.'

'But some people say she was just divorced. And I don't want my daughters associating with that kind of people.'

Virginia removed her blue gaze from her mother's boots to the little mantle trimmed with swansdown. 'I should think you'd roast with that thing on,' she remarked.

'Jinny! Now you listen to what I say,' her mother ineffectually called after her.

Nan St George had taken no part in the conversation; at first she had hardly heeded what was said. Such wrangles between mother and daughter were of daily, almost hourly, occurrence; Mrs St George's only way of guiding her children was to be always crying out to them not to do this or that. Nan St George, at sixteen, was at the culminating phase of a passionate admiration for her elder sister. Virginia was all that her junior longed to be: perfectly beautiful, completely self-possessed, calm and sure of herself. Nan, whose whole life was a series of waves of the blood, hot rushes of enthusiasm, icy chills of embarrassment and self-depreciation, looked with envy and admiration at her goddess-like elder. The only thing she did not quite like about Virginia was the latter's tone of superiority with her mother; to get the better of Mrs St George was too easy, too much like what Colonel St George called 'shooting a bird sitting'. Yet so strong was Virginia's influence that in her presence Nan always took the same tone with their mother, in the secret hope of attracting her sister's favourable notice. She had even gone so far as to mime for Virginia (who was no mimic) Mrs St George looking shocked at an untidy stocking ('mother wondering where we were brought up'), Mrs St George smiling in her sleep in church ('mother listening to the angels'), or Mrs St George doubtfully mustering new arrivals ('mother smelling a drain'). But Virginia took such demonstrations for granted, and when poor Nan afterwards, in an agony of remorse, stole back alone to her mother, and whispered through penitent kisses: 'I didn't mean to be naughty to you, Mamma,' Mrs St George, raising a nervous hand to her crimped bandeaux, would usually reply apprehensively: 'I'm sure you didn't, darling; only don't get my hair all in a muss again.'

Expiation unresponded to embitters the blood, and something within Nan shrank and hardened with each of these rebuffs. But she now seldom exposed herself to them, finding it easier to follow Virginia's lead and ignore their parent's admonitions. At the moment, however, she was actually wavering in her allegiance to Virginia. Since she had seen Conchita Closson she was no longer sure that features and complexion were woman's crowning glory. Long before Mrs St George and Mrs Elmsworth had agreed on a valuation of the newcomer Nan had fallen under her spell. From the day when she had first seen her come whistling around the corner of the verandah, her restless little head crowned by a flapping Leghorn hat with a rose under the brim, and dragging after her a reluctant poodle with a large red bow, Nan had felt the girl's careless power. What would Mrs St George have said if one of her daughters had strolled along the verandah whistling, and dragging a grotesque-looking toy-shop animal at her heels? Miss Closson seemed troubled by no such considerations. She sat down on the upper step of the verandah, pulled a lump of molasses candy from her pocket, and invited the poodle to 'get up and waltz for it'; which the uncanny animal did by rising on his hind legs and performing a series of unsteady circles before his mistress while she licked the molasses from her fingers. Every rocking-chair on the verandah stopped creaking as its occupant sat upright to view the show. 'Circus performance!' Mrs St George commented to Mrs Elmsworth; and the latter retorted with her vulgar laugh: 'Looks as if the two of 'em were used to showing off, don't it?'

Nan overheard the comments, and felt sure the two mothers were mistaken. The Closson girl was obviously unaware that anyone was looking at her and her absurd dog; it was that absence of self-consciousness which fascinated Nan. Virginia was intensely self-conscious; she really thought just as much as her mother of 'what people would say'; and even Lizzy Elmsworth, though she was so much cleverer at concealing her thoughts, was not really simple and natural; she merely affected unaffectedness. It frightened Nan a little to find herself thinking these things; but they forced themselves upon her, and when Mrs St George issued the order that her daughters were not to associate with 'the strange girl' (as if they didn't all know her name!) Nan felt a rush of anger. Virginia sauntered on, probably content to have shaken her mother's confidence in the details of her dress (a matter of much anxious thought to Mrs St George); but Nan stopped short.

'Why can't I go with Conchita if she wants me to?'

Mrs St George's faintly withered pink turned pale. 'If she *wants you to?* Annabel St George, what do you mean by talking to me that way? What on earth do you care for what a girl like that *wants?*'

Nan ground her heels into the crack between the verandah boards. 'I think she's lovely.'

Mrs St George's small nose was wrinkled with disdain. The small mouth under it drooped disgustedly.

She was 'mother smelling a drain'.

'Well, when that new governess comes next week I guess you'll find she feels just the way I do about those people. And you'll have to do what *she* tells you, anyhow,' Mrs St George helplessly concluded.

A chill of dismay rushed over Nan. The new governess! She had never really believed in that remote bogey. She had an idea that Mrs St George and Virginia had cooked up the legend between them, in order to be able to say 'Annabel's governess', as they had once heard that tall proud Mrs Eglinton from New York, who had stayed only one night at the hotel, say to the landlord: 'You must be sure to put my daughter's governess in the room next to her.' Nan had never believed that the affair of the governess would go beyond talking; but now she seemed to hear the snap of the handcuffs on her wrists.

'A governess – me?'

Mrs St George moistened her lips nervously. 'All stylish girls have governesses the year before they come out.'

'I'm not coming out next year – I'm only sixteen,' Nan protested.

'Well, they have them for two years before. That Eglinton girl had.'

'Oh, that Eglinton girl! She looked at us all as if we weren't there.'

'Well, that's the way for a lady to look at strangers,' said Mrs St George heroically.

Nan's heart grew black within her. 'I'll kill her if she tries to interfere with me.'

'You'll drive down to the station on Monday to meet her,' Mrs St George shrilled back, defiant. Nan turned on her heel and walked away.

# TWO

THE CLOSSON GIRL HAD ALREADY DISAPPEARED WITH HER dog, and Nan suspected that she had taken him for a game of ball in the rough field adjoining the meagre grounds of the hotel. Nan went down the steps of the porch, and crossing the drive espied the slim Conchita whirling a ball high over-head while the dog spun about frantically at her feet. Nan had so far exchanged only a few shy words with her, and in ordi-nary circumstances would hardly have dared to join her now. But she had reached an acute crisis in her life, and her need for sympathy and help overcame her shyness. She vaulted over the fence into the field and went up to Miss Closson.

'That's a lovely dog,' she said.

Miss Closson flung the ball for her poodle, and turned with a smile to Nan. 'Isn't he a real darling?'

Nan stood twisting one foot about the other. 'Have you ever had a governess?' she asked abruptly.

Miss Closson opened with a stare of wonder the darkly fringed eyes which shone like pale aquamarines on her small dusky face. 'Me? A governess? Mercy, no – what for?'

'That's what I say! My mother and Virginia have cooked it up between them. I'm going to have one next week.'

'Land's sake! You're not? She's coming here?' Nan nodded sulkily.

'*Well* –' Conchita murmured.

'What'll I do about it – what would you?' Nan burst out, on the brink of tears.

Miss Closson drew her lids together meditatively; then she stooped with deliberation to the poodle, and threw the ball for him again.

'I said I'd kill her,' broke from Nan in a hoarse whisper.

The other laughed. 'I wouldn't do that; not right off, anyhow. I'd get round her first.'

'Get round her? How can I? I've got to do whatever she wants.'

'No, you haven't. Make her want whatever *you* want.'

'How can I? Oh, can I call you Conchita? It's such a lovely name. Mine's Annabel, really, but everybody calls me Nan . . . Well, but how can I get round that governess? She'll try to make me learn lists of dates . . . that's what she's paid for.'

Conchita's expressive face became one grimace of disapproval. 'Well, I should hate that like castor-oil. But perhaps she won't. I knew a girl at Rio who had a governess, and she was hardly any older than the girl, and she used to . . . well, carry messages and letters for her, the governess did . . . and in the evening she used to slip out to . . . to see a friend . . . and she and the girl knew all each other's secrets; so you see they couldn't tell on each other, neither one of them couldn't . . .'

'Oh, I see,' said Nan, with a feigned air of knowingness. But she was suddenly conscious of a queer sensation in her throat, almost of physical sickness. Conchita's laughing eyes seemed whispering to her through half-drawn lids. She admired Conchita as much as ever – but she was not sure she liked her at that moment.

Conchita was obviously not aware of having produced an unfavourable impression. 'Out in Rio I knew a girl who got married that way. The governess carried her notes for her . . . Do you want to get married?' she asked abruptly.

Nan flushed and stared. Getting married was an inexhaustible theme of confidential talk between her sister and the Elmsworth girls; but she felt herself too young and inexperienced to take part in their discussions. Once, at one of the hotel dances, a young fellow called Roy Gilling had picked up her handkerchief, and refused to give it back. She had seen him raise it meaningly to his young moustache before he slipped it into his pocket; but the incident had left her annoyed and bewildered rather than excited, and she had not been sorry when soon afterwards he rather pointedly transferred his attentions to Mabel Elmsworth. She knew Mabel Elmsworth had already been kissed behind a door; and Nan's own sister Virginia had too, Nan suspected. She herself had no definite prejudices in the matter; she simply felt unprepared as yet to consider matrimonial plans. She stooped to stroke the poodle, and answered, without looking up: 'Not to anybody I've seen yet.'

The other considered her curiously. 'I suppose you like love-making better, eh?' She spoke in a soft drawl, with a languid rippling of the Rs.

Nan felt her blood mounting again; one of her quick blushes steeped her in distress. Did she – didn't she – like 'love-making', as this girl crudely called it (the others always spoke of it as flirting)? Nan had not been subjected to any warmer advances than Mr Gilling's, and the obvious answer was that she didn't know, having had no experience of such matters; but she had the reluctance of youth to confess to its youthfulness, and she also felt that her likes and dislikes were no business of this strange girl's. She gave a vague laugh and said loftily, 'I think it's silly.'

Conchita laughed too; a low deliberate laugh, full of repressed and tantalizing mystery. Once more she flung the ball for her intently watching poodle; then she thrust a hand into a fold of her dress, and pulled out a crumpled packet of cigarettes. 'Here – have one! Nobody'll see us out here,' she suggested amicably.

Nan's heart gave an excited leap. Her own sister and the Elmsworth girls already smoked in secret, removing the traces of their indiscretion by consuming little highly perfumed pink lozenges furtively acquired from the hotel barber; but they had never offered to induct Nan into these forbidden rites, which, by awful oaths, they bound her not to reveal to their parents. It was Nan's first cigarette, and while her fingers twitched for it she asked herself in terror: 'Suppose it should make me sick right before her?'

But Nan, in spite of her tremors, was not the girl to refuse what looked like a dare, nor even to ask if in this open field they were really safe from unwanted eyes. There was a clump of low shrubby trees at the farther end, and Conchita strolled there and mounted the fence-rail, from which her slender uncovered ankles dangled gracefully. Nan swung up beside her, took a cigarette, and bent towards the match which her companion proffered. There was an awful silence while she put the forbidden object to her lips and drew a frightened breath; the acrid taste of the tobacco struck her palate sharply, but in another moment a pleasant fragrance filled her nose and throat. She puffed again, and knew she was going to like it. Instantly her mood passed from timidity to triumph, and she wrinkled her nose critically and threw back her head, as her father did when he was tasting a new brand of cigar. 'These are all right – where do you get them?' she inquired with a careless air; and then, suddenly forgetful of the experience her tone implied, she rushed on in a breathless little-girl voice: 'Oh, Conchita, won't you show me how you make those lovely rings? Jinny doesn't really do them right, nor the Elmsworth girls either.'

Miss Closson in turn threw back her head with a smile. She drew a deep breath, and removing the cigarette from her lips, curved them to a rosy circle through which she sent a wreath of misty smoke-rings. 'That's how,' she laughed, and pushed the packet into Nan's hands. 'You can practise at night,' she said good-humouredly, as she jumped from the rail.

Nan wandered back to the hotel, so much elated by her success as a smoker that her dread of the governess grew fainter. On the hotel steps she was further reassured by the glimpse, through the lobby doors, of a tall broad-shouldered man in a Panama hat and light grey suit who, his linen duster over his arm, his portmanteaux at his feet, had paused to light a big cigar and shake hands with the clerk. Nan gave a start of joy. She had not known that her father was arriving that afternoon, and the mere sight of him banished all her cares. Nan had a blind faith in her father's faculty for helping people out of difficulties – a faith based not on actual experience (for Colonel St George usually dealt with difficulties by a wave of dismissal which swept them into somebody else's lap), but on his easy contempt for feminine fusses, and his way of saying to his youngest daughter: 'You just call on me, child, when things want straightening out.' Perhaps he would straighten out even this nonsense about the governess; and meanwhile the mere thought of his large powerful presence, his big cologne-scented hands, his splendid yellow moustache and easy rolling gait, cleared the air of the cobwebs in which Mrs St George was always enveloped.

'Hullo, daughter! What's the news?' The Colonel greeted Nan with a resounding kiss, and stood with one arm about her, scrutinizing her lifted face.

'I'm glad you've come, father,' she said, and then shrank back a little, fearful lest a whiff of cigarette smoke should betray her.

'Your mother taking her afternoon nap, I suppose?' the Colonel continued jovially. 'Well, come along with me. See here, Charlie' (to the clerk), 'send those things right along to my room, will you? There's something in them of interest to this young lady.'

The clerk signalled to a black porter, and preceded by his bags the Colonel mounted the stairs with Nan.

'Oh, father! It's lovely to have you! What I want to ask you is –'

But the Colonel was digging into the depths of one of the portmanteaux and scattering over the bed various parts of a showy but somewhat crumpled wardrobe. 'Here now; you wait,' he puffed, pausing to mop his broad white forehead with a fine cambric handkerchief. He pulled out two parcels, and beckoned to Nan. 'Here's some fancy notions for you and Jinny; the girl in the store said it was what the Newport belles are wearing this summer. And this is for your mother, when she wakes up.' He took the tissue-paper wrappings from a small red-morocco case and pressed the spring of the lid. Before Nan's dazzled eyes lay a diamond brooch formed of a spray of briar-roses. She gave an admiring gasp. 'Well, how's that for style?' laughed her father.

'Oh, father –' She paused, and looked at him with a faint touch of apprehension.

'Well?' the Colonel repeated. His laugh had an emptiness under it, like the hollow under a loud wave; Nan knew the sound.

'Is it a present for mother?' she asked doubtfully.

'Why, who'd you think it was for – not you?' he joked, his voice slightly less assured.

Nan twisted one foot about the other. 'It's terribly expensive, isn't it?'

'Why, you critical imp, you – what's the matter if it is?'

'Well, the last time you brought mother a piece of jewellery there was an all-night row after it, about cards or something,' said Nan judicially.

The Colonel burst out laughing, and pinched her chin. 'Well, well! You fear the Greeks, eh, do you? How does it go? *Timeo Danaos . . .*'

'What Greeks?'

Her father raised his handsome ironic eyebrows. Nan knew he was proud of his far-off smattering of college culture, and wished she could have understood the allusion. 'Haven't they even taught you that much Latin at your school? Well, I guess your mother's right; you *do* need a governess.'

Nan paled, and forgot the Greeks. 'Oh, father; that's what I wanted to speak to you about –'

'What about?'

'That governess. I'm going to hate her, you know. She's going to make me learn lists of dates, the way the Eglinton girl had to. And mother'll fill her up with silly stories about us, and tell her we musn't do this, and we mustn't say that. I don't believe she'll even let me go with Conchita Closson, because mother says Mrs Closson's divorced.'

The Colonel looked up sharply. 'Oh, your mother says that, does she? She's down on the Clossons? I supposed she would be.' He picked up the morocco case and examined the brooch critically. 'Yes; that's a good piece; Black, Starr and Frost. And I don't mind telling you that you're right; it cost me a pretty penny. But I've got to persuade your mother to be polite to Mrs Closson – see?' He wrinkled up his face in the funny way he had, and took his daughter by the shoulders. 'Business matter, you understand – strictly between ourselves. I need Closson; got to have him. And he's fretted to death about the way all the women cold-shoulder his wife … I'll tell you what, Nan; suppose you and I form a league, defensive and offensive? You help me to talk round your mother, and get her to be decent to Mrs Closson, and persuade the others to be, and to let the girl go round with all of you; and I'll fix it up with the governess so you don't have to learn too many dates.'

Nan uttered a cry of joy. Already the clouds were lifting. 'Oh, father, you're perfectly grand! I knew everything would be all right as soon as you got here! I'll do all I can about mother – and you'll tell the governess I'm to go round all I like with Conchita?' She flung herself into the Colonel's comforting embrace.

# THREE

MRS ST GEORGE, HAD SHE LOOKED BACK FAR ENOUGH, COULD have recalled a time when she had all of Nan's faith in the Colonel's restorative powers; when to carry her difficulties to him seemed the natural thing, and his way of laughing at them gave her the illusion that they were solved. Those days were past; she had long been aware that most of her difficulties came from the Colonel instead of being solved by him. But she admired him as much as ever – thought him in fact even handsomer than when, before the Civil War, he had dawned on her dazzled sight at a White Sulphur Springs ball, in the uniform of a captain of militia; and now that he had become prominent in Wall Street, where life seemed to grow more feverish every day, it was only natural that he should require a little relaxation, though she deplored its always meaning poker and whisky, and sometimes, she feared, the third element celebrated in the song. Though Mrs St George was now a worried middle-aged woman with grown-up daughters, it cost her as much to resign herself to this as when she had first found in her husband's pocket a letter she was not meant to read. But there was nothing to be done about it, or about the whisky and poker, and the visits to establishments where game and champagne were served at all hours, and gentlemen who had won at roulette or the races supped in meretricious company. All this had long since been part of Mrs St George's consciousness, yet she was half consoled, when the Colonel joined his family at Long Branch or Saratoga, by the knowledge that all the other worried and middle-aged wives in the long hotel dining-room envied her her splendid husband.

And small wonder, thought Mrs St George, contemptuously picturing the gentlemen those ladies had to put up with: that loud red-faced Elmsworth, who hadn't yet found out that big lumps of black whisker were no longer worn except by undertakers, or the poor dyspeptic Closson, who spent such resigned and yawning hours beside the South American woman to whom he was perhaps not married at all. Closson was particularly obnoxious to Mrs St George; much as she despised Mrs Closson, she could almost have pitied her for having nothing better to show as a husband – even if he was that, as Mrs St George would add in her confidential exchanges with Mrs Elmsworth.

Even now, though of late the Colonel had been so evasive and unsatisfactory, and though she wasn't yet sure if he would turn up for the morrow's races, Mrs St George reflected thankfully that if he *did* she wouldn't have to appear in the hotel dining-room with a man about whom a lady need feel apologetic. But when, after her siesta, as she was rearranging her hair before going back to the verandah, she heard his laugh outside her door, her slumbering apprehensions started up. 'He's too cheerful,' she thought, nervously folding away her dressing-gown and slippers; for when the Colonel was worried he was always in the highest spirits.

'Well, my dear! Thought I'd surprise the family, and see what you were all up to. Nan's given me a fairly good report, but I haven't run down Jinny yet.' He laid a hand on his wife's greying blond hair, and brushed her care-worn forehead with the tip of his moustache; a ritual gesture which convinced him that he had kissed her, and Mrs St George that she had been kissed.

She looked up at him with admiring eyes.

'That governess is coming on Monday,' she began. At the moment of his last successful 'turn-over', a few months earlier, his wife had wrung from him the permission to engage a governess; but now she feared a renewal of the discussion about the governess's salary, and yet she knew the girls, and Nan especially, must have some kind of social discipline. 'We've got to have her,' Mrs St George added.

The Colonel was obviously not listening. 'Of course, of course,' he agreed, measuring the room with his large strides (his inability to remain seated was another trial to his sedentary wife). Suddenly he paused before her and fumbled in his pocket, but produced nothing from it. Mrs St George noted the gesture, and thought: 'It's the coal bill! But he *knew* I couldn't get it down any lower . . .'

'Well, well, my dear,' the Colonel continued, 'I don't know what you've all been up to, but I've had a big stroke of luck, and it's only fair you three girls should share in it.' He jerked the morocco case out of another pocket.

'Oh, Colonel,' his wife gasped as he pressed the spring.

'Well, take it – it's for you!' he joked.

Mrs St George gazed blankly at the glittering spray; then her eyes filled, and her lip began to tremble. 'Tracy . . .' she stammered. It was years since she had called him by his name. 'But you oughtn't to,' she protested, 'with all our expenses . . . It's too grand – it's like a wedding present . . .'

'Well, we're married, ain't we?' The Colonel laughed resonantly. 'There's the first result of my turn-over, madam. And I brought the girls some gimcracks too. I gave Nan the parcel; but I haven't seen Jinny. I suppose she's off with some of the other girls.'

Mrs St George detached herself from ecstatic contemplation of the jewel. 'You mustn't spoil the girls, Colonel. I've got my hands full with them. I want you to talk to them seriously about not going with that Closson girl . . .'

Colonel St George blew a faint whistle through his moustache, and threw himself into the rocking-chair facing his wife's. 'Going with the Closson girl? Why, what's the matter with the Closson girl? She's as pretty as a peach, anyhow.'

'I guess your own daughters are pretty enough without having to demean themselves running after that girl. I can't keep Nan away from her.' Mrs St George knew that Nan was the Colonel's favourite, and she spoke with an inward tremor. But it would never do to have this fashionable new governess (who had been with the Russell Parmores of Tarrytown, and with the Duchess of Tintagel in England) imagine that her new charges were hand in glove with the Clossons.

Colonel St George tilted himself back in his chair, felt for a cigar and lit it thoughtfully. (He had long since taught Mrs St George that smoking in her bedroom was included among his marital rights.) 'Well,' he said, 'what's wrong with the Clossons, my dear?'

Mrs St George felt weak and empty inside. When he looked at her in that way, half laughing, half condescending, all her reasons turned to a puff of mist. And there lay the jewel on the dressing-table – and timorously she began to understand. But the girls must be rescued, and a flicker of maternal ardour stirred in her. Perhaps in his large careless way her husband had simply brushed by the Clossons without heeding them.

'I don't know any of the particulars, naturally. People *do* say . . . but Mrs Closson (if that's her name) is not a woman I could ever associate with, so I haven't any means of knowing . . .'

The Colonel gave his all-effacing laugh. 'Oh, well – if you haven't any means of knowing, we'll fix that up all right. But I've got business reasons for wanting you to make friends with Mrs Closson first; we'll investigate her history afterwards.'

Make friends with Mrs Closson! Mrs St George looked at her husband with dismay. He wanted her to do the thing that would most humiliate her; and it was so important to him that he had probably spent his last dollar on this diamond bribe. Mrs St George was not unused to such situations; she knew that a gentleman's financial situation might at any moment necessitate compromises and concessions. All the ladies of her acquaintance were inured to them; up one day, down the next, as the secret gods of Wall Street decreed. She measured her husband's present need by the cost of the probably unpaid for jewel and her heart grew like water.

'But, Colonel –'

'Well, what's wrong with the Clossons, anyhow? I've done business with Closson off and on for some years now, and I don't know a squarer fellow. He's just put me on to a big thing, and if you're going to wreck the whole business by turning up your nose at his wife . . .'

Mrs St George gathered strength to reply: 'But, Colonel, the talk is that they're not even married . . .'

Her husband jumped up and stood before her with flushed face and irritated eyes. 'If you think I'm going to let my making a big rake-off depend on whether the Clossons had a parson to tie the knot, or only the town clerk . . .'

'I've got the girls to think of,' his wife faltered.

'It's the girls I'm thinking of, too. D'you suppose I'd sweat and slave downtown the way I do if it wasn't for the girls?'

'But I've got to think of the girls they go with, if they're to marry nice young men.'

'The nice young men'll show up in larger numbers if I can put this deal through. And what's the matter with the Closson girl? She's as pretty as a picture.'

Mrs St George marvelled once more at the obtuseness of the most brilliant men. Wasn't that one of the very reasons for not encouraging the Closson girl?

'She powders her face, and smokes cigarettes . . .'

'Well, don't our girls and the two Elmsworths do as much? I'll swear I caught a whiff of smoke when Nan kissed me just now.'

Mrs St George grew pale with horror. 'If you'll say that of your daughters you'll say anything!' she protested.

There was a knock at the door, and without waiting for it to be answered Virginia flew into her father's arms. 'Oh, father, how sweet of you! Nan gave me the locket. It's too lovely; with my monogram on it – and in diamonds!'

She lifted her radiant lips, and he bent to them with a smile. 'What's that new scent you're using, Miss St George? Or have you been stealing one of your papa's lozenges?' He sniffed and then held her at arm's-length, watching her quick flush of alarm, and the way in which her deeply fringed eyes pleaded with his.

'See here, Jinny. Your mother says she don't want you to go with the Closson girl because she smokes. But I tell her I'll answer for it that you and Nan would never follow such a bad example – eh?'

Their eyes and their laugh met. Mrs St George turned from the sight with a sense of helplessness. 'If he's going to let them smoke now . . .'

'I don't think your mother's fair to the Closson girl, and I've told her so. I want she should be friends with Mrs Closson. I want her to begin right off. Oh, here's Nan,' he added, as the door opened again. 'Come along, Nan; I want you to stick up for your friend Conchita. You like her, don't you?'

But Mrs St George's resentment was stiffening. She could fight for her daughters, helpless as she was for herself. 'If you're going to rely on the girls to choose who they associate with! They say the girl's name isn't Closson at all. Nobody knows what it is, or who any of them are. And the brother travels round with a guitar tied with ribbons. No nice girls will go with your daughters if you want them seen everywhere with those people.'

The Colonel stood frowning before his wife. When he frowned she suddenly forgot all her reasons for opposing him, but the blind instinct of opposition remained. 'You wouldn't invite the Clossons to join us at supper tonight?' he suggested.

Mrs St George moistened her dry lips with her tongue. 'Colonel –'

'You won't?'

'Girls, your father's joking,' she stammered, turning with a tremulous gesture to her daughters. She saw Nan's eyes darken, but Virginia laughed – a laugh of complicity with her father. He joined in it.

'Girls, I see your mother's not satisfied with the present I've brought her. She's not as easily pleased as you young simpletons.' He waved his hand to the dressing-table, and Virginia caught up the morocco box.

'Oh, mother – is this for *you*? Oh, I never saw anything so beautiful! You must invite Mrs Closson, just to see how envious it makes her. I guess that's what father wants you to do – isn't it?'

The Colonel looked at her sympathetically. 'I've told your mother the plain truth. Closson's put me on to a good thing, and the only return he wants is for you ladies to be a little humane to his women-folk. Is that too unreasonable? He's coming today, by the afternoon train, bringing two young fellows with him, by the way – his step-son and a young Englishman who's been working out in Brazil on Mrs Closson's estancia. The son of an earl, or something. How about that, girls? Two new dancing-partners! And you ain't any too well off in that line, are you?' This was a burning question, for it was common knowledge that, if their dancing-partners were obscure and few, it was because all the smart and eligible young men of whom Virginia and the Elmsworths read in the 'society columns' of the newspapers had deserted Saratoga for Newport.

'Mother knows we generally have to dance with each other,' Virginia murmured sulkily.

'Yes – or with the beaux from Buffalo!' Nan laughed.

'Well, I call that mortifying; but of course, if your mother disapproves of Mrs Closson, I guess the young fellows that Closson's bringing'll have to dance with the Elmsworth girls instead of you.'

Mrs St George stood trembling beside the dressing-table. Virginia had put down the box, and the diamonds sparkled in a sunset ray that came through the slats of the shutters.

Mrs St George did not own many jewels, but it suddenly occurred to her that each one marked the date of a similar episode. Either a woman, or a business deal – something she had to be indulgent about. She liked trinkets as well as any woman, but at that moment she wished that all of hers were at the bottom of the sea. For each time she had yielded – as she knew she was going to yield now. And her husband would always think that it was because he had bribed her . . .

The readjustment of seats necessary to bring together the St George and Closson parties at the long hotel supper table caused a flutter in the room. Mrs St George was too conscious of it not to avoid Mrs Elmsworth's glance of surprise; but she could not deafen herself to Mrs Elmsworth's laugh. She had always thought the woman had an underbred laugh. And to think that, so few seasons ago, she had held her chin high in passing Mrs Elmsworth on the verandah, just as she had done till this very afternoon – and how much higher! – passing Mrs Closson. Now Mrs Elmsworth, who did not possess the art of the lifted chin, but whispered and nudged and giggled where a 'lady' would have sailed by – now it would be in her power to practise on Mrs St George these vulgar means of reprisal. The diamond spray burned like hot lead on Mrs St George's breast; yet through all her misery there pierced the old thrill of pride as the Colonel entered the dining-room in her wake, and she saw him reflected in the other women's eyes. Ah, poor Mrs Elmsworth, with her black-whiskered undertaker, and Mrs Closson with her cipher of a husband – all the other ladies, young or elderly, of whom not one could boast a man of Colonel St George's quality! Evidently, like Mrs St George's diamonds, he was a costly possession, but (unlike the diamonds, she suspected) he had been paid for – oh, how dearly! – and she had a right to wear him with her head high.

But in the eyes of the other guests it was not only the Colonel's entrance that was reflected. Mrs St George saw there also the excitement and curiosity occasioned by the regrouping of seats, and the appearance, behind Mrs Closson – who came in with her usual somnambulist's walk, and thick-lashed stare – of two young men, two authentic new dancers for the hotel beauties. Mrs St George knew all about them. The little olive-faced velvet-eyed fellow, with the impudently curly black hair, was Teddy de Santos-Dios, Mr Closson's Brazilian step-son, over on his annual visit to the States; the other, the short heavy-looking young man with a low forehead pressed down by a shock of drab hair, an uncertain mouth under a thick drab moustache, and small eyes, slow, puzzled, not unkindly yet not reliable, was Lord Richard Marable, the impecunious younger son of an English marquess, who had picked up a job on the Closson estancia, and had come over for his holiday with Santos-Dios. Two 'foreigners', and certainly ineligible ones, especially the little black popinjay who travelled with his guitar – but, after all, dancers for the girls, and therefore not wholly unwelcome even to Mrs St George, whose heart often ached at the thought of the Newport ball-rooms, where black coat-tails were said to jam every doorway; while at Saratoga the poor girls –

Ah, but there they were, the girls! – the privileged few whom she grouped under that designation. The fancy had taken them to come in late, and to arrive all together; and

now, arm-in-arm, a blushing bevy, they swayed across the
threshold of the dining-room like a branch hung with blos-
soms, drawing the dull middle-aged eyes of the other guests
from lobster salad and fried chicken, and eclipsing even the
refulgent Colonel – happy girls, with two new dancers for the
weekend, they had celebrated the unwonted wind-fall by
extra touches of adornment: a red rose in the fold of a fichu, a
loose curl on a white shoulder, a pair of new satin slippers, a
fresh, moiré ribbon.

Seeing them through the eyes of the new young men Mrs
St George felt their collective grace with a vividness almost
exempt from envy. To her, as to those two foreigners, they
embodied 'the American girl', the world's highest achievement; and she was as ready to enjoy Lizzy Elmsworth's brilliant darkness, and that dry sparkle of Mab's, as much as her
own Virginia's roses, and Nan's alternating frowns and dimples. She was even able to recognize that the Closson girl's
incongruous hair gilded the whole group like a sunburst.
Could Newport show anything lovelier, she wondered half-
bitterly, as she seated herself between Mr Closson and young
Santos-Dios.

Mrs Closson, from the Colonel's right, leaned across the
table with her soft ambiguous smile. 'What lovely diamonds,
Mrs St George! I wish I hadn't left all mine in the safe at
New York!'

Mrs St George thought: 'She means the place isn't worth
bringing jewels to. As if she ever went out anywhere in New
York!' But her eyes wandered beyond Mrs Closson to Lord
Richard Marable; it was the first time she had ever sat at
table with anyone even remotely related to a British nobleman, and she fancied the young man was ironically observing
the way in which she held her fork. But she saw that his eyes,
which were sand-coloured like his face, and sandy-lashed,
had found another occupation. They were fixed on Conchita
Closson, who sat opposite to him; they rested on her

unblinkingly, immovably, as if she had been a natural object, a landscape or a cathedral, that one had travelled far to see, and had the right to look at as long as one chose. 'He's drinking her up like blotting paper. I thought they were better brought up over in England!' Mrs St George said to herself, austerely thankful that he was not taking such liberties with *her* daughters ('but men always know the difference,' she reflected), and suddenly not worrying any longer about how she held her fork.

# FOUR

MISS LAURA TESTVALLEY STOOD ON THE WOODEN PLATFORM of the railway station at Saratoga Springs, NY, and looked about her. It was not an inspiriting scene; but she had not expected that it would be, and would not have greatly cared if it had. She had been in America for eighteen months, and it was not for its architectural or civic beauties that she had risked herself so far. Miss Testvalley had small means, and a derelict family to assist; and her successful career as a governess in the households of the English aristocracy had been curtailed by the need to earn more money. English governesses were at a premium in the United States, and one of Miss Testvalley's former pupils, whose husband was attached to the British Legation in Washington, had recommended her to Mrs Russell Parmore, a cousin of the Eglintons and the van der Luydens – the best, in short, that New York had to offer. The salary was not as high as Miss Testvalley had hoped for; but her ex-pupil at the Legation had assured her that among the 'new' coal and steel people, who could pay more, she would certainly be too wretched. Miss Testvalley was not sure of this. She had not come to America in search of distinguished manners any more than of well-kept railway stations; but she decided on reflection that the Parmore household might be a useful spring-board, and so it proved. Mrs Russell

Parmore was certainly very distinguished, and so were her pallid daughter and her utterly rubbed-out husband; and how could they know that to Miss Testvalley they represented at best a milieu of retired colonials at Cheltenham, or the household of a minor canon in a cathedral town? Miss Testvalley had been used to a more vivid setting, and accustomed to social dramas and emotions which Mrs Russell Parmore had only seen hinted at in fiction; and as the pay was low, and the domestic economies were painful (Mrs Russell Parmore would have thought it ostentatious and vulgar to live largely), Miss Testvalley, after conscientiously 'finishing' Miss Parmore (a young lady whom Nature seemed scarcely to have begun), decided to seek, in a different field, ampler opportunities of action. She consulted a New York governesses' agency, and learned that the 'new people' would give 'almost anything' for such social training as an accomplished European governess could impart. Miss Testvalley fixed a maximum wage, and in a few days was notified by the agency that Mrs Tracy St George was ready to engage her. 'It was Mrs Russell Parmore's reference that did it,' said the black-wigged lady at the desk as they exchanged fees and congratulations. 'In New York that counts more than all your Duchesses'; and Miss Testvalley again had reason to rate her own good sense at its just value. Life at the Parmores', on poor pay and a scanty diet, had been a weary business; but it had been worth while. Now she had in her pocket the promise of eighty dollars a month, and the possibility of a more exciting task; for she understood that the St Georges were very 'new', and the prospect of comparing the manners and customs of the new and the not-new might be amusing. 'I wonder,' she thought ironically, 'if the Duchess would see the slightest difference . . .' the Duchess meaning always *hers*, the puissant lady of Tintagel, where Miss Testvalley had spent so many months shivering with cold, and bandaging the chilblains of the younger girls, while the other daughters, with their particular 'finishing' duenna, accompanied their parents from one ducal residence to another. The Duchess of Tintagel, who had beaten Miss Testvalley's salary well-nigh down to the level of an upper housemaid's, who had so often paid it after an embarrassingly long delay, who had been surprised that a governess should want a fire in her room, or a hot soup for her school-room dinner – the Duchess was now (all unknown to herself) making up for her arrears towards Miss Testvalley. By giving Mrs Parmore the chance to say, when she had friends to dine: 'I happen to know, for instance, that at Tintagel Castle there are only open fires, and the halls and corridors are not heated at all', Miss Testvalley had gained several small favours from her parsimonious employer. By telling her, in the strictest confidence, that their Graces had at one time felt a good deal of anxiety about their only son – oh, a simple sweet-natured young man if ever there was one; but then, the temptations which beset a marquess! – Miss Testvalley had obtained from Mrs Parmore a letter of recommendation which placed her at the head of the educational sisterhood in the United States.

Miss Testvalley needed this, and every other form of assistance she could obtain. It would have been difficult for either Mrs Parmore or the Duchess of Tintagel to imagine how poor she was, or how many people had (or so she thought) a lien on her pitiful savings. It was the penalty of the family glory. Miss Testvalley's grandfather was the illustrious patriot, Gennaro Testavaglia of Modena, fomenter of insurrections, hero of the Risorgimento, author of those once famous historical novels, *Arnaldo da Brescia* and *La Donna della Fortezza*, but whose fame lingered in England chiefly because he was the cousin of the old Gabriele Rossetti, father of the decried and illustrious Dante Gabriel. The Testavaglias, fleeing from the Austrian inquisition, had come to England at the same time as the Rossettis, and contracting their impossible name to the scope of English lips, had intermarried with other exiled revolutionaries and antipapists, producing sons who were artists and agnostics, and daughters who were evangelicals of the strictest pattern, and governesses in the highest families. Laura Testvalley had obediently followed the family tradition; but she had come after the heroic days of evangelical great ladies who required governesses to match; competition was more active, there was less demand for drawing-room Italian and prayerful considerations on the Collects, and more for German and the natural sciences, in neither of which Miss Testvalley excelled. And in the intervening years the mothers and aunts of the family had grown rheumatic and impotent, the heroic old men lingered on in their robust senility, and the drain on the younger generation grew heavier with every year. At thirty-nine Laura had found it impossible, on her English earnings, to keep the grandmother (wife of the Risorgimento hero), and to aid her own infirm mother in supporting an invalid brother and a married sister with six children, whose husband had disappeared in the wilds of Australia. Laura was sure that it was not her vocation to minister to others, but she had been forced into the task early, and continued in it from family pride – and because, after all, she belonged to the group, and the Risorgimento and the Pre-Raphaelites were her chief credentials. And so she had come to America.

At the Parmores' she had learned a good deal about one phase of American life, and she had written home some droll letters on the subject; but she had suspected from the first that the real America was elsewhere, and had been tempted and amused by the idea that among the Wall Street parvenus she might discover it. She had an unspoiled taste for oddities and contrasts, and nothing could have been more alien to her private sentiments than the family combination of revolutionary radicalism, Exeter Hall piety, and awestruck reverence for the aristocratic households in which the Testvalley governesses earned the keep of their ex-carbonari. 'If I'd been a man,' she sometimes thought, 'Dante Gabriel might not have been the only cross in the family.' And the idea obscurely comforted her when she was correcting her pupils' compositions, or picking up the dropped stitches in their knitting.

She was used to waiting in strange railway stations, her old black beaded 'dolman' over her arm, her modest horse-hair box at her feet. Servants often forget to order the fly which is to fetch the governess, and the lady herself, though she may have meant to come to the station, is not infrequently detained by shopping or calling. So Miss Testvalley, without impatience, watched the other travellers drive off in the spidery high-wheeled vehicles in which people bounced across the humps and ruts of the American country roads. It was the eve of the great race-week, and she was amused by the showy garb of the gentlemen and the much-flounced elegance of their ladies, though she felt sure Mrs Parmore would have disdained them.

One by one the travellers scattered, their huge 'Saratogas' (she knew that expression also) hoisted into broken-down express-carts that crawled off in the wake of the owners; and at last a new dust-cloud formed down the road and floated slowly nearer, till there emerged from it a lumbering vehicle of the kind which Miss Testvalley knew to be classed as hotel hacks. As it drew up she was struck by the fact that the driver, a small dusky fellow in a white linen jacket and a hat-brim of exotic width, had an orange bow tied to his whip, and a beruffled white poodle with a bigger orange bow perched between himself and the shabby young man in overalls who shared his seat; while from within she felt herself laughingly surveyed by two tiers of bright young eyes. The driver pulled up with a queer guttural cry to his horses, the poodle leapt down and began to dance on his hind legs, and out of the hack poured a spring torrent of muslins, sash-ends, and bright cheeks under swaying hat-brims. Miss Testvalley found herself in a circle of nymphs shaken by hysterical laughter, and as she stood there, small, brown, interrogative, there swept through her mind a shred of verse which Dante Gabriel used to be fond of reciting:

*Whence came ye, merry damsels, whence came ye,*
*So many and so many, and such glee?*

and she smiled at the idea that Endymion should greet her at the Saratoga railway station. For it was clearly in search of her that the rabble rout had come. The dancing nymphs hailed her with joyful giggles, the poodle sprang on her with dusty paws, and then turned a somersault in her honour, and from the driver's box came the twang of a guitar and the familiar wail of: *Nita, Juanita, ask thy soul if we must part?*

'No, certainly not!' cried Miss Testvalley, tossing up her head towards the driver, who responded with doffed sombrero and hand on heart. 'That is to say!' she added, 'if my future pupil is one of the young ladies who have joined in this very flattering welcome!'

The enchanted circle broke, and the nymphs, still hand in hand, stretched a straight line of loveliness before her. 'Guess which!' chimed simultaneously from five pairs of lips, while five deep curtsies swept the platform; and Miss Testvalley drew back a step and scanned them thoughtfully.

Her first thought was that she had never seen five prettier girls in a row; her second (tinged with joy) that Mrs Russell Parmore would have been scandalized by such an exhibition, on the Saratoga railway platform, in full view of departing travellers, gazing employees, and delighted station loafers; her third that, whichever of the beauties was to fall to her lot, life in such company would be infinitely more amusing than with the Parmores. And still smiling she continued to examine the mirthful mocking faces.

No dominant beauty, was her first impression; no proud angelic heads, ready for coronets or halos, such as she was used to in England; unless indeed the tall fair girl with such heaps of wheat-coloured hair and such gentian-blue eyes – or the very dark one, who was too pale for her black hair, but had the small imperious nose of a Roman empress ... yes, those two were undoubtedly beautiful, yet they were not beauties. They seemed rather to have reached the last height of prettiness, and to be perched on that sunny lower slope, below the cold divinities. And with the other three, taken one by one, fault might have been found on various counts; for the one in the striped pink and white organdy, though she looked cleverer than the others, had a sharp nose, and her laugh showed too many teeth; and the one in white, with a big orange-coloured sash the colour of the poodle's bow (no doubt she was his mistress) was sallow and redhaired, and you had to look into her pale starry eyes to forget that she was too tall, and stooped a little. And as for the fifth, who seemed so much younger – hardly more than a child – her small face was such a flurry of frowns and dimples that Miss Testvalley did not know how to define her.

'Well, young ladies, my first idea is that I wish you were all to be my pupils; and the second –' she paused, weighed the possibilities and met the eyes – 'the second is that this is Miss Annabel St George, who is, I believe, to be my special charge.' She put her hand on Nan's arm.

'How did you know?' burst from Nan, on the shrill note of a netted bird; and the others broke into laughter.

'Why, you silly, we told you so! Anybody can see you're nothing but a baby!'

Nan faced about, blazing and quivering. 'Well, if I'm a baby, what I want is a nurse, and not a beastly English governess!'

Her companions laughed again and nudged each other; then, abashed, they glanced at the newcomer, as if trying to read in her face what would come next.

Miss Testvalley laughed also. 'Oh, I'm used to both jobs,'

she rejoined briskly. 'But meanwhile hadn't we better be getting off to the hotel? Get into the carriage, please, Annabel,' she said with sudden authority.

She turned to look for her trunk; but it had already been shouldered by the nondescript young man in overalls, who hoisted it to the roof of the carriage, and then, jumping down, brushed the soot and dust off his hands. As he did so Miss Testvalley confronted him, and her hand dropped from Nan's arm.

'Why – Lord Richard!' she exclaimed; and the young man in overalls gave a sheepish laugh. 'I suppose at home they all think I'm in Brazil,' he said in an uncertain voice.

'I know nothing of what they think,' retorted Miss Testvalley drily, following the girls into the carriage. As they drove off, Nan, who was crowded in between Mab Elmsworth and Conchita, burst into sudden tears. 'I didn't mean to call you "beastly",' she whispered, stealing a hand towards the new governess; and the new governess, clasping the hand, answered with her undaunted smile: 'I didn't hear you call me so, my dear.'

# FIVE

MRS ST GEORGE HAD GONE TO THE RACES WITH HER HUSBAND
- an ordeal she always dreaded and yet prayed for. Colonel St
George, on these occasions, was so handsome, and so splendid in his light racing suit and grey top hat, that she enjoyed
a larger repetition of her triumph in the hotel dining-room;
but when this had been tasted to the full there remained her
dread of the mysterious men with whom he was hail-fellow-
well-met in the paddock, and the dreadful painted women in
open carriages, who leered and beckoned (didn't she see
them?) under the fringes of their sunshades.

She soon wearied of the show, and would have been glad
to be back rocking and sipping lemonade on the hotel verandah; yet when the Colonel helped her into the carriage, suggesting that if she wanted to meet the new governess it was
time to be off, she instantly concluded that the rich widow at
the Congress Springs Hotel, about whom there was so much
gossip, had made him a secret sign, and was going to carry
him off to the gambling rooms for supper – if not worse. But
when the Colonel chose his arts were irresistible, and in
another moment Mrs St George was driving away alone, her
heart heavy with this new anxiety superposed on so many
others.

When she reached the hotel all the frequenters of the

verandah, gathered between the columns of the porch, were greeting with hysterical laughter a motley group who were pouring out of the familiar vehicle from which Mrs St George had expected to see Nan descend with the dreaded and longed-for governess. The party was headed by Teddy de Santos-Dios, grotesquely accoutred in a hotel waiter's white jacket, and twanging his guitar to the antics of Conchita's poodle, while Conchita herself, the Elmsworth sisters and Mrs St George's own two girls, danced up the steps surrounding a small soberly garbed figure, whom Mrs St George instantly identified as the governess. Mrs Elmsworth and Mrs Closson stood on the upper step, smothering their laughter in lace handkerchiefs; but Mrs St George sailed past them with set lips, pushing aside a shabby-looking young man in overalls who seemed to form part of the company.

'Virginia – Annabel,' she gasped, 'what is the meaning . . . Oh, Miss Testvalley – what *must* you think?' she faltered with trembling lips.

'I think it very kind of Annabel's young friends to have come with her to meet me,' said Miss Testvalley; and Mrs St George noted with bewilderment and relief that she was actually smiling, and that she had slipped her arm through Nan's.

For a moment Mrs St George thought it might be easier to deal with a governess who was already on such easy terms with her pupil; but by the time Miss Testvalley, having removed the dust of travel, had knocked at her employer's door, the latter had been assailed by new apprehensions. It would have been comparatively simple to receive, with what Mrs St George imagined to be the dignity of a duchess, a governess used to such ceremonial; but the disconcerting circumstances of Miss Testvalley's arrival, and the composure with which she met them, had left Mrs St George with her dignity on her hands. Could it be –? But no; Mrs Russell Parmore, as well as the Duchess, answered for Miss

Testvalley's unquestionable respectability. Mrs St George fanned herself nervously.

'Oh, come in. Do sit down, Miss Testvalley.' (Mrs St George had expected someone taller, more majestic. She would have thought Miss Testvalley insignificant, could the term be applied to anyone coming from Mrs Parmore.) 'I don't know how my daughters can have been induced to do anything so – so undignified. Unfortunately the Closson girl –.' She broke off, embarrassed by the recollection of the Colonel's injunctions.

'The tall young girl with auburn hair? I understand that one of the masqueraders was her brother.'

'Yes; her half-brother. Mrs Closson is a Brazilian' – but again Mrs St George checked the note of disparagement. 'Brazilian' was bad enough, without adding anything pejorative. 'The Colonel – Colonel St George – has business relations with Mr Closson. I never met them before . . .'

'Ah,' said Miss Testvalley.

'And I'm sure my girls and the Elmsworths would never . . .'

'Oh, quite so; I understood. I've no doubt the idea was Lord Richard's.'

She uttered the name as though it were familiar to her, and Mrs St George caught at Lord Richard. 'You knew him already? He appears to be a friend of the Clossons.'

'I knew him in England; yes. I was with Lady Brightlingsea for two years – as his sisters' governess.'

Mrs St George gazed awestruck down this new and resonant perspective. 'Lady Brittlesey?' (It was thus that Miss Testvalley had pronounced the name.)

'The Marchioness of Brightlingsea; his mother. It's a very large family. I was with two of the younger daughters. Lady Honoria and Lady Ulrica Marable. I think Lord Richard is the third son. But one saw him at home so very seldom . . .'

Mrs St George drew a deep breath. She had not bargained for this glimpse into the labyrinth of the peerage, and she felt a little dizzy, as though all the Brightlingseas and the Marables were in the room, and she ought to make the proper gestures, and didn't even know what to call them without her husband's being there to tell her. She wondered whether the experiment of an English governess might not after all make life too complicated. And this one's eyebrows were so black and ironical.

'Lord Richard,' continued Miss Testvalley, 'always has to have his little joke.' Her tone seemed to dismiss him, and all his titled relations with him. Mrs St George was relieved. 'But your daughter Annabel – perhaps,' Miss Testvalley continued, 'you would like to give me some general idea of the stage she has reached in her different studies?' Her manner was now distinctly professional, and Mrs St George's spirits drooped again. If only the Colonel had been there – as he would have been, but for that woman! Or even Nan herself ... Mrs St George looked helplessly at the governess. But suddenly an inspiration came to her. 'I have always left these things to the girls' teachers,' she said with majesty.

'Oh, quite –' Miss Testvalley assented.

'And their father; their father takes a great interest in their studies – when time permits ...' Mrs St George continued. 'But of course his business interests ... which are enormous ...'

'I think I understand,' Miss Testvalley softly agreed.

Mrs St George again sighed her relief. A governess who understood without the need of tiresome explanations – was it not more than she had hoped for? Certainly Miss Testvalley looked insignificant; but the eyes under her expressive eyebrows were splendid, and she had an air of firmness. And the miracle was that Nan should already have taken a fancy to her. If only the other girls didn't laugh her out of it! 'Of course,' Mrs St George began again, 'what I attach most importance to is that my girls should be taught to – to behave like ladies.'

Miss Testvalley murmured: 'Oh, yes. Drawing-room accomplishments.'

'I may as well tell you that I don't care very much for the girls they associate with here. Saratoga is not what it used to be. In New York of course it will be different. I hope you can persuade Annabel to study.'

She could not think of anything else to say, and the governess, who seemed singularly discerning, rose with a slight bow, and murmured: 'If you will allow me . . .'

Miss Testvalley's room was narrow and bare; but she had already discovered that the rooms of summer hotels in the States were all like that; the luxury and gilding were reserved for the public parlours. She did not much mind; she had never been used to comfort, and her Italian nature did not crave it. To her mind the chief difference between the governess's room at Tintagel, or at Allfriars, the Brightlingsea seat, and those she had occupied since her arrival in America, was that the former were larger (and therefore harder to heat) and were furnished with threadbare relics of former splendour, and carpets in which you caught your heel; whereas at Mrs Parmore's, and in this big hotel, though the governess's quarters were cramped, they were neat and the furniture was in good repair. But this afternoon Miss Testvalley was perhaps tired, or oppressed by the heat, or perhaps only by an unwonted sense of loneliness. Certainly it was odd to find one's self at the orders of people who wished their daughters to be taught to 'behave like ladies'. (The alternative being – what, she wondered? Perhaps a disturbing apparition like Conchita Closson.)

At any rate, Miss Testvalley was suddenly aware of a sense of loneliness, of far-away-ness, of a quite unreasonable yearning for the dining-room at the back of a certain shabby house at Denmark Hill, where her mother, in a widow's cap of white crape, sat on one side of the scantily filled grate, turning with rheumatic fingers the pages of the Reverend

Frederick Maurice's sermons, while, facing her across the hearth, old Gennaro Testavaglia, still heavy and powerful in his extreme age, brooded with fixed eyes in a big parchment-coloured face, and repeated over and over some forgotten verse of his own revolutionary poems. In that room, with its chronic smell of cold coffee and smouldering coals, of Elliman's liniment and human old age, Miss Testvalley had spent some of the most disheartening hours of her life. 'Le mie prigioni,' she had once called it; yet was it not for that detested room that she was homesick!

Only fifteen minutes in which to prepare for supper! (She had been warned that late dinners were still unknown in American hotels.) Miss Testvalley, setting her teeth against the vision of the Denmark Hill dining-room, went up to the chest of drawers on which she had already laid out her mod-est toilet appointments; and there she saw, between her yel-lowish-backed brush and faded pincushion, a bunch of freshly gathered geraniums and mignonette. The flowers had certainly not been there when she had smoothed her hair before waiting on Mrs St George; nor had they, she was sure, been sent by that lady. They were not bought flowers, but flowers lovingly gathered; and someone else must have entered in Miss Testvalley's absence, and hastily deposited the humble posy.

The governess sat down on the hard chair beside the bed, and her eyes filled with tears. Flowers, she had noticed, did not abound in the States; at least not in summer. In winter, in New York, you could see them banked up in tiers in the damp heat of the florists' windows; plumy ferns, forced lilac, and those giant roses, red and pink, which rich people offered to each other so lavishly in long white cardboard boxes. It was very odd; the same ladies who exchanged these costly tributes in mid-winter lived through the summer without a flower, or with nothing but a stiff bed of dwarf foliage plants before the door, or a tub or two of the inevitable hydrangeas. Yet someone had apparently managed to snatch these flowers from the meagre border before the hotel porch, and had put them there to fill Miss Testvalley's bedroom with scent and colour. And who could have done it but her new pupil?

QUARTER of an hour later Miss Testvalley, her thick hair rebraided and glossed with brilliantine, her black merino exchanged for a plum-coloured silk with a crochet lace collar, and lace mittens on her small worn hands, knocked at the door of the Misses St George. It opened, and the governess gave a little 'oh' of surprise. Virginia stood there, a shimmer of ruffled white drooping away from her young throat and shoulders. On her heaped-up wheat-coloured hair lay a wreath of cornflowers; and a black velvet ribbon with a locket hanging from it intensified her fairness like the black stripe on a ring-dove's throat.

'What elegance for a public dining-room!' thought Miss Testvalley; and then reflected: 'But no doubt it's her only chance of showing it.'

Virginia opened wondering blue eyes, and the governess explained: 'The supper-bell has rung, and I thought you and your sister might like me to go down with you.'

'Oh –' Virginia murmured; and added: 'Nan's lost her slipper. She's hunting for it.'

'Very well; shall I help her? And you'll go down and excuse us to your mamma?'

Virginia's eyes grew wider. 'Well, I guess mother's used to waiting,' she said, as she sauntered along the corridor to the staircase.

Nan St George lay face downward on the floor, poking with a silk parasol under the wardrobe. At the sound of Miss Testvalley's voice she raised herself sulkily. Her small face was flushed and frowning. ('None of her sister's beauty,' Miss Testvalley thought.) 'It's there, but I can't get at it,' Nan proclaimed.

'My dear, you'll tumble your lovely frock –'

'Oh, it's not lovely. It's one of Jinny's last year's organdies.'

'Well, it won't improve it to crawl about on the floor. Is your shoe under the wardrobe? Let me try to get it. My silk won't be damaged.'

Miss Testvalley put out her hand for the sunshade, and Nan scrambled to her feet. 'You can't reach it,' she said, still sulkily. But Miss Testvalley, prostrate on the floor, had managed to push a thin arm under the wardrobe, and the parasol presently reappeared with a little bronze slipper on its tip. Nan gave a laugh.

'Well, you *are* handy!' she said.

Miss Testvalley echoed the laugh. 'Put it on quickly, and let me help you to tidy your dress. And, oh dear, your sash is untied –' She spun the girl about, retied the sash and smoothed the skirt with airy touches; for all of which, she noticed, Nan uttered no word of thanks.

'And your handkerchief, Annabel?' In Miss Testvalley's opinion no lady should appear in the evening without a scrap of lace-edged cambric, folded into a triangle and held between gloved or mittened finger-tips. Nan shrugged. 'I never know where my handkerchiefs are – I guess they get lost in the wash, wandering round in hotels the way we do.'

Miss Testvalley sighed at this nomadic wastefulness. Perhaps because she had always been a wanderer herself she loved orderly drawers and shelves, and bunches of lavender between delicately fluted under-garments.

'Do you always live in hotels, my dear?'

'We did when I was little. But father's bought a house in New York now. Mother made him do it because the Elmsworths did. She thought maybe, if we had one, Jinny'd be invited out more; but I don't see much difference.'

'Well, I shall have to help you to go over your linen,' the governess continued; but Nan showed no interest in the offer. Miss Testvalley saw before her a cold impatient little face – and yet . . .

'Annabel,' she said, slipping her hand through the girl's thin arm, 'how did you guess I was fond of flowers?'

The blood rose from Nan's shoulders to her cheeks, and a half-guilty smile set the dimples racing across her face. 'Mother said we'd acted like a lot of savages, getting up that circus at the station – and what on earth would you think of us?'

'I think that I shall like you all very much; and you especially, because of those flowers.'

Nan gave a shy laugh. 'Lord Richard said you'd like them.'

'Lord Richard?'

'Yes. He says in England everybody has a garden, with lots of flowers that smell sweet. And so I stole them from the hotel border . . . He's crazy about Conchita, you know. Do you think she'll catch him?'

Miss Testvalley stiffened. She felt her upper lip lengthen, though she tried to smile. 'I don't think it's a question that need concern us, do you?'

Nan stared. 'Well, she's my greatest friend – after Jinny, I mean.'

'Then we must wish her something better than Lord Richard. Come, my dear, or those wonderful American griddle-cakes will all be gone.'

EARLY in her career Miss Testvalley had had to learn the difficult art of finding her way about – not only as concerned the tastes and temper of the people she lived with, but the topography of their houses. In those old winding English dwellings, half-fortress, half-palace, where suites and galleries of stately proportions abruptly tapered off into narrow twists and turns, leading to unexpected rooms tucked away in unaccountable corners, and where school-room and nurseries were usually at the far end of the labyrinth, it behoved the governess to blaze her trail by a series of private aids to memory. It was important, in such houses, not only to know the way you were meant to take, but the many you were expected to avoid, and a young governess turning too often down the passage leading to the young gentlemen's wing, or getting into the way of the master of the house in his dignified descent to the breakfast-room, might suddenly have her services dispensed with. To anyone thus trained the simple plan of an American summer hotel offered no mysteries; and when supper was over and, after a sultry hour or two in the red and gold ball-room, the St George ladies ascended to their apartments, Miss Testvalley had no difficulty in finding her way up another flight to her own room. She was already aware that it was in the wing of the hotel, and had noted that from its window she could look across into that from which, before supper, she had seen Miss Closson signal to her brother and Lord Richard, who were smoking on the gravel below.

It was no business of Miss Testvalley's to keep watch on what went on in the Closson rooms – or would not have been, she corrected herself, had Nan St George not spoken of Conchita as her dearest friend. Such a tie did seem to the governess to require vigilance. Miss Closson was herself an unknown quantity, and Lord Richard was one only too well known to Miss Testvalley. It was therefore not unnatural that, after silence had fallen on the long corridors of the hotel, the governess, finding sleep impossible in her small suffocating room, should put out her candle, and gaze across from her window at that from which she had seen Conchita lean.

Light still streamed from it, though midnight was past, and presently came laughter, and the twang of Santos-Dios's guitar, and a burst of youthful voices joining in song. Was her pupil's among them? Miss Testvalley could not be sure; but soon, detaching itself from Teddy de Santos-Dios's reedy tenor, she caught the hoarse baritone of another voice.

Imprudent children! It was bad enough to be gathered at that hour in a room with a young man and a guitar; but at least the young man was Miss Closson's brother, and Miss Testvalley had noticed, at the supper table, much exchange of civilities between the St Georges and the Clossons. But Richard Marable – that was inexcusable, that was scandalous! The hotel would be ringing with it tomorrow . . .

Ought not Miss Testvalley to find some pretext for knocking at Conchita's door, gathering her charges back to safety, and putting it in their power to say that their governess had assisted at the little party? Her first impulse was to go; but governesses who act on first impulses seldom keep their places. 'As long as there's so much noise,' she thought, 'there can't be any mischief . . .' and at that moment, in a pause of the singing, she caught Nan's trill of little-girl laughter. Miss Testvalley started up, and went to her door; but once more she drew back. Better wait and see – interfering might do more harm than good. If only some exasperated neighbour did not ring to have the rejoicings stopped!

At length music and laughter subsided. Silence followed. Miss Testvalley, drawing an austere purple flannel garment over her night-dress, unbolted her door and stole out into the passage. Where it joined the main corridor she paused and waited. A door had opened half-way down the corridor – Conchita's door – and the governess saw a flutter of light dresses, and heard subdued laughter and good nights. Both the St George and Elmsworth families were lodged below, and in the weak glimmer of gas she made sure of four girls hurrying toward her wing. She drew back hastily. Glued to her door she listened, and heard a heavy but cautious step passing by, and a throaty voice humming 'Champagne Charlie'. She drew a breath of relief, and sat down before her glass to finish her toilet for the night.

Her hair carefully waved on its pins, her evening prayer recited, she slipped into bed and blew out the light. But still

sleep did not come, and she lay in the sultry darkness and listened, she hardly knew for what. At last she heard the same
heavy step returning cautiously, passing her door, gaining
once more the main corridor – the step she would have
known in a thousand, the step she used to listen for at
Allfriars after midnight, groping down the long passage to
the governess's room.

She started up. Forgetful of crimping-pins and bare feet,
she opened her door again. The last flicker of gas had gone
out, and secure in the blackness she crept after the heavy
step to the corner. It sounded ahead of her half-way down the
long row of doors; then it stopped, a door opened . . . and
Miss Testvalley turned back on leaden feet . . .

Nothing of that fugitive adventure at Allfriars had ever
been known. Of that she was certain. An ill-conditioned
youth, the boon companion of his father's grooms, and a
small brown governess, ten years his elder, and known to be
somewhat curt and distant with everyone except her pupils
and their parents – who would ever have thought of associating the one with the other? The episode had been brief; the
peril was soon over; and when, the very same year, Lord
Richard was solemnly banished from his father's house, it was
not because of his having once or twice stolen down the
school-room passage at undue hours; but for reasons so far
more deplorable that poor Lady Brightlingsea, her reserve
utterly broken down, had sobbed out on Miss Testvalley's
breast: 'Anything, anything else I know his father would
have forgiven.' (Miss Testvalley wondered . . . )

# SIX

WHEN COLONEL ST GEORGE BOUGHT HIS HOUSE IN MADISON Avenue it seemed to him fit to satisfy the ambitions of any budding millionaire. That it had been built and decorated by one of the Tweed ring, who had come to grief earlier than his more famous fellow-criminals, was to Colonel St George convincing proof that it was a suitable setting for wealth and elegance. But social education is acquired rapidly in New York, even by those who have to absorb it through the cracks of the sacred edifice; and Mrs St George had already found out that no one lived in Madison Avenue, that the front hall should have been painted Pompeian red with a stencilled frieze, and not with naked Cupids and humming birds on a sky-blue ground, and that basement dining-rooms were unknown to the fashionable. So much she had picked up almost at once from Jinny and Jinny's school-friends; and when she called on Mrs Parmore to enquire about the English governess, the sight of the Parmore house, small and simple as it was, completed her disillusionment.

But it was too late to change. The Colonel, who was insensitive to details, continued to be proud of his house; even when the Elmsworths, suddenly migrating from Brooklyn, had settled themselves in Fifth Avenue he would not admit his mistake, or feel the humiliation of the contrast.

And yet what a difference it made to a lady to be able to say 'Fifth Avenue' in giving her address to Black, Starr and Frost, or to Mrs Connelly, the fashionable dress-maker! In establishments like that they classed their customers at once, and 'Madison Avenue' stood at best for a decent mediocrity.

Mrs St George at first ascribed to this unfortunate locality her failure to make a social situation for her girls; yet after the Elmsworths had come to Fifth Avenue she noted with satisfaction that Lizzy and Mabel were not asked out much more than Virginia. Of course Mr Elmsworth was an obstacle; and so was Mrs Elmsworth's laugh. It was difficult – it was even painful – to picture the Elmsworths dining at the Parmores' or the Eglintons'. But the St Georges did not dine there either. And the question of ball-going was almost as discouraging. One of the young men whom the girls had met at Saratoga had suggested to Virginia that he might get her a card for the first Assembly; but Mrs St George, when sounded, declined indignantly, for she knew that in the best society girls did not go to balls without their parents.

These subscription balls were a peculiar source of bitterness to Mrs St George. She could not understand how her daughters could be excluded from entertainment for which one could buy a ticket. She knew all about the balls from her hairdresser, the celebrated Katie Wood. Katie did everybody's hair, and innocently planted dagger after dagger in Mrs St George's anxious breast by saying: 'If you and Jinny want me next Wednesday week for the first Assembly you'd better say so right off, because I've got every minute bespoke already from three o'clock on', or, 'If you're invited to the opening night of the Opera, I might try the new chignon with the bunch of curls on the left shoulder', or worse still, 'I suppose Jinny belongs to the Thursday Evening Dances, don't she? The débutantes are going to wear wreaths of apple-blossom or rose-buds a good deal this winter – or forget-me-not would look lovely, with her eyes.'

Lovely, indeed. But if Virginia had not been asked to belong, and if Mrs St George had vainly tried to have her own name added to the list of the Assembly balls, or to get a box for the opening night of the Opera, what was there to do but to say indifferently: 'Oh, I don't know if we shall be here – the Colonel's thinking a little of carrying us off to Florida if he can get away . . .' knowing all the while how much the hairdresser believed of that excuse, and also aware that, in speaking of Miss Eglinton and Miss Parmore, Katie did not call them by their Christian names . . .

Mrs St George could not understand why she was subjected to this cruel ostracism. The Colonel knew everybody – that is, all the gentlemen he met downtown, or at his clubs, and he belonged to many clubs. Their dues were always having to be paid, even when the butcher and the grocer were clamouring. He often brought gentlemen home to dine, and gave them the best champagne and Madeira in the cellar; and they invited him back, but never included Mrs St George and Virginia in their invitations.

It was small comfort to learn one day that Jinny and Nan had been invited to act as Conchita Closson's bridesmaids. She thought it unnatural that the Clossons, who were strangers in New York, and still camping at the Fifth Avenue Hotel, should be marrying their daughter before Virginia was led to the altar. And then the bridegroom! – well, everybody knew that he was only a younger son, and that in England, even in the great aristocratic families, younger sons were of small account unless they were clever enough to make their own way – an ambition which seemed never to have troubled Dick Marable. Moreover, there were dark rumours about him, reports of warning discreetly transmitted through the British Legation in Washington, and cruder tales among the clubs. Still, nothing could alter the fact that Lord Richard Marable was the son of the Marquess of Brightlingsea, and that his mother had been a Duke's daughter – and who knows whether the Eglintons and Parmores, though they thanked heaven their dear girls would never be exposed to such risks, were not half envious of the Clossons? But then there was the indecent haste of it. The young people had met for the first time in August; and they were to be married in November! In good society it was usual for a betrothal to last at least a year; and among the Eglintons and Parmores even that time allowance was thought to betray an undue haste. 'The young people should be given time to get to know each other,' the mothers of Fifth Avenue decreed; and Mrs Parmore told Miss Testvalley, when the latter called to pay her respects to her former employer, that she for her part hoped her daughter would never consent to an engagement of less than two years. 'But I suppose, dear Miss Testvalley, that among the people you're with now there are no social traditions.'

'None except those they are making for themselves,' Miss Testvalley was tempted to rejoin; but that would not have been what she called a 'governess's answer', and she knew a governess should never be more on her guard than when conversing with a former employer. Especially, Miss Testvalley thought, when the employer had a long nose with a slight droop, and pale lips like Mrs Parmore's. She murmured that there were business reasons, she understood; Mr Closson was leaving shortly for Brazil.

'Ah, so they *say*. But of course, the rumours one hears about this young man ... a son of Lord Brightlingsea's, I understand? But, Miss Testvalley, you were with the Brightlingseas; you must have known him?'

'It's a very big family, and when I went there the sons were already scattered. I usually remained at Allfriars with the younger girls.'

Mrs Parmore nodded softly. 'Quite so. And by that time this unfortunate young man had already begun his career of dissipation in London. He *has* been dissipated, I believe?'

'Lately I think he's been trying to earn his living on Mr Closson's plantation in Brazil.'

'Poor young man! Do his family realize what a deplorable choice he has made? Whatever his past may have been, it's a pity he should marry in New York, and leave it again, without having any idea of it beyond what can be had in the Closson set. If he'd come in different circumstances, we should all have been so happy ... Mr Parmore would have put him down at his clubs ... he would have been invited everywhere ... Yes, it does seem unfortunate ... But of course no one knows the Clossons.'

'I suppose the young couple will go back to Brazil after the marriage,' said Miss Testvalley evasively.

Mrs Parmore gave an ironic smile. 'I don't imagine Miss Closson is marrying the son of a marquess to go and live on a plantation in Brazil. When I took Alida to Mrs Connelly's to order her dress for the Assembly, Mrs Connelly told me she'd heard from Mrs Closson's maid that Mr Closson meant to give the young couple a house in London. Do you suppose this is likely? They can't keep up any sort of establishment in London without a fairly large income; and I hear Mr Closson's position in Wall Street is rather shaky.'

Miss Testvalley took refuge in one of her Italian gestures of conjecture. 'Governesses, you know, Mrs Parmore, hear so much less gossip than dress-makers and ladies'-maids; and I'm not Miss Closson's governess.'

'No; fortunately for you! For I believe there were rather unpleasant rumours at Saratoga. People were bound to find a reason for such a hurried marriage ... But your pupils have been asked to be bridesmaids, I understand?'

'The girls got to know each other last summer. And you know how exciting it is, especially for a child of Annabel St George's age, to figure for the first time in a wedding procession.'

'Yes. I suppose they haven't many chances ... But

shouldn't you like to come upstairs and see Alida's Assembly dress? Mrs Connelly has just sent it home, and your pupils might like to hear about it. White tulle, of course – nothing will ever replace white tulle for a débutante, will it?'

Miss Testvalley, after that visit, felt that she had cast in her lot once for all with the usurpers and the adventurers. Perhaps because she herself had been born in exile, her sympathies were with the social as well as the political outcasts – with the weepers by the waters of Babylon rather than those who barred the doors of the Assembly against them. Describe Miss Parmore's white tulle to her pupils, indeed! What she meant – but how accomplish it? – was to get cards for the Assembly for Mrs St George and Virginia, and to see to it that the latter's dress outdid Miss Parmore's as much as her beauty over-shadowed that young woman's.

But how? Through Lord Richard Marable? Well, that was perhaps not impossible ... Miss Testvalley had detected, in Mrs Parmore, a faint but definite desire to make the young man's acquaintance, even to have him on the list of her next dinner. She would like to show him, poor young fellow, her manner implied, that there are houses in New York where a scion of the English aristocracy may feel himself at home, and discover (though, alas, too late!) that there are American girls comparable to his own sisters in education and breeding.

Since the announcement of Conchita's engagement, and the return of the two families to New York, there had been a good deal of coming and going between the St George and Closson households – rather too much to suit Miss Testvalley. But she had early learned to adapt herself to her pupils' whims while maintaining her authority over them, and she preferred to accompany Nan to the Fifth Avenue Hotel rather than let her go there without her. Virginia, being 'out', could come and go as she pleased; but among the

Parmores and Eglintons, in whose code Mrs St George was profoundly versed, girls in the school-room did not walk about New York alone, much less call at hotels, and Nan, fuming yet resigned – for she had already grown unaccountably attached to her governess – had to submit to Miss Testvalley's conducting her to the Closson apartment, and waiting below when she was to be fetched. Sometimes, at Mrs Closson's request, the governess went in with her charge. Mrs Closson was almost always in her sitting-room, since leaving it necessitated encasing her soft frame in stays and a heavily whale-boned dress; and she preferred sitting at her piano, or lying on the sofa with a novel and a cigarette, in an atmosphere of steam-heat and heavily scented flowers, and amid a litter of wedding presents and bridal finery. She was a good-natured woman, friendly and even confidential with everybody who came her way, and when she caught sight of Miss Testvalley behind her charge, often called to her to come in and take a look at the lovely dress Mrs Connelly had just sent home, or the embossed soup-tureen of Baltimore silver offered by Mr Closson's business friends. Miss Testvalley did not always accept; but sometimes she divined that Mrs Closson wished to consult her, or to confide in her, and, while her pupil joined the other girls, she would clear the finery from a chair and prepare to receive Mrs Closson's confidences – which were usually connected with points of social etiquette, indifferent to the lady herself, but preoccupying to Mr Closson.

'He thinks it's funny that Dick's family haven't cabled, or even written. Do they generally do so in England? I tell Mr Closson there hasn't been time yet – I'm so bad about answering letters myself that I can't blame anybody else for not writing! But Mr Closson seems to think it's meant for a slight. Why should it be? If Dick's family are not satisfied with Conchita, they will be when they see her, don't you think so?' Yes, certainly, Miss Testvalley thought so. 'Well, then – what's the use of worrying? But Mr Closson is a business man, and he expects everybody to have business habits. I don't suppose the Marquess is in business, is he?'

Miss Testvalley said no, she thought not; and for a moment there flickered up in Mrs Closson a languid curiosity to know more of her daughter's future relatives. 'It's a big family, isn't it? Dick says he can never remember how many brothers and sisters he has; but I suppose that's one of his jokes . . . He's a great joker, isn't he; like my Ted! Those two are always playing tricks on everybody. But how many brothers and sisters are there, really?'

Miss Testvalley, after a moment's calculation, gave the number as eight; Lord Seadown, the heir, Lord John, Lord Richard – and five girls; yes, there were five girls. Only one married as yet; the Lady Camilla. Her own charges, the Ladies Honoria and Ulrica, were now out; the other two were still in the school-room. Yes; it was a large family – but not so very large, as English families went. Large enough, however, to preoccupy Lady Brightlingsea a good deal – especially as concerned the future of her daughters.

Mrs Closson listened with her dreamy smile. Her attention had none of the painful precision with which Mrs St George tried to master the details of social life in the higher spheres, nor of the eager curiosity gleaming under Mrs Parmore's pale eyelashes. Mrs Closson really could not see that there was much difference between one human being and another, except that some had been favoured with more leisure than others – and leisure was her idea of heaven.

'I should think Lady Brightlingsea would be worn out, with all those girls to look after. I don't suppose she's had much time to think about the boys.'

'Well, of course she's devoted to her sons too.'

'Oh, I suppose so. And you say the other two sons are not married?' No, not as yet, Miss Testvalley repeated.

A flicker of interest was again perceptible between Mrs

Closson's drowsy lids. 'If they don't either of them marry, Dick will be the Marquess some day, won't he?'

Miss Testvalley could not restrain a faint amusement. 'But Lord Seadown is certain to marry. In those great houses it's a family obligation for the heir to marry.'

Mrs Closson's head sank back contentedly. 'Mercy! How many obligations they all seem to have. I guess Conchita'll be happier just making a love-match with Lord Richard. He's passionately in love with her, isn't he?' Mrs Closson pursued with her confidential smile.

'It would appear so, certainly,' Miss Testvalley rejoined.

'All I want is that she should be happy; and he *will* make her happy, won't he?' the indulgent mother concluded, as though Miss Testvalley's words had completely reassured her.

At that moment the door was flung open, and the bride herself whirled into the room. 'Oh, mother!' Conchita paused to greet Miss Testvalley; her manner, like her mother's, was always considerate and friendly. 'You're not coming to take Nan away already, are you?' Reassured by Miss Testvalley, she put her hands on her hips and spun lightly around in front of the two ladies.

'Mother! Isn't it a marvel? – It's my Assembly dress,' she explained, laughing, to the governess.

It was indeed a marvel; the money these American mothers spent on their daughters' clothes never ceased to astonish Miss Testvalley; but while her appreciative eye registered every costly detail her mind was busy with the incredible fact that Conchita Closson – 'the Closson girl' in Mrs Parmore's vocabulary – had contrived to get an invitation to the Assembly, while her own charges, who were so much lovelier and more lovable . . . But here they were, Virginia, Nan, and Lizzy Elmsworth, all circling gaily about the future bride, applauding, criticizing, twitching as critically at her ruffles and ribbons as though these were to form a part of their own adornment. Miss Testvalley, looking closely, saw no trace of envy in their radiant faces, though Virginia's was perhaps a trifle sad. 'So they've not been invited to the ball, and Conchita *has*,' she reflected, and felt a sudden irritation against Miss Closson.

But the irritation did not last. This was Mrs Parmore's doing, the governess was sure; to secure Lord Richard she had no doubt persuaded the patronesses of the Assembly – that stern tribunal – to include his fiancée among their guests. Only – how had she, or the others, managed to accept the idea of introducing the fiancée's mother into their hallowed circle? The riddle was answered by Mrs Closson herself. 'First I was afraid I'd have to take Conchita – just imagine it! Get up out of my warm bed in the middle of the night, and rig myself up in satin and whale-bones, and feathers on my head – they say I'd have had to wear feathers!' Mrs Closson laughed luxuriously over this plumed and armoured vision, 'But luckily they didn't even invite me. They invited my son instead – it seems in New York a girl can go to a ball with her brother, even to an Assembly ball . . . and Conchita was so crazy to accept that Mr Closson said we'd better let her . . .'

Conchita spun around again, her flexible arms floating like a dancer's on her outspread flounces. 'Oh, girls, it's a perfect shame you're not coming too! They ought to have invited all my bridesmaids, oughtn't they, Miss Testvalley?' She spoke with evident good will, and the governess reflected how different Miss Parmore's view would have been, had she been invited to an exclusive entertainment from which her best friends were omitted. But then no New York entertainment excluded Miss Parmore's friends.

Miss Testvalley, as she descended the stairs, turned the problem over in her mind. She had never liked her girls (as she already called them) as much as she did at that moment. Nan, of course, was a child, and could comfort herself with the thought that her time for ball-going had not yet come;

but Virginia – well, Virginia, whom Miss Testvalley had not altogether learned to like, was behaving as generously as her sister. Her quick hands had displaced the rose-garland on Conchita's shoulder, rearranging it in a more becoming way. Conchita was careless about her toilet, and had there been any malice in Virginia she might have spoilt her friend's dress instead of improving it. No act of generosity appealed in vain to Miss Testvalley, and as she went down the stairs to the hotel entrance she muttered to herself: 'If I only could – if I only knew how!'

# SEVEN

SHE WAS SO BUSY WITH HER THOUGHTS THAT SHE WAS startled by the appearance, at the foot of the stairs, of a young man who stood there visibly waiting.

'Lord Richard!' she exclaimed, almost as surprised as when she had first recognized him, disguised in grimy overalls, at the Saratoga station.

Since then she had, of necessity, run across him now and then, at the St Georges' as well as at Mrs Closson's; but if he had not perceptibly avoided her, neither had he sought her out, and for that she was thankful. The Lord Richard chapter was a closed one, and she had no wish to reopen it. She had paid its cost in some brief fears and joys, and one night of agonizing tears; but perhaps her Italian blood had saved her from ever, then or after, regarding it as a moral issue. In her busy life there was no room for dead love-affairs; and besides, did the word 'love' apply to such passing follies? Fatalistically, she had registered the episode and pigeon-holed it. If ever she were to know an abiding grief it must be caused by one that engaged the soul.

Lord Richard stood before her awkwardly. He was always either sullen or too hearty, and she hoped he was not going to be hearty. But perhaps since those days life had formed him . . .

'I saw you go upstairs just now – and I waited.'

'You waited? For me?'

'Yes,' he muttered, still more awkwardly. 'Could I speak to you?'

Miss Testvalley reflected. She could not imagine what he wanted, but experience told her that it would almost certainly be something disagreeable. However, it was not her way to avoid issues – and perhaps he only wanted to borrow money. She could not give him much, of course . . . but if it were only that, so much the better. 'We can go in there, I suppose,' she said, pointing to the door of the public sitting-room. She lifted the *portière* and, finding the room empty, led the way to a ponderous rosewood sofa. Lord Richard shambled after her, and seated himself on the other side of the table before the sofa.

'You'd better be quick – there are always people here receiving visitors.'

The young man, thus admonished, was still silent. He sat sideways on his chair, as though to avoid facing Miss Testvalley. A frown drew the shock of drab hair still lower over his low forehead, and he pulled nervously at his drab moustache.

'Well?' said Miss Testvalley.

'I – look here. I'm no hand at explaining . . . never was . . . But you were always a friend of mine . . .'

'I've no wish to be otherwise.'

His frown relaxed slightly. 'I never know how to say things . . .'

'What is it you wish to say?'

'I – well, Mr Closson asked me yesterday if there was any reason why I shouldn't marry Conchita.'

His eyes still avoided her, but she kept hers resolutely on his face. 'Do you know what made him ask?'

'Well, you see – there's been no word from home. I rather fancy he expected the governor to write, or even to cable. They seem to do such a lot of cabling in this country, don't they?'

Miss Testvalley reflected. 'How long ago did you write? Has there been time enough for an answer to come? It's not likely that your family would cable.'

Lord Richard looked embarrassed; which meant, she suspected, that his letter had not been sent as promptly as he had let the Clossons believe. Sheer dilatoriness might even have kept him from sending it at all. 'You have written, I suppose?' she enquired sternly.

'Oh, yes, I've written.'

'And told them everything – I mean about Miss Closson's family?'

'Of course,' he repeated, rather sulkily. 'I haven't got much of a head for that kind of thing; but I got Santos-Dios to write it all out for me.'

'Then you'll certainly have an answer. No doubt it's on the way now.'

'It ought to be. But Mr Closson's always in such a devil of a hurry. Everybody's in a hurry in America. He asked me if there was any reason why my people shouldn't write.'

'Well – is there?'

Lord Richard turned in his chair, and glanced at her with an uncomfortable laugh. 'You must see now what I'm driving at.'

'No, I don't. Unless you count on me to reassure the Clossons?'

'No –. Only, if they should take it into their heads to question you . . .'

She felt a faint shiver of apprehension. To question her – about what? Did he imagine that anyone, at this hour, and at this far end of the world, would disinter that old unhappy episode? If this was what he feared, it meant her career to begin all over again, those poor old ancestors of Denmark Hill without support or comfort, and no one on earth to help her to her feet . . . She lifted her head sternly. 'Nonsense, Lord Richard – speak out.'

'Well, the fact is, I know my mother blurted out all that stupid business to you before I left Allfriars – I mean about the cheque,' he muttered half-audibly.

Miss Testvalley suddenly became aware that her heart had stopped beating by the violent plunge of relief it now gave. Her whole future, for a moment, had hung there in the balance. And after all, it was only the cheque he was thinking of. Now she didn't care what happened! She even saw, in a flash, that she had him at a disadvantage, and her past fear nerved her to use her opportunity.

'Yes, your mother did, as you say, blurt out something . . .'

The young man, his elbows on the table, had crossed his hands and rested his chin on them. She knew what he was waiting for – but she let him wait.

'I was a poor young fool – I didn't half know what I was doing . . . My father was damned hard on me, you know.'

'I think he was,' said Miss Testvalley.

Lord Richard lifted his head and looked at her. He hardly ever smiled, but when he did his face cleared, and became almost boyish again, as though a mask had been removed from it. 'You're a brick, Laura – you always were.'

'We're not here to discuss my merits, Lord Richard. Indeed you seem to have doubted them a moment ago.' He stared, and she remembered that subtlety was always lost on him. 'You imagined, knowing that I was in your mother's confidence, that I might betray it. Was that it?'

His look of embarrassment returned. 'I – you're so hard on a fellow . . .'

'I don't want to be hard on you. But, since you suspected I might tell your secrets, you must excuse my suspecting *you* –'

'Me? Of what?'

Miss Testvalley was silent. A hundred thoughts rushed through her brain – preoccupations both grave and trivial. It had always been thus with her, and she could never see that it was otherwise with life itself, where unimportant trifles and grave anxieties so often darkened the way with their joint shadows. At Nan St George's age, Miss Testvalley, though already burdened with the care and responsibilities of middle life, had longed with all Nan's longing to wear white tulle and be invited to a ball. She had never been invited to a ball, had never worn white tulle; and now, at nearly forty, and scarred by hardships and disappointments, she still felt that early pang, still wondered what, in life, ought to be classed as trifling, and what as grave. She looked again at Lord Richard. 'No,' she said, 'I've only one stipulation to make.'

He cleared his throat. 'Er – yes?'

'Lord Richard – are you truly and sincerely in love with Conchita?'

The young man's sallow face crimsoned to the roots of his hair, and even his freckled hands, with their short square fingers, grew red. 'In love with her?' he stammered. 'I . . . I never saw a girl that could touch her . . .'

There was something curiously familiar about the phrase; and she reflected that the young man had not renewed his vocabulary. Miss Testvalley smiled faintly. 'Conchita's very charming,' she continued. 'I wouldn't for the world have anything – anything that I could prevent – endanger her happiness.'

Lord Richard's flush turned to a sudden pallor. 'I – I swear to you I'd shoot myself sooner than let anything harm a hair of her head.'

Miss Testvalley was silent again. Lord Richard stirred uneasily in his chair, and she saw that he was trying to interpret her meaning. She stood up and gathered her old beaded dolman about her shoulders. 'I mean to believe you, Lord Richard,' she announced abruptly. 'I hope I'm not wrong.'

'Wrong? God bless you, Laura.' He held out his blunt hand. 'I'll never forget – never.'

'Never forget your promise about Conchita. That's all I ask.' She began to move toward the door, and slowly, awk-

wardly, he moved at her side. On the threshold she turned
back to him. 'No, it's not all – there's something else.' His
face clouded again, and his look of alarm moved her. Poor
blundering boy that he still was! Perhaps his father *had* been
too hard on him.

'What I'm going to ask is a trifle . . . yet at that age nothing
is a trifle . . . Lord Richard, I'll back you up through thick and
thin if you'll manage to get Miss Closson's bridesmaids
invited to the Assembly ball next week.'

He looked at her in bewilderment. 'The Assembly ball?'

'Yes. They've invited you, I know; and your fiancée. In
New York it's considered a great honour – almost' (she
smiled) 'like being invited to Court in England . . .'

'Oh, come,' he interjected. 'There's nothing like a Court
here.'

'No; but this is the nearest approach. And my two girls,
the St Georges, and their friends the Elmsworths, are not
very well known in the fashionable set which manages the
Assemblies. Of course they can't all be invited; and indeed
Nan is too young for balls. But Virginia St George and Lizzy
Elmsworth ought not to be left out. Such things hurt young
people cruelly. They've just been helping Conchita to
arrange her dress, knowing all the while they were not going
themselves. I thought it charming of them . . .'

Lord Richard stood before her in perplexity. 'I'm dreadfully
sorry. It is hard on them, certainly. I'd forgotten all about that
ball. But can't their parents –?'

'Their parents, I'm afraid, are the obstacle.'

He bent his puzzled eyes on the ground, but at length light
seemed to break on him. 'Oh, I see. They're not in the right
set? They seem to think a lot about sets in the States, don't
they?'

'Enormously. But as you've been invited – through Mrs
Parmore, I understand – and Mr de Santos-Dios also, you
two, between you, can certainly get invitations for Virginia

and Lizzy. You can count on me, Lord Richard, and I shall count on you. I've never asked you a favour before, have I?'

'Oh, but I say – I'd do anything, of course. But how the devil can I, when I'm a stranger here?'

'Because you're a stranger – because you're Lord Richard Marable. I should think you need only ask one of the patronesses. Or that clever monkey Santos-Dios will help you, as he has with your correspondence.' Lord Richard reddened. 'In any case,' Miss Testvalley continued, 'I don't wish to know how you do it; and of course you must not say that it's my suggestion. Any mention of that would ruin everything. But you must get those invitations, Lord Richard.'

She held him for a second with her quick decisive smile, just touched his hand, and walked out of the hotel.

NEW York society in the seventies was a nursery of young beauties, and Mrs Parmore and Mrs Eglinton would have told any newcomer from the old world that he would see at an Assembly ball faces to outrival all the court beauties of Europe. There were rumours, now and then, that others even surpassing the Assembly standard had been seen at the Opera (on off-nights, when the fashionable let, or gave away, their boxes, or at such promiscuous annual entertainments as the Charity ball, the Seventh Regiment ball, and so on). And of late, more particularly, people had been talking of a Miss Closson, daughter or step-daughter of a Mr Closson, who was a stock-broker or railway-director – or was he a coffee planter in South America? The facts about Mr Closson were few and vague, but he had a certain notoriety in Wall Street and on the fashionable race-courses, and had now come into newspaper prominence through the engagement of his daughter (or step-daughter) to Lord Richard Marable, a younger son of the Marquess of Brightlingsea ... (No, my dear, you must pronounce it Brittlesey.) Some of the fashionable young men had met Miss Closson, and spoken favourably, even enthusiastically, of her charms; but then young men are always attracted by novelty, and by a slight flavour of, shall we say fastness, or anything just a trifle off-colour?

The Assembly ladies felt it would be surprising if any Miss Closson could compete in loveliness with Miss Alida Parmore, Miss Julia Vandercamp, or, among the married, with the radiant Mrs Casimir Dulac, or Mrs Fred Alston, who had been a van der Luyden. They were not afraid, as they gathered on the shining floor of Delmonico's ball-room, of any challenge to the supremacy of these beauties.

Miss Closson's arrival was, nevertheless, awaited with a certain curiosity. Mrs Parmore had been very clever about her invitation. It was impossible to invite Lord Richard without his fiancée, since their wedding was to take place the following week; and the ladies were eager to let a scion of the British nobility see what a New York Assembly had to show. But to invite the Closson parents was obviously impossible. No one knew who they were, or where they came from (beyond the vague tropical background), and Mrs Closson was said to be a divorcée, and to lie in bed all day smoking enormous cigars. But Mrs Parmore, whose daughter's former governess was now with a family who knew the Clossons, had learned that there was a Closson step-son, a clever little fellow with a Spanish name, who was a great friend of Lord Richard's, and was to be his best man; and of course it was perfectly proper to invite Miss Closson with her own brother. One or two of the more conservative patronesses had indeed wavered, and asked what further concessions this might lead to; but Mrs Parmore's party gained the day, and rich was their reward, for at the eleventh hour Mrs Parmore was able to announce that Lord Richard's sisters, the Ladies Ulrica and Honoria, had unexpectedly arrived for their brother's wedding, and were anxious, they too – could anything be more gratifying? – to accompany him to the ball.

Their appearance, for a moment, overshadowed Miss

Closson's; yet perhaps (or so some of the young men said afterwards) each of the three girls was set off by the charms of the others. They were so complementary in their graces, each seemed to have been so especially created by Providence, and adorned by coiffeur and dressmaker, to make part of that matchless trio, that their entrance was a sight long remembered, not only by the young men thronging about them to be introduced but by the elderly gentlemen who surveyed them from a distance with critical and reminiscent eyes. The patronesses, whose own daughters risked a momentary eclipse, were torn between fears and admiration; but after all these lovely English girls, one so dazzlingly fair, the other so darkly vivid, who framed Miss Closson in their contrasting beauty were only transient visitors; and Miss Closson was herself soon to rejoin them in England, and might some day, as the daughter-in-law of a marquess, remember gratefully that New York had set its social seal on her.

No such calculations troubled the dancing men. They had found three new beauties to waltz with – and how they waltzed! The rumour that London dancing was far below the New York standard was not likely to find credit with anyone who had danced with the Ladies Marable. The tall fair one – was she the Lady Honoria? – was perhaps the more harmonious in her movements; but the Lady Ulrica, as befitted her flashing good looks, was as nimble as a gipsy; and if Conchita Closson polka-ed and waltzed as well as the English girls, these surpassed her in the gliding elegance of the square dances.

At supper they were as bewitching as on the floor. Nowhere in the big supper-room, about the flower-decked tables, was the talk merrier, the laughter louder (a shade too loud, perhaps? – but that may have been the fault of the young men), than in the corner where the three girls, enclosed in a dense bodyguard of admirers, feasted on champagne and terrapin. As Mrs Eglinton, with some bitterness, afterwards remarked to Mrs Parmore, it was absurd to say that English girls had no conversation, when these charming creatures had chattered all night like magpies. She hoped it would teach their own girls that there were moments when a little innocent *abandon* was not unsuitable.

IN the small hours of the same night a knock at her door waked Miss Testvalley out of an uneasy sleep. She sat up with a start, and lighting her candle beheld a doleful little figure in a beribboned pink wrapper.

'Why, Annabel – aren't you well?' she exclaimed, setting down her candle beside the Book of Common Prayer and the small volume of poems which always lay together on her night-table.

'Oh, don't call me Annabel, please! I can't sleep, and I feel so lonely . . . !'

'My poor Nan! Come and sit on the bed. What's the matter, child? You're half frozen!' Miss Testvalley, thankful that before going to bed she had wound her white net scarf over her crimping-pins, sat up and drew the quilt around her pupil.

'I'm not frozen; I'm just lonely. I *did* want to go to that ball,' Nan confessed, throwing her arms about her governess.

'Well, my dear, there'll be plenty of other balls for you when the time comes.'

'Oh, but will there? I'm not a bit sure; and Jinny's not either. She only got asked to this one because Lord Richard fixed it up. I don't know how he did it; but I suppose those old Assembly scare-crows are such snobs –'

'Annabel!'

'Oh, bother! When you know they are. If they hadn't been, wouldn't they have invited Jinny and Lizzy long ago to all their parties?'

'I don't think that question need trouble us. Now that your sister and Lizzy Elmsworth have been seen they're sure to be invited again; and when your turn comes . . .'

Suddenly she felt herself pushed back against her pillows by her pupil's firm young hands. 'Miss Testvalley! How can you talk like that, when you know the only way they got invited –'

Miss Testvalley, rearing herself up severely, shook off Nan's clutch. 'Annabel! I've no idea how they were invited; I can't imagine what you mean. And I must ask you not to be impertinent.'

Nan gazed at her for a moment, and then buried her face among the pillows in a wild rush of laughter.

'Annabel!' the governess repeated, still more severely; but Nan's shoulders continued to shake with mirth.

'My dear, you told me you'd waked me up because you felt lonely. If all you wanted was someone to giggle with, you'd better go back to bed, and wait for your sister to come home.'

Nan lifted a penitent countenance to her governess. 'Oh, she won't be home for hours. And I promise I won't laugh any more. Only it *is* so funny! But do let me stay a little longer; please! Read aloud to me, there's a darling; read me some poetry, won't you?'

She wriggled down under the bed-quilt, and crossing her arms behind her, laid her head back against them, so that her brown curls overflowed on the pillow. Her face had grown wistful again, and her eyes were full of entreaty.

Miss Testvalley reached out for *Hymns Ancient and Modern*. But after a moment's hesitation she put it back beside the prayer-book, and took up instead the volume of poetry which always accompanied her on her travels.

'Now listen; listen very quietly, or I won't go on.' Almost solemnly she began to read.

> *The blessèd damozel leaned out*
> *From the gold bar of Heaven:*
> *Her eyes were deeper than the depth*

*Of waters stilled at even;*
  *She had three lilies in her hand,*
    *And the stars in her hair were seven.*

Miss Testvalley read slowly, chantingly, with a rich murmur of vowels, and a lingering stress on the last word of the last line, as though it symbolized something grave and mysterious. *Seven . . .*

'That's lovely,' Nan sighed. She lay motionless, her eyes wide, her lips a little parted.

*Her robe, ungirt from clasp to hem,*
  *No wrought flowers did adorn,*
    *But a white rose of Mary's gift . . .*

'I shouldn't have cared much for that kind of dress, should you? I suppose it had angel sleeves, if she was in heaven. When I go to my first ball I want to have a dress that *fits*; and I'd like it to be pale blue velvet, embroidered all over with seed-pearls, like I saw . . .'

'My dear, if you want to tálk about ball-dresses, I should advise you to go to the sewing-room and get the maid's copy of *Butterick's Magazine*,' said Miss Testvalley icily.

'No, no! I want to hear the poem – I do! Please read it to me, Miss Testvalley. See how good I am.'

Miss Testvalley resumed her reading. The harmonious syllables flowed on, weaving their passes about the impatient young head on the pillow. Presently Miss Testvalley laid the book aside, and folding her hands continued her murmur of recital.

*And still she bowed herself and stooped*
  *Out of the circling charm;*
*Until her bosom must have made*
  *The bar she leaned on warm . . .*

She paused, hesitating for the next line, and Nan's drowsy

eyes drifted to her face. 'How heavenly! But you know it all by heart.'

'Oh, yes; I know it by heart.'

'I never heard anything so lovely. Who wrote it?'

'My cousin, Dante Gabriel.'

'Your own cousin?' Nan's eyes woke up.

'Yes, dear. Listen:

*And the lilies lay as if asleep*
  *Along her bended arm . . .*

*The sun was gone now; the curled moon*
  *Was like a little feather . . .*

'Do you mean to say he's your very own cousin? Aren't you madly in love with him, Miss Testvalley?'

'Poor Dante Gabriel! My dear, he's a widower, and very stout – and has caused all the family a good deal of trouble.'

Nan's face fell. 'Oh – a widower? What a pity . . . If I had a cousin who was a poet I should be madly in love with him. And I should desert my marble palace to flee with him to the isles of Greece.'

'Ah – and when are you going to live in a marble palace?'

'When I'm an ambassadress, of course. Lord Richard says that ambassadresses . . . Oh, darling, don't stop! I do long to hear the rest . . . I do, really . . .'

Miss Testvalley resumed her recital, sinking her voice as she saw Nan's lids gradually sink over her questioning eyes till at last the long lashes touched her cheeks. Miss Testvalley murmured on, ever more softly, to the end; then, blowing out the candle, she slid down to Nan's side so gently that the sleeper did not move. 'She might have been my own daughter,' the governess thought, composing her narrow frame to rest, and listening in the darkness to Nan's peaceful breathing.

Miss Testvalley did not fall asleep herself. She lay speculating rather nervously over the meaning of her pupil's hysterical burst of giggling. She was delighted that Lord Richard had succeeded in getting invitations to the ball for Virginia and Lizzy Elmsworth; but she could not understand why Nan regarded his having done so as particularly droll. Probably, she reflected, it was because the invitations had been asked for and obtained without Mrs St George's knowledge. Everything was food for giggles when that light-hearted company were together, and nothing amused them more than to play a successful trick on Mrs St George. In any case, the girls had had their evening – and a long evening it must have been, since the late winter dawn was chilling the windows when Miss Testvalley at length heard Virginia on the stairs.

LORD Richard Marable, as it turned out, had underrated his family's interest in his projected marriage. No doubt, as Miss Testvalley had surmised, his announcement of the event had been late in reaching them; but the day before the wedding a cable came. It was not, however, addressed to Lord Richard, or to his bride, but to Miss Testvalley, who, having opened it with surprise (for she had never before received a cable) read it in speechless perplexity.

Is she black his anguished mother Selina Brightlingsea.

For some time the governess pored in vain over this cryptic communication; but at last light came to her, and she leaned her head back against her chair and laughed. She understood just what must have happened. Though there were two splendid globes, terrestrial and celestial, at opposite ends of the Allfriars library, no one in the house had ever been known to consult them; and Lady Brightlingsea's geographical notions, even measured by the family standard, were notoriously hazy. She could not imagine why anyone should ever want to leave England, and her idea of the Continent was one enormous fog from which two places called Paris and

Rome indistinctly emerged; while the whole Western hemisphere was little more clear to her than to the forerunners of Columbus. But Miss Testvalley remembered that on one wall of the Vandyke saloon, where the family sometimes sat after dinner, there hung a great tapestry, brilliant in colour, rich and elaborate in design, in the foreground of which a shapely young negress flanked by ruddy savages and attended by parakeets and monkeys was seen offering a tribute of tropical fruits to a lolling divinity. The housekeeper, Miss Testvalley also remembered, in showing this tapestry to visitors, on the day when Allfriars was open to the public, always designated it as 'The Spanish Main and the Americas –' and what could be more natural than that poor bewildered Lady Brightlingsea should connect her son's halting explanations with this instructive scene?

Miss Testvalley pondered for a long time over her reply; then, for once forgetting to make a 'governess's answer', she cabled back to Lady Brightlingsea: 'No, but comely.'

BOOK

II

# EIGHT

ON A JUNE AFTERNOON OF THE YEAR 1875 ONE OF THE biggest carriages in London drew up before one of the smallest houses in Mayfair – the very smallest in that exclusive quarter, its occupant, Miss Jacqueline March, always modestly averred.

The tiny dwelling, a mere two-windowed wedge, with a bulging balcony under a striped awning, had been newly painted a pale buff, and freshly festooned with hanging pink geraniums and intensely blue lobelias. The carriage, on the contrary, a vast old-fashioned barouche of faded yellow, with impressive armorial bearings, and coachman and footman to scale, showed no signs of recent renovation; and the lady who descended from it was, like her conveyance, large and rather shabby though undeniably impressive.

A freshly starched parlour-maid let her in with a curtsey of recognition. 'Miss March is in the drawing-room, my lady.' She led the visitor up the narrow stairs and announced from the threshold: 'Please, Miss, Lady Brightlingsea.'

Two ladies sat in the drawing-room in earnest talk. One of the two was vaguely perceived by Lady Brightlingsea to be small and brown, with burning black eyes which did not seem to go with her stiff purple poplin and old-fashioned beaded dolman.

The other lady was also very small, but extremely fair and elegant, with natural blond curls touched with grey, and a delicate complexion. She hurried hospitably forwards.

'Dearest Lady Brightlingsea! What a delightful surprise! – You're not going to leave us, Laura?'

It was clear that the dark lady addressed as Laura was meant to do exactly what her hostess suggested she should not. She pressed the latter's hand in a resolute brown kid glove, bestowed a bow and a slanting curtsey on the Marchioness of Brightlingsea, and was out of the room with the ease and promptness of a person long practised in self-effacement.

Lady Brightlingsea sent a vague glance after the retreating figure. 'Now who was that, my dear? I seem to know . . .'

Miss March, who had a touch of firmness under her deprecating exterior, replied without hesitation: 'An old friend, dear Lady Brightlingsea, Miss Testvalley, who used to be governess to the Duchess's younger girls at Tintagel.'

Lady Brightlingsea's long pale face grew still vaguer. 'At Tintagel? Oh, but of course. It was I who recommended her to Blanche Tintagel . . . Testvalley? The name is so odd. She was with us, you know; she was with Honoria and Ulrica before Madame Championnet finished them.'

'Yes. I remember you used to think well of her. I believe it was at Allfriars I first met her.'

Lady Brightlingsea looked plaintively at Miss March. Her face always grew plaintive when she was asked to squeeze one more fact – even one already familiar – into her weary and over-crowded memory. 'Oh, yes . . . oh, yes!'

Miss March, glancing brightly at her guest, as though to reanimate the latter's failing energy, added: 'I wish she could have stayed. You might have been interested in her experiences in America.'

'In America?' Lady Brightlingsea's vagueness was streaked by a gleam of interest. 'She's been in America?'

'In the States. In fact, I think she was governess to that new beauty who's being talked about a good deal just now. A Miss St George – Virginia St George. You may have heard of her?'

Lady Brightlingsea sighed at this new call upon her powers of concentration. 'I hear of nothing but Americans. My son's house is always full of them.'

'Oh, yes; and I believe Miss St George is a particular friend of Lady Richard's.'

'Very likely. Is she from the same part of the States – from Brazil?'

Miss March, who was herself a native of the States, had in her youth been astonished at enquiries of this kind, and slightly resentful of them; but long residence in England, and a desire to appear at home in her adopted country, had accustomed her to such geography as Lady Brightlingsea's. 'Slightly farther north, I think,' she said.

'Ah? But they make nothing of distances in those countries, do they? Is this new young woman rich?' asked Lady Brightlingsea abruptly.

Miss March reflected, and then decided to say: 'According to Miss Testvalley the St Georges appear to live in great luxury.'

Lady Brightlingsea sank back wearily. 'That means nothing. My daughter-in-law's people do that too. But the man has never paid her settlements. Her step-father, I mean – I never can remember any of their names. I don't see how they can tell each other apart, all herded together, without any titles or distinctions. It's unfortunate that Richard did nothing about settlements; and now, barely two years after their marriage, the man says he can't go on paying his step-daughter's allowance. And I'm afraid the young people owe a great deal of money.'

Miss March heaved a deep sigh of sympathy. 'A bad coffee-year, I suppose.'

'That's what he says. But how can one tell? Do you suppose those other people would lend them the money?'

Miss March counted it as one of the many privileges of living in London that two or three times a year her friend Lady Brightlingsea came to see her. In Miss March's youth a great tragedy had befallen her – a sorrow which had darkened all her days. It had befallen her in London, and all her American friends – and they were many – had urged her to return at once to her home in New York. A proper sense of dignity, they insisted, should make it impossible for her to remain in a society where she had been so cruelly, so publicly offended. Miss March listened, hesitated – and finally remained in London. 'They simply don't know,' she explained to an American friend who also lived there, 'what they're asking me to give up.' And the friend sighed her assent.

'The first years will be difficult,' Miss March had continued courageously, 'but I think in the end I shan't be sorry.' And she was right. At first she had been only a poor little pretty American who had been jilted by an eminent nobleman; yes, and after the wedding-dress was ordered – the countermanding of that wedding-dress had long been one of her most agonizing memories. But since the unhappy date over thirty years had slipped by; and gradually, as they passed, and as people found out how friendly and obliging she was, and what a sweet little house she lived in, she had become the centre of a circle of warm friends, and the oracle of transatlantic pilgrims in quest of a social opening. These pilgrims had learned that Jacky March's narrow front door led straight into the London world, and a number had already slipped in through it. Miss March had a kind heart, and could never resist doing a friend a good turn; and if her services were sometimes rewarded by a cheque, or a new drawing-room carpet, or a chinchilla tippet and muff, she saw no harm in this way of keeping herself and her house in good shape.

'After all, if my friends are kind enough to come here, I want my house and myself, tiny as we both are, to be presentable.'

All this passed through Miss March's active mind while she sat listening to Lady Brightlingsea. Even should friendship so incline them, she doubted if the St George family would be able to come to the aid of the young Dick Marables, but there might be combinations, arrangements – who could tell? Laura Testvalley might enlighten her. It was never Miss March's policy to oppose a direct refusal to a friend.

'Dear Lady Brightlingsea, I'm so dreadfully distressed at what you tell me.'

'Yes. It's certainly very unlucky. And most trying for my husband. And I'm afraid poor Dick's not behaving as well as he might. After all, as he says, he's been deceived.'

Miss March knew that this applied to Lady Richard's money and not to her morals, and she sighed again. 'Mr St George was a business associate of Mr Closson's at one time, I believe. Those people generally back each other up. But of course they all have their ups and downs. At any rate I'll see, I'll make enquiries . . .'

'Their ways are so odd, you know,' Lady Brightlingsea pursued. It never seemed to occur to her that Miss March was one of 'them', and Miss March emitted a murmur of sympathy, for these new people seemed as alien to her as to her visitor. 'So very odd. And they speak so fast – I can't understand them. But I suppose one would get used to that. What I *cannot* see is their beauty – the young girls, I mean. They toss about so – they're never still. And they don't know how to carry themselves.' She paused to add in a lower tone: 'I believe my daughter-in-law dances to some odd instrument – quite like a ballet dancer. I hope her skirts are not as short. And sings in Spanish. Is Spanish their native language still?'

Miss March, despairing of making it clear to Lady Brightlingsea that Brazil was not one of the original Thirteen States, evaded this by saying: 'You must remember they've not had the social training which only a Court can give. But some of them seem to learn very quickly.'

'Oh, I hope so,' Lady Brightlingsea exclaimed, as if clutching at a floating spar. Slowly she drew herself up from the sofa-corner. She was so tall that the ostrich plumes on her bonnet might have brushed Miss March's ceiling had they not drooped instead of towering. Miss March had often wondered how her friend managed to have such an air of majesty when everything about her flopped and dangled. 'Ah – it's their secret,' she thought, and rejoiced that at least she could recognize and admire the attribute in her noble English friends. So many of her travelling compatriots seemed not to understand, or even to perceive, the difference. They were the ones who could not see what she 'got out' of her little London house, and her little London life.

Lady Brightlingsea stood in the middle of the room, looking uncertainly about her. At last she said: 'We're going out of town in a fortnight. You must come down to Allfriars later, you know.'

Miss March's heart leapt up under her trim black satin bodice. (She wore black often, to set off her still fair complexion.) She could never quite master the excitement of an invitation to Allfriars. In London she did not expect even to be offered a meal; the Brightlingseas always made a short season, and there were so many important people whom they had to invite. Besides, being asked down to stay in the country, *en famille*, was really much more flattering – more intimate. Miss March felt herself blushing to the roots of her fair curls. 'It's so kind of you, dear Lady Brightlingsea. Of course you know there's nothing I should like better. I'm never as happy anywhere as at Allfriars.'

Lady Brightlingsea gave a mirthless laugh. 'You're not like my daughter-in-law. She says she'd as soon spend a month in the family vault. In fact she'd never be with us at all if they hadn't had to let their house for the season.'

Miss March's murmur of horror was inarticulate. Words failed her. These dreadful new Americans – would London ever be able to educate them? In her confusion she followed Lady Brightlingsea to the landing without speaking. There her visitor suddenly turned towards her. 'I wish we could marry Seadown,' she said.

This allusion to the heir of the Brightlingseas was a fresh surprise to Miss March. 'But surely – in Lord Seadown's case it will be only too easy,' she suggested with a playful smile.

Lady Brightlingsea produced no answering smile. 'You must have heard, I suppose, of his wretched entanglement with Lady Churt. It's much worse, you know, than if she were a disreputable woman. She costs him a great deal more, I mean. And we've tried everything . . . But he won't look at a nice girl . . .' She paused, her wistful eyes bent entreatingly on Miss March's responsive face. 'And so, in sheer despair, I thought perhaps, if this friend of my daughter-in-law's is rich, really rich, it might be better to try . . . There's something about these foreigners that seems to attract the young men.'

Yes – there was, as Jacky March had reason to know. Her own charm had been subtler and more discreet, and in the end it had failed her; but the knowledge that she had possessed it gave her a feeling of affinity with this new band of marauders, social aliens though they were: the wild gipsy who had captured Dick Marable, and her young friends who, two years later, had come out to look over the ground, and do their own capturing.

Miss March, who was always on her watch-tower, had already sighted and classified them; the serenely lovely Virginia St George, whom Lady Brightlingsea had singled out for Lord Seadown, and her younger sister Nan, negligible as yet compared with Virginia, but odd and interesting too, as her sharp little observer perceived. It was a novel kind of invasion, and Miss March was a-flutter with curiosity, and with an irrepressible sympathy. In Lady Brightlingsea's company she had quite honestly blushed for the crude intruders; but freed from the shadow of the peerage she felt herself mysteriously akin to them, eager to know more of their plans, and even to play a secret part in the adventure.

Miss Testvalley was an old friend, and her arrival in London with a family of obscure but wealthy Americans had stirred the depths of Miss March's social curiosity. She knew from experience that Miss Testvalley would never make imprudent revelations concerning her employers, much less betray their confidence; but her shrewd eye and keen ear must have harvested, in the transatlantic field, much that would be of burning interest to Miss March, and the latter was impatient to resume their talk. So far, she knew only that the St George girls were beautiful, and their parents rich, yet that fashionable New York had rejected them. There was much more to learn, and there was also this strange outbreak of Lady Brightlingsea's to hint at, if not reveal, to Miss Testvalley.

It was certainly a pity that their talk had been interrupted by Lady Brightlingsea; yet Miss March would not for the world have missed the latter's visit, and above all, her unexpected allusion to her eldest son. For years Miss March had carried in her bosom the heavy weight of the Marable affairs, and this reference to Seadown had thrown her into such agitation that she sat down on the sofa and clasped her small wrinkled hands over her anxious heart. Seadown to marry an American – what news to communicate to Laura Testvalley!

Miss March rose and went quickly to her miniature writing-desk. She wrote a hurried note in her pretty flowing script, sealed it with silver-grey wax, and rang for the beruffled parlour-maid. Then she turned back into the room. It was crowded with velvet-covered tables and quaint corner-shelves, all laden with photographs in heavy silver or morocco frames, surmounted by coronets, from the baronial to the ducal – one, even, royal (in a place of honour by itself, on the mantel). Most of these photographs were of young or middle-aged women, with long necks and calm imperious faces, crowned with diadems or nodded over by court feathers. 'Selina Brightlingsea', 'Blanche Tintagel', 'Elfrida Marable', they were signed in tall slanting hands. The handwriting was as uniform as the features, and nothing but the signatures seemed to differentiate these carven images. But in a corner by itself (pushed behind a lamp at Lady Brightlingsea's arrival) was one, 'To Jacky from her friend Idina Churt', which Miss March now drew forth and studied with a furtive interest. What chance had an untaught transatlantic beauty against this reprehensible creature, with her tilted nose and impertinent dark fringe? Yet, after studying the portrait for a while, Miss March, as she set it down, simply murmured, 'Poor Idina.'

# NINE

IN THE LONG SUMMER TWILIGHT A FATHER AND SON WERE
pacing the terrace of an old house called Honourslove, on
the edge of the Cotswolds. The irregular silver-grey building,
when approached from the village by a drive winding under
ancient beech trees, seemed, like so many old dwellings in
England, to lie almost in a hollow, screened to the north by
hanging woods, and surveying from its many windows only
its own lawns and trees; but the terrace on the other front
overlooked an immensity of hill and vale, with huddled village roofs and floating spires. Now, in the twilight, though
the sky curved above so clear and luminous, everything
below was blurred, and the spires were hardly distinguishable
from the tree-trunks; but to the two men strolling up and
down before the house long familiarity made every fold of
the landscape visible.

The Cotswolds were in the blood of the Thwartes, and
their rule at Honourslove reached back so far that the present baronet, Sir Helmsley Thwarte, had persuaded himself
that only by accident (or treachery – he was given to suspecting treachery) had their title to the estate dropped out of
Domesday.

His only son, Guy, was not so sure; but, as Sir Helmsley
said, the young respect nothing and believe in nothing, least

of all in the validity of tradition. Guy did, however, believe in Honourslove, the beautiful old place which had come to be the first and last article of the family creed. Tradition, as embodied in the ancient walls and the ancient trees of Honourslove, seemed to him as priceless a quality as it did to Sir Helmsley; and indeed he sometimes said to himself that if ever he succeeded to the baronetcy he would be a safer and more vigilant guardian than his father, who loved the place and yet had so often betrayed it.

'I'd have shot myself rather than sell the Titian,' Guy used to think in moments of bitterness. 'But then my father's sure to outlive me – so what's the odds?'

As they moved side by side that summer evening it would have been hard for a looker-on to decide which had the greater chance of longevity; the heavy vigorous man approaching the sixties, a little flushed after his dinner and his bottle of Burgundy, but obliged to curb his quick stride to match his son's more leisurely gait; or the son, tall and lean, and full of the balanced energy of the hard rider and quick thinker.

'You don't adapt yourself to the scene, sir. It's an insult to Honourslove to treat the terrace as if it were the platform at Euston, and you were racing for your train.'

Sir Helmsley was secretly proud of his own activity, and nothing pleased him better than his son's disrespectful banter on his over-youthfulness. He slackened his pace with a gruff laugh.

'I suppose you young fellows expect the grey-beards to drag their gouty feet and lean on staves, as they do in *Oedipe-roi* at the *Français*.'

'Well, sir, as your beard's bright auburn, that strikes me as irrelevant.' Guy knew this would not be unwelcome either; but a moment later he wondered if he had not overshot the mark. His father stopped short and faced him. 'Bright auburn, indeed? Look here, my dear fellow, what is there behind this indecent flattery?' His voice hardened. 'Not another bill to be met – eh?'

Guy gave a short laugh. He *had* wanted something; and had perhaps resorted to flattery in the hope of getting it; but his admiration for his brilliant and impetuous parent, even when not disinterested, was sincere.

'A bill –?' He laughed again. That would have been easier – though it was never easy to confess a lapse to Sir Helmsley. Guy had never learned to take his father's tropical fits of rage without wincing. But to make him angry about money would have been less dangerous; and, at any rate, the young man was familiar with the result. It always left him seared, but still upright; whereas . . .

'Well?'

'Nothing, sir.'

The father gave one of his angry 'foreign' shrugs (reminiscent of far-off Bohemian days in the Quartier Latin), and the two men walked on in silence.

There were moments during their talks – and this was one – when the young man felt that, if each could have read the other's secret mind, they would have found little to unite them except a joint love of their house and the land it stood on. But that love was so strong, and went so deep, that it sometimes seemed to embrace all the divergences. Would it now, Guy wondered? 'How the devil shall I tell him?' he thought.

The two had paused, and stood looking out over the lower terraces to the indistinct blue reaches beyond. Lights were beginning to prick the dusk, and every roof which they revealed had a name and a meaning to Guy Thwarte. Red Farm, where the famous hazel copse was, Ausprey with its decaying Norman church, Little Ausprey with the old heronry at the Hall, Odcote, Sudcote, Lowdon, the ancient borough with its market-cross and its rich minster – all were thick with webs of memory for the youth whose people had so long been rooted in their soil. And those frail innumerable webs tightened about him like chains at the thought that in a few weeks he was to say goodbye to it all, probably for many months.

After preparing for a diplomatic career, and going through a first stage at the Foreign Office, and a secretaryship in Brazil, Guy Thwarte had suddenly decided that he was not made for diplomacy, and braving his father's wrath at this unaccountable defection had settled down to a period of hard drudgery with an eminent firm of civil engineers who specialized in railway building. Though he had a natural bent for the work he would probably never have chosen it had he not hoped it would be a quick way to wealth. The firm employing him had big contracts out for building railways in Far Eastern and South American lands, and Guy's experience in Brazil had shown him that in those regions there were fortunes to be made by energetic men with a practical knowledge of the conditions. He preferred making a fortune to marrying one, and it was clear that sooner or later a great deal of money would be needed to save Honourslove and keep it going. Sir Helmsley's financial ventures had been even costlier than his other follies, and the great Titian which was the glory of the house had been sold to cover the loss of part of the fortune which Guy had inherited from his mother, and which, during his minority, had been in Sir Helmsley's imprudent hands. The subject was one never touched upon between father and son, but it had imperceptibly altered their relations, though not the tie of affection between them.

The truth was that the son's case was hardly less perplexing than the father's. Contradictory impulses strove in both. Each had the same love for the ancient habitation of their race, which enchanted but could not satisfy them, each was anxious to play the part fate had allotted to him, and each was dimly conscious of an inability to remain confined in it,

and painfully aware that their secret problems would have
been unintelligible to most men of their own class and kind.
Sir Helmsley had been a grievous disappointment to the
county, and it was expected that Guy should make up for his
father's short-comings by conforming to the accepted standards, should be a hard rider, a good shot, a conscientious
landlord and magistrate, and should in due time (and as soon
as possible) marry a wife whose settlements would save
Honourslove from the consequences of Sir Helmsley's follies.

The county was not conscious of anything incomprehensible about Guy. Sir Helmsley had dabbled dangerously in
forbidden things; but Guy had a decent reputation about
women, and it was incredible that a man so tall and well set-
up, and such a brilliant point-to-point rider, should mess
about with poetry or painting. Guy knew what was expected
of him, and secretly agreed with his observers that the path
they would have him follow was the right one for a man in
his situation. But since Honourslove had to be saved, he
would rather try to save it by his own labour than with a rich
woman's money.

Guy's stage of drudgery as an engineer was now over, and
he had been chosen to accompany one of the members of the
firm on a big railway-building expedition in South America.
His knowledge of the country, and the fact that his diplomatic training had included the mastering of two or three
foreign languages, qualified him for the job, which promised
to be lucrative as well as adventurous, and might, he hoped,
lead to big things. Sir Helmsley accused him of undergoing
the work only for the sake of adventure; but, aggrieved
though he was by his son's decision, he respected him for
sticking to it. 'I've been only a brilliant failure myself,' he
had grumbled at the end of their discussion; and Guy had
laughed back: 'Then I'll try to be a dingy success.'

The memory of this talk passed through the young man's
mind, and with it the new impulse which, for the last week,

had never been long out of his thoughts, and now threatened to absorb them. Struggle as he would, there it was, fighting in him for control. 'As if my father would ever listen to reason!' But was this reason? He leaned on the balustrade, and let his mind wander over the rich darkness of the countryside.

Though he was not yet thirty, his life had been full of dramatic disturbances; indeed, to be the only son of Sir Helmsley Thwarte was in itself a potential drama. Sir Helmsley had been born with the passionate desire to be an accomplished example of his class: the ideal English squire, the model landowner, crack shot, leader and champion in all traditionally British pursuits and pleasures; but a contrary streak in his nature was perpetually driving him towards art and poetry and travel, odd intimacies with a group of painters and decorators of socialistic tendencies, reckless dalliance with ladies, and a loud contempt for the mental inferiority of his county neighbours. Against these tendencies he waged a spasmodic and unavailing war, accusing and excusing himself in the same breath, and expecting his son to justify his vagaries, and to rescue him from their results. During Lady Thwarte's life the task had been less difficult; she had always, as Guy now understood, kept a sort of cold power over her husband. To Guy himself she remained an enigma; the boy had never found a crack through which to penetrate beyond the porcelain-like surface of her face and mind. But while she lived things had gone more smoothly at Honourslove. Her husband's oddest experiments had been tried away from home, and had never lasted long; her presence, her power, her clear conception of what the master of Honourslove ought to be, always drew him back to her and to conformity.

Guy summed it up by saying to himself, 'If she'd lived the Titian never would have gone.' But she had died, and left the two men and their conflicting tendencies alone in the old house ... Yes; she had been the right mistress for such a house. Guy was thinking of that now, and knew that the same thought was in his father's mind, and that his own words had roused it to the pitch of apprehension. Who was to come after her? father and son were both thinking.

'Well, out with it!' Sir Helmsley broke forth abruptly.

Guy straightened himself with a laugh. 'You seem to expect a confession of bankruptcy or murder. I'm afraid I shall disappoint you. All I want is to have you ask some people to tea.'

'Ah – ? Some "people"?' Sir Helmsley puffed dubiously at his cigar. 'I suppose they've got names and a local habitation?'

'The former, certainly. I can't say as to the rest. I ran across them the other day in London, and as I know they're going to spend next Sunday at Allfriars I thought –'

Sir Helmsley Thwarte drew the cigar from his lips, and looked along it as if it were a telescope at the end of which he saw an enemy approaching.

'Americans?' he queried, in a shrill voice so unlike his usual impressive baritone that it had been known to startle servants and trespassers almost out of their senses, and even in his family to cause a painful perturbation.

'Well – yes.'

'Ah,' – said Sir Helmsley again. Guy proffered no remark, and his father broke out irritably: 'I suppose it's because you know how I hate the whole spitting tobacco-chewing crew, the dressed-up pushing women dragging their reluctant back-woodsmen after them, that you suggest polluting my house, and desecrating our last few days together, by this barbarian invasion – eh?'

There had been a time when his father's outbursts, even when purely rhetorical, were so irritating to Guy that he could meet them only with silence. But the victory of choosing his career had given him a lasting advantage. He smiled, and said, 'I don't seem to recognize my friends from your description.'

'Your friends – your friends? How many of them are there?'

'Only two sisters – the Miss St Georges. Lady Richard would drive them over, I imagine.'

'Lady Richard? What's she? Some sort of West Indian octoroon, I believe?'

'She's very handsome, and has auburn hair.'

Sir Helmsley gave an angry laugh. 'I suppose you think the similarity in our colouring will be a tie between us.'

'Well, sir, I think she'll amuse you.'

'I hate women who try to amuse me.'

'Oh, she won't try – she's too lazy.'

'But what about the sisters?'

Guy hesitated. 'Well, the rumour is that the eldest is going to marry Seadown.'

'Seadown – marry Seadown? Good God, are the Brightlingseas out of their minds? It was well enough to get rid of Dick Marable at any price. There wasn't a girl in the village safe from him, and his father was forever buying people off. But Seadown – Seadown marry an American! There won't be a family left in England without that poison in their veins.'

Sir Helmsley walked away a few paces and then returned to where his son was standing. 'Why do you want these people asked here?'

'I – I like them,' Guy stammered, suddenly feeling as shamefaced as a guilty schoolboy.

'Like them!' In the darkness, the young man felt his father's nervous clutch on his arm. 'Look here, my boy – you know all the plans I had for you. Plans – dreams, they turned out to be! I wanted you to be all I'd meant to be myself. The enlightened landlord, the successful ambassador, the model MP, the ideal MFH. The range was wide enough – or ought to have been. Above all, I wanted you to have a steady career on an even keel. Just the reverse of the crazy example I've set you.'

'You've set me the example of having too many talents to keep any man on an even keel. There's not much danger of my following you in that.'

'Let's drop compliments, Guy. You're a gifted fellow; too much so, probably, for your job. But you've more persistency than I ever had, and I haven't dared to fight your ideas because I could see they were more definite than mine. And now –'

'Well, sir?' his son queried, forcing a laugh.

'And now – are you going to wreck everything, as I've done so often?' He paused, as if waiting for an answer; but none came. 'Guy, why do you want those women here? Is it because you've lost your head over one of them? I've a right to an answer, I think.'

Guy Thwarte appeared to have none ready. Too many thoughts were crowding through his mind. The first was: 'How like my father to corner me when anybody with a lighter hand would have let the thing pass unnoticed! But he's always thrown himself against life head foremost ...' The second: 'Well, and isn't that what I'm doing now? It's the family folly, I suppose ... Only, if he'd said nothing ... When I spoke I really hadn't got beyond ... well, just wanting to see her again ... and now ...'

Through the summer dark he could almost feel the stir of his father's impatience. 'Am I to take your silence as an answer?' Sir Helmsley challenged him.

Guy relieved the tension with a laugh. 'What nonsense! I ask you to let me invite some friends and neighbours to tea ...'

'To begin with, I hate these new-fangled intermediate meals. Why can't people eat enough at luncheon to last till dinner?'

'Well, sir, to dine and sleep, if you prefer.'

'Dine and sleep? A pack of strange women under my roof?' Sir Helmsley gave a grim laugh. 'I should like to see Mrs

Bolt's face if she were suddenly told to get their rooms ready! Everything's a foot deep in dust and moths, I imagine.'

'Well, it might be a good excuse for a clean-up,' rejoined his son good-humouredly. But Sir Helmsley ignored this.

'For God's sake, Guy – you're not going to bring an American wife to Honourslove? I shan't shut an eye tonight unless you tell me.'

'And you won't shut an eye if I tell you "yes"?'

'Damn it, man – don't fence.'

'I'm not fencing, sir; I'm laughing at your way of jumping at conclusions. I shan't take any wife till I get back from South America; and there's not much chance that this one would wait for me till then – even if I happened to want her to.'

'Ah, well. I suppose, this last week, if you were to ask me to invite the devil I should have to do it.'

From her post of observation in the window of the house-keeper's room, Mrs Bolt saw the two red cigar-tips pass along the front of the house and disappear. The gentlemen were going in, and she could ring to have the front door locked, and the lights put out everywhere but in the baronet's study and on the stairs.

Guy followed his father across the hall, and into the study. The lamp on the littered writing-table cast a circle of light on crowded bookshelves, on Sienese predellas, and bold unsteady watercolours and charcoal sketches by Sir Helmsley himself. Over the desk hung a small jewel-like picture in a heavy frame, with D.G. Rossetti inscribed beneath. Sir Helmsley glanced about him, selected a pipe from the rack, and filled and lit it. Then he lifted up the lamp.

'Well, Guy, I'm going to assume that you mean to have a good night's sleep.'

'The soundest, sir.'

Lamp in hand, Sir Helmsley moved towards the door. He paused – was it voluntarily? – half-way across the room, and the lamplight touched the old yellow marble of the carved mantel, and struck upwards to a picture above it, set in elaborate stucco scrolls. It was the portrait of a tall thin woman in white, her fair hair looped under a narrow diadem. As she looked forth from the dim background, expressionless, motionless, white, so her son remembered her in their brief years together. She had died, still young, during his last year at Eton – long ago, in another age, as it now seemed. Sir Helmsley, still holding the lifted lamp, looked up too. 'She was the most beautiful woman I ever saw,' he said abruptly – and added, as if in spite of himself, 'But utterly unpaintable; even Millais found her so.'

Guy offered no comment, but went up the stairs in silence after his father.

# TEN

THE ST GEORGE GIRLS HAD NEVER SEEN ANYTHING AS BIG AS the house at Allfriars except a public building, and as they drove towards it down the long avenue, and had their first glimpse of Inigo Jones's most triumphant expression of the Palladian dream, Virginia said with a little shiver: 'Mercy – it's just like a gaol.'

'Oh, no – a palace,' Nan corrected.

Virginia gave an impatient laugh. 'I'd like to know where you've ever seen a palace.'

'Why, hundreds of times, I have, in my dreams.'

'You mustn't tell your dreams. Miss Testvalley says nothing bores people so much as being told other people's dreams.'

Nan said nothing, but an iron gate seemed to clang shut in her; the gate that was so often slammed by careless hands. As if anyone could be bored by such dreams as hers!

'Oh,' said Virginia, 'I never saw anything so colossal. Do you suppose they live all over it? I guess our clothes aren't half dressy enough. I told mother we ought to have something better for the afternoon than those mauve organdies.'

Nan shot a side-glance at the perfect curve of her sister's cheek. 'Mauve's the one colour that simply murders me. But nobody who sees you will bother to notice what you've got on.'

'You little silly, you, shut up ... Look, there's Conchita and the poodle!' cried Virginia in a burst of reassurance. For there, on the edge of the drive, stood their friend, in a crumpled but picturesque yellow muslin and flapping garden hat, and a first glance at her smiling waving figure assured the two girls of her welcome. They sprang out, leaving the brougham to be driven on with maid and luggage, and instantly the trio were in each other's arms.

'Oh, girls, girls – I've been simply pining for you! I can't believe you're really here!' Lady Richard cried, with a tremor of emotion in her rich Creole voice.

'Conchita! Are you really glad?' Virginia drew back and scanned her anxiously. 'You're lovelier than ever; but you look terribly tired. Don't she look tired, Nan?'

'Don't talk about me. I've looked like a fright ever since the baby was born. But he's a grand baby, and they say I'll be all right soon. Jinny, darling, you can't think how I've missed you both! Little Nan, let me have a good look at you. How big your eyes have grown ... Jinny, you and I must be careful, or this child will crowd us out of the running ...'

Linked arm in arm, the three loitered along the drive, the poodle caracoling ahead. As they approached the great gateway, Conchita checked their advance. 'Look, girls! It is a grand house, isn't it?'

'Yes; but I'm not a bit afraid any more,' Nan laughed, pressing her arm.

'Afraid? What were you afraid of?'

'Virginia said you'd be as grand as the house. She didn't believe you'd be really glad to see us. We were scared blue of coming.'

'Nan – you little idiot!'

'Well, you did say so, Jinny. You said we must expect her to be completely taken up with her lords and ladies.'

Conchita gave a dry little laugh. 'Well, you wait,' she said.

Nan stood still, gazing up at the noble façade of the great

house. 'It is grand. I'm so glad I'm not afraid of it,' she murmured, following the other two up the steps between the mighty urns and columns of the doorway.

IT was a relief to the girls – though somewhat of a surprise – that there was no one to welcome them when they entered the big domed hall hung with tall family portraits and moth-eaten trophies of the chase. Conchita, seeing that they hesitated, said, 'Come along to your room – you won't see any of the in-laws till dinner'; and they went with her up the stairs, and down a succession of long corridors, glad that the dread encounter was postponed. Miss Jacky March, to whom they had been introduced by Miss Testvalley, had assured them that Lady Brightlingsea was the sweetest and kindest of women; but this did not appear to be Conchita's view, and they felt eager to hear more of her august relatives before facing them at dinner.

In the room with dark heavy bed-curtains and worn chintz armchairs which had been assigned to the sisters, the lady's-maid was already shaking out their evening toilets. Nan had wanted to take Miss Testvalley to Allfriars, and had given way to a burst of childish weeping when it was explained to her that girls who were 'out' did not go visiting with their governesses. Maids were a new feature in the St George household, and when, with Miss Jacky March's aid, Laura Testvalley had run down a paragon, and introduced her into the family, Mrs St George was even more terrified than the girls. But Miss Testvalley laughed. 'You were afraid of me once,' she said to Virginia. 'You and Nan must get used to being waited on, and having your clothes kept in order. And don't let the woman see that you're not used to it. Behave as if you'd never combed your own hair or rummaged for your stockings. Try and feel that you're as good as any of these people you're going about with,' the dauntless governess ordained.

'I guess we're as good as anybody,' Virginia replied haughtily. 'But they act differently from us, and we're not used to them yet.'

'Well, act in your own way, as you call it – that will amuse them much more than if you try to copy them.'

After deliberating with the maid and Conchita over the choice of dinner-dresses, they followed their friend along the corridor to her own bedroom. It was too late to disturb the baby, who was in the night-nursery in the other wing; but in Conchita's big shabby room, after inspecting everything it contained, the sisters settled themselves down happily on a wide sofa with broken springs. Dinner at Allfriars was not till eight, and they had an hour ahead of them before the dressing-gong. 'Tell us about everything, Conchita darling,' Virginia commanded.

'Well, you'll find only a family party, you know. They don't have many visitors here, because they have to bleed themselves white to keep the place going, and there's not much left for entertaining. They're terribly proud of it – they couldn't imagine living in any other way. At least my father-in-law couldn't. He thinks God made Allfriars for him to live in, and Frenshaw – the other place, in Essex; but he doesn't understand why God gave him so little money to do it on. He's so busy thinking about that, that he doesn't take much notice of anybody. You mustn't mind. My mother-in-law's good natured enough; only she never can think of anything to say to people she isn't used to. Dick talks a little when he's here; but he so seldom is, what with racing and fishing and shooting. I believe he's at Newmarket now; but he seldom keeps me informed of his movements.' Her aquamarine eyes darkened as she spoke her husband's name.

'But aren't your sisters-in-law here?' Virginia asked.

Conchita smiled. 'Oh, yes, poor dears; there's nowhere else for them to go. But they're too shy to speak when my mother-in-law doesn't; sometimes they open their mouths to begin, but they never get as far as the first sentence. You must get used to an ocean of silence, and just swim about in it as well as you can. I haven't drowned yet, and you won't. Oh – and Seadown's here this week. I think you'll like him; only he doesn't say much either.'

'Who does talk, then?' Nan broke in, her spirits sinking at this picture of an Allfriars evening.

'Well, I do; too much so, my mother-in-law says. But this evening you two will have to help me out. Oh, and the Rector thinks of something to say every now and then; and so does Jacky March. She's just arrived, by the way. You know her, don't you?'

'That little Miss March with the funny curls, that Miss Testvalley took us to see?'

'Yes. She's an American, you know – but she's lived in England for years and years. I'll tell you something funny – only you must swear not to let on. She was madly in love with Lord Brightlingsea – with my father-in-law. Isn't that a good one?' said Conchita with her easy laugh.

'Mercy! In love? But she must be sixty,' cried Virginia, scandalized.

'Well', said Nan gravely, 'I can imagine being in love at sixty.'

'There's nothing crazy you can't imagine,' her sister retorted. 'But can you imagine being in love with Miss March?'

'Oh, she wasn't sixty when it happened,' Conchita continued. 'It was ages and ages ago. She says they were actually engaged, and that he jilted her after the wedding-dress was ordered; and I believe he doesn't deny it. But of course he forgot all about her years ago; and after a time she became a great friend of Lady Brightlingsea's, and comes here often, and gives all the children the loveliest presents. Don't you call that funny?'

Virginia drew herself up. 'I call it demeaning herself; it

shows she hasn't any proper pride. I'm sorry she's an American.'

Nan sat brooding in her corner. 'I think it just shows she loves him better than she does her pride.'

The two elder girls laughed, and she hung her head with a sudden blush. 'Well', said Virginia, 'if mother heard that she'd lock you up.'

The dressing-gong boomed through the passages, and the sisters sprang up and raced back to their room.

THE Marquess of Brightlingsea stood with his coat-tails to the monumental mantelpiece of the red drawing-room, and looked severely at his watch. He was still, at sixty, a splendid figure of a man, firm-muscled, well set-up, with the sloping profile and coldly benevolent air associated, in ancestral por-traits, with a tie-wig, and ruffles crossed by an Order. Lord Brightlingsea was a just man, and having assured himself that it still lacked five minutes to eight he pocketed his watch with a milder look, and began to turn about busily in the empty shell of his own mind. His universe was a brilliantly illuminated circle extending from himself at its centre to the exact limit of his occupations and interests. These comprised his dealings with his tenantry and his man of business, his local duties as Lord Lieutenant of the County and MFH, and participation in the manly sports suitable to his rank and age. The persons ministering to these pursuits were necessarily in the foreground, and the local clergy and magistracy in the middle distance, while his family clung in a precarious half-light on the periphery, and all beyond was blackness. Lady Brightlingsea considered it her duty to fish out of this outer darkness, and drag for a moment into the light, any person or obligation entitled to fix her husband's attention; but they always faded back into night as soon as they had served their purpose.

Lord Brightlingsea had learned from his valet that several

guests had arrived that afternoon, his own eldest son among them. Lord Seadown was seldom at Allfriars except in the hunting season, and his father's first thought was that if he had come at so unlikely a time it was probably to ask for money. The thought was excessively unpleasant, and Lord Brightlingsea was eager to be rid of it, or at least to share it with his wife, who was more used to such burdens. He looked about him impatiently; but Lady Brightlingsea was not in the drawing-room, nor in the Vandyke saloon beyond. Lord Brightlingsea, as he glanced down the length of the saloon, said to himself: 'Those tapestries ought to be taken down and mended' – but that too was an unpleasant thought, associated with much trouble and expense, and therefore belonging distinctly to his wife's province. Lord Brightlingsea was well aware of the immense value of the tapestries, and knew that if he put them up for sale all the big London dealers would compete for them; but he would have kicked out of the house anyone who approached him with an offer. 'I'm not sunk as low as Thwarte,' he muttered to himself, shuddering at the sacrilege of the Titian carried off from Honourslove to the auction-room.

'Where the devil's your mother?' he asked, as a big-boned girl in a faded dinner-dress entered the drawing-room.

'Mamma's talking with Seadown, I think; I saw him go into her dressing-room,' Lady Honoria Marable replied.

Lord Brightlingsea cast an unfavourable glance on his daughter. ('If her upper teeth had been straightened when she was a child we might have had her married by this time,' he thought. But that again was Lady Brightlingsea's affair.)

'It's an odd time for your mother to be talking in her dressing-room. Dinner'll be on the table in a minute.'

'Oh, I'm sure Mamma will be down before the others. And Conchita's always late, you know.'

'Conchita knows that I won't eat my soup cold on her account. Who are the others?'

'No one in particular. Two American girls who are friends of Conchita's.'

'H'm. And why were they invited, may I ask?'

Honoria Marable hesitated. All the girls feared their father less than they did their mother, because she remembered and he did not. Honoria feared him least of all, and when Lady Brightlingsea was not present was almost at her ease with him. 'Mamma told Conchita to ask them down, I think. She says they're very rich. I believe their father's in the American army. They call him "Colonel".'

'The American army? There isn't any. And they call dentists "Colonel" in the States.' But Lord Brightlingsea's countenance had softened. 'Seadown . . .' he thought. If that were the reason for his son's visit, it altered the situation, of course. And, much as he disliked to admit such considerations to his mind, he repeated carelessly: 'You say these Americans are very rich?'

'Mamma has heard so. I think Miss March knows them, and she'll be able to tell her more about them. Miss March is here too, you know.'

'Miss March?' Lord Brightlingsea's sloping brow was wrinkled in an effort of memory. He repeated: 'March – March. Now that's a name I know . . .'

Lady Honoria smiled. 'I should think so, Papa!'

'Now why? Do you mean that I know her too?'

'Yes. Mamma told me to be sure to remind you.'

'Remind me of what?'

'Why, that you jilted her, and broke her heart. Don't you remember? You're to be particularly nice to her, Papa; and be sure not to ask her if she's ever seen Allfriars before.'

'I – what? Ah, yes, of course . . . That old nonsense! I hope I'm "nice", as you call it, to everyone who comes to my house,' Lord Brightlingsea rejoined, pulling down the lapels of his dress-coat, and throwing back his head majestically.

At the same moment the drawing-room door opened

again, and two girls came into the room. Lord Brightlingsea, gazing at them from the hearth, gave a faint exclamation, and came forward with extended hand. The elder and taller of the two advanced to meet it.

'You're Lord Brightlingsea, aren't you? I'm Miss St George, and this is my sister Annabel,' the young lady said, in a tone that was fearless without being familiar.

Lord Brightlingsea fixed on her a gaze of undisguised benevolence. It was a long time since his eyes had rested on anything so fresh and fair, and he found the sensation very agreeable. It was a pity, he reflected, that his eldest son lacked his height, and had freckles and white eyelashes. 'Gad,' he thought, 'if I were Seadown's age . . .'

But before he could give further expression to his approval another guest had appeared. This time it was someone vaguely known to him; a small elderly lady, dressed with a slightly antiquated elegance, who came towards him reddening under her faint touch of rouge. 'Oh, Lord Brightlingsea –' and, as he took her trembling little hand he repeated to himself: 'My wife's old friend, of course; Miss March. The name's perfectly familiar to me – what the deuce else did Honoria say I was to remember about her?'

# ELEVEN

WHEN THE ST GEORGE GIRLS, FOLLOWING CANDLE IN HAND the bedward procession headed by Lady Brightlingsea, had reached the door of their room, they could hardly believe that the tall clock ticking so loudly in the corner had not gone back an hour or two.

'Why, is it only half-past ten?' Virginia exclaimed.

Conchita, who had followed them in, threw herself on the sofa with a laugh. 'That's what I always think when I come down from town. But it's not the clocks at Allfriars that are slow; my father-in-law sees to that. It's the place itself.' She sighed. 'In London the night's just beginning. And the worst of it is that when I'm here I feel as dead with sleep by ten o'clock as if I'd been up till daylight.'

'I suppose it's the struggling to talk,' said Nan irrepressibly.

'That, and the awful certainty that when anybody does speak nothing will be said that one hasn't heard a million times before. Poor little Miss March! What a fight she put up; but it's no use. My father-in-law can never think of anything to say to her. – Well, Jinny, what did you think of Seadown?'

Virginia coloured; the challenge was a trifle too direct. 'Why, I thought he looked pretty sad, too; like all the others.'

'Well, he *is* sad, poor old Seedy. The fact is – it's no mystery – he's tangled up with a rapacious lady who can't afford to let him go; and I suspect he's so sick of it that if any nice girl came along and held out her hand . . .'

Virginia, loosening her bright tresses before the mirror, gave them a contemptuous toss. 'In America girls don't have to hold out their hands –'

'Oh, I mean, just be kind; show him a little sympathy. He isn't easy to amuse; but I saw him laugh once or twice at things Nan said.'

Nan sat up in surprise. 'Me? Jinny says I always say the wrong thing.'

'Well, you know, that rather takes in England. They're so tired of the perfectly behaved Americans who are afraid of using even a wrong word.'

Virginia gave a slightly irritated laugh. 'You'd better hold your hand out, Nan, if you want to be Conchita's sister-in-law.'

'Oh, misery! What I like is just chattering with people I'm not afraid of – like that young man we met the other day in London who said he was a friend of yours. He lives somewhere near here, doesn't he?'

'Oh, Guy Thwarte. Rather! He's one of the most fascinating detrimentals in England.'

'What's a detrimental?'

'A young man that all the women are mad about, but who's too poor to marry. The only kind left for the married women, in fact – so hands off, please, my dear. Not that I want Guy for myself,' Conchita added with her lazy laugh. 'Dick's enough of a detrimental for me. What I'm looking for is a friend with a settled income that he doesn't know how to spend.'

'Conchita!' Virginia exclaimed, flushed with disapproval.

Lady Richard rose from the sofa. 'So sorry! I forgot you little Puritans weren't broken in yet. Goodnight, dears. Breakfast at nine sharp; and don't forget family prayers.' She stopped on the threshold to add in a half-whisper: 'Don't forget, either, that the day after tomorrow we're going to drive over to call on him – the detrimental, I mean. And even if you don't care about him, you'll see the loveliest place in all England.'

'WELL, it was true enough, what Conchita said about nobody speaking,' Virginia remarked when the two sisters were alone. 'Did you ever know anything as awful as that dinner? I couldn't think of a word to say. My voice just froze in my throat.'

'I didn't mind so much, because it gave me a chance to look,' Nan rejoined.

'At what? All I saw was a big room with cracks in the ceiling, and bits of plaster off the walls. And after dinner, when those great bony girls showed us albums with views of the Rhine, I thought I should scream. I wonder they didn't bring out a magic lantern!'

Nan was silent. She knew that Virginia's survey of the world was limited to people, the clothes they wore, and the carriages they drove in. Her own universe was so crammed to bursting with wonderful sights and sounds that, in spite of her sense of Virginia's superiority – her beauty, her ease, her self-confidence – Nan sometimes felt a shamefaced pity for her. It must be cold and lonely, she thought, in such an empty colourless world as her sister's.

'But the house is terribly grand, don't you think it is? I like to imagine all those people on the walls, in their splendid historical dresses, walking about in the big rooms. Don't you believe they come down at night sometimes?'

'Oh, shut up, Nan. You're too old for baby-talk . . . Be sure you look under the bed before you blow out the candle . . .'

Virginia's head was already on the pillow, her hair over-flowing it in ripples of light.

'Do come to bed, Nan. I hate the way the furniture creaks. Isn't it funny there's no gas? I wish we'd told that maid to sit up for us.' She waited a moment, and then went on: 'I'm sorry for Lord Seadown. He looks so scared of his father; but I thought Lord Brightlingsea was very kind, really. Did you see how I made him laugh?'

'I saw they couldn't either of them take their eyes off you.'

'Oh, well – if they have nobody to look at but those daughters

I don't wonder,' Virginia murmured complacently, her lids sinking over her drowsy eyes.

Nan was not drowsy. Unfamiliar scenes and faces always palpitated in her long afterwards; but the impact of new scenes usually made itself felt before that of new people. Her soul opened slowly and timidly to her kind, but her imagination rushed out to the beauties of the visible world; and the decaying majesty of Allfriars moved her strangely. Splendour neither frightened her, nor made her self-assertive as it did Virginia; she never felt herself matched against things greater than herself, but softly merged in them; and she lay awake, thinking of what Miss Testvalley had told her of the history of the ancient abbey, which Henry VIII had bestowed on an ancestor of Lord Brightlingsea's, and of the tragic vicissitudes following on its desecration. She lay for a long time listening to the mysterious sounds given forth by old houses at night, the undefinable creakings, rustlings and sighings which would have frightened Virginia had she remained awake, but which sounded to Nan like the long murmur of the past breaking on the shores of a sleeping world.

IN a majestic bedroom at the other end of the house the master of Allfriars, in dressing-gown and slippers, appeared from his dressing-room. On his lips was a smile of retrospective satisfaction seldom seen by his wife at that hour.

'Well, those two young women gave us an unexpectedly lively evening – eh, my dear? Remarkably intelligent, that eldest girl; the beauty, I mean. I'm to show her the pictures tomorrow morning. By the way, please send word to the Vicar that I shan't be able to go to the vestry meeting at eleven; he'd better put it off till next week . . . What are you to tell him? Why – er – unexpected business . . . And the little one, who looks such a child, had plenty to say for herself too. She seemed to know the whole history of the place. Now, why can't our girls talk like that?'

'You've never encouraged them to chatter,' replied Lady Brightlingsea, settling a weary head on a longed-for pillow; and her lord responded by a growl. As if talk were necessarily chatter! Yet as such Lord Brightlingsea had always regarded it when it issued from the lips of his own family. How little he had ever been understood by those nearest him, he thought; and as he composed himself to slumber in his half of the vast bed, his last conscious act was to murmur over: 'The Hobbema's the big black one in the red drawing-room, between the lacquer cabinets; and the portrait of Lady Jane Grey that they were asking about must be the one in the octagon room, over the fire-place.' For Lord Brightlingsea was determined to shine as a connoisseur in the eyes of the young lady for whom he had put off the vestry meeting.

THE terrace of Honourslove had never looked more beautiful than on the following Sunday afternoon. The party from Allfriars – Lady Richard Marable, her brother-in-law Lord Seadown, and the two young ladies from America – had been taken through the house by Sir Helmsley and his son, and after a stroll along the shady banks of the Love, murmuring in its little glen far below, had returned by way of the gardens to the chapel hooded with ivy at the gates of the park. In the gardens they had seen the lavender-borders, the hundreds of feet of rosy brick hung with peaches and nectarines, the old fig-tree heavy with purple fruit in a sheltered corner; and in the chapel, with its delicately traceried roof and dark oaken stalls, had lingered over kneeling and recumbent Thwartes, Thwartes in cuirass and ruff, in furred robes, in portentous wigs, their stiffly farthingaled ladies at their sides, and baby Thwartes tucked away overhead in little marble cots. And now, turning back to the house, they were looking out from the terrace over the soft reaches of country bathed in afternoon light.

After the shabby vastness of Allfriars everything about Honourslove seemed to Nan St George warm, cared-for, exquisitely intimate. The stones of the house, the bricks of the walls, the very flags of the terrace, were so full of captured sunshine that in the darkest days they must keep an inner brightness. Nan, though too ignorant to single out the details of all this beauty, found herself suddenly at ease with the soft mellow place, as though some secret thread of destiny attached her to it.

Guy Thwarte, somewhat to her surprise, had kept at her side during the walk and the visit to the chapel. He had not said much, but with him also Nan had felt instantly at ease. In his answers to her questions she had detected a latent passion for every tree and stone of the beautiful old place – a sentiment new to her experience, as a dweller in houses without histories, but exquisitely familiar to her imagination. They had walked together to the far end of the terrace before she noticed that the others, guided by Sir Helmsley, were passing through the glass doors into the hall. Nan turned to follow, but her companion laid his hand on her arm. 'Stay,' he said quietly.

Without answering she perched herself on the ledge of the balustrade, and looked up at the long honey-coloured front of the house, with the great carven shield above the door, and the quiet lines of cornice and window-frames.

'I wanted you to see it in this light. It's the magic hour,' he explained.

She turned her glance from the house to his face. 'I see why Conchita says it's the most beautiful place in England.'

He smiled. 'I don't know. I suppose if one were married to a woman one adored, one would soon get beyond her beauty. That's the way I feel about Honourslove. It's in my bones.'

'Oh, then you understand!' she exclaimed.

'Understand –?'

Nan coloured a little; the words had slipped out. 'I mean about the *beyondness* of things. I know there's no such word . . .'

'There's such a feeling. When two people have reached it together it's – well, they *are* "beyond".' He broke off. 'You see now why I wanted you to come to Honourslove,' he said in an odd new voice.

She was still looking at him thoughtfully. 'You knew I'd understand.'

'Oh, everything!'

She sighed for pleasure; but then: 'No. There's one thing I don't understand. How you go away and leave it all for so long.'

He gave a nervous laugh. 'You don't know England. That's part of our sense of beyondness: I'd do more than that for those old stones.'

Nan bent her eyes to the worn flags on the terrace. 'I see; that was stupid of me.'

For no reason at all the quick colour rushed to her temples again, and the young man coloured too. 'It's a beautiful view,' she stammered, suddenly self-conscious.

'It depends who looks at it!' he said.

She dropped to her feet, and turned to gaze away over the shimmering distances. Guy Thwarte said nothing more, and for a long while they stood side by side without speaking, each seeing the other in every line of the landscape.

Sɪʀ Helmsley, after fulminating in advance against the foreign intruders, had been all smiles on their arrival. Guy was used to such sudden changes of the paternal mood, and knew that feminine beauty could be counted on to produce them. His father could never, at the moment, hold out against deep lashes and brilliant lips, and no one knew better than Virginia St George how to make use of such charms.

'That red-haired witch from Brazil has her wits about her,' Sir Helmsley mumbled that evening over his after-dinner cigar. 'I don't wonder she stirs them up at Allfriars. Gad, I should think Master Richard Marable had found his match . . . But your St George girl is a goddess . . . *patuit dea* – I think I like 'em better like that . . . divinely dull . . . just the quiet bearers of their own beauty, like the priestesses in a

Panathenaic procession . . .' He leaned back in his armchair, and looked sharply across the table at his son, who sat with bent head, drawing vague arabesques on the mahogany. 'Guy, my boy – that kind are about as expensive to acquire as the Venus of Milo; and as difficult to fit into domestic life.'

Guy Thwarte looked up with an absent smile. 'I daresay that's what Seadown's thinking, sir.'

'Seadown?'

'Well, I suppose your classical analogies are meant to apply to the eldest Miss St George, aren't they?'

Father and son continued to look at each other, the father perplexed, the son privately amused. 'What? Isn't it the eldest –?' Sir Helmsley broke out.

Guy shook his head, and his father sank back with a groan. 'Good Lord, my boy! I thought I understood you. Sovran beauty . . . and that girl has it . . .'

'I suppose so, sir.'

'You *suppose* –?'

Guy held up his head and cleared his throat. 'You see, sir, it happens to be the younger one –'

'The younger one? I didn't even notice her. I imagined you were taking her off my hands so that I could have a better chance with the beauties.'

'Perhaps in a way I was,' said Guy. 'Though I think you might have enjoyed talking to her almost as much as gazing at the goddess.'

'H'm. What sort of talk?'

'Well, she came to a dead point before the Rossetti in the study, and at once began to quote "The Blessed Damozel".'

'That child? So the Fleshly School has penetrated to the backwoods! Well, I don't know that it's exactly the best food for the family breakfast-table.'

'I imagine she came on it by chance. It appears she has a wonderful governess who's a cousin of the Rossettis.'

'Ah, yes. One of old Testavaglia's descendants, I suppose. What a queer concatenation of circumstances, to doom an

Italian patriot to bring up a little Miss Jonathan!'

'I think it was rather a happy accident to give her someone with whom she could talk of poetry.'

'Well – supposing you were to leave that to her governess? Eh? I say, Guy, you don't mean –?'

His son paused before replying. 'I've nothing to add to what I told you the other day, sir. My South American job comes first; and God knows what will have become of her when I get back. She's barely nineteen and I've only seen her twice . . .'

'Well, I'm glad you remember that,' his father interjected. 'I never should have, at your age.'

'Oh, I've given it thought enough, I can assure you,' Guy rejoined, still with his quiet smile.

Sir Helmsley rose from his chair. 'Shall we finish our smoke on the terrace?'

They went out together into the twilight, and strolled up and down, as their habit was, in silence. Guy Thwarte knew that Sir Helmsley's mind was as crowded as his own with urgent passionate thoughts clamouring to be expressed. And there were only three days left in which to utter them! To the young man his father's step and his own sounded as full of mystery as the tread of the coming years. After a while they made one of their wonted pauses, and stood leaning against the balustrade above the darkening landscape.

'Eh, well – what are you thinking of?' Sir Helmsley broke out, with one of his sudden jerks of interrogation.

Guy pondered. 'I was thinking how strange and far-off everything here seems to me already. I seem to see it all as sharply as things in a dream.'

Sir Helmsley gave a nervous laugh. 'H'm. And I was thinking that the strangest thing about it all was to hear common sense spoken about a young woman under the roof of Honourslove.' He pressed his son's arm, and then turned abruptly away, and they resumed their walk in silence; for in truth there was nothing more to be said.

# TWELVE

A DARK-HAIRED GIRL WHO WAS SO HANDSOME THAT THE heads nearest her were all turned her way, stood impatiently at a crowded London street-corner. It was a radiant afternoon of July; and the crowd which had checked her advance had assembled to see the fine ladies in their state carriages on the way to the last Drawing-room of the season.

'I don't see why they won't let us through. It's worse than a village circus,' the beauty grumbled to her companion, a younger girl who would have been pretty save for that dazzling proximity, but who showed her teeth too much when she laughed. She laughed now.

'What's wrong with just staying where we are, Liz? It beats any Barnum show I ever saw, and the people are ever so much more polite. Nobody shoves you. Look at that antique yellow coach coming along now, with the two powdered giants hanging on at the back. Oh, Liz! – and the old mummy inside! I guess she dates way back beyond the carriage. But look at her jewels, will you? My goodness – and she's got a real live crown on her head!'

'Shut up, Mab – everybody's looking at you,' Lizzy Elmsworth rejoined, still sulkily, though in spite of herself she was beginning to be interested in the scene.

The younger girl laughed again. 'They're looking at *you*,

you silly. It rests their eyes, after all the scarecrows in those circus-chariots. Liz, why do you suppose they dress up like queens at the waxworks, just to go to an afternoon party?'

'It's not an ordinary party. It's the Queen's Drawing-room.'

'Well, I'm sorry for the Queen if she has to feast her eyes for long on some of these beauties ... Oh, good; the carriages are moving! Better luck next time. This next carriage isn't half as grand, but maybe it's pleasanter inside ... Oh!' Mab Elmsworth suddenly exclaimed, applying a sharp pinch to her sister's arm.

'"Oh" what? I don't see anything so wonderful –'

'Why, look, Lizzy! Reach up on your tip-toes. In the third carriage – if it isn't the St George girls! Look, *look!* When they move again they'll see us.'

'Nonsense. There are dozens of people between us. Besides, I don't believe it is ... How in the world should they be here?'

'Why, I guess Conchita fixed it up. Or don't they present people through our Legation?'

'You have to have letters to the Minister. Who on earth'd have given them to the St Georges?'

'I don't know; but there they are. Oh, Liz, look at Jinny, will you? She looks like a queen herself – a queen going to her wedding, with that tulle veil and the feathers ... Oh, mercy, and there's little Nan! Well, the headdress isn't as becoming to her – she hasn't got the *style*, has she? Now, Liz! The carriages are moving ... I'm not tall enough – you reach up and wave. They're sure to see us if you do.'

Lizzy Elmsworth did not move. 'I can survive not being seen by the St George girls,' she said coldly. 'If only we could get out of this crowd.'

'Oh, just wait till I squeeze through, and make a sign to them! There –. Oh, thank you so much ... Now they see me! Jinny – Nan – do look! It's Mab ...'

Lizzy caught her sister by the arm. 'You're making a show

of us; come away,' she whispered angrily.

'Why, Liz . . . Just wait a second . . . I'm sure they saw us . . .'

'I'm sure they didn't want to see us. Can't you understand? A girl screaming at the top of her lungs from the side-walk . . . Please come when I tell you to, Mabel.'

At that moment Virginia St George turned her head towards Mab's gesticulating arm. Her face, under its halo of tulle and arching feathers, was so lovely that the eyes in the crowd deserted Lizzy Elmsworth. 'Well, they're not *all* mummies going to Court,' a man said good-naturedly; and the group about him laughed.

'Come away, Mabel,' Miss Elmsworth repeated. She did not know till that moment how much she would dislike seeing the St George girls in the glory of their Court feathers. She dragged her reluctant sister through a gap in the crowd, and they turned back in the direction of the hotel where they were staying.

'Now I hope you understand that they saw us, *and didn't want to see us!*'

'Why, Liz, what's come over you? A minute ago you said they couldn't possibly see us.'

'Now I'm sure they did, and made believe not to. I should have thought you'd have had more pride than to scream at them that way among all those common people.'

The two girls walked on in silence.

MRS St George had been bitterly disappointed in her attempt to launch her daughters in New York. Scandalized though she was by Virginia's joining in the wretched practical joke played on the Assembly patronesses by Lord Richard Marable and his future brother-in-law, she could not think that such a prank would have lasting consequences. The difficulty, she believed, lay with Colonel St George. He was too free and easy, too much disposed to behave as if Fifth Avenue and Wall Street were one. As a social figure no one took him seriously (except certain women she could have named, had it not demeaned her even to think of them), and by taking up with the Clossons, and forcing her to associate publicly with that divorced foreigner, he had deprived her girls of all chance of social recognition. Miss Testvalley had seen it from the first. She too was terribly upset about the ball; but she did not share Mrs St George's view that Virginia and Nan, by acting as bridesmaids to Conchita Closson, had increased the mischief. At the wedding their beauty had been much remarked; and, as Miss Testvalley pointed out, Conchita had married into one of the greatest English families, and if ever the girls wanted to do a London season, knowing the Brightlingseas would certainly be a great help.

'A London season?' Mrs St George gasped, in a tone implying that her burdens and bewilderments were heavy enough already.

Miss Testvalley laughed. 'Why not? It might be much easier than New York; you ought to try,' that intrepid woman declared.

Mrs St George, in her bewilderment, repeated this to her eldest daughter; and Virginia, who was a thoughtful girl, turned the matter over in her mind. The New York experiment, though her mother regarded it as a failure, had not been without its compensations; especially the second winter, when Nan emerged from the school-room. There was no doubt that Nan supplemented her sister usefully; she could always think of something funny or original to say, whereas there were moments when Virginia had to rely on the length of her eyelashes and the lustre of her lips, and trust to them to plead for her. Certainly the two sisters made an irresistible pair. The Assembly ladies might ignore their existence, but the young men did not; and there were jolly little dinners and gay theatre-parties in plenty to console the exiled beauties. Still, it was bitter to be left out of all the most exclusive entertainments, to have not a single invitation to Newport, to be unbidden to the Opera on the fashionable nights. With Mrs St George it rankled more than with her daughters. With the approach of the second summer she had thought of hiring a house at Newport; but she simply didn't dare – and it was then that Miss Testvalley made her bold suggestion.

'But I've never been to England. I wouldn't know how to get to know people. And I couldn't face a strange country all alone.'

'You'd soon make friends, you know. It's easier sometimes in foreign countries.'

Virginia here joined in. 'Why shouldn't we try, mother? I'm sure Conchita'd be glad to get us invitations. She's awfully good-natured.'

'Your father would think we'd gone crazy.'

Perhaps Mrs St George hoped he would; it was always an added cause for anxiety when her husband approved of holiday plans in which he was not to share. And that summer she knew he intended to see the Cup Races off Newport, with a vulgar drinking crowd, Elmsworth and Closson among them, who had joined him in chartering a steam-yacht for the occasion.

Colonel St George's business association with Mr Closson had turned out to be an exceptionally fruitful one, and he had not failed to remind his wife that its pecuniary results had already justified him in asking her to be kind to Mrs Closson. 'If you hadn't, how would I have paid for this European trip, I'd like to know, and all the finery for the girls' London season?' he had playfully reminded her, as he pressed the steamer-tickets and a letter of credit into her reluctant hand.

Mrs St George knew then that the time for further argument was over. The letter of credit, a vaguely understood instrument which she handled as though it were an explosive, proved that his decision was irrevocable. The pact with Mr Closson had paid for the projected European tour, and would also, Mrs St George bitterly reflected, help to pay for the charter of the steam-yacht, and the champagne orgies on board, with ladies in pink bonnets. All this was final, unchangeable, and she could only exhale her anguish to her daughters and their governess.

'Now your father's rich his first idea is to get rid of us, and have a good time by himself.'

Nan flushed up, longing to find words in defence of the Colonel; and Virginia spoke for her. 'How silly, mother! Father feels it's only fair to give us a chance in London. You know perfectly well that if we get on there we'll be invited everywhere when we get back to New York. That's why father wants us to go.'

'But I simply couldn't go to England all alone with you girls,' Mrs St George despairingly repeated.

'But we won't be alone. Of course Miss Testvalley'll come too!' Nan interrupted.

'Take care, Nan! If I do, it will be to try to get you on with your Italian,' said the governess. But they were all aware that by this time she was less necessary to her pupils than to their mother. And so, they hardly knew how, they had all (with Colonel St George's too-hearty encouragement) drifted, or been whirled, into this wild project; and now, on a hot July afternoon, when Mrs St George would have been so happy sipping her lemonade in friendly company on the Grand Union verandah, she sat in the melancholy exile of a London hotel, and wondered when the girls would get back from that awful performance they called a Drawing-room.

There had been times – she remembered ruefully – when she had not been happy at Saratoga, had felt uncomfortable in the company of the dubious Mrs Closson, and irritated by the vulgar exuberance of Mrs Elmsworth; but such was her present loneliness that she would have welcomed either with open arms. And it was precisely as this thought crossed her mind that the buttons knocked on the door to ask if she would receive Mrs Elmsworth.

'Oh, my dear!' cried poor Mrs St George, falling on her visitor's breast; and two minutes later the ladies were mingling their loneliness, their perplexities, their mistrust of all things foreign and unfamiliar, in an ecstasy of interchanged confidences.

THE confidences lasted so long that Mrs Elmsworth did not return to her hotel until after her daughters. She found them alone in the dark shiny sitting-room which so exactly resembled the one inhabited by Mrs St George, and saw at once that they were out of humour with each other if not with the world. Mrs Elmsworth disliked gloomy faces, and on this occasion felt herself entitled to resent them, since it was to please her daughters that she had left her lazy pleasant cure at Bad Ems to give them a glimpse of the London season.

'Well, girls, you look as if you were just home from a funeral,' she remarked, breathing heavily from her ascent of the hotel stairs, and restraining the impulse to undo the upper buttons of her strongly whale-boned Paris dress.

'Well, we are. We've seen all the old corpses in London dressed up for that circus they call a Drawing-room,' said her eldest daughter.

'They weren't all corpses, though,' Mab interrupted. 'What do you think, mother? We saw Jinny and Nan St George, rigged out to kill, feathers and all, in the procession!'

Mrs Elmsworth manifested no surprise. 'Yes, I know. I've just been sitting with Mrs St George, and she told me the girls had gone to the Drawing-room. She said Conchita Marable fixed it up for them. So you see it's not so difficult, after all.'

Lizzy shrugged impatiently. 'If Conchita has done it for them we can't ask her to do it again for us. Besides, it's too late; I saw in the paper it was the last Drawing-room. I told you we ought to have come a month ago.'

'Well, I wouldn't worry about that,' said her mother good-naturedly. 'There was a Miss March came in while I was with Mrs St George – such a sweet little woman. An American; but she's lived for years in London, and knows everybody. Well, she said going to a Drawing-room didn't really amount to anything; it just gave the girls a chance to dress up and see a fine show. She says the thing is to be in the Prince of Wales's set. That's what all the smart women are after. And it seems that Miss March's friend, Lady Churt, is very intimate with the Prince and has introduced Conchita to him, and he's crazy about her Spanish songs. Isn't that funny, girls?'

'It may be very funny. But I don't see how it's going to help us,' Lizzy grumbled.

Mrs Elmsworth gave her easy laugh. 'Well, it won't, if you don't help yourselves. If you think everybody's against you, they will be against you. But that Miss March has invited you and Mabel to take tea at her house next week – it seems everybody in England takes tea at five. In the country-houses the women dress up for it, in things they call "tea-gowns". I wish we'd known that when we were ordering our clothes in Paris. But Miss March will tell you all about it, and a lot more besides.'

LIZZY Elmsworth was not a good-tempered girl, but she was too intelligent to let her temper interfere with her opportunities. She hated the St George girls for having got ahead of her in their attack on London, but was instantly disposed to profit by the breach they had made. Virginia St George was not clever, and Lizzy would be able to guide her; they could be of the greatest use to each other, if the St Georges could be made to enter into the plan. Exactly what plan, Lizzy herself did not know; but she felt instinctively that, like their native country, they could stand only if they were united.

Mrs St George, in her loneliness, had besought Mrs Elmsworth to return the next afternoon. She didn't dare invite Lizzy and Mab, she explained, because her own girls were being taken to see the Tower of London by some of their new friends (Lizzy's resentment stirred again as she listened); but if Mrs Elmsworth would just drop in and sit with her, Mrs St George thought perhaps Miss March would be coming in too, and then they would talk over plans for the rest of the summer. Lizzy understood at once the use to which Mrs St George's loneliness might be put. Mrs Elmsworth was lonely too; but this did not greatly concern her daughter. In the St George and Elmsworth circles unemployed mothers were the rule; but Lizzy saw that, by pooling their solitudes, the two ladies might become more contented, and therefore more manageable. And having come to lay siege to London Miss Elmsworth was determined, at all costs, not to leave till the citadel had fallen.

'I guess I'll go with you,' she announced, when her mother rose to put on her bonnet for the call.

'Why, the girls won't be there; she told me so. She says they'll be round to see you tomorrow,' said Mrs Elmsworth, surprised.

'I don't care about the girls; I want to see that Miss March.'

'Oh, well,' her mother agreed. Lizzy was always doing things she didn't understand, but Mab usually threw some light on them afterwards. And certainly, Mrs Elmsworth reflected, it became her eldest daughter to be in one of her mysterious moods. She had never seen Lizzy look more goddess-like than when they ascended Mrs St George's stairs together.

Miss March was not far from sharing Mrs Elmsworth's opinion. When the Elmsworth ladies were shown in, Miss March was already sitting with Mrs St George. She had returned on the pretext of bringing an invitation for the girls to visit Holland House; but in reality she was impatient to see the rival beauty. Miss Testvalley, the day before, had told her all about Lizzy Elmsworth, whom some people thought, in her different way, as handsome as Virginia, and who was certainly cleverer. And here she was, stalking in ahead of her mother, in what appeared to be the new American style, and carrying her slim height and small regal head with an assurance which might well eclipse Virginia's milder light.

Miss March surveyed her with the practised eye of an old frequenter of the marriage-market.

'Very fair girls usually have a better chance here; but Idina Churt is dark – perhaps, for that reason, this girl might be more likely . . .' Miss March lost herself in almost maternal musings. She often said to herself (and sometimes to her most intimate friends) that Lord Seadown seemed to her like her own son; and now, as she looked on Lizzy Elmsworth's dark splendour, she murmured inwardly: 'Of course we must find out first what Mr Elmsworth would be prepared to do . . .'

To Mrs Elmsworth, whom she greeted with her most persuasive smile, she said engagingly: 'Mrs St George and I have such a delightful plan to suggest to you. Of course you won't want to stay in London much longer. It's so hot and crowded; and before long it will be a dusty desert. Mrs St George tells me that you're both rather wondering where to go next, and I've suggested that you should join her in hiring a lovely little cottage on the Thames belonging to a friend of mine, Lady Churt. It could be had at once, servants and all – the most perfect servants – and I've stayed so often with Lady Churt that I know just how cool and comfortable and lazy one can be there. But I was thinking more especially of your daughters and their friends . . . The river's a paradise at their age . . . the punting by moonlight, and all the rest . . .'

Long-past memories of the river's magic brought a sigh to Miss March's lips; but she turned it into a smile as she raised her forget-me-not eyes to Lizzy Elmsworth's imperial orbs. Lizzy returned the look, and the two immediately understood each other.

'Why, mother, that sounds perfectly lovely. You'd love it

too, Mrs St George, wouldn't you?' Lizzy smiled, stooping gracefully to kiss her mother's friend. She had no idea what punting was, but the fact that it was practised by moonlight suggested the exclusion of rheumatic elders, and a free field – or river, rather – for the exercise of youthful arts. And in those she felt confident of excelling.

# THIRTEEN

THE LAWN BEFORE LADY CHURT'S COTTAGE (OR BUNGALOW, AS the knowing were beginning to say) spread sweetly to the Thames at Runnymede. With its long deck-like verandah, its awnings stretched from every window, it seemed to Nan St George a fairy galleon making, all sails set, for the river. Swans, as fabulous to Nan as her imaginary galleon, sailed majestically on the silver flood; and boats manned by beautiful bare-armed athletes sped back and forth between the flat grass-banks.

At first Nan was the only one of the party on whom the river was not lost. Virginia's attention travelled barely as far as the circles of calceolarias and lobelias dotting the lawn, and the vases of red geraniums and purple petunias which flanked the door; she liked the well-kept flowers and bright turf, and found it pleasant, on warm afternoons, to sit under an ancient cedar and play at the new-fangled tea-drinking into which they had been initiated by Miss March, with the aid of Lady Churt's accomplished parlour-maid. Lizzy Elmsworth and Mab also liked the tea-drinking, but were hardly aware of the great blue-green boughs under which the rite was celebrated. They had grown up between city streets and watering-place hotels, and were serenely unconscious of the 'beyondness' of which Nan had confided her mysterious sense to Guy Thwarte.

The two mothers, after their first bewildered contact with Lady Churt's servants, had surrendered themselves to these accomplished guides, and lapsed contentedly into their old watering-place habits. To Mrs St George and Mrs Elmsworth the cottage at Runnymede differed from the Grand Union at Saratoga only in its inferior size, and more restricted opportunities for gossip. True, Miss March came down often with racy tit-bits from London, but the distinguished persons concerned were too remote to interest the exiles. Mrs St George missed even the things she had loathed at Saratoga – the familiarity of the black servants, the obnoxious sociability of Mrs Closson, and the spectacle of the race-course, with ladies in pink bonnets lying in wait for the Colonel. Mrs Elmsworth had never wasted her time in loathing anything. She would have been perfectly happy at Saratoga and in New York if her young ladies had been more kindly welcomed there. She privately thought Lizzy hard to please, and wondered what her own life would have been if she had turned up her nose at Mr Elmsworth, who was a clerk in the village grocery-store when they had joined their lot; but the girls had their own ideas, and since Conchita Closson's marriage (an unhappy affair, as it turned out) had roused theirs with social ambition, Mrs Elmsworth was perfectly willing to let them try their luck in England, where beauty such as Lizzy's (because it was rarer, she supposed) had been known to raise a girl almost to the throne. It would certainly be funny, she confided to Mrs St George, to see one of their daughters settled at Windsor Castle (Mrs St George thought it would be exceedingly funny to see one of Mrs Elmsworth's); and Miss March, to whom the confidence was passed on, concluded that Mrs Elmsworth was imperfectly aware of the difference between the ruler of England and her subjects.

'Unfortunately their Royal Highnesses are all married,' she said with her instructive little laugh.

Mrs Elmsworth replied vaguely: 'Oh, but aren't there

plenty of other dukes?' If there were, she could trust Lizzy, her tone implied; and Miss March, whose mind was now set on uniting the dark beauty to Lord Seadown, began to wonder if she might not fail again, this time not as in her own case, but because of the young lady's too-great ambition.

Mrs Elmsworth also missed the friendly bustle of the Grand Union, the gentlemen coming from New York on Saturdays with the Wall Street news, and the flutter caused in the dining-room when it got round that Mr Elmsworth had made another hit on the market; but she soon resigned herself to the routine of bezique with Mrs St George. At first she too was chilled by the silent orderliness of the household; but though both ladies found the maid-servants painfully unsociable, and were too much afraid of the cook ever to set foot in the kitchen, they enjoyed the absence of domestic disturbances, and the novel experience of having every wish anticipated.

Meanwhile the bungalow was becoming even more attractive than when its owner inhabited it. Parliament sat exceptionally late that year, and many were the younger members of both Houses, chafing to escape to Scotland, and the private secretaries and minor government officials, still chained to their desks, who found compensations at the cottage on the Thames. Reinforced by the guardsmen quartered at Windsor, they prolonged the river season in a manner unknown to the oldest inhabitants. The weather that year seemed to be in connivance with the American beauties, and punting by moonlight was only one of the midsummer distractions to be found at Runnymede.

To Lady Richard Marable the Thames-side cottage offered a happy escape from her little house in London, where there were always duns to be dealt with, and unpaid servants to be coaxed to stay. She came down often always bringing the right people with her, and combining parties, and inventing amusements, which made invitations to the cottage as sought-after as cards to the Royal enclosure. There was not an ounce of jealousy in Conchita's easy nature. She was delighted with the success of her friends, and proud of the admiration they excited. 'We've each got our own line', she said to Lizzy Elmsworth, 'and if we only back each other up we'll beat all the other women hands down. The men are blissfully happy in a house where nobody chaperons them, and they can smoke in every room, and gaze at you and Virginia, and laugh at my jokes, and join in my nigger songs. It's too soon yet to know what Nan St George and Mab will contribute; but they'll probably develop a line of their own, and the show's not a bad one as it is. If we stick to the rules of the game, and don't play any low-down tricks on each other', ('Oh, Conchita!' Lizzy protested, with a beautiful pained smile) 'we'll have all London in our pocket next year.'

No one followed the Runnymede revels with a keener eye than Miss Testvalley. The invasion of England had been her own invention, and from a thousand little signs she already knew it would end in conquest. But from the outset she had put her charges on their guard against a too-easy triumph. The young men were to be allowed as much innocent enjoyment as they chose; but Miss Testvalley saw to it that they remembered the limits of their liberty. It was amusement enough to be with a group of fearless and talkative girls, who said new things in a new language, who were ignorant of tradition and unimpressed by distinctions of rank; but it was soon clear that their young hostesses must be treated with the same respect, if not with the same ceremony, as English girls of good family.

Miss Testvalley, when she persuaded the St Georges to come to England, had rejoiced at the thought of being once more near her family; but she soon found that her real centre of gravity was in the little house at Runnymede. She performed the weekly pilgrimage to Denmark Hill in the old spirit of filial piety; but the old enthusiasm was lacking. Her venerable relatives (thanks to her earnings in America) were now comfortably provided for; but they had grown too placid, too static, to occupy her. Her natural inclination was for action and conflict, and all her thoughts were engrossed by her young charges. Miss March was an admirable lieutenant, supplying the social experience which Miss Testvalley lacked; and between them they administered the cottage at Runnymede like an outpost in a conquered province.

Miss March, who was without Miss Testvalley's breadth of vision, was slightly alarmed by the audacities of the young ladies, and secretly anxious to improve their social education.

'I don't think they understand *yet* what a duke is,' she sighed to Miss Testvalley, after a Sunday when Lord Seadown had unexpectedly appeared at the cottage with his cousin, the young Duke of Tintagel.

Miss Testvalley laughed. 'So much the better! I hope they never will. Look at the well brought-up American girls who've got the peerage by heart, and spend their lives trying to be taken for members of the British aristocracy. Don't they always end by marrying curates or army-surgeons – or just not marrying at all?'

A reminiscent pink suffused Miss March's cheek. 'Yes . . . sometimes; perhaps you're right . . . But I don't think I shall ever quite get used to Lady Richard's Spanish dances; or to the peculiar words in some of her songs.'

'Lady Richard's married, and needn't concern us,' said Miss Testvalley. 'What attracts the young men is the girls' naturalness, and their not being afraid to say what they think.' Miss March sighed again, and said she supposed that was the new fashion; certainly it gave the girls a better chance . . .

Lord Seadown's sudden appearance at the cottage seemed in fact to support Miss Testvalley's theory. Miss March remembered Lady Churt's emphatic words when the lease had been concluded. 'I'm ever so much obliged to you, Jacky. You've got me out of an awfully tight place by finding tenants for me, and getting such a good rent out of them. I only hope your American beauties will want to come back next year. But I've forbidden Seadown to set foot in the place while they're there, and if Conchita Marable coaxes him down you must swear you'll let me know, and I'll see it doesn't happen again.'

Miss March had obediently sworn; but she saw now that she must conceal Lord Seadown's visits instead of denouncing them. Poor Idina's exactions were obviously absurd. If she chose to let her house she could not prevent her tenants from receiving anyone they pleased; and it was clear that the tenants liked Seadown, and that he returned the sentiment, for after his first visit he came often. Lady Churt, luckily, was in Scotland; and Miss March trusted to her remaining there till the lease of the cottage had expired.

The Duke of Tintagel did not again accompany his friend. He was a young man of non-committal appearance and manner, and it was difficult to say what impression the American beauties made on him; but, to Miss March's distress, he had apparently made little if any on them.

'They don't seem in the least to realize that he's the 'greatest match in England,' Miss March said with a shade of impatience. 'Not that there would be the least chance ... I understand the Duchess has already made her choice; and the young Duke is a perfect son. Still, the mere fact of his coming ...'

'Oh, he came merely out of curiosity. He's always been rather a dull young man, and I daresay all the noise and the nonsense simply bewildered him.'

'Oh, but you know him, of course, don't you? You were at Tintagel before you went to America. Is it true that he always does what his mother tells him?'

'I don't know. But the young men about whom that is said

usually break out sooner or later,' replied the governess with a shrug.

About this time she began to wonder if the atmosphere of Runnymede were not a little too stimulating for Nan's tender sensibilities. Since Teddy de Santos-Dios, who had joined his sister in London, had taken to coming down with her for Sundays, the fun had grown fast and furious. Practical jokes were Teddy's chief accomplishment, and their preparation involved rather too much familiarity with the upper ranges of the house, too much popping in and out of bedrooms, and too many screaming midnight pillow-fights. Miss Testvalley saw that Nan, whose feelings always rushed to extremes, was growing restless and excited, and she felt the need of shielding the girl and keeping her apart. That the others were often noisy, and sometimes vulgar, did not disturb Miss Testvalley; they were obviously in pursuit of husbands, and had probably hit on the best way of getting them. Seadown was certainly very much taken by Lizzy Elmsworth; and two or three of the other young men had fallen victims to Virginia's graces. But it was too early for Nan to enter the matrimonial race, and when she did, Miss Testvalley hoped it would be for different reasons, and in a different manner. She did not want her pupil to engage herself after a night of champagne and song on the river; her sense of artistic fitness rejected the idea of Nan's adopting the same methods as her elders.

Mrs St George was slightly bewildered when the governess suggested taking her pupil away from the late hours and the continuous excitements at the cottage. It was not so much the idea of parting from Nan, as of losing the moral support of the governess's presence, that troubled Mrs St George. 'But, Miss Testvalley, why do you want to go away? I never know how to talk to those servants, and I never can remember the titles of the young men that Conchita brings down, or what I ought to call them.'

'I'm sure Miss March will help you with all that. And I do

think Nan ought to get away for two or three weeks. Haven't you noticed how thin she's grown? And her eyes are as big as saucers. I know a quiet little place in Cornwall where she could have some bathing, and go to bed every night at nine.'

To everyone's surprise, Nan offered no objection. The prospect of seeing new places stirred her imagination, and she seemed to lose all interest in the gay doings at the cottage when Miss Testvalley told her that, on the way, they would stop at Exeter, where there was a very beautiful cathedral.

'And shall we see some beautiful houses too? I love seeing houses that are so ancient and so lovely that the people who live there have them in their bones.'

Miss Testvalley looked at her pupil sharply. 'What an odd expression! Did you find it in a book?' she asked; for the promiscuity of Nan's reading sometimes alarmed her.

'Oh, no. It was what that young Mr Thwarte said to me about Honourslove. It's why he's going away for two years – so that he can make a great deal of money, and come back and spend it on Honourslove.'

'H'm – from what I've heard, Honourslove could easily swallow a good deal more than he's likely to make in two years, or even ten,' said Miss Testvalley. 'The father and son are both said to be very extravagant, and the only way for Mr Guy Thwarte to keep up his ancestral home will be to bring a great heiress back to it.'

Nan looked thoughtful. 'You mean, even if he doesn't love her?'

'Oh, well, I daresay he'll love her – or be grateful to her, at any rate.'

'I shouldn't think gratitude was enough,' said Nan with a sigh. She was silent again for a while, and then added: 'Mr Thwarte has read all your cousin's poetry – Dante Gabriel's, I mean.'

Miss Testvalley gave her a startled glance. 'May I ask how you happened to find that out?'

'Why, because there's a perfectly beautiful picture by your cousin in Sir Helmsley's study, and Mr Thwarte showed it to me. And so we talked of his poetry too. But Mr Thwarte thinks there are other poems even more wonderful than "The Blessed Damozel". Some of the sonnets in *The House of Life*, I mean. Do you think they're more beautiful, Miss Testvalley?'

The governess hesitated; she often found herself hesitating over the answers to Nan's questions. 'You told Mr Thwarte that you'd read some of those poems?'

'Oh, yes; I told him I'd read every one of them.'

'And what did he say?'

'He said . . . he said he'd felt from the first that he and I would be certain to like the same things; and he *loved* my liking Dante Gabriel. I told him he was your cousin, and that you were devoted to him.'

'Ah – well, I'm glad you told him that, for Sir Helmsley Thwarte is an old friend of my cousin's, and one of his best patrons. But you know, Nan, there are people who don't appreciate his poetry – don't see how beautiful it is; and I'd rather you didn't proclaim in public that you've read it all. Some people are so stupid that they wouldn't exactly understand a young girl's caring for that kind of poetry. You see, don't you, dear?'

'Oh, yes. They'd be shocked, I suppose, because it's all about love. But that's why I like it, you know,' said Nan composedly.

Miss Testvalley made no answer, and Nan went on in a thoughtful voice, 'Shall we see some other places as beautiful as Honourslove?'

The governess reflected. She had not contemplated a round of sightseeing for her pupil, and Cornwall did not seem to have many sights to offer. But at length she said: 'Well,

Trevennick is not so far from Tintagel. If the family are away I might take you there, I suppose. You know the old Tintagel was supposed to have been King Arthur's castle.'

Nan's face lit up. 'Where the Knights of the Round Table were? Oh, Miss Testvalley, can we see that too? And the mere where he threw his sword Excalibur? Oh, couldn't we start tomorrow, don't you think?'

Miss Testvalley felt relieved. She had been slightly disturbed by Nan's allusion to Honourslove, and the unexpected glimpse it gave of an exchange of confidences between Guy Thwarte and her pupil; but she saw that in another moment the thought of visiting the scenes celebrated in Tennyson's famous poems had swept away all other fancies. *The Idylls of the King* had been one of Nan's magic casements, and Miss Testvalley smiled to herself at the ease with which the girl's mind flitted from one new vision to another.

'A child still, luckily,' she thought, sighing, she knew not why, at what the future might hold for Nan when childish things should be put away.

# FOURTEEN

THE DUKE OF TINTAGEL WAS A YOUNG MAN BURDENED WITH scruples. This was probably due to the fact that his father, the late Duke, had had none. During all his boyhood and youth the heir had watched the disastrous effects of not considering trifles. It was not that his father had been either irresponsible or negligent. The late Duke had no vices; but his virtues were excessively costly. His conduct had always been governed by a sense of the overwhelming obligations connected with his great position. One of these obligations, he held, consisted in keeping up his rank; the other, in producing an heir. Unfortunately the Duchess had given him six daughters before a son was born, and two more afterwards in the attempt to provide the heir with a younger brother; and though daughters constitute a relatively small charge on a great estate, still a Duke's daughters cannot (or so their parent thought) be fed, clothed, educated and married at as low a cost as young women of humbler origin. The Duke's other obligation, that of keeping up his rank, had involved him in even heavier expenditure. Hitherto Longlands, the seat in Somersetshire, had been thought imposing enough even for a duke; but its owner had always been troubled by the fact that the new castle at Tintagel, built for his great-grandfather in the approved Gothic style of the day, and with the avowed intention of surpassing Inveraray, had never been inhabited. The expense of completing it, and living in it in suitable state, appeared to have discouraged its creator; and for years it stood abandoned on its Cornish cliff, a sadder ruin than the other, until it passed to the young Duke's father. To him it became a torment, a reproach, an obsession; the Duke of Tintagel must live at Tintagel as the Duke of Argyll lived at Inveraray, with a splendour befitting the place; and the carrying out of this resolve had been the late Duke's crowning achievement.

His young heir, who had just succeeded him, had as keen a sense as his father of ducal duties. He meant, if possible, to keep up in suitable state both Tintagel and Longlands, as well as Folyat House, his London residence; but he meant to do so without the continual drain on his fortune which his father had been obliged to incur. The new Duke hoped that, by devoting all his time and most of his faculties to the care of his estates and the personal supervision of his budget, he could reduce his cost of living without altering its style; and the indefatigable Duchess, her numerous daughters notwithstanding, found time to second the attempt. She was not the woman to let her son forget the importance of her aid; and though a perfect understanding had always reigned between them, recent symptoms made it appear that the young Duke was beginning to chafe under her regency.

Soon after his visit to Runnymede he and his mother sat together in the Duchess's boudoir in the London house, a narrow lofty room on whose crowded walls authentic Raphaels were ultimately mingled with watercolours executed by the Duchess's maiden aunts, and photographs of shooting-parties at the various ducal estates. The Duchess invariably arranged to have this hour alone with her son, when breakfast was over, and her daughters (of whom death or marriage had claimed all but three) had gone their different ways. The Duchess had always kept her son to herself, and the Ladies Clara, Ermyntrude and Almina Folyat would never have dreamed of intruding on them.

At present, as it happened, all three were in the country, and Folyat House had put on its summer sack-cloth; but the Duchess lingered on, determined not to forsake her son till he was released from his Parliamentary duties.

'I was hoping', she said, noticing that the Duke had twice glanced at the clock, 'that you'd manage to get away to Scotland for a few days. Isn't it possible? The Hopeleighs particularly wanted you to go to them at Loch Skarig. Lady Hopeleigh wrote yesterday to ask me to remind you . . .'

The Duchess was small of stature, with firm round cheeks, a small mouth and quick dark eyes under an anxiously wrinkled forehead. She did not often smile, and when, as now, she attempted it, the result was a pucker similar to the wrinkles on her brow. 'You know that someone else will be very grieved if you don't go,' she insinuated archly.

The Duke's look passed from faint ennui to marked severity. He glanced at the ceiling, and made no answer.

'My dear Ushant,' said the Duchess, who still called him by the title he had borne before his father's death, 'surely you can't be blind to the fact that poor Jean Hopeleigh's future is in your hands. It is a serious thing to have inspired such a deep sentiment . . .'

The Duke's naturally inexpressive face had become completely expressionless, but his mother continued: 'I only fear it may cause you a lasting remorse . . .'

'I will never marry anyone who hunts me down for the sake of my title,' exclaimed the Duke abruptly.

His mother raised her neat dark eyebrows in a reproachful stare. 'For your title? But, my dear Ushant, surely Jean Hopeleigh . . .'

'Jean Hopeleigh is like all the others. I'm sick of being tracked like a wild animal,' cried the Duke, who looked excessively tame.

The Duchess gave a deep sigh. 'Ushant –'
'Well?'

'You haven't – it's not possible – formed an imprudent attachment? You're not concealing anything from me?' The Duke's smiles were almost as difficult as his mother's; but his muscles made an effort in that direction. 'I shall never form an attachment until I meet a girl who doesn't know what a duke is!'

'Well, my dear, I can't think where one could find a being so totally ignorant of everything on which England's greatness rests,' said the Duchess impressively.

'Then I shan't marry.'

'Ushant –'

'I'm sorry, mother –'

She lifted her sharp eyes to his. 'You remember that the roof at Tintagel has still to be paid for?'

'Yes.'

'Dear Jean's settlements would make all that so easy. There's nothing the Hopeleighs wouldn't do . . .'

The Duke interrupted her. 'Why not marry me to a Jewess? Some of those people in the City could buy up the Hopeleighs and not feel it.'

The Duchess drew herself up. Her lips trembled, but no word came. Her son stalked out of the room. From the threshold he turned to say: 'I shall go down to Tintagel on Friday night to go over the books with Blair.' His mother could only bend her head; his obstinacy was beginning to frighten her.

THE Duke got into the train on the Friday with a feeling of relief. His high and continuous sense of his rank was combined with a secret desire for anonymity. If he could have had himself replaced in the world of fashion and politics by a mechanical effigy of the Duke of Tintagel, while he himself went obscurely about his private business, he would have been a happier man. He was as firmly convinced as his mother that the greatness of England rested largely on her dukes. The Dukes of Tintagel had always had a strong sense of public obligation; and the young Duke was determined not to fall below their standard. But his real tastes were for small matters, for the minutiae of a retired and leisurely existence. As a little boy his secret longing had been to be a clock-maker; or rather (since their fabrication might have been too delicate a business) a man who sold clocks and sat among them in his little shop, watching them, doctoring them, taking their temperature, feeling their pulse, listening to their chimes, oiling, setting and regulating them. The then Lord Ushant had never avowed this longing to his parents; even in petticoats he had understood that a future duke can never hope to keep a clock-shop. But often, wandering through the great saloons and interminable galleries of Longlands and Tintagel, he had said to himself with a beating heart: 'Some day I'll wind all these clocks myself, every Sunday morning before breakfast.'

Later he felt that he would have been perfectly happy as a country squire, arbitrating in village disputes, adjusting differences between vicar and school-master, sorting fishing-tackle, mending broken furniture, doctoring the dogs, rearranging his collection of stamps; instead of which fate had cast him for the centre front of the world's most brilliant social stage.

Undoubtedly his mother had been a great help. She enjoyed equally the hard work and the pompous ceremonial incumbent on conscientious Dukes; and the poor young Duke was incorrigibly conscientious. But his conscience could not compel him to accept a marriage arranged by his mother. That part of his life he intended to arrange for himself. His departure for Tintagel was an oblique reply to the Duchess's challenge. She had told him to go to Scotland, and he was going to Cornwall instead. The mere fact of being seated in a train which was hurrying westward was a declaration of independence. The Duke longed above all to be free, to decide for himself; and though he was ostensibly going to Tintagel on estate business, his real purpose was to think over his future in solitude.

If only he might have remained unmarried! Not that he was without the feelings natural to young men; but the kind of marriage he was expected to make took no account of such feelings. 'I won't be hunted – I won't!' the Duke muttered as the train rushed westward, seeing himself as a panting quarry pursued by an implacable pack of would-be duchesses. Was there no escape? Yes. He would dedicate his public life entirely to his country, but in private he would do as he chose. Valiant words, and easy to speak when no one was listening; but with his mother's small hard eyes on him, his resolves had a way of melting. Was it true that if he did not offer himself to Jean Hopeleigh the world might accuse him of trifling with her? If so, the sooner he married someone else the better. The chief difficulty was that he had not yet met anyone whom he really wanted to marry.

Well, he would give himself at least three days in which to think it all over, out of reach of the Duchess's eyes . . .

A salt mist was drifting to and fro down the coast as the Duke, the next afternoon, walked along the cliffs towards the ruins of the old Tintagel. Since early morning he had been at work with Mr Blair, the agent, going into the laborious question of reducing the bills for the roof of the new castle, and examining the other problems presented by the administration of his great domain. After that, with agent and housekeeper, he had inspected every room in the castle, carefully examining floors and ceilings, and seeing to it that Mr Blair recorded the repairs to be made, but firmly hurrying past the innumerable clocks, large and small, loud and soft, which, from writing-table and mantel-shelf and cabinet-top, cried out to him for attention. 'Have you a good man for the clocks?' he had merely asked, with an affectation of indifference; and when the housekeeper replied: 'Oh, yes, your Grace. Mr Trelly from Wadebridge comes once a week, the same that his late Grace always employed,' he had passed on with a distinct feeling of disappointment; for probably a man of that sort would resent anyone else's winding the clocks – a sentiment the Duke could perfectly appreciate.

Finally, wearied by these labours, which were as much out of scale with his real tastes as the immense building itself, he had lunched late and hastily on bread and cheese, to the despair of the housekeeper, who had despatched a groom before daybreak to scour Wadebridge for delicacies.

The Duke's afternoon was his own and, his meagre repast over, he set out for a tramp. The troublesome question of his marriage was still foremost in his mind; for after inspecting the castle he felt more than ever the impossibility of escaping from his ducal burdens. Yet how could the simple-hearted girl of whom he was in search be induced to share the weight of these great establishments? It was unlikely that a young woman too ignorant of worldly advantages to covet his title would be attracted by his responsibilities. Why not remain unmarried, as he had threatened, and let the title and the splendours go to the elderly clergyman who was his heir presumptive? But no – that would be a still worse failure in duty. He must marry, have children, play the great part assigned to him.

As he walked along the coast towards the ruined Tintagel he shook off his momentary cowardice. The westerly wind blew great trails of fog in from the sea, and now and then, between them, showed a mass of molten silver, swaying heavily, as though exhausted by a distant gale. The Duke thought of the stuffy heat of London, and the currents of his blood ran less sedately. He would marry, yes; but he would choose his own wife, and choose her away from the world, in some still backwater of rural England. But here another difficulty lurked. He had once, before his father's death, lit on a girl who fitted ideally into his plan: the daughter of a naval officer's widow, brought up in a remote Norfolk village. The Duke had found a friend to introduce him, had called, had talked happily with the widow of parochial matters, had shown her what was wrong with her clock, and had even contrived to be left alone with the young lady. But the young lady could say no more than 'Yes' and 'No', and she placed even these monosyllables with so little relevance that face to face with her he was struck dumb also. He did not return, and the young lady married a curate.

The memory tormented him now. Perhaps, if he had been patient, had given her time – but no, he recalled her blank bewildered face, and thought what a depressing sight it would be every morning behind the tea-urn. Though he sought simplicity he dreaded dullness. Dimly conscious that he was dull himself, he craved the stimulus of a quicker mind; yet he feared a dull wife less than a brilliant one, for with the latter how could he maintain his superiority? He remembered his discomfort among those loud rattling young women whom his cousin Seadown had taken him to see at Runnymede. Very handsome they were, each in her own way; nor was the Duke insensible to beauty. One especially, the fair one, had attracted him. She was less noisy than the others, and would have been an agreeable sight at the break-fast-table; and she carried her head in a way to show off the Tintagel jewels. But marry an American –? The thought was inconceivable. Besides, supposing she should want to sur-round herself with all those screaming people, and supposing he had to invite the mother – he wasn't sure which of the two elderly ladies with dyed fringes was the mother – to Longlands or Tintagel whenever a child was born? From this glimpse into an alien world the Duke's orderly imagination recoiled. What he wanted was an English bride of ancient lineage and Arcadian innocence; and somewhere in the British Isles there must be one awaiting him . . .

# FIFTEEN

AFTER THEIR EARLY SWIM THE MORNING HAD TURNED SO damp and foggy that Miss Testvalley said to Nan: 'I believe this would be a good day for me to drive over to Polwhelly and call at the vicarage. You can sit in the garden a little while if the sun comes out.'

The vicarage at Polwhelly had been Miss Testvalley's chief refuge during her long lonely months at Tintagel with her Folyat pupils, and Nan knew that she wished to visit her old friends. As for Nan herself, after the swim and the morning walk, she preferred to sit in the inn garden, sheltered by a tall fuchsia hedge, and gazing out over the headlands and the sea. She had not even expressed the wish to take the short walk along the cliffs to the ruins of Tintagel; and she had apparently forgotten Miss Testvalley's offer to show her the modern castle of the same name. She seemed neither listless nor unwell, the governess thought, but lulled by the strong air, and steeped in a lazy beatitude; and this was the very mood Miss Testvalley had sought to create in her.

But an hour or two after Trevennick's only fly had carried off Miss Testvalley, the corner where Nan sat became a balcony above a great sea-drama. A twist of the wind had whirled away the fog, and there of a sudden lay the sea in a metallic glitter, with white clouds storming over it, hiding and then revealing the fiery blue sky between. Sit in the shelter of the fuchsia hedge on such a day? Not Nan! Her feet were already dancing on the sunbeams, and in another minute the gate had swung behind her, and she was away to meet the gale on the downs above the village.

WHEN the Duke of Tintagel reached the famous ruin from which he took his name, another freak of the wind had swept the fog in again. The sea was no more than a hoarse sound on an invisible shore, and he climbed the slopes through a cloud filled with the stormy clash of sea-birds. To some minds the change might have seemed to befit the desolate place; but the Duke, being a good landlord, thought only: 'More rain, I suppose; and that is certain to mean a loss on the crops.'

But the walk had been exhilarating, and when he reached the upper platform of the castle, and looked down through a break in the fog at the savage coastline, a feeling of pride and satisfaction crept through him. He liked the idea that a place so ancient and renowned belonged to him, was a mere milestone in his race's long descent; and he said to himself: 'I owe everything to England. Perhaps after all I ought to marry as my mother wishes . . .'

He had thought he had the wild place to himself, but as he advanced towards the edge of the platform he perceived that his solitude was shared by a young lady who, as yet unaware of his presence, stood wedged in a coign of the ramparts, absorbed in the struggle between wind and sea.

The Duke gave an embarrassed cough; but between the waves and the gulls the sound did not carry far. The girl remained motionless, her profile turned seaward, and the Duke was near enough to study it in detail.

She had not the kind of beauty to whirl a man off his feet, and his eye was free to note that her complexion, though now warmed by the wind, was naturally pale, that her nose was a trifle too small, and her hair a tawny uncertain mixture of dark and fair. Nothing overpowering in all this; but being overpowered was what the Duke most dreaded. He went in fear of the terrible beauty that is born and bred for the straw-berry leaves, and the face he was studying was so grave yet so happy that he felt somehow reassured and safe. This girl, at any rate, was certainly not thinking of dukes; and in the eyes she presently turned to him he saw not himself but the sea.

He raised his hat, and she looked at him, surprised but not disturbed. 'I didn't know you were there,' she said simply.

'The grass deadens one's steps . . .' the Duke apologized.

'Yes. And the birds scream so – and the wind.'

'I'm afraid I startled you.'

'Oh, no. I didn't suppose the place belonged to me . . .' She continued to scrutinize him gravely, and he wondered whether a certain fearless gravity were not what he liked best in woman. Then suddenly she smiled, and he changed his mind.

'But I've seen you before, haven't I?' she exclaimed. 'I'm sure I have. Wasn't it at Runnymede?'

'At Runnymede?' he stammered, his heart sinking. The smile, then, had after all been for the Duke!

'Yes. I'm Nan St George. My mother and Mrs Elmsworth have taken a little cottage there – Lady Churt's cottage. A lot of people come down from London to see my sister Virginia and Liz Elmsworth, and I have an idea you came one day – didn't you? There are so many of them – crowds of young men; and always changing. I'm afraid I can't remember all their names. But didn't Teddy de Santos-Dios bring you down the day we had that awful pillow-fight? I know – you're a Mr Robinson.'

In an instant the Duke's apprehensive mind registered a succession of terrors. First, the dread that he had been recog-nized and marked down; then the more deadly fear that, though this had actually happened, his quick-witted antago-nist was clever enough to affect an impossible ignorance. A

Mr Robinson! For a fleeting second the Duke tried to feel what it would be like to be a Mr Robinson . . . a man who might wind his own clocks when he chose. It did not feel as agreeable as the Duke had imagined – and he hastily re-became a duke.

Yet would it not be safer to accept the proffered alias? He wavered. But no; the idea was absurd. If this girl, though he did not remember ever having seen her, had really been at Runnymede the day he had gone there, it was obvious that, though she might not identify him at the moment (a thought not wholly gratifying to his vanity), she could not long remain in ignorance. His face must have betrayed his embarrassment, for she exclaimed: 'Oh, then, you're not Mr Robinson? I'm so sorry! Virginia (that's my sister; I don't believe you've forgotten *her*) – Virginia says I'm always making stupid mistakes. And I know everybody hates being taken for somebody else; and especially for a Mr Robinson. But won't you tell me your name?'

The Duke's confusion increased. But he was aware that hesitation was ridiculous. There was no help for it; he had to drag himself into the open. 'My name's Tintagel.'

Nan's eyebrows rose in surprise, and her smile enchanted him again. 'Oh, how perfectly splendid! Then of course you know Miss Testvalley?'

The Duke stared. He had never seen exactly that effect produced by the announcement of his name. 'Miss Testvalley?'

'Oh, don't you know her? How funny! But aren't you the brother of those girls whose governess she was? They used to live at Tintagel. I mean Clara and Ermie and Mina . . .'

'Their governess?' It suddenly dawned on the Duke how little he knew about his sisters. The fact of being regarded as a mere appendage to these unimportant females was a still sharper blow to his vanity; yet it gave him the reassurance that even now the speaker did not know she was addressing a duke. Incredible as such ignorance was, he was constrained to recognize it. 'She knows me only as their brother,' he thought. 'Or else,' he added, 'she knows who I am, and doesn't care.'

At first neither alternative was wholly pleasing; but after a moment's reflection he felt a glow of relief. 'I remember my sisters had a goveness they were devoted to,' he said, with a timid affability.

'I should think so! She's perfectly splendid. Did you know she was Dante Gabriel Rossetti's own cousin?' Nan continued, her enthusiasm rising, as it always did when she spoke of Miss Testvalley.

The Duke's perplexity deepened; and it annoyed him to have to grope for his answers in conversing with this prompt young woman. 'I'm afraid I know very few Italians –'

'Oh, well, you wouldn't know *him*; he's very ill, and hardly sees anybody. But don't you love his poetry? Which sonnet do you like best in *The House of Life*? I have a friend whose favourite is the one that begins: *When do I love thee most, belovèd one?*'

'I – the fact is, I've very little time to read poetry,' the Duke faltered.

Nan looked at him incredulously. 'It doesn't take much time if you really care for it. But lots of people don't – Virginia doesn't . . . Are you coming down soon to Runnymede? Miss Testvalley and I are going back next week. They just sent me here for a little while to get a change of air and some bathing, but it was really because they thought Runnymede was too exciting for me.'

'Ah,' exclaimed the Duke, his interest growing, 'you don't care for excitement, then?' (The lovely child!)

Nan pondered the question. 'Well, it all depends . . . Everything's exciting, don't you think so? I mean sunsets and poetry, and swimming out too far in a rough sea . . . But I don't believe I care as much as the others for practical jokes:

frightening old ladies by dressing up as burglars with dark lanterns, or putting wooden rattlesnakes in people's beds – do *you?*'

It was the Duke's turn to hesitate. 'I – well, I must own that such experiences are unfamiliar to me; but I can hardly imagine being amused by them.'

His mind revolved uneasily between the alternatives of disguising himself as a burglar or listening to a young lady recite poetry; and to bring the talk back to an easier level he said: 'You're staying in the neighbourhood?'

'Yes. At Trevennick, at the inn. I love it here, don't you? You live somewhere near here, I suppose?'

Yes, the Duke said: his place wasn't above three miles away. He'd just walked over from there . . . He broke off, at a loss how to go on; but his interlocutor came to the rescue.

'I suppose you must know the vicar at Polwhelly? Miss Testvalley's gone to see him this afternoon. That's why I came up here alone. I promised and swore I wouldn't stir out of the inn garden – but how could I help it, when the sun suddenly came out?'

'How indeed?' echoed the Duke, attempting one of his difficult smiles. 'Will your governess be very angry, do you think?'

'Oh, fearfully, at first. But afterwards she'll understand. Only I do want to get back before she comes in, or she'll be worried . . .' She turned back to the rampart for a last look at the sea; but the deepening fog had blotted out everything. 'I must really go,' she said, 'or I'll never find my way down.'

The Duke's gaze followed her. Was this a tentative invitation to guide her back to the inn? Should he offer to do so? Or would the governess disapprove of this even more than of her charge's wandering off alone in the fog? 'If you'll allow me – may I see you back to Trevennick?' he suggested.

'Oh, I wish you would. If it's not too far out of your way?'

'It's – it's on my way,' the Duke declared, lying hurriedly;

and they started down the steep declivity. The slow descent was effected in silence, for the Duke's lie had exhausted his conversational resources, and his companion seemed to have caught the contagion of his shyness. Inwardly he was thinking: 'Ought I to offer her a hand? Is it steep enough – or will she think I'm presuming?'

He had never before met a young lady alone in a ruined castle, and his mind, nurtured on precedents, had no rule to guide it. But nature cried aloud in him that he must somehow see her again. He was still turning over the best means of effecting another meeting – an invitation to the castle, a suggestion that he should call on Miss Testvalley – when, after a slippery descent from the ruins, and an arduous climb up the opposite cliff, they reached the fork of the path where it joined the lane to Trevennick.

'Thank you so much; but you needn't come any further. There's the inn just below,' the young lady said, smiling.

'Oh, really? You'd rather –? Mayn't I –?'

She shook her head. 'No; really,' she mimicked him lightly; and with a quick wave of dismissal she started down the lane.

The Duke stood motionless, looking irresolutely after her, and wondering what he ought to have said or done. 'I ought to have contrived a way of going as far as the inn with her,' he said to himself, exasperated by his own lack of initiative. 'It comes of being always hunted, I suppose,' he added, as he watched her slight outline lessen down the hill.

Just where the descent took a turn towards the village, Nan encountered a familiar figure panting upwards.

'Annabel – I've been hunting for you everywhere!'

Annabel laughed and embraced her duenna. 'You weren't expected back so soon.'

'You promised me faithfully that you'd stay in the garden. And in this drenching fog –'

'Yes; but the fog blew away after you'd gone, and I thought

that let me off my promise. So I scrambled up to the castle – that's all.'

'That's all? Over a mile away, and along those dangerous slippery cliffs?'

'Oh, it was all right. There was a gentleman there who brought me back.'

'A gentleman – in the ruins?'

'Yes. He says he lives somewhere round here.'

'How often have I told you not to let strangers speak to you?'

'He didn't. I spoke to him. But he's not really a stranger, darling; he thinks he knows you.'

'Oh, he does, does he?' Miss Testvalley gave a sniff of incredulity.

'I saw he wanted to ask if he could call,' Nan continued, 'but he was too shy. I never saw anybody so scared. I don't believe he's been around much.'

'I daresay he was shocked by your behaviour.'

'Oh, no. Why should he have been? He just stayed with me while we were getting up the cliff; after that I said he mustn't come any farther. Why, there he is still – at the top of the lane, where I left him. I suppose he's been watching to see that I got home safely. Don't you call that sweet of him?'

Miss Testvalley released herself from her pupil's arm. Her eyes were not only keen but far-sighted. They followed Nan's glance, and rested on the figure of a young man who stood above them on the edge of the cliff. As she looked he turned slowly away.

'Annabel! Are you sure that was the gentleman?'

'Yes . . . He's funny. He says he has no time to read poetry. What do you suppose he does instead?'

'But it's the Duke of Tintagel!' Miss Testvalley suddenly declared.

'The Duke? That young man?' It was Nan's turn to give an incredulous laugh. 'He said his name was Tintagel, and that he was the brother of those girls at the castle; but I thought of course he was a younger son. He never said he was the Duke.'

Miss Testvalley gave an impatient shrug. 'They don't go about shouting out their titles. The family name is Folyat. And he has no younger brother, as it happens.'

'Well, how was I to know all that? Oh, Miss Testvalley,' exclaimed Nan, spinning around on her governess, 'but if he's the Duke he's the one Miss March wants Jinny to marry!'

'Miss March is full of brilliant ideas.'

'I don't call that one particularly brilliant. At least not if I was Jinny, I shouldn't. I think', said Nan, after a moment's pondering, 'that the Duke's one of the stupidest young men I ever met.'

'Well', rejoined her governess severely, 'I hope he thinks nothing worse than that of you.'

# SIXTEEN

THE MR ROBINSON FOR WHOM NAN ST GEORGE HAD MISTAKEN the Duke of Tintagel was a young man much more confident of his gifts, and assured as to his future, than that retiring nobleman. There was nothing within the scope of his understanding which Hector Robinson did not know, and mean at some time to make use of. His grandfather had been first a miner and then a mine-owner in the North; his father, old Sir Downman Robinson, had built up one of the biggest cotton industries in Lancashire, and been rewarded with a knighthood, and Sir Downman's only son meant to turn the knighthood into a baronetcy, and the baronetcy into a peerage. All in good time.

Meanwhile, as a partner in his father's big company, and director in various city enterprises, and as Conservative MP for one of the last rotten boroughs in England, he had his work cut out for him, and could boast that his thirty-five years had not been idle ones.

It was only on the social side that he had hung fire. In coming out against his father as a Conservative, and thus obtaining without difficulty his election to Lord Saltmire's constituency, Mr Robinson had flattered himself that he would secure a footing in society as readily as in the City. Had he made a miscalculation? Was it true that fashion had turned towards Liberalism, and that a young Liberal MP was more likely to find favour in the circles to which Mr Robinson aspired?

Perhaps it was true; but Mr Robinson was a Conservative by instinct, by nature, and in his obstinate self-confidence was determined that he would succeed without sacrificing his political convictions. And at any rate, when it came to a marriage, he felt reasonably sure that his Conservatism would recommend him in the families from which he intended to choose his bride.

Mr Robinson, surveying the world as his oyster, had already (if the figure be allowed) divided it into two halves, each in a different way designed to serve his purpose. The one, which he labelled Mayfair, held out possibilities of immediate success. In that set, which had already caught the Heir to the Throne in its glittering meshes, there were ladies of the highest fashion who, in return for pecuniary favours, were ready and even eager to promote the ascent of gentlemen with short pedigrees and long purses. As a Member of Parliament he had a status which did away with most of the awkward preliminaries; and he found it easy enough to pick up, among his masculine acquaintances, an introduction to that privileged group beginning to be known as 'the Marlborough set'.

But it was not in this easygoing world that he meant to marry. Socially as well as politically Mr Robinson was a true Conservative, and it was in the duller half of the London world, the half he called 'Belgravia', that he intended to seek a partner. But into those uniform cream-coloured houses where dowdy dowagers ruled, and flocks of marriageable daughters pined for a suitor approved by the family, Mr Robinson had not yet forced his way. The only interior known to him in that world was Lord Saltmire's, and in this he was received on a strictly Parliamentary basis. He had made the immense mistake of not immediately recognizing the fact, and of imagining, for a mad moment, that the Earl of Saltmire, who had been so ready to endow him with a seat in Parliament, would be no less disposed to welcome him as a brother-in-law. But Lady Audrey de Salis, plain, dowdy, and one of five unmarried sisters, had refused him curtly and all too definitely; and the shock had thrown him back into the arms of Mayfair. Obviously he had aspired too high, or been too impatient; but it was in his nature to be aspiring and impatient, and if he was to succeed it must be on the lines of his own character.

So he had told himself as he looked into his glass on the morning of his first visit to the cottage at Runnymede, whither Teddy de Santos-Dios was to conduct him. Mr Robinson saw in his mirror the energetic reddish features of a young man with a broad short nose, a dense crop of brown hair, and a heavy brown moustache. He had been among the first to recognize that whiskers were going out, and had sacrificed as handsome a pair as the City could show. When Mr Robinson made up his mind that a change was coming, his principle was always to meet it half-way; and so the whiskers went. And it did make him look younger to wear only the fashionable moustache. With that, and a flower in the buttonhole of his Poole coat, he could take his chance with most men, though he was aware that the careless unselfconsciousness of the elect was still beyond him. But in time he would achieve that too.

Certainly he could not have gone to a better school than the bungalow at Runnymede. The young guardsmen, the budding MPs and civil servants who frequented it, were all of the favoured caste whose ease of manner Mr Robinson envied; and nowhere were they so easy as in the company of the young women already familiar to fashionable London as 'the Americans'. Mr Robinson returned from that first visit enchanted and slightly bewildered, but with the fixed resolve to go back as often as he was invited. Before the day was over he had lent fifty pounds to Teddy de Santos-Dios, and lost another fifty at poker to the latter's sister, Lady Richard Marable, thus securing a prompt invitation for the following week; and after that he was confident of keeping the foothold he had gained.

But if the young ladies enchanted him he saw in the young men his immediate opportunity. Lady Richard's brother-in-law, Lord Seadown, was, for instance, one of the golden youths to whom Mr Robinson had vainly sought an introduction. Lord Richard Marable, Seadown's younger brother, he did know; but Lord Richard's acquaintance was easy to make, and led nowhere, least of all in the direction of his own family. At Runnymede Lord Richard was seldom visible; but Lord Seadown, who was always there, treated with brotherly cordiality all who shared the freedom of the cottage. There were others too, younger sons of great houses, officers quartered at Windsor or Aldershot, young Parliamentarians and minor Government officials reluctantly detained in town at the season's end, and hailing with joy the novel distractions of Runnymede; there was even – on one memorable day – the young Duke of Tintagel, a shrinking neutral-tinted figure in that highly coloured throng.

'Now if *I* were a Duke –' Robinson thought, viewing with pity the unhappy nobleman's dull clothes and embarrassed manner; but he contrived an introduction to his Grace, and even a few moments of interesting political talk, in which the Duke took eager refuge from the call to play blindman's-buff with the young ladies. All this was greatly to the good, and Mr Robinson missed no chance to return to Runnymede.

On a breathless August afternoon he had come down from London, as he did on most Saturdays, and joined the party about the tea-table under the big cedar. The group was smaller than usual. Miss March was away visiting friends in the Lake country, Nan St George was still in Cornwall with her governess, Mrs St George and Mrs Elmsworth, exhausted by the heat, had retired to the seclusion of their bedrooms, and only Virginia St George and the two Elmsworth girls, under the doubtful chaperonage of Lady Richard Marable, sat around the table with their usual guests – Lord Seadown, Santos-Dios, Hector Robinson, a couple of young soldiers from Windsor, and a caustic young civil servant, the Honourable Miles Dawnly, who could always be trusted to bring down the latest news from London – or, at that season, from Scotland, Homburg or Marienbad, as the case might be.

Mr Robinson by this time felt quite at home among them. He agreed with the others that it was far too hot to play tennis or even croquet, or to go on the river before sunset, and he lay contentedly on the turf under the cedar, thinking his own thoughts, and making his own observations, while he joined in the languid chatter about the tea-table.

Of observations there were always plenty to be made at Runnymede. Robinson, by this time, had in his hands most of the threads running from one to another of these careless smiling young people. It was obvious, for instance, that Miles Dawnly, who had probably never lost his balance before, was head-over-ears in love with Conchita Marable, and that she was 'playing' him indolently and amusedly, for want of a bigger fish. But the neuralgic point in the group was the growing rivalry between Lizzy Elmsworth and Virginia St George. Those two inseparable friends were gradually becoming estranged; and the reason was not far to seek. It was between them now, in the person of Lord Seadown, who lay at their feet, plucking up tufts of clover, and gazing silently skyward through the dark boughs of the cedar. It had for some time been clear to Robinson that the susceptible young man was torn between Virginia St George's exquisite profile and Lizzy Elmsworth's active wit. He needed the combined stimulus of both to rouse his slow imagination, and Robinson saw that while Virginia had the advantage as yet, it might at any moment slip into Lizzy's quick fingers. And Lizzy saw this too.

Suddenly Mabel Elmsworth, at whose feet no one was lying, jumped up and declared that if she sat still a minute longer she would take root. 'Walk down to the river with me, will you, Mr Robinson? There may be a little more air there than under the trees.'

Robinson had no particular desire to walk to the river, or anywhere else, with Mab Elmsworth. She was jolly and conversable enough, but minor luminaries never interested him when stars of the first magnitude were in view. However, he was still tingling with the resentment aroused by the Lady Audrey de Salis's rejection, and in the mood to compare unfavourably that silent and large-limbed young woman with the swift nymphs of Runnymede. At Runnymede they all seemed to live, metaphorically, from hand to mouth. Everything that happened seemed to be improvised, and this suited his own impetuous pace much better than the sluggish tempo of the Saltmire circle. He rose, therefore, at Mabel's summons, wondering what the object of the invitation could be. Was she going to ask him to marry her? A little shiver ran down his spine; for all he knew, that might be the way they did it in the States. But her first words dispelled his fear.

'Mr Robinson, Lord Seadown's a friend of yours, isn't he?'

Robinson hesitated. He was far too intelligent to affect to be more intimate with anyone than he really was, and after a moment he answered: 'I haven't known him long; but everybody who comes here appears to be on friendly terms with everybody else.'

His companion frowned slightly. 'I wish they really were! But what I wanted to ask you was – have you ever noticed anything particular between Lord Seadown and my sister?'

Robinson stopped short. The question took him by surprise. He had already noticed, in these free-mannered young women, a singular reticence about their family concerns, a sort of moral modesty that seemed to constrain them to

throw a veil over matters freely enough discussed in aristocratic English circles. He repeated: 'Your sister?'

'You probably think it's a peculiar question. Don't imagine
I'm trying to pump you. But everybody must have seen that
he's tremendously taken with Lizzy, and that Jinny St George
is doing her best to come between them.'

Robinson's embarrassment deepened. He did not know
where she was trying to lead him. 'I should be sorry to think
that of Miss St George, who appears to be so devoted to your
sister.'

Mabel Elmsworth laughed impatiently. 'I suppose that's
the proper thing to say. But I'm not asking you to take sides –
I'm not even blaming Virginia. Only it's been going on now
all summer, and what I say is it's time he chose between
them, if he's ever going to. It's very hard on Lizzy, and it's not
fair that he should make two friends quarrel. After all, we're
all alone in a strange country, and I daresay our ways are not
like yours, and may lead you to make mistakes about us. All I
wanted to ask is, if you couldn't drop a hint to Lord
Seadown.'

Hector Robinson looked curiously at this girl, who might
have been pretty in less goddess-like company, and who
spoke with such precocious wisdom on subjects delicate to
touch. 'By Jove, she'd make a good wife for an ambitious
man,' he thought. He did not mean himself, but he reflected
that the man who married her beautiful sister might be glad
enough, at times, to have such a counsellor at his elbow.

'I think you're right about one thing, Miss Elmsworth.
Your ways are so friendly, so kind, that a fellow, if he wasn't
careful, might find himself drawn two ways at once –'

Mabel laughed. 'Oh, you mean: we flirt. Well, it's in our
blood, I suppose. And no one thinks the worse of a girl for it
at home. But over here it may seem undignified; and perhaps
Lord Seadown thought he had the right to amuse himself
without making up his mind. But in America, when a girl has

shown that she really cares, it puts a gentleman on his honour, and he understands that the game has gone on long enough.'

'I see.'

'Only, we've nobody here to say this to Lord Seadown' (Mabel seemed tacitly to assume that neither mother could be counted on for the purpose – not at least in such hot weather), 'and so I thought –'

Mr Robinson murmured, 'Yes – yes –' and after a pause went on, 'But Lord Seadown is Lady Richard's brother-in-law. Couldn't she –?'

Mabel shrugged. 'Oh, Conchita's too lazy to be bothered. And if she took sides, it would be with Jinny St George, because they're great friends, and she'd want all the money she can get for Seadown. Colonel St George is a very rich man nowadays.'

'I see,' Mr Robinson again murmured. It was out of the question that he should speak on such a matter to Lord Seadown, and he did not know how to say this to anyone as inexperienced as Mabel Elmsworth. 'I'll think it over – I'll see what can be done,' he pursued, directing his steps towards the group under the cedar in his desire to cut the conversation short.

As he approached he thought what a pretty scene it was: the young women in their light starched dresses and spreading hats, the young men in flannel boating suits, stretched at their feet on the turf, and the afternoon sunlight filtering through the dark boughs in dapplings of gold.

Mabel Elmsworth walked beside him in silence, clearly aware that her appeal had failed; but suddenly she exclaimed: 'There's a lady driving in that I've never seen before . . . She's stopping the carriage to get out and join Conchita. I suppose it's a friend of hers, don't you?'

Calls from ladies, Mr Robinson had already noticed, were rare and unexpected at the cottage. If a guardsman had leapt from the station fly Mabel, whether she knew him or not, would have remained unperturbed; but the sight of an unknown young woman of elegant appearance filled her with excitement and curiosity. 'Let's go and see,' she exclaimed.

The visitor, who was dark-haired, with an audaciously rouged complexion, and the kind of nose which the Laureate had taught his readers to describe as tip-tilted, was personally unknown to Mr Robinson also; but thanks to the Bond Street photographers and the new society journals her features were as familiar to him as her reputation.

'Why, it's Lady Churt – it's your landlady!' he exclaimed, with a quick glance of enquiry at his companion. The tie between Seadown and Lady Churt had long been notorious in their little world, and Robinson instantly surmised that the appearance of the lady might have a far from favourable bearing on what Mabel Elmsworth had just been telling him. But Mabel hurried forward without responding to his remark, and they joined the party just as Lady Churt was exchanging a cordial hand-clasp with Lady Richard Marable.

'Darling!'

'Darling Idina, what a surprise!'

'Conchita, dearest – I'd no idea I should find you here! Won't you explain me, please, to these young ladies – my tenants, I suppose?' Lady Churt swept the group with her cool amused glance, which paused curiously, and as Robinson thought somewhat anxiously, on Virginia St George's radiant face.

'She looks older than in her photographs – and hunted, somehow,' Robinson reflected, his own gaze resting on Lady Churt.

'I'm Lady Churt – your landlady, you know,' the speaker continued affably, addressing herself to Virginia and Lizzy. 'Please don't let me interrupt this delightful party. Mayn't I join it instead? What a brilliant idea to have tea out here in hot weather! I always used to have it on the terrace. But you

Americans are so clever at arranging things.' She looked
about her, mustering the group with her fixed metallic smile.
With the exception of Hector Robinson the young men were
evidently all known to her, and she found an easy word of
greeting for each. Lord Seadown was the last that she named.

'Ah, Seadown – so you're here too? Now I see why you
forgot that you were lunching with me in town today. I must
say you chose the better part!' She dropped into the deep
basket-chair which Santos-Dios had pushed forward, and
held out her hand for a proffered mint julep. 'No tea, thanks
– not when one of Teddy's demoralizing mixtures is available
... You see, I know what to expect when I come here ... A
cigarette, Seadown? I hope you've got my special supply
with you, even if you've forgotten our engagement?' She
smiled again upon the girls. 'He spoils me horribly, you
know, by always remembering to carry about my particular
brand.'

Seadown, with flushed face and lowering brow, produced
the packet, and Lady Churt slipped the contents into her cig-
arette-case. 'I do hope I'm not interrupting some delightful
plan or other? Perhaps you were all going out on the river? If
you were, you mustn't let me delay you, for I must be off
again in a few minutes.'

Everyone protested that it was much too hot to move, and
Lady Churt continued: 'Really – you had no plans? Well, it *is*
pleasanter here than anywhere else. But perhaps I'm dreadfully in the way. Seadown's looking at me as if I were ...' She
turned her glance laughingly towards Virginia St George.
'The fact is, I'm not at all sure that landladies have a right to
intrude on their tenants unannounced. I daresay it's really
against the law.'

'Well, if it is, you must pay the penalty by being detained
at our pleasure,' said Lady Richard gaily; and after a
moment's pause Lizzy Elmsworth came forward. 'Won't you
let me call my mother and Mrs St George, Lady Churt? I'm

sure they'd be sorry not to see you. It was so hot after luncheon that they went up to their rooms to rest.'

'How very wise of them! I wouldn't disturb them for the world.' Lady Churt set down her empty glass, and bent over the lighting of a cigarette. 'Only you really mustn't let me interfere for a moment with what you were all going to do. You see,' she added, turning about with a smile of challenge, 'you see, though my tenants haven't yet done me the honour of inviting me down, I've heard what amusing things are always going on here, and what wonderful ways you've found of cheering up the poor martyrs to duty who can't get away to the grouse and the deer – and I may as well confess that I'm dreadfully keen to learn your secrets.'

Robinson saw that this challenge had a slightly startling effect on the three girls, who stood grouped together with an air of mutual defensiveness unlike their usual easy attitude. But Lady Richard met the words promptly. 'If your tenants haven't invited you down, Idina dear, I fancy it's only because they were afraid to have you see how rudimentary their arts are compared to their landlady's. So many delightful people had already learnt the way to the cottage that there was nothing to do but to leave the door unlatched. Isn't that your only secret, girls? If there's any other –' she too glanced about her with a smile – 'well, perhaps it's *this*; but this, remember, *is* a secret, even from the stern Mammas who are taking their siesta upstairs.'

As she spoke she turned to her brother. 'Come, Teddy – if everybody's had tea, what about lifting the tray and things on to the grass, and putting this table to its real use?' Two of the young men sprang to her aid, and in a moment tray and tea-cloth had been swept away, and the green baize top of the folding table had declared its original purpose.

'Cards? Oh, how jolly!' cried Lady Churt. She drew a seat up to the table, while Teddy de Santos-Dios, who had disappeared into the house, hurried back with a handful of packs.

'But this is glorious! No wonder my poor little cottage has become so popular. What – poker? Oh, by all means. The only game worth playing – I took my first lesson from Seadown last week . . . Seadown, I had a little *porte-monnaie* somewhere, didn't I? Or did I leave it in the fly? Not that I've much hope of finding anything in it but some powder and a few pawn tickets . . . Oh, Seadown, will you come to my rescue? Lend me a fiver, there's a darling – I hope I'm not going to lose more than that.'

Lord Seadown who, since her arrival, had maintained a look of gloomy detachment, drew forth his notecase with an embarrassed air. She received it with a laugh. 'What? *Carte blanche?* What munificence! But let me see –.' She took up the notecase, ran her fingers through it, and drew out two or three five-pound notes. 'Heavens, Seadown, what wealth! How am I ever to pay you back if I lose? Or even if I win, when I need so desperately every penny I can scrape together?' she slipped the notes into her purse, which the observant Hector Robinson, alert for the chance of making himself known to the newcomer, had hastened to retrieve from the fly. Lady Churt took the purse with a brief nod for the service rendered, and a long and attentive look at the personable Hector; then she handed back Lord Seadown's notecase. 'Wish me luck, my dear! Perhaps I may manage to fleece one or two of these hardened gamblers.'

The card-players, laughing, settled themselves about the table. Lady Churt and Lady Richard sat on opposite sides, Lord Seadown took a seat next to his sister-in-law, and the other men disposed themselves as they pleased. Robinson, who did not care to play, had casually placed himself behind Lady Churt, and the three girls, resisting a little banter and entreaty, declared that they also preferred to walk about and look on at the players.

The game began in earnest, and Lady Churt opened with the supernaturally brilliant hand which often falls to the lot of the novice. The stakes (the observant Robinson noticed) were higher than usual, the players consequently more intent. It was one of those afternoons when thunder invisibly amasses itself behind the blue, and as the sun drooped slowly westward it seemed as though the card-table under the cedar-boughs were overhung by the same feverish hush as the sultry lawns and airless river.

Lady Churt's luck did not hold. Too quickly elated, she dashed ahead towards disaster. Robinson was not long in discovering that she was too emotional for a game based on dissimulation, and no match for such seasoned players as Lady Richard and Lady Richard's brother. Even the other young men had more experience, or at any rate more self-control, than she could muster; and though her purse had evidently been better supplied than she pretended, the time at length came when it was nearly empty.

But at that very moment her luck turned again. Robinson could not believe his eyes. The hand she held could hardly be surpassed; she understood enough of the game to seize her opportunity, and fling her last notes into the jackpot presided over by Teddy de Santos-Dios's glossy smile and supple gestures. There was more money in the jackpot than Robinson had ever seen on the Runnymede card-table, and a certain breathlessness overhung the scene, as if the weight of the thundery sky were in the lungs of the players.

Lady Churt threw down her hand, and leaned back with a sparkle of triumph in eyes and lips. But Miles Dawnly, with an almost apologetic gesture, had spread his cards upon the table.

'Begorra! A royal flush –' a young Irish lieutenant gasped out. The groups about the table stared at each other. It was one of those moments which make even seasoned poker-players gasp. For a short interval of perplexity Lady Churt was silent; then the exclamations of the other players brought home to her the shock of her disaster.

'It's the sort of game that fellows write about in their memoirs,' murmured Teddy, almost awestruck; and the lucky winner gave an embarrassed laugh. It was almost incredible to him too.

Lady Churt pushed back her chair, nearly colliding with the attentive Robinson. She tried to laugh. 'Well, I've learnt my lesson! Lost Seadown's last copper, as well as my own. Not that he need mind; he's won more than he lent me. But I'm completely ruined – down and out, as I believe you say in the States. I'm afraid you're all too clever for me, and one of the young ladies had better take my place,' she added with a drawn smile.

'Oh, come, Idina, don't lose heart!' exclaimed Lady Richard, deep in the game, and annoyed at the interruption.

'Heart, my dear? I assure you I've never minded parting with that organ. It's losing the shillings and pence that I can't afford.'

Miles Dawnly glanced across the table at Lizzy Elmsworth, who stood beside Hector Robinson, her keen eyes bent on the game. 'Come, Miss Elmsworth, if Lady Churt is really deserting us, won't you replace her?'

'Do, Lizzy,' cried Lady Richard; but Lizzy shook her head, declaring that she and her friends were completely ignorant of the game.

'What, even Virginia?' Conchita laughed. 'There's no excuse for her, at any rate, for her father is a celebrated poker-player. My respected parent always says he'd rather make Colonel St George a handsome present than sit down at poker with him.'

Virginia coloured at the challenge, but Lizzy, always quicker at the uptake, intervened before she could answer.

'You seem to have forgotten, Conchita, that girls don't play cards for money in America.'

Lady Churt turned suddenly towards Virginia St George, who was standing behind her. 'No. I understand the game you young ladies play has fewer risks, and requires only two players,' she said, fixing her vivid eyes on the girl's bewildered face. Robinson, who had drawn back a few steps, was still watching her intently. He said to himself that he had never seen a woman so angry, and that certain small viperine heads darting forked tongues behind their glass cases at the Zoo would in future always remind him of Lady Churt.

For a moment Virginia's bewilderment was shared by the others about the table; but Conchita, startled out of her absorption in the game, hastily assumed the air of one who is vainly struggling to repress a burst of ill-timed mirth. 'How frightfully funny you are, Idina! I do wish you wouldn't make me laugh so terribly in this hot weather!'

Lady Churt's colour rose angrily. 'I'm glad it amuses you to see your friends lose their money,' she said. 'But unluckily I can't afford to make the fun last much longer.'

'Oh, nonsense, darling! Of course your luck will turn. It's been miraculous already. Lend her something to go on with, Seadown, do . . .'

'I'm afraid Seadown can't go on either. I'm sorry to be a spoil-sport, but I must really carry him off. As he forgot to lunch with me today it's only fair that he should come back to town for dinner.'

Lord Seadown, who had relapsed into an unhappy silence, did not break it in response to this; but Lady Richard once more came to his rescue. 'We love your chaff, Idina; and we hope the idea of carrying off Seadown is only a part of it. You say he was engaged to lunch with you today; but isn't there a mistake about dates? Seedy, in his family character as my brother-in-law, brought me down here for the weekend, and I'm afraid he's got to wait and see me home on Monday. You wouldn't suppose my husband would mind my travelling alone, would you, considering how much he does it himself – or professes to; but as a matter of fact he and my father-in-law, who disagree on so many subjects, are quite agreed that

I'm not to have any adventures if they can help it. And so you see ... But sit down again, darling, do. Why should you hurry away? If you'll only stop and dine you'll have an army of heroes to see you back to town; and Seadown's society at dinner.'

The effect of this was to make Lady Churt whiten with anger under her paint. She glanced sharply from Lady Richard to Lord Seadown.

'Yes; do, Idina,' the latter at length found voice to say.

Lady Churt threw back her brilliant head with another laugh. 'Thanks a lot for your invitation, Conchita darling – and for yours too, Seadown. It's really rather amusing to be asked to dine in one's own house ... But today I'm afraid I can't. I've got to carry you back to London with me, Seadown, whoever may have brought you here. The fact is – she turned another of her challenging glances on Virginia St George – 'the fact is, it's time your hostesses found out that you don't go with the house; at least not when I'm not living in it. That ought to have been explained to them, perhaps –'

'Idina ...' Lord Seadown muttered in anguish.

'Oh, I'm not blaming anybody! It's such a natural mistake. Lord Seadown comes down so continually when I'm here,' Lady Churt pursued, her eyes still on Virginia's burning face, 'that I suppose he simply forgot the house was let, and went on coming from the mere force of habit. I do hope, Miss St George, his being here hasn't inconvenienced you? Come along, Seadown, or we'll miss our train; and please excuse yourself to these young ladies, who may think your visits were made on their account – mayn't they?'

A startled silence followed. Even Conchita's ready tongue seemed to fail her. She cast a look of interrogation at her brother-in-law, but his gaze remained obstinately on the ground, and the other young men had discreetly drawn back from the scene of action.

Virginia St George stood a little way from her friends. Her

head was high, her cheeks burning, her blue eyes dark with indignation. Mr Robinson, intently following the scene, wondered whether it were possible for a young creature to look more proud and beautiful. But in another moment he found himself reversing his judgement; for Mr Robinson was all for action, and suddenly, swiftly, the other beauty, Virginia's friend and rival, had flung herself into the fray.

'Virginia! What are you waiting for? Don't you see that Lord Seadown has no right to speak till you do? Why don't you tell him at once that he has your permission to announce your engagement?' Lizzy Elmsworth cried with angry fervour.

Mr Robinson hung upon this dialogue with the breathless absorption of an experienced play-goer discovering the gifts of an unknown actress. 'By Jove – by Jove,' he murmured to himself. His talk with Mabel Elmsworth had made clear to him the rivalry he had already suspected between the two beauties, and he could measure the full significance of Lizzy's action.

'By Jove – she knew she hadn't much of a chance with Seadown, and quick as lightning she decided to back up the other girl against the common enemy.' His own admiration, which, like Seadown's, had hitherto wavered between the two beauties, was transferred in a flash, and once for all, to Lizzy. 'Gad, she looks like an avenging goddess – I can almost hear the arrow whizzing past! What a party-leader she'd make,' he thought; and added, with inward satisfaction: 'Well, she won't be thrown away on this poor nonentity, at all events.'

Virginia St George still stood uncertain, her blue entreating eyes turned with a sort of terror on Lady Churt.

'Seadown!' the latter repeated with an angry smile.

The sound of his name seemed to rouse the tardy suitor. He lifted his head, and his gaze met Virginia's, and detected her tears. He flushed to his pale eyebrows.

'This is all a mistake, a complete mistake ... I mean,' he

stammered, turning to Virginia, 'it's just a joke of Lady Churt's – who's such an old friend of mine that I know she'll want to be the first to congratulate me . . . if you'll only tell her that she may.'

He went up to Virginia, and took possession of her trembling hand. Virginia left it in his; but with her other hand she drew Lizzy Elmsworth to her.

'Oh, Lizzy,' she faltered.

Lizzy bestowed on her a kiss of congratulation, and drew back with a little laugh. Mr Robinson, from his secret observatory, guessed exactly what was passing through her mind. 'She's begun to realize that she's thrown away her last hope of Seadown; and very likely she repents her rashness. But the defence of the clan before everything; and I daresay he wasn't the only string to her bow.'

Lady Churt stood staring at the two girls with a hard bright intensity which, as the silence lengthened, made Mr Robinson conscious of a slight shiver down his spine. At length she too broke into a laugh. 'Really –' she said, 'really . . .' She was obviously struggling for the appropriate word. She found it in another moment.

'Engaged? Engaged to Seadown? What a delightful surprise! Almost as great a one, I suspect, to Seadown as to Miss St George herself. Or is it only another of your American jokes – just a way you've invented of keeping Seadown here over Sunday? Well, for my part you're welcome either way . . .' She paused and her quick ironic glance travelled from face to face. 'But if it's serious, you know – then of course I congratulate you, Seadown. And you too, Miss St George.' She went up to Virginia, and looked her straight in the eyes. 'I congratulate you, my dear, on your cleverness, on your good looks, on your success. But you must excuse me for saying that I know Seadown far too well to congratulate you on having caught him for a husband.'

She held out a gloved hand rattling with bracelets, just

touched Virginia's shrinking fingers, and stalked past Lord Seadown without seeming to see him.

'Conchita, darling, how cleverly you've staged the whole business. We must really repeat it the next time there are tableaux vivants at Stafford House.' Her eyes took a rapid survey of the young men. 'And now I must be off. Mr Dawnly, will you see me to my fly?'

Mr Robinson turned from the group with a faint smile as Miles Dawnly advanced to accompany Lady Churt. 'What a titbit for Dawnly to carry back to town!' he thought. 'Poor woman . . . She'll have another try for Seadown, of course – but the game's up, and she probably knows it. I thought she'd have kept her head better. But what fools the cleverest of them can be . . .' He had the excited sense of having assisted at a self-revelation such as the polite world seldom offers. Every accent of Lady Churt's stinging voice, every lift of her black eyebrows and tremor of her red lips, seemed to bare her before him in her avidity, her disorder, her social arrogance and her spiritual poverty. The sight curiously readjusted Mr Robinson's sense of values, and his admiration for Lizzy Elmsworth grew with his pity for her routed opponent.

ぐ CHAPTER ぐ

# SEVENTEEN

UNDER THE FIXED SMILE OF THE FOLYAT RAPHAEL THE DUCHESS of Tintagel sat at breakfast opposite two of her many daughters, the Ladies Almina Folyat and Gwendolen de Lurey.

When the Duke was present he reserved to himself the right to glance through the morning papers between his cup of tea and his devilled kidneys; but in his absence his mother exercised the privilege, and had the *Morning Post* placed before her as one of her jealously guarded rights.

She always went straight to the Court Circular, and thence (guided by her mother's heart) to the Fashionable Marriages; and now, after a brief glance at the latter, she threw down the journal with a sudden exclamation.

'Oh, Mamma, what is it?' both daughters cried in alarm. Lady Almina thought wistfully: 'Probably somebody else she had hopes of for Ermie or me is engaged,' and Lady Gwendolen de Lurey, who had five children, and an invalid husband with a heavily mortgaged estate, reflected, as she always did when she heard of a projected marriage in high life, that when her own engagement had been announced everyone took it for granted that Colonel de Lurey would inherit within the year the immense fortune of a paralysed uncle – who after all was still alive. 'So there's no use planning in advance,' Lady Gwendolen concluded wearily, glanc-

ing at the clock to make sure it was not yet time to take her
second girl to the dentist (the children always had to draw
lots for the annual visit to the dentist, as it was too expensive
to take more than one a year).

'What is it, Mamma?' the daughters repeated apprehensively.

The Duchess laid down the newspaper, and looked first at
one and then at the other. 'It is – it is – that I sometimes
wonder what we bring you all up for!'

'Mamma!'

'Yes; the time, and the worry, and the money –'

'But what in the world has happened, Mamma?'

'What has happened? Only that Seadown is going to
marry an American! That a – what's the name? – a Miss
Virginia St George of New York is going to be premier
Marchioness of England!' She pushed the paper aside, and
looked up indignantly at the imbecile smile of the
Raphael Madonna. 'And nobody cares!' she ended bitterly, as though including that insipid masterpiece in her
reproach.

Lady Almina and Lady Gwendolen repeated with astonishment: 'Seadown?'

'Yes; your cousin Seadown – who used to be at Longlands
so often at one time that I had hoped . . .'

Lady Almina flushed at the hint, which she took as a personal reproach, and her married sister, seeing her distress,
intervened: 'Oh, but Mamma, you know perfectly well that
for years Seadown has been Idina Churt's property, and
nobody has had a chance against her.'

The Duchess gave her dry laugh. 'Nobody? It seems this
girl had only to lift a finger –'

'I daresay, Mamma, they use means in the States that a
well-bred English girl wouldn't stoop to.'

The Duchess stirred her tea angrily. 'I wish I knew what
they are!' she declared, unconsciously echoing the words of

an American President when his most successful general was accused of intemperance.

Lady Gwendolen, who had exhausted her ammunition, again glanced at the clock. 'I'm afraid, Mamma, I must ask you to excuse me if I hurry off with Clare to the dentist. It's half-past nine – and in this house I'm always sure Ushant keeps the clocks on time . . .'

The Duchess looked at her with unseeing eyes. 'Oh, Ushant –!' she exclaimed. 'If you can either of you tell me where Ushant is – or why he's not in London, when the House has not risen – I shall be much obliged to you!'

Lady Gwendolen had slipped away under cover of this outburst, and the Duchess's unmarried daughter was left alone to weather the storm. She thought, 'I don't much mind, if only Mamma lets me alone about Seadown.'

Lady Almina Folyat's secret desire was to enter an Anglican Sisterhood, and next to the grievance of her not marrying, she knew none would be so intolerable to her mother as her joining one of these High Church masquerades, as the evangelical Duchess would have called it. 'If you want to dress yourself up, why don't you go to a fancy-ball?' the Duchess had parried her daughter's first approach to the subject; and since then Lady Almina had trembled, and bided her time in silence. She had always thought, she could not tell why, that perhaps when Ushant married he might take her side – or at any rate set her the example of throwing off their mother's tyranny.

'Seadown marrying an American! I pity poor Selina Brightlingsea; but she has never known how to manage her children.' The Duchess folded the *Morning Post*, and gathered up her correspondence. Her morning duties lay before her, stretching out in a long monotonous perspective to the moment when all Ushant's clocks should simultaneously strike the luncheon hour. She felt a sudden discouragement when she thought of it – she to whom the duties of her sta-

tion had for over thirty years been what its pleasures would
have been to other women. Well – it was a joy, even now, to
do it all for Ushant, neglectful and ungrateful as he had lately
been; and she meant to go on with the task unflinchingly till
the day when she could put the heavy burden into the hands
of his wife. And what a burden it seemed to her that morning!

She reviewed it all, as though it lay outlined before her on
some vast chart: the treasures, the possessions, the heirlooms:
the pictures, the jewels – Raphaels, Correggios, Ruysdaels,
Vandykes and Hobbemas, the Folyat rubies, the tiaras, the
legendary Ushant diamond, the plate, the great gold service
for royal dinners, the priceless porcelain, the gigantic ranges
of hot-houses at Longlands; and then the poor, the charities,
the immense distribution of coal and blankets, committee
meetings, bazaar openings, foundation layings; and last, but
not least onerous, the recurring Court duties, inevitable as
the turn of the seasons. She had been Mistress of the Robes,
and would be so again; and her daughter-in-law, of course,
could be no less. The Duchess smiled suddenly at the
thought of what Seadown's prospects might have been if he
had been a future Duke, and obliged to initiate his American
wife into the official duties of her station! 'It will be bad
enough for his poor mother as it is – but fancy having to prepare a Miss St George of New York for her duties as Mistress
of the Robes. But no – the Queen would never consent. The
Prime Minister would have to be warned . . . But what nonsense I'm inventing!' thought the Duchess, pushing back her
chair, and ringing to tell the butler that she would see the
groom-of-the-chambers that morning before the housekeeper.

'No message from the Duke, I suppose?' she asked, as the
butler backed towards the threshold.

'Well, your Grace, I was about to mention to your Grace
that his Grace's valet has just received a telegram instructing

him to take down a couple of portmanteaux to Tintagel, where his Grace is remaining for the present.'

The door closed, and the Duchess sat looking ahead of her blindly. She had not noticed that her second daughter had also disappeared, but now a sudden sense of being alone – quite alone and unwanted – overwhelmed her, and her little piercing black eyes grew dim.

'I hope', she murmured to herself, 'this marriage will be a warning to Ushant.' But this hope had no power to dispel her sense of having to carry her immense burden alone.

When the Duke finally joined his mother at Longlands he had surprisingly little to say about his long stay at Tintagel. There had been a good many matters to go into with Blair; and he had thought it better to remain till they were settled. So much he said, and no more; but his mere presence gradually gave the Duchess the comfortable feeling of slipping back with him into the old routine.

The shooting-parties had begun, and as usual, in response to long-established lists of invitations, the guns were beginning to assemble. The Duchess always made out these lists; her son had never expressed any personal preference in the matter. Though he was a moderately good shot he took no interest in the sport, and, as often as he could, excused himself on the ground of business. His cousins Seadown and Dick Marable, both ardent sportsmen and excellent shots, used often to be asked to replace him on such occasions; and he always took it for granted that Seadown would be invited, though Dick Marable no longer figured on the list.

After a few days, therefore, he said to his mother: 'I'm afraid I shall have to go up to town tomorrow morning for a day or two.'

'To town? Are you never going to allow yourself a proper holiday?' she protested.

'I shan't be away long. When is Seadown coming? He can replace me.'

The Duchess's tight lips grew tighter. 'I doubt if Seadown comes. In fact, I've done nothing to remind him. So soon after his engagement, I could hardly suggest it could I?'

The Duke's passive countenance showed a faint surprise. 'But surely, if you invite the young lady –'

'And her Mamma? And her sister? I understand there's a sister –' the Duchess rejoined ironically.

'Yes,' said the Duke, the slow blood rising to his face, 'there's a sister.'

'Well, you know how long in advance our shooting-parties are made up; even if I felt like adding three unknown ladies to my list, I can't think where I could put them.'

Knowing the vast extent of the house, her son received this in a sceptical silence. At length he said: 'Has Seadown brought Miss St George to see you?'

'No. Selina Brightlingsea simply wrote me a line. I fancy she's not particularly eager to show off the future Marchioness.'

'Miss St George is wonderfully beautiful,' the Duke murmured.

'My dear Ushant, nothing will convince me that our English beauties can be surpassed. – But since you're here will you glance at the seating of tonight's dinner-table. The Hopeleighs, you remember, are arriving . . .'

'I'm afraid I'm no good at dinner-tables. Hadn't you better consult one of the girls?' replied the Duke, ignoring the mention of the expected guests; and as he turned to leave the room his mother thought, with a sinking heart:

'I might better have countermanded the Hopeleighs. He has evidently got wind of their coming, and now he's running away from them.'

The cottage at Runnymede stood dumb and deserted-looking as the Duke drove up to it. The two mothers, he knew, were in London, with the prospective bride and her friends Lizzy and Mab, who were of course to be among her bridesmaids. In view of the preparations for her daughter's approaching marriage, Mrs St George had decided to take a small house in town for the autumn, and, as the Duke also knew, she had chosen Lady Richard Marable's, chiefly because it was near Miss Jacky March's modest dwelling, and because poor Conchita was more than ever in need of ready money.

The Duke of Tintagel was perfectly aware that he should find neither Mrs St George nor her eldest daughter at Runnymede; but he was not in quest of either. If he had not learned, immediately on his return to Longlands, that Jean Hopeleigh and her parents were among the guests expected there, he might never have gone up to London, or taken the afternoon train to Staines. It took the shock of an imminent duty to accelerate his decisions; and to run away from Jean Hopeleigh had become his most urgent duty.

He had not returned to the cottage since the hot summer day when he had avoided playing blindman's-buff with a bevy of noisy girls only by letting himself be drawn into a tiresome political discussion with a pushing young man whose name had escaped him.

Now the whole aspect of the place was changed. The house seemed empty, the bright awnings were gone, and a cold grey mist hung in the cedar-boughs and hid the river. But the Duke found nothing melancholy in the scene. He had a healthy indifference to the worst vagaries of the British climate, and the mist reminded him of the day when, in the fog-swept ruins of Tintagel, he had come on the young lady whom it had been his exquisite privilege to guide back to Trevennick. He had called at the inn the next day, to reintroduce himself to the young lady's governess, and to invite them both to the new Tintagel; and for a fortnight his visits to the inn at Trevennick, and theirs to the ducal seat, had been frequent and protracted. But, though he had spent with them long hours which had flown like minutes, he had never got beyond saying to himself: 'I shan't rest till I've found an

English girl exactly like her.' And to be sure of not mistaking the copy he had continued his study of the original.

Miss Testvalley was alone in the little upstairs sitting-room at Runnymede. For some time past she had craved a brief respite from her arduous responsibilities, but now that it had come she was too agitated to profit by it.

It was startling enough to be met, on returning home with Nan, by the announcement of Virginia's engagement; and when she had learned of Lady Churt's dramatic incursion she felt that the news she herself had to impart must be postponed – the more so as, for the moment, it was merely a shadowy affair of hints, apprehensions, divinations.

If Miss Testvalley could have guessed the consequences of her proposal to give the St George girls a season in England, she was not sure she would not have steered Mrs St George back to Saratoga. Not that she had lost her taste for battle and adventure; but she had developed a tenderness for Nan St George, and an odd desire to shelter her from the worldly glories her governess's rash advice had thrust upon the family. Nan was different, and Miss Testvalley could have wished a different future for her; she felt that Belgravia and Mayfair, shooting-parties in great country houses, and the rest of the fashionable routine to which Virginia and the Elmsworth girls had taken so promptly, would leave Nan bewildered and unsatisfied. What kind of life would satisfy her, Miss Testvalley did not profess to know. The girl, for all her flashes of precocity, was in most ways immature, and the governess had a feeling that she must shape her own fate, and that only unhappiness could come of trying to shape it for her. So it was as well that at present there was no time to deal with Nan.

Virginia's impending marriage had thrown Mrs St George into a state of chaotic despair. It was too much for her to cope with – too complete a revenge on the slights of Mrs

Parmore and the cruel rebuff of the Assembly ladies. 'We might better have stayed in New York,' Mrs St George wailed, aghast at the practical consequences of a granted prayer.

Miss Jacky March and Conchita Marable soon laughed her out of this. The trembling awe with which Miss March spoke of Virginia's privilege in entering into one of the greatest families in England woke a secret response in Mrs St George. She, who had suffered because her beautiful daughters could never hope to marry into the proud houses of Eglinton or Parmore, was about to become the mother-in-law of an earl, who would one day (in a manner as unintelligible to Mrs St George as the development of the embryo) turn into the premier Marquess of England. The fact that it was all so unintelligible made it seem more dazzling. 'At last Virginia's beauty will have a worthy setting,' Miss March exulted; and when Mrs St George anxiously murmured, 'But look at poor Conchita. Her husband drinks, and behaves dreadfully with other women, and she never seems to have enough money –' Miss March calmed her with the remark: 'Well, you ask her if she'd rather be living in Fifth Avenue, with more money than she'd know how to spend.'

Conchita herself confirmed this. 'Seadown's always been the good boy of the family. He'll never give Jinny any trouble. After all, that hateful entanglement with Idina Churt shows how quiet and domestic he really is. That was why she held him so long. He likes to sit before the same fire every evening ... Of course with Dick it's different. The family shipped him off to South America because they couldn't keep him out of scrapes. And if I took a sentimental view of marriage I'd sit up crying half the night ... But I'll tell you what, Mrs St George; even that's worthwhile in London. In New York, if a girl's unhappily married there's nothing to take her mind off it; whereas here there's never really time to think about it. And of course Jinny won't have my worries, and she'll have a position that Dick wouldn't have given me even if he'd been a model son and husband.'

Most of this was beyond Mrs St George's grasp: but the gist of it was consoling, and even flattering. After all, if it was the kind of life Jinny wanted, and if even poor Conchita, and that wretched Jacky March, who'd been so cruelly treated, agreed that London was worth the price – well, Mrs St George supposed it must be; and anyhow Mrs Parmore and Mrs Eglinton must be rubbing their eyes at this very minute over the announcement of Virginia's engagement in the New York papers. All that London could give, in rank, in honours, in social glory, was only, to Mrs St George, a knife to stab New York with – and that weapon she clutched with feverish glee. 'If only her father rubs the Brightlingseas into those people he goes with at Newport,' she thought vindictively.

THE bell rung by the Duke tinkled languidly and long before a flurried maid appeared; and the Duke, accustomed to seeing double doors fly open on velvet carpets at his approach, thought how pleasant it would be to live in a cottage with too few servants, and have time to notice that the mat was shabby, and the brass knocker needed polishing.

Mrs St George and Mrs Elmsworth were up in town. Yes, he knew that; but might he perhaps see Miss Testvalley? He muttered his name as if it were a term of obloquy, and the dazzled maid curtsied him into the drawing-room and rushed up to tell the governess.

'Did you tell his Grace that Miss Annabel was in London too?' Miss Testvalley asked.

No, the maid replied; but his Grace had not asked for Miss Annabel.

'Ah –' murmured the governess. She knew her man well enough by this time to be aware that this looked serious. 'It was me he asked for?' And the maid, evidently sharing her astonishment, declared that it was.

'Oh, your Grace, there's no fire!' Miss Testvalley exclaimed, as she entered the drawing-room a moment later and found her visitor standing close to the icy grate. 'No, I won't ring. I can light a fire at least as well as any house-maid.'

'Not for me, please,' the Duke protested. 'I dislike over-heated rooms.' He continued to stand near the hearth. 'The – the fact is, I was just noticing, before you came down, that this clock appears to be losing about five minutes a day; that is, supposing it to be wound on Sunday mornings.'

'Oh, your Grace – would you come to our rescue? That clock has bothered Mrs St George and Mrs Elmsworth ever since we came here –'

But the Duke had already opened the glass case, and with his ear to the dial was sounding the clock as though it were a human lung. 'Ah – I thought so!' he exclaimed in a tone of quiet triumph; and for several minutes he continued his deli-cate manipulations, watched attentively by Miss Testvalley, who thought: 'If ever he nags his wife – and I should think he might be a nagger – she will only have to ask him what's wrong with the drawing-room clock. And how many clocks there must be, at Tintagel and Longlands and Folyat House!'

'There – but I'm afraid it ought to be sent to a profes-sional,' said the Duke modestly, taking the seat designated by Miss Testvalley.

'I'm sure it will be all right. Your Grace is so wonderful with clocks.' The Duke was silent, and Miss Testvalley con-cluded that doctoring the time-piece had been prompted less by an irrepressible impulse than by the desire to put off weightier matters. 'I'm so sorry', she said, 'that there's no one here to receive you. I suppose the maid told you that our two ladies have taken a house in town for a few weeks, to prepare for Miss St George's wedding.'

'Yes, I've heard of that,' said the Duke, almost solemnly. He cast an anxious glance about him, as if in search of something; and Miss Testvalley thought it proper to add:

'And your young friend Annabel has gone to London with her sister.'

'Ah –' said the Duke laboriously.

He stood up, walked back to the hearth, gazed at the passive face of the clock, and for a moment followed the smooth movement of the hands. Then he turned to Miss Testvalley. 'The wedding is to take place soon?'

'Very soon; in about a month. Colonel St George naturally wants to be present, and business will take him back to New York before December. In fact, it was at first intended that the wedding should take place in New York –'

'Oh –' murmured the Duke, in the politely incredulous tone of one who implies: 'Why attempt such an unheard-of experiment?'

Miss Testvalley caught his meaning and smiled. 'You know Lord and Lady Richard were married in New York. It seems more natural that a girl should be married from her own home.'

The Duke looked doubtful. 'Have they the necessary churches?' he asked.

'Quite adequate,' said Miss Testvalley drily.

There was another and heavier silence before the Duke continued, 'And does Mrs St George intend to remain in London, or will she take a house in the country?'

'Oh, neither. After the wedding Mrs St George will go to her own house in New York. She will sail immediately with the Colonel.'

'Immediately –' echoed the Duke. He hesitated. 'And Miss Annabel –?'

'Naturally goes home with her parents. They wish her to have a season in New York.'

This time the silence closed in so oppressively that it seemed as though it had literally buried her visitor. She felt an impulse to dig him out, but repressed it.

At length the Duke spoke in a hoarse unsteady voice. 'It would be impossible for me – er – to undertake the journey to New York.'

Miss Testvalley gave him an amused glance. 'Oh, it's set-tled that Lord Seadown's wedding is to be in London.'

'I – I don't mean Seadown's. I mean – my own,' said the Duke. He stood up again, walked the length of the room and came back to her. 'You must have seen, Miss Testvalley . . . It has been a long struggle, but I've decided . . .'

'Yes?'

'To ask Miss Annabel St George –'

Miss Testvalley stood up also. Her heart was stirred with an odd mixture of curiosity and sympathy. She really liked the Duke – but could Annabel ever be brought to like him?

'And so I came down today, in the hope of consulting with you –'

Miss Testvalley interrupted him. 'Duke, I must remind you that arranging marriages for my pupils is not included in my duties. If you wish to speak to Mrs St George –'

'But I don't!' exclaimed the Duke. He looked so startled that for a moment she thought he was about to turn and take flight. It would have been a relief to her if he had. But he coughed nervously, cleared his throat, and began again.

'I've always understood that in America it was the custom to speak first to the young lady herself. And knowing how fond you are of Miss St George, I merely wished to ask –'

'Yes, I am very fond of her,' Miss Testvalley said gravely.

'Quite so. And I wished to ask if you had any idea whether her . . . her feelings in any degree corresponded with mine,' faltered the anxious suitor.

Miss Testvalley pondered. What should she say? What could she say? What did she really wish to say? She could not, at the moment, have answered any of these questions; she knew only that, as life suddenly pressed closer to her charge, her impulse was to catch her fast and hold her tight.

'I can't reply to that, your Grace. I can only say that I don't know.'

'You don't know?' repeated the Duke in surprise.

'Nan in some ways is still a child. She judges many things as a child would –'

'Yes! That's what I find so interesting . . . so unusual . . .'

'Exactly. But it makes your question unanswerable. How can one answer for a child who can't yet answer for herself?'

The Duke looked crestfallen. 'But it's her childish innocence, her indifference to money and honours and – er – that kind of thing, that I value so immensely . . .'

'Yes. But you can hardly regard her as a rare piece for your collection.'

'I don't know, Miss Testvalley, why you should accuse me of such ideas . . .'

'I don't accuse you, your Grace. I only want you to understand that Nan is one thing now, but may be another, quite different, thing in a year or two. Sensitive natures alter strangely after their first contact with life.'

'Ah, but I should make it my business to shield her from every contact with life!'

'I'm sure you would. But what if Nan turned out to be a woman who didn't want to be shielded?'

The Duke's countenance expressed the most genuine dismay. 'Not want to be shielded? I thought you were a friend of hers,' he stammered.

'I am. A good friend, I hope. That's why I advise you to wait, to give her time to grow up.'

The Duke looked at her with a hunted eye, and she suddenly thought, 'Poor man! I daresay he's trying to marry her against someone else. Running away from the fatted heiress . . . But Nan's worth too much to be used as an alternative.'

'To wait? But you say she's going back to the States immediately.'

'Well, to wait till she returns to England. She probably will, you know.'

'Oh, but I can't wait!' cried the Duke, in the astonished tone of the one who has never before been obliged to.

Miss Testvalley smiled. 'I'm afraid you must say that to Annabel herself, not to me.'

'I thought you were my friend. I hoped you'd advise me . . .'

'You don't want me to advise you, Duke. You want me to agree with you.'

The Duke considered this for some time without speaking; then he said: 'I suppose you've no objection to giving me the London address?' and the governess wrote it down for him with her same disciplined smile.

# EIGHTEEN

Longlands House, October 25

To Sir Helmsley Thwarte, Bart.
Honourslove, Lowdon, Glos.

MY DEAR SIR HELMSLEY,

It seems an age since you have given Ushant and me the pleasure of figuring among the guns at Longlands; but I hope next month you will do us that favour.

You are, as you know, always a welcome guest; but I will not deny that this year I feel a special need for your presence. I suppose you have heard that Selina Brightlingsea's eldest boy is marrying an American – so that there will soon be two daughters-in-law of that nationality in the family. I make no comment beyond saying that I fail to see why the virtue and charms of our English girls are not sufficient to satisfy the hearts of our young men. It is useless, I suppose, to argue such matters with the interested parties; one can only hope that when experience has tested the more showy attractions of the young ladies from the States, the enduring qualities of our own daughters will reassert themselves. Meanwhile I am selfishly glad that it is poor Selina, and not I, on whom such a trial has been imposed.

But to come to the point. You know Ushant's exceptionally high standards, especially in family matters, and
will not be surprised to hear that he feels we ought to do
our cousinly duty toward the Brightlingseas by inviting
Seadown, his fiancée, and the latter's family (a Colonel
and Mrs St George, and a younger daughter), to
Longlands. He says it would not matter half as much if
Seadown were marrying one of our own kind; and though
I do not quite follow this argument, I respect it, as I do all
my dear son's decisions. You see what is before me, therefore; and though you may not share Ushant's view, I hope
your own family feeling will prompt you to come and help
me out with all these strange people.

The shooting is especially good this year, and if you
could manage to be with us from the 10th to the 18th of
November, Ushant assures me the sport will be worthy of
your gun.

Believe me

Yours very sincerely
BLANCHE TINTAGEL

Longlands House, November 15
To Guy Thwarte Esqre
Care of the British Consulate General
Rio Janeiro
(To be forwarded)
MY DEAR BOY,

Look on the above address and marvel! You who know
how many years it is since I have allowed myself to be
dragged into a Longlands shooting-party will wonder what
can have caused me to succumb at last.

Well – queerly enough, a sense of duty! I have, as you
know, my (rare) moments of self-examination and

remorse. One of these penitential phases coincided with Blanche Tintagel's invitation, and as it was reinforced by a moving appeal to my tribal loyalty, I thought I ought to respond and I did. After all, Tintagel is our Duke, and Longlands is our Dukery, and we local people ought all to back each other up in subversive times like these.

The reason of Blanche's cry for help will amuse you. Do you remember, one afternoon just before you left for Brazil, having asked me to invite to Honourslove two American young ladies, friends of Lady Dick Marable's, who were staying at Allfriars? You were so urgent that my apprehensions were aroused; and I imagine rightly. But being soft-hearted I yielded, and Lady Richard appeared with an enchantress, and the enchantress's younger sister, who seemed to me totally eclipsed by her elder, though you apparently thought otherwise. I've no doubt you will recall the incident.

Well – Seadown is to marry the beauty, a Miss St George, of New York. Rumours, of course, are rife about the circumstances of the marriage. Seadown is said to have been trapped by a clever manoeuvre; but as this report probably emanates from Lady Churt – the Ariadne in the case – it need not be taken too seriously. We know that American business men are 'smart', but we also know that their daughters are beautiful; and having seen the young lady who has supplanted Ariadne, I have no difficulty in believing that her 'beaux yeux' sufficed to let Seadown out of prison – for friends and foes agree that the affair with the relentless Idina had become an imprisonment. They also say that Papa St George is very wealthy, and that consideration must be not without weight – its weight in gold – to the Brightlingseas. I hope they will not be disappointed, but as you know I am no great believer in transatlantic fortunes – though I trust, my dear fellow, that the one you are now amassing is beyond suspicion.

Otherwise I should find it hard to forego your company much longer.

It's an odd chance that finds me in an atmosphere so different from that of our shabby old house, on the date fixed for the despatch of my monthly chronicle. But I don't want to miss the South American post, and it may amuse you to have a change from the ordinary small beer of Honourslove. Certainly the contrast is not without interest; and perhaps it strikes me the more because of my disintegrating habit of seeing things through other people's eyes, so that at this moment I am viewing Longlands, not as a familiar and respected monument, but as the unheard-of and incomprehensible phenomenon that a great English country-seat offers to the unprejudiced gaze of the American backwoodsman and his females. I refer to the St George party, who arrived the day before yesterday, and are still in the first flush of their bewilderment.

The Duchess and her daughters are of course no less bewildered. They have no conception of a society not based on aristocratic institutions, with Inveraray, Welbeck, Chatsworth, Longlands and so forth as its main supports; and their guests cannot grasp the meaning of such institutions or understand the hundreds of minute observances forming the texture of an old society. This has caused me, for the first time in my life, to see from the outside at once the absurdity and the impressiveness of our great ducal establishments, the futility of their domestic ceremonial, and their importance as custodians of historical tradition and of high (if narrow) social standards. My poor friend Blanche would faint if she knew that I had actually ventured to imagine what an England without dukes might be, perhaps may soon be; but she would be restored to her senses if she knew that, after weighing the evidence for and against, I have decided that, having been afflicted with dukes, we'd better keep 'em. I need hardly add that such problems do not trouble the St Georges, who have not yet reached the stage of investigating social origins.

I can't imagine how the Duchess and the other ladies deal with Mrs St George and her daughters during the daily absence of the guns; but I have noticed that American young ladies cannot be kept quiet for an indefinite time by being shown views of Vesuvius and albums of family watercolours.

Luckily it's all right for the men. The shooting has never been better, and Seadown, who is in his element, has had the surprise of finding that his future father-in-law is not precisely out of his. Colonel St George is a good shot; and it is not the least part of the joke that he is decidedly bored by covert shooting, an institution as new to him as dukedoms, and doesn't understand how a man who respects himself can want to shoot otherwise than over a dog. But he accommodates himself well enough to our effete habits and is in fact a big good-natured easygoing man, with a kind of florid good looks, too new clothes, and a collection of funny stories, some of which are not new enough.

As to the ladies, what shall I say? The beauty *is* a beauty, as I discovered (you may remember) the moment she appeared at Honourslove. She is precisely what she was then: the obvious, the finished exemplar, of what she professes to be. And, as you know, I have always had a preference for the icily regular. Her composure is unshakeable; and under a surface of American animation I imagine she is as passive as she looks. She giggles with the rest, and says: 'Oh, girls', but on her lips such phrases acquire a classic cadence. I suspect her of having a strong will and knowing all the arts of exaction. She will probably get whatever she wants in life, and will give in return only her beautiful profile. I don't believe her soul has a full face. If I

were in Seadown's place I should probably be as much in
love with her as he is. As a rule I don't care for interesting
women; I mean in the domestic relation. I prefer a fine fig-
urehead embodying a beautiful form, a solid bulk of usage
and conformity. But I own that figureheads lack conversation . . .

Your little friend is not deficient in this respect; and she
is also agreeable to look upon. Not beautiful; but there is a
subtler form of loveliness, which the unobservant confuse
with beauty, and which this young Annabel is on the way
to acquire. I say 'on the way' because she is still a bundle
of engaging possibilities rather than a finished picture. Of
the mother there is nothing to say, for that excellent lady
evidently requires familiar surroundings to bring out such
small individuality as she possesses. In the unfamiliar she
becomes invisible; and Longlands and she will never be
visible to each other.

Most amusing of all is to watch our good Blanche, her
faithful daughters, and her other guests, struggling with
the strange beings suddenly thrust upon them. Your little
friend (the only one with whom one can converse, by the
way) told me that when Lady Brightlingsea heard of Dick
Marable's engagement to the Brazilian beauty she cabled
to the St Georges' governess: 'Is she black?' Well, the attitude of Longlands toward its transatlantic guests is not
much more enlightened than Selina Brightlingsea's. Their
bewilderment is so great that, when one of the girls spoke
of archery clubs being fashionable in the States, somebody
blurted out: 'I suppose the Indians taught you?'; and I am
constantly expecting them to ask Mrs St George how she
heats her wigwam in winter.

The only exceptions are Seadown, who contributes little beyond a mute adoration of the beauty, and our host,
young Tintagel. Strange to say, he seems curiously alert
and informed about his American visitors; so much so

**Miss Testvalley**

Cherie Lunghi

Characters' names in brackets
are those used in the television series

**Conchita**

Mira Sorvino

❧

**Lord and Lady
Brightlingsea**

Dinsdale Landen and

Rosemary Leach

❧

**Seadown and
Virginia**
Mark Tandy and
Alison Elliott

❧

**Idina Churt
(Idina Hatton)**
Jenny Agutter

❧

**Nan**

Carla Gugino

☙

**Colonel St George**

Peter Michael Goetz

❧

**Mrs St George**

Gwen Humble

❧

RIGHT

**Miss March**
Connie Booth

❧

**Ushant (Julius) and
the Dowager Duchess**
James Frain and
Sheila Hancock

❧

**Lizzy**

Rya Kihlstedt

∞

**Hector**

Richard Huw

∞

**Sir Helmsley Thwarte**

**(Sir Helmsley Thwaite)**

Michael Kitchen

**Guy Thwarte**

**(Guy Thwaite)**

Greg Wise

that I'm wondering if his including them in the party is due only to a cousinly regard for Seadown. My short study of the case has almost convinced me that his motives are more interested. His mother, of course, has no suspicion of this – when did our Blanche ever begin to suspect anything until it was emblazoned across the heavens? The first thing she said to me (in explaining the presence of the St Georges) was that, since so many of our young eligibles were beginning to make these mad American marriages, she thought that Tintagel should see a few specimens at close quarters. *Sancta simplicitas*! If this is her object, I fear the specimens are not well-chosen. I suspect that Tintagel had them invited because he's very nearly, if not quite, in love with the younger girl, and being a sincere believer in the importance of dukes, wants her family to see what marriage with an English duke means.

How far the St Georges are aware of all this, I can't say. The only one I suspect of suspecting it is the young Annabel; but these Americans, under their forthcoming manner, their surface gush, as some might call it, have an odd reticence about what goes on underneath. At any rate the young lady seems to understand something of her environment, which is a sealed book to the others. She has been better educated than her sister, and has a more receptive mind. It seems as though someone had sown in a bare field a sprinkling of history, poetry and pictures, and every seed had shot up in a flowery tangle. I fancy the sower is the little brown governess of whom you spoke (her pupil says she is little and brown). Miss Annabel asks so many questions about English life in town and country, about rules, customs, traditions, and their why and wherefore, that I sometimes wonder if she is not preparing for a leading part on the social stage; then a glimpse of utter simplicity dispels the idea, and I remember that all her country people are merciless questioners, and conclude that she has the national habit, but exercises it more intelligently than the others. She is intensely interested in the history of this house, and has an emotional sense at least of its beauties; perhaps the little governess – that odd descendant of old Testavaglia's – has had a hand in developing this side also of her pupil's intelligence.

Miss Annabel seems to be devoted to this Miss Testvalley, who is staying on with the family though both girls are out, and one on the brink of marriage, and who is apparently their guide in the world of fashion – odd as such a role seems for an Italian revolutionary. But I understood she had learned her way about the great world as governess in the Brightlingsea and Tintagel households. Her pupil, by the way, tells me that Miss Testvalley knows all about the circumstances in which my D.G. Rossetti was painted, and knows also the mysterious replica with variants which is still in D.G.'s possession, and which he has never been willing to show me. The girl, the afternoon she came to Honourslove, apparently looked closely enough at my picture to describe it in detail to her governess, who says that in the replica the embroidered border of the cloak is *peach-coloured* instead of blue ...

All this has stirred up the old collector in me, and when the St Georges go to Allfriars, where they have been asked to stay before the wedding, Miss Annabel has promised to try to have the governess invited, and to bring her to Honourslove to see the picture. What a pity you won't be there to welcome them! The girl's account of the Testavaglia and her family excites my curiosity almost as much as this report about the border of the cloak.

After the above, which reads, I flatter myself, not unlike a page of Saint Simon, the home chronicle will seem tamer than ever. Mrs Bolt has again upset everything in my study by having it dusted. The chestnut mare has foaled, and we're getting on with the ploughing. We are having too much rain – but when haven't we too much rain in England? The new grocer at Little Ausprey threatens to leave, because he says his wife and the non-conformist minister – but there, you always pretend to hate village scandals, and as I have, for the moment, none of my own to tempt your jaded palate, I will end this confession of an impenitent but blameless parent.

Your aff^te'

H.T.

P.S. The good Blanche asked anxiously about you – your health, plans and prospects, the probable date of your return; and I told her I would give a good deal to know myself. Do you suppose she has her eye on you for Ermie or Almina? Seadown's defection was a hard blow; and if I'm right about Tintagel, Heaven help her!

BOOK

 III

# NINETEEN

THE WINDOWS OF THE CORREGGIO ROOM AT LONGLANDS overlooked what was known as the Duchess's private garden, a floral masterpiece designed by the great Sir Joseph Paxton, of Chatsworth and Crystal Palace fame. Beyond an elaborate cast-iron fountain swarmed over by chaste divinities, and surrounded by stars and crescents of bedding plants, an archway in the wall of yew and holly led down a grass avenue to the autumnal distances of the home park. Mist shrouded the slopes dotted with mighty trees, the bare woodlands, the lake pallidly reflecting a low uncertain sky. Deer flitted spectrally from glade to glade, and on remoter hillsides blurred clusters of sheep and cattle were faintly visible. It had rained heavily in the morning, it would doubtless rain again before night; and in the Correggio room the drip of water sounded intermittently from the long reaches of roof-gutter and from the creepers against the many-windowed house-front.

The Duchess, at the window, stood gazing out over what seemed a measureless perspective of rain-sodden acres. Then, with a sigh, she turned back to the writing-table and took up her pen. A sheet of paper lay before her, carefully inscribed in a small precise hand:

To a Dowager Duchess.
To a Duchess.
To a Marchioness.
To the wife of a Cabinet Minister who has no rank by
    birth.
To the wife of a Bishop.
To an Ambassador.

The page was inscribed: 'Important', and under each head-line was a brief formula for beginning and ending a letter. The Duchess scrutinized this paper attentively; then she glanced over another paper bearing a list of names, and finally, with a sigh, took from a tall mahogany stand a sheet of notepaper with 'Longlands House' engraved in gold under a ducal coronet, and began to write.

After each note she struck a pencil line through one of the names on the list, and then began another note. Each was short, but she wrote slowly, almost laboriously, like a consci-entious child copying out an exercise; and at the bottom of the sheet she inscribed her name, after assuring herself once more that the formula preceding her signature corresponded with the instructions before her. At length she reached the last note, verified the formula, and for the twentieth time wrote out underneath: 'Annabel Tintagel'.

There before her, in orderly sequence, lay the invitations to the first big shooting-party of the season at Longlands, and she threw down her pen with another sigh. For a minute or two she sat with her elbows on the desk, her face in her hands; then she uncovered her eyes and looked again at the note she had just signed.

'Annabel Tintagel,' she said slowly, 'who *is* Annabel Tintagel?'

The question was one which she had put to herself more than once during the last months, and the answer was always the same: she did not know. Annabel Tintagel was a strange

figure with whom she lived, and whose actions she watched
with a cold curiosity, but with whom she had never arrived at
terms of intimacy, and never would. Of that she was now sure.

There was another perplexing thing about her situation.
She was now, to all appearances, Annabel Tintagel, and had
been so for over two years; but before that she had been
Annabel St George, and the figure of Annabel St George,
her face and voice, her likes and dislikes, her memories and
moods, all that made up her tremulous little identity, though
still at the new Annabel's side, no longer composed the central Annabel, the being with whom this strange new
Annabel of the Correggio room at Longlands, and the
Duchess's private garden, felt herself really one. There were
moments when the vain hunt for her real self became so perplexing and disheartening that she was glad to escape from it
into the mechanical duties of her new life. But in the intervals she continued to grope for herself, and to find no one.

To begin with, what had caused Annabel St George to
turn into Annabel Tintagel? That was the central problem!
Yet how could she solve it, when she could no longer question that elusive Annabel St George, who was still so near to
her, yet as remote and unapproachable as a plaintive ghost?

Yes – ghost. That was it. Annabel St George was dead, and
Annabel Tintagel did not know how to question the dead,
and would therefore never be able to find out why and how
that mysterious change had come about . . .

'The greatest mistake,' she mused, her chin resting on her
clasped hands, her eyes fixed unseeingly on the dim reaches
of the park, 'the greatest mistake is to think that we ever
know why we do things . . . I suppose the nearest we can ever
come to it is by getting what old people call "experience".
But by the time we've got that we're no longer the persons
who did the things we no longer understand. The trouble is, I
suppose, that we change every moment; and the things we
did stay.'

Of course she could have found plenty of external reasons; a succession of incidents, leading, as a trail leads across a desert, from one point to another of the original Annabel's career. But what was the use of recapitulating these points, when she was no longer the Annabel whom they had led to this splendid and lonely room set in the endless acres of Longlands?

The curious thing was that her uncertainty and confusion of mind seemed to have communicated themselves to the new world into which she found herself transplanted – and that she was aware of the fact. 'They don't know what to make of me, and why should they, when I don't know what to make of myself?' she had once said, in an unusual burst of confidence, to her sister Virginia, who had never really understood her confidences, and who had absently rejoined, studying herself while she spoke in her sister's monumental cheval glass, and critically pinching her waist between thumb and forefinger: 'My dear, I've never yet met an Englishman or an Englishwoman who didn't know what to make of a duchess, if only they had the chance to try. The trouble is you don't give them the chance.'

Yes; Annabel supposed it was that. Fashionable London had assimilated with surprising rapidity the lovely transatlantic invaders. Hostesses who only two years ago would have shuddered at the clink of tall glasses and the rattle of cards, now threw their doors open to poker-parties, and offered intoxicating drinks to those to whom the new-fangled afternoon tea seemed too reminiscent of the schoolroom. Hands trained to draw from a Broadwood the dulcet cadences of 'La Sonnambula' now thrummed the banjo to 'Juanita' or 'The Swanee River'. Girls, and even young matrons, pinned up their skirts to compete with the young men in the new game of lawn-tennis on lordly lawns, smoking was spreading from the precincts reserved for it to dining-room and library (it was even rumoured that 'the Americans'

took sly whiffs in their bedrooms!). Lady Seadown was said
to be getting up an amateur nigger-minstrel performance for
the Christmas party at Allfriars, and as for the wild games
introduced into country-house parties, there was no denying
that, even after a hard day's hunting or shooting, they could
tear the men from their after-dinner torpor.

A blast of outer air had freshened the stagnant atmosphere
of Belgravian drawing-rooms, and while some sections of
London society still shuddered (or affected to shudder) at 'the
Americans', others, and the uppermost among them, openly
applauded and imitated them. But in both groups the young
Duchess of Tintagel remained a figure apart. The Dowager
Duchess spoke of her as 'my perfect daughter-in-law', but
praise from the Dowager Duchess had about as much zest as a
Sunday-school diploma. In the circle where the pace was set by
Conchita Marable, Virginia Seadown and Lizzy Elmsworth
(now married to the brilliant young Conservative member of
Parliament, Mr Hector Robinson), the circle to which, by kinship and early associations, Annabel belonged, she was as
much a stranger as in the straitest fastnesses of the peerage.
'Annabel has really managed,' Conchita drawled with her slow
smile, 'to be considered unfashionable among the unfashionable –' and the phrase clung to the young Duchess, and cata-
logued her once for all.

One side of her loved, as much as the others did, dancing,
dressing up, midnight romps, practical jokes played on the
pompous and elderly; but the other side, the side which had
dominated her since her arrival in England, was passionately
in earnest and beset with vague dreams and ambitions, in
which a desire to better the world alternated with a longing
for solitude and poetry.

If her husband could have kept her company in either of
these regions she might not have given a thought to the rest
of mankind. But in the realm of poetry the Duke had never
willingly risked himself since he had handed up his Vale at

Eton, and a great English nobleman of his generation could hardly conceive that he had anything to learn regarding the management of his estates from a little American girl whose father appeared to be a cross between a stock-broker and a professional gambler, and whom he had married chiefly because she seemed too young and timid to have any opinions on any subject whatever.

'The great thing is that I shall be able to form her,' he had said to his mother, on the dreadful day when he had broken the news of his engagement to the horrified Duchess; and the Duchess had replied, with a flash of unwonted insight:

'You're very skilful, Ushant; but women are not quite as simple as clocks.'

As simple as clocks. How like a woman to say that! The Duke smiled. 'Some clocks are not at all simple,' he said with an air of superior knowledge.

'Neither are some women,' his mother rejoined; but there both thought it prudent to let the discussion drop.

ANNABEL stood up and looked about the room. It was large and luxurious, with walls of dark green velvet framed in heavily carved and gilded oak. Everything about its decoration and furnishings – the towering malachite vases, the ponderous writing-table supported on winged geniuses in ormolu, the heavily foliaged wall-lights, the Landseer portrait, above the monumental chimney-piece, of her husband as a baby, playing with an elder sister in a tartan sash – all testified to a sumptuous 're-doing', doubtless dating from the day when the present Dowager had at last presented her lord with an heir. A stupid oppressive room – somebody else's room not Annabel's . . . But on three of the velvet-panelled walls hung the famous Correggios; in the half-dusk of an English November they were like rents in the clouds, tunnels of radiance reaching to pure sapphire distances. Annabel looked at the golden limbs, the parted lips gleaming with laughter, the abandonment of young bodies under shimmering foliage. On dark days – and there were many – these pictures were her sunlight. She speculated about them, wove stories around them, and hung them with snatches of verse from Miss Testvalley's poet-cousin. How was it they went?

> Beyond all depth away
> The heat lies silent at the brink of day:
> Now the hand trails upon the viol-string
> That sobs, and the brown faces cease to sing,
> Sad with the whole of pleasure.

Were there such beings anywhere, she wondered, save in the dreams of poets and painters, such landscapes, such sunlight? The Correggio room had always been the reigning Duchess's private boudoir, and at first it had surprised Annabel that her mother-in-law should live surrounded by scenes before which Mrs St George would have veiled her face. But gradually she understood that in a world as solidly buttressed as the Dowager Duchess's by precedents, institutions and traditions, it would have seemed far more subversive to displace the pictures than to hear the children's Sunday-school lessons under the laughter of those happy pagans. The Correggio room had always been the Duchess's boudoir, and the Correggios had always hung there. 'It has always been like that,' was the Dowager's invariable answer to any suggestion of change; and she had conscientiously brought up her son in the same creed.

Though she had been married for over two years it was for her first big party at Longlands that the new Duchess was preparing. The first months after her marriage had been spent at Tintagel, in a solitude deeply disapproved of by the Duke's mother, who for the second time found herself powerless to influence her son. The Duke gave himself up with a sort of dogged abandonment to the long dreamed-of delights of solitude and domestic bliss. The ducal couple (as the

Dowager discovered with dismay, on her first visit to them)
lived like any middle-class husband and wife, tucked away in
a wing of the majestic pile where two butlers and ten footmen should have been drawn up behind the dinner-table,
and a groom-of-the-chambers have received the guests in the
great hall. Groom-of-the-chambers, butlers and footmen had
all been relegated to Longlands, and to his mother's dismay
only two or three personal servants supplemented the under-
studies who had hitherto sufficed for Tintagel's simple needs
on his trips to Cornwall.

Even after their return to London and Longlands the
young couple continued to disturb the Dowager Duchess's
peace of mind. The most careful and patient initiation into
the functions of the servants attending on her had not kept
Annabel from committing what seemed to her mother-in-
law inexcusable, perhaps deliberate blunders; such as asking
the groom-of-the-chambers to fetch her a glass of water, or
bidding one of the under house-maids to lace up her dinner-
dress when her own maid was accidentally out of hearing.

'It's not that she's *stupid*, you know, my dear,' the Dowager
avowed to her old friend Miss Jacky March, 'but she puts one
out, asking the reason of things that have nothing to do with
reason – such as why the housekeeper doesn't take her meals
with the upper servants, but only comes in for dessert. What
would happen next, as I said to her, in a house where the
housekeeper *did* take her meals with the upper servants? That
sort of possibility never occurs to the poor child; yet I really
can't call her stupid. I often find her with a book in her hand.
I think she thinks too much about things that oughtn't to be
thought about,' wailed the bewildered Duchess. 'And the
worst of it is that dear Ushant doesn't seem to know how to
help her . . .' her tone implying that, in any case, such a task
should not have been laid on him. And Miss Jacky March
murmured her sympathy.

## CHAPTER

# TWENTY

THOSE QUIET MONTHS IN CORNWALL, WHICH ALREADY SEEMED so much more remote from the actual Annabel than her girl-hood at Saratoga, had been of her own choosing. She did not admit to herself that her first sight of the ruins of the ancient Tintagel had played a large part in her wooing; that if the Duke had been only the dullest among the amiable but dull young men who came to the bungalow at Runnymede she would hardly have given him a second thought. But the idea of living in that magic castle by the sad western sea had secretly tinged her vision of the castle's owner; and she had thought that he and she might get to know each other more readily there than anywhere else. And now, in looking back, she asked herself if it were not her own fault that the weeks at Tintagel had not brought the expected understanding. Instead, as she now saw, they had only made husband and wife more unintelligible to each other. To Annabel, the Cornish castle spoke with that rich low murmur of the past which she had first heard in its mysterious intensity the night when she had lain awake in the tapestried chamber at Allfriars, beside the sleeping Virginia, who had noticed only that the room was cold and shabby. Though the walls of Tintagel were relatively new, they were built on ancient foundations, and crowded with the treasures of the past; and near by was the mere of Excalibur, and from her windows she could see the dark grey sea, and sometimes, at nightfall, the mysterious barge with black sails putting out from the ruined castle to carry the dead King to Avalon.

Of all this, nothing existed for her husband. He saw the new Tintagel only as a costly folly of his father's, which family pride obliged him to keep up with fitting state, in spite of the unfruitful acres that made its maintenance so difficult. In shouldering these cares, however, he did not expect his wife to help him, save by looking her part as a beautiful and angelically pure young Duchess, whose only duties consisted in bestowing her angelic presence on entertainments for the tenantry and agricultural prize-givings. The Duke had grown up under the iron rod of a mother who, during his minority, had managed not only his property, but his very life, and he had no idea of letting her authority pass to his wife. Much as he dreaded the duties belonging to his great rank, deeply as he was oppressed by them, he was determined to perform them himself, were it ever so hesitatingly and painfully, and not to be guided by anyone else's suggestions.

To his surprise such suggestions were not slow in coming from Annabel. She had not yet learned that she was expected to remain a lovely and adoring looker-on, and in her daily drives over the estate (in the smart pony-chaise with its burnished trappings and gay piebald ponies) she often, out of sheer loneliness, stopped for a chat at toll-gates, farmhouses and cottages, made purchases at the village shops, scattered toys and lollipops among the children, and tried to find out from their mothers what she could do to help them. It had filled her with wonder to learn that for miles around, both at Longlands and Tintagel, all these people in the quaint damp cottages and the stuffy little shops were her husband's tenants and dependants; that he had the naming of the rectors and vicars of a dozen churches, and that even the old men and women in the mouldy almshouses were there by virtue of his bounty. But when she had grasped the extent of his power it seemed to her that to help and befriend those who depended on him was the best service she could render him. Nothing in her early bringing-up had directed her mind towards any kind of organized beneficence, but she had always been what she called 'sorry for people', and it seemed to her that there was a good deal to be sorry about in the lot of these people who depended solely, in health and sickness, on a rich man's whim.

The discovery that her interest in them was distasteful to the Duke came to her as a great shock, and left a wound that did not heal. Coming in one day, a few months after their marriage, from one of her exploring expeditions, she was told that his Grace wished to speak to her in his study, and she went in eagerly, glad to seize the chance of telling him at once about the evidences of neglect and poverty she had come upon that very afternoon.

'Oh, Ushant, I'm so glad you're in! Could you come with me at once to the Linfrys' cottage, down by St Gildas's; you know, that damp place under the bridge, with the front covered with roses? The eldest boy's down with typhoid, and the drains ought to be seen to at once if all the younger ones are not to get it.' She spoke in haste, too much engrossed in what she had to say to notice the Duke's expression. It was his silence that roused her; and when she looked at him she saw that his face wore what she called its bolted look – the look she most disliked to see on it. He sat silent, twisting an ivory paper-cutter between his fingers.

'May I ask who told you this?' he said at length, in a voice like his mother's when she was rebuking an upper house-maid.

'Why, I found it out myself. I've just come from there.'

The Duke stood up, knocking the paper-cutter to the floor.

'You've been there? Yourself? To a house where you tell me there is typhoid fever? In your state of health? I confess,

Annabel –' His lips twitched nervously under his scanty blond moustache.

'Oh, bother my state of health! I feel all right, really I do. And you know the doctors have ordered me to walk and drive every day.'

'But not go and sit with Mrs Linfry's sick children, in a house reeking with disease.'

'But, Ushant, I just had to! There was no one else to see about them. And if the house reeks with disease, whose fault is it but ours? They've no sick-nurse, and nobody to help the mother, or tell her what to do; and the doctor comes only every other day.'

'Is it your idea, my dear, that I should provide every cottage on my estates, here and elsewhere, with a hospital nurse?' the Duke asked ironically.

'Well, I wish you would! At least there ought to be a nurse in every village, and two in the bigger ones; and the doctor ought to see his patients every day; and the drains – Ushant, you must come with me *at once* and smell the drains!' cried Nan in a passion of entreaty.

She felt the Duke's inexpressive eyes fixed coldly on her.

'If your intention is to introduce typhoid fever at Tintagel, I can imagine no better way of going about it,' he began. 'But perhaps you don't realize that, though it may not be as contagious as typhus, the doctors are by no means sure . . .'

'Oh, but they *are* sure; only ask them! Typhoid comes from bad drains and infected milk. It can't hurt you in the least to go down and see what's happening at the Linfrys'; and you ought to, because they're your own tenants. Won't you come with me now? The ponies are not a bit tired, and I told William to wait –'

'I wish you would not call Armson by his Christian name; I've already told you that in England head grooms are called by their surnames.'

'Oh, Ushant, what *can* it matter? I call you by your surname, but I never can remember about the others. And the only thing that matters now . . .'

The Duke walked to the hearth, and pulled the embroidered bell-rope beside the chimney. To the footman who appeared he said: 'Please tell Armson that her Grace will not require the pony-chaise any longer this afternoon.'

'But –' Annabel burst out; then she stood silent till the door closed on the servant. The Duke remained silent also.

'Is that your answer?' she asked at length, her breath coming quickly.

He lifted a more friendly face. 'My dear child, don't look so tragic. I'll see Blair; he shall look into the drains. But do try to remember that these small matters concern my agent more than they do me, and that they don't concern you at all. My mother was very much esteemed and respected at Tintagel, but though she managed my affairs so wisely; it never occurred to her to interfere directly with the agent's business, except as regards Christmas festivities, and the annual school-treat. Her holding herself aloof increased the respect that was felt for her; and my wife could not do better than to follow her example.'

Annabel stood staring at her husband without speaking. She was too young to understand the manifold inhibitions, some inherited, some peculiar to his own character, which made it impossible for him to act promptly and spontaneously; but she knew him to be by nature not an unkind man, and this increased her bewilderment.

Suddenly a flood of words burst from her. 'You tell me to be careful about my health in the very same breath that you say you can't be bothered about these poor people, and that their child's dying is a small matter, to be looked after by the agent. It's for the sake of your own child that you forbid me to go to see them – but I tell you I don't want a child if he's to be brought up with such ideas, if he's to be taught, as you have been, that it's right and natural to live in a palace with fifty servants, and not care for the people who are slaving for him on his own land, to make his big income bigger! I'd rather be dead than see a child of mine taught to grow up as – as you have!'

She broke down and dropped into a seat, hiding her face in her hands. Her husband looked at her without speaking. Nothing in his past experience had prepared him for such a scene, and the consciousness that he did not know how to deal with it increased his irritation. Had Annabel gone mad – or was it only what the doctors called her 'condition'? In either case he felt equally incapable of resolute and dignified action. Of course, if he were told that it was necessary, owing to her 'condition', he would send these Linfrys – a shiftless lot – money and food, would ask the doctor to see the boy oftener; though it went hard with him to swallow his own words, and find himself again under a woman's orders. At any rate, he must try to propitiate Annabel, to get her into a more amenable mood; and as soon as possible must take her back to Longlands, where she would be nearer a London physician, accustomed to bringing dukes into the world.

'Annabel,' he said, going up to her, and laying his hand on her bent head.

She started to her feet. 'Let me alone,' she exclaimed, and brushed past him to the door. He heard her cross the hall and go up the stairs in the direction of her own rooms; then he turned back to his desk. One of the drawing-room clocks stood there before him, disembowelled; and as he began (with hands that still shook a little) to put it cautiously together, he remembered his mother's comment: 'Women are not always as simple as clocks.' Had she been right?

After a while he laid aside the works of the clock and sat staring helplessly before him. Then it occurred to him that Annabel, in her present mood, was quite capable of going contrary to his orders, and sending for a carriage to drive her back to the Linfrys'– or Heaven knew where. He rang again, and asked for his own servant. When the man came the Duke confided to him that her Grace was in a somewhat nervous state, and that the doctors wished her to be kept quiet, and not to drive out again that afternoon. Would Bowman therefore see the head coachman at once, and explain that, even if her Grace should ask for a carriage, some excuse must be found ... they were not, of course, to say anything to implicate the Duke, but it must be so managed that her Grace should not be able to drive out again that day.

Bowman acquiesced, with the look of respectful compassion which his face often wore when he was charged with his master's involved and embarrassed instructions; and the Duke, left alone, continued to sit idly at his writing-table.

Annabel did not reappear that afternoon; and when the Duke, on his way up to dress for dinner, knocked at her sitting-room door, she was not there. He went on to his own dressing-room, but on the way met his wife's maid, and asked if her Grace were already dressing.

'Oh, no, your Grace. I thought the Duchess was with your Grace . . .'

A little chill caught him about the heart. It was nearly eight o'clock, for they dined late at Tintagel; and the maid had not yet seen her mistress! The Duke said with affected composure: 'Her Grace was tired this afternoon. She may have fallen asleep in the drawing-room –' though he could imagine nothing less like the alert and restless Annabel.

Oh, no, the maid said again; her Grace had gone out on foot two or three hours ago, and had not yet returned.

'On foot?'

'Yes, your Grace. Her Grace asked for her pony-carriage; but I understood there were orders –'

The Duke interrupted irritably, 'The doctor's orders were that her Grace should not go out at all today.'

The maid lowered her lids as if to hide her incredulous eyes, and he felt that she was probably acquainted with every

detail of the day's happenings. The thought sent the blood up
to the roots of his pale hair, and he challenged her nervously.
'You must at least know which way her Grace said she was
going.'

'The Duchess said nothing to me, your Grace. But I understand she sent to the stables, and finding she could not have
a carriage walked away through the park.'

'That will do . . . there's been some unfortunate misunder-
standing about her Grace's orders,' stammered the Duke,
turning away to his dressing-room.

The day had been raw and cloudy, and with the dusk rain
had begun, and was coming down now in a heavy pour that
echoed through the narrow twisting passages of the castle
and made their sky-lights rattle. And in this icy downpour
his wife, his Duchess, the expectant mother of future dukes,
was wandering somewhere on foot, alone and unprotected.
Anger and alarm contended in the Duke. If anyone had told
him that marrying a simple unworldly girl, hardly out of the
school-room, would add fresh complications to a life already
over-burdened with them, he would have scoffed at the idea.
Certainly he had done nothing to deserve such a fate. And
he wondered now why he had been so eager to bring it upon
himself. Though he had married for love only a few months
before, he was now far more concerned with Annabel as the
mother of his son than for her own sake. The first weeks with
her had been very sweet – but since then her presence in his
house had seemed only to increase his daily problems and
bothers. The Duke rang and ordered Bowman to send to the
stables for the station-brougham, and when it arrived he
drove down at breakneck speed to the Linfrys' cottage. But
Nan was not there. The Duke stared at Mrs Linfry blankly.
He did not know where to go next, and it mortified him to
reveal his distress and uncertainty to the coachman. 'Home!'
he ordered angrily, getting into the carriage again; and the
dark drive began once more. He was half-way back when the

carriage stopped with a jerk, and the coachman, scrambling down from the box, called to him in a queer frightened voice.

The Duke jumped out and saw the man lifting a small dripping figure into the brougham. 'By the mercy of God, your Grace . . . I think the Duchess has fainted . . .'

'Drive like the devil . . . stop at the stables to send a groom for the doctor,' stammered the Duke, pressing his wife in his arms. The rest of the way back was as indistinct to him as to the girl who lay so white on his breast. Bowed over her in anguish, he remembered nothing till the carriage drove under the echoing gate-tower at Tintagel, and lights and servants pressed confusedly about them. He lifted Annabel out, and she opened her eyes and took a few steps alone across the hall. 'Oh – am I here again?' she said, with a little laugh; then she swayed forward, and he caught her as she fell . . .

To the Duchess of Tintagel who was signing the last notes of invitation for the Longlands shooting-party, the scene at Tintagel and what had followed now seemed as remote and legendary as the tales that clung about the old ruins of Arthur's castle. Annabel had put herself hopelessly in the wrong. She had understood it without being told, she had acknowledged it and wept over it at the time; but the irremediable had been done, and she knew that never, in her husband's eyes, would any evidence of repentance atone for that night's disaster.

The miscarriage which had resulted from her mad expedition through the storm had robbed the Duke of a son; of that he was convinced. He, the Duke of Tintagel, wanted a son, he had a right to expect a son, he would have had a son, if this woman's criminal folly had not destroyed his hopes. The physicians summoned in consultation spoke of the necessity of many months of repose . . . even they did not seem to understand that a Duke must have an heir, that it is the purpose for which dukes make the troublesome effort of marrying.

It was now more than a year since that had happened, and after long weeks of illness a new Annabel – a third Annabel – had emerged from the ordeal. Life had somehow, as the months passed, clumsily readjusted itself. As far as words went, the Duke had forgiven his wife; they had left the solitude of Tintagel as soon as the physicians thought it possible for the Duchess to be moved; and now, in their crowded London life, and at Longlands, where the Dowager had seen to it that all the old ceremonial was re-established, the ducal pair were too busy, too deeply involved in the incessant distractions and obligations of their station, to have time to remember what was over and could not be mended.

But Annabel gradually learned that it was not only one's self that changed. The ceaseless mysterious flow of days wore down and altered the shape of the people nearest one, so that one seemed fated to be always a stranger among strangers. The mere fact, for instance, of Annabel St George's becoming Annabel Tintagel had turned her mother-in-law, the Duchess of Tintagel, into a Dowager Duchess, over whose diminished head the mighty roof of Longlands had shrunk into the modest shelter of a lovely little rose-clad dower-house at the gates of the park. And everyone else, as far as Annabel's world reached, seemed to have changed in the same way.

That, at times, was the most perplexing part of it. When, for instance, the new Annabel tried to think herself back on to the verandah of the Grand Union Hotel, waiting for her father and his stock-broker friends to return from the races, or in the hotel ball-room with the red damask curtains, dancing with her sister, with Conchita Closson and the Elmsworth girls, or with the obscure and infrequent young men who now and then turned up to partner their wasted loveliness – when she thought, for instance, of Roy Gilling, and the handkerchief she had dropped, and he had kissed and hidden in his pocket – it was like looking at the flickering figures of the magic lanterns she used to see at children's parties. What was left, now, of those uncertain apparitions, and what relation, say, did the Conchita Closson who had once seemed so ethereal and elusive, bear to Lady Dick Marable, beautiful still, though she was growing rather too stout, but who had lost her lovely indolence and detachment, and was now perpetually preoccupied about money, and immersed in domestic difficulties and clandestine consolations; or to Virginia, her own sister Virginia, who had seemed to Annabel so secure, so aloof, so disdainful of everything but her own pleasures, but who, as Lady Seadown, was enslaved to that dull half-asleep Seadown, absorbed in questions of rank and precedence, and in awe – actually in awe – of her father-in-law's stupid arrogance, and of Lady Brightlingsea's bewildered condescensions?

Yes; changed, every one of them, vanished out of recognition, as the lost Annabel of the Grand Union had vanished. As she looked about her, the only figures which seemed to have preserved their former outline were those of her father and his business friends; but that, perhaps, was because she so seldom saw them, because when they appeared, at long intervals, for a hurried look at transatlantic daughters and grandchildren, they brought New York with them, solidly and loudly, remained jovially unconscious of any change of scene and habits greater than that between the east and west shores of the Hudson, and hurried away again, leaving behind them cheques and christening mugs, and unaware to the last that they had been farther from Wall Street than across the ferry.

Ah, yes – and Laura Testvalley, her darling old Val! She too had remained her firm sharp-edged self. But then she too was usually away, she had not suffered the erosion of daily contact. The real break with the vanished Annabel had come, the new Annabel sometimes thought, when Miss Testvalley, her task at the St Georges' ended, had vanished into the seclusion of another family which required 'finishing'. Miss Testvalley, since she had kissed the bride after the great Tintagel wedding, nearly three years ago, had reappeared only at long intervals, and as it were under protest. It was one of her principles – as she had often told Annabel – that a governess should not hang about her former pupils. Later they might require her – there was no knowing, her subtle smile implied; but once the school-room was closed, she should vanish with the tattered lesson-books, the dreary school-room food, the cod-liver oil and the chilblain cures.

Perhaps, Annabel thought, if her beloved Val had remained with her, they might between them have rescued the old Annabel, or at least kept up communications with her ghost – a faint tap now and then against the walls which had built themselves up about the new Duchess. But as it was, there was the new Duchess isolated in her new world, no longer able to reach back to her past, and not having yet learned how to communicate with her present.

She roused herself from these vain musings, and took up her pen. A final glance at the list had shown her that one invitation had been forgotten – or, if not forgotten, at least postponed.

DEAR MR THWARTE,

The Duke tells me you have lately come back to England, and he hopes so much that you can come to Longlands for our next shooting-party, on the 18th. He asks me to say that he is anxious to have a talk with you about the situation at Lowdon. He hopes you intend to stand if Sir Hercules Loft is obliged to resign, and wishes you to know that you will have his full support.

Yours sincerely

ANNABEL TINTAGEL

Underneath she added: 'P.S. Perhaps you'd remember me if I signed Nan St George.' But what was the sense of that, when there was no longer anyone of that name? She tore the note up, and rewrote it without adding the postscript.

# TWENTY-ONE

GUY THWARTE HAD NOT BEEN BACK AT HONOURSLOVE LONG
enough to expect a heavy mail beside his breakfast plate. His
four years in Brazil had cut him off more completely than he
had realized from his former life; and he was still in the somewhat painful stage of picking up the threads.

'Only one letter? Lucky devil, I envy you!' grumbled Sir
Helmsley, taking his seat at the other end of the table and impatiently pushing aside a stack of newspapers, circulars and letters.

The young man glanced with a smile at his father's correspondence. He knew so well of what it consisted: innumerable bills, dunning letters, urgent communications from
bookmakers, tradesmen, the chairman of political commit-
tees or art exhibitions, scented notes from enamoured ladies,
or letters surmounted by mysterious symbols from astrologers,
palmists or alchemists – for Sir Helmsley had dabbled in
most of the arts, and bent above most of the mysteries. But
today, as usual, his son observed, the bills and the dunning
letters predominated. Guy would have to put some order into
that; and probably into the scented letters too.

'Yes, I'm between two worlds yet – "powerless to be born"
kind of feeling,' he said as he took up the solitary note beside
his own plate. The writing was unknown to him, and he
opened the envelope with indifference.

'Oh, my dear fellow – don't say that; don't say "powerless",'
his father rejoined, half-pleadingly, but with a laugh. 'There's
such a lot waiting to be done; we all expect you to put your
hand to the plough without losing a minute. I was lunching
at Longlands the other day and had a long talk with Ushant.
With old Sir Hercules Loft in his dotage for the last year,
there's likely to be a vacancy at Lowdon at any minute, and
the Duke's anxious to have you look over the ground without
losing any time, especially as that new millionaire from
Glasgow is said to have some chance of getting in.'

'Oh, well –' Guy was glancing over his letter while his
father spoke. He knew Sir Helmsley's great desire was to see
him in the House of Commons, an ambition hitherto curbĕd
by the father's reduced fortune, but brought into the foreground again since the son's return from exile with a substantial bank account.

Guy looked up from his letter. 'Tintagel's been talking to
you about it, I see.'

'You see? Why – has he written to you already?'

'No. But she has. The new American Duchess – the little
girl I brought here once, you remember?' He handed the letter to his father, whose face expressed a growing satisfaction
as he read.

'Well – that makes it plain sailing. You'll go to Longlands,
of course?'

'To Longlands?' Guy hesitated. 'I don't know. I'm not sure
I want to.'

'But if Tintagel wants to see you about the seat? You ought
to look over the ground. There may not be much time to lose.'

'Not if I'm going to stand – certainly.'

'If!' shouted Sir Helmsley, bringing down his fist with a
crash that set the Crown Derby cups dancing. 'Is that what
you're not sure of? I thought we were agreed before you went
away that it was time there was a Thwarte again in the
House of Commons.'

'Oh – before I went away,' Guy murmured. His father's challenge, calling him back suddenly to his old life, the traditional life of a Thwarte of Honourslove, had shown him for the first time how far from it all he had travelled in the last years, how remote had become the old sense of inherited obligations which had once seemed the very marrow of his bones.

'Now you've made your pile, as they say, out there,' Sir Helmsley continued, attempting a lighter tone, but unable to disguise his pride in the incredible fact of his son's achievement – a Thwarte who had made money! – 'now that you've made your pile, isn't it time to think of a career? In my simplicity, I imagined it was one of your principal reasons for exiling yourself.'

'Yes, I suppose it was,' Guy acquiesced.

After this, for a while, father and son faced one another in silence across the breakfast-table, each, as is the way of the sensitive, over-conscious of the other's thoughts. Guy, knowing so acutely what was expected of him, was vainly struggling to become again the young man who had left England four years earlier; but strive as he would he could not yet fit himself into his place in the old scheme of things. The truth was, he was no longer the Guy Thwarte of four years ago, and would probably never recover that lost self. The break had been too violent, the disrupting influences too powerful. Those dark rich stormy years of exile lay like a raging channel between himself and his old life, and his father's summons only drove him back upon himself.

'You'll have to give me time, sir – I seem to be on both sides of the globe at once,' he muttered at length with bent head.

Sir Helmsley stood up abruptly, and walking around the table laid a hand on his son's shoulder. 'My dear fellow, I'm so sorry. It seems so natural to have you back that I'd forgotten the roots you've struck over there . . . I'd forgotten the grave . . .'

Guy's eyes darkened, and he nodded. 'All right, sir . . .' He stood up also. 'I think I'll take a turn about the stables.' He put the letter from Longlands into his pocket, and walked out alone onto the terrace. As he stood there, looking out over the bare November landscape, and the soft blue hills fading into a low sky, the sense of kinship between himself and the soil began to creep through him once more. What a power there was in these accumulated associations, all so low-pitched, soft and unobtrusive, yet which were already insinuating themselves through his stormy Brazilian years, and sapping them of their reality! He felt himself becoming again the school-boy who used to go nutting in the hazel-copses of the Red Farm, who fished and bathed in the dark pools of the Love, stole nectarines from the walled gardens, and went cub-hunting in the autumn dawn with his father, glorying in Sir Helmsley's horsemanship, and racked with laughter at his jokes – the school-boy whose heart used to beat to bursting at that bend of the road from the station where you first sighted the fluted chimney-stacks of Honourslove.

He walked across the terrace, and turning the flank of the house passed under the sculptured lintel of the chapel. A smell of autumn rose from the cold paving, where the kneeling Thwartes elbowed each other on the narrow floor, and under the recumbent effigies the pillows almost mingled their stony fringes. How many there were, and how faithfully hand had joined hand in the endless work of enlarging and defending the family acres! Guy's glance travelled slowly down the double line, from the armoured effigy of the old fighting Thwarte who had built the chapel to the Thornycroft image of his own mother, draped in her marble slumber, just as the boy had seen her, lying with drawn lids, on the morning when his father's telegram had called him back from Eton. How many there were – and all these graves belonged to him, all were linked to the same soil and to one another in an old community of land and blood; together for all time, and kept warm by each other's nearness. And that far-off grave which also belonged to him – the one to which his father had alluded – how remote and lonely it was, off there under tropic skies, among other graves that were all strange to him.

He sat down and rested his face against the back of the bench in front of him. The sight of his mother's grave had called up that of his young Brazilian wife, and he wanted to shut out for a moment all those crowding Thwartes, and stand again beside her far-off headstone. What would life at Honourslove have been if he had brought Paquita home with him instead of leaving her among the dazzling white graves at Rio? He sat for a long time, thinking, remembering, trying to strip his mind of conventions and face the hard reality underneath. It was inconceivable to him now that, in the first months of his marriage, he had actually dreamed of sev-ering all ties with home, and beginning life anew as a Brazilian mine-owner. He saw that what he had taken for a slowly matured decision had been no more than a passionate impulse; and its resemblance to his father's headlong experi-ments startled him as he looked back. His mad marriage had nearly deflected the line of his life – for a little pale face with ebony hair and curving black lashes he would have sold his birthright. And long before the black lashes had been drawn down over the quiet eyes he had known that he had come to the end of that adventure . . .

All his life, and especially since his mother's death, Guy Thwarte had been fighting against his admiration for his father, and telling himself that it was his duty to be as little like him as possible; yet more than once he had acted exactly as Sir Helmsley would have acted, or snatched himself back just in time. But in Brazil he had not been in time . . .

'One brilliant man's enough in a family,' he said to himself as he stood up and left the chapel.

Forgetting his projected visit to the stables, he turned back to the house, and crossing the hall, opened the door of his father's study. There he found Sir Helmsley seated at his easel, retouching a delicately drawn watercolour copy of the little Rossetti Madonna above his desk. Sir Helmsley, whose own work was incurably amateurish, excelled in the art of copying, or rather interpreting, the work of others; and his watercolour glowed with the deep brilliance of the original picture.

As his son entered he laid down his palette with an embarrassed laugh. 'Well, what do you think of it – eh?'

'Beautiful. I'm glad you've not given up your painting.'

'Eh –? Oh, well, I don't do much of it nowadays. But I'd promised this little thing to Miss Testvalley,' the baronet stammered, reddening handsomely above his auburn beard.

Guy echoed, bewildered, 'Miss Testvalley?'

Sir Helmsley coughed and cleared his throat. 'That governess, you know – or perhaps you don't. She was with the little new Duchess of Tintagel before her marriage; came here with her one day to see my Rossettis. She's Dante Gabriel's cousin; didn't I tell you? Remarkable woman – one of the few relations the poet is always willing to see. She persuaded him to sell me a first study of the *Bocca Baciata*, and I was doing this as a way of thanking her. She's with Augusta Glenloe's girls; I see her occasionally when I go over there.'

Sir Helmsley imparted this information in a loud almost challenging voice, as he always did when he had to communicate anything unexpected or difficult to account for. Explaining was a nuisance, and somewhat of a derogation. He resented anything that made it necessary, and always spoke as if his interlocutor ought to have known beforehand the answer to the questions he was putting.

After his bad fall in the hunting-field, the year before Guy's return from Brazil, the county had confidently expected that the lonely widower would make an end by marrying either his hospital nurse or the Gaiety girl who had brightened his solitude during his son's absence. One or the other of these conclusions to a career over-populated by the fair sex appeared inevitable in the case of a brilliant and unsteady widower. Coroneted heads had been frequently shaken over what seemed a foregone conclusion; and Guy had shared these fears. And behold, on his return, he found the nurse gone, the Gaiety girl expensively pensioned off, and the baronet, slightly lame, but with youth renewed by six months of enforced seclusion, apparently absorbed in a little brown governess who wore violet poplin and heavy brooches of Roman mosaic, but who (as Guy was soon to observe) had eyes like torches, and masses of curly-edged dark hair which she was beginning to braid less tightly, and to drag back less severely from her broad forehead.

Guy stood looking curiously at his father. The latter's bluster no longer disturbed him; but he was uncomfortably reminded of certain occasions when Sir Helmsley, on the brink of an imprudent investment or an impossible marriage, had blushed and explained with the same volubility. Could this outbreak be caused by one of the same reasons? But no! A middle-aged governess? It was unthinkable. Sir Helmsley had always abhorred the edifying, especially in petticoats; and with his strong well-knit figure, his handsome auburn head, and a complexion clear enough for blushes, he still seemed, in spite of his accident, built for more alluring prey. His real interest, Guy concluded, was no doubt in the Rossetti kinship, and all that it offered to his insatiable imagination. But it made the son wonder anew what other mischief his inflammable parent had been up to during his own long absence. It would clearly be part of his business to look into his father's sentimental history, and keep a sharp eye on his future. With these thoughts in his mind, Guy stood smiling down paternally on his father.

'Well, sir, it's all right,' he said. 'I've thought it over, and

I'll go to Longlands; when the time comes I'll stand for Lowdon.'

His father returned the look with something filial and obedient in his glance. 'My dear fellow, it's all right indeed. That's what I've always expected of you.'

GUY wandered out again, drawn back to the soil of Honourslove as a sailor is drawn to the sea. He would have liked to go over all its acres by himself, yard by yard, inch by inch, filling his eyes with the soft slumbrous beauty, his hands with the feel of wrinkled tree-boles, the roughness of sodden autumnal turf, his nostrils with the wine-like smell of dead leaves. The place was swathed in folds of funereal mist shot with watery sunshine, and he thought of all the quiet women who had paced the stones of the terrace on autumn days, worked over the simple-garden and among the roses, or sat in the oak parlour at their accounts or their needle-work speaking little, thinking much, dumb and nourishing as the heaps of faded leaves which mulched the soil for coming seasons.

The 'little Duchess's' note had evoked no very clear memory when he first read it; but as he wandered down the glen through the fading heath and bracken he suddenly recalled their walk along the same path in its summer fragrance, and how they had stayed alone on the terrace when the rest of the party followed Sir Helmsley through the house. They had leaned side by side on the balustrade, he remembered, looking out over that dear scene, and speaking scarcely a word; and yet, when she had gone, he knew how near they had been ... He even remembered thinking, as his steamer put out from the docks at Liverpool, that on the way home, after he had done his job in Brazil, he would stop a few days in New York to see her. And then he had heard – with wonder and incredulity – the rumour of her ducal marriage; a rumour speedily confirmed by letters and newspapers from home.

That girl – and Tintagel! She had given Guy the momentary sense of being the finest instrument he had ever had in his hand; an instrument from which, when the time came, he might draw unearthly music. Not that he had ever seriously considered the possibility of trying his chance with her; but he had wanted to keep her image in his heart, as something once glimpsed, and giving him the measure of his dreams. And now it was poor little Tintagel who was to waken those melodies; if indeed he could! For a few weeks after the news came it had blackened Guy's horizon; but he was far away, he was engrossed in labours and pleasures so remote from his earlier life that the girl's pale image had become etherealized, and then had faded out of existence. He sat down on the balustrade of the terrace, in the corner where they had stood together, and pulling out her little note, reread it.

'The writing of a school-girl . . . and the language of dicta-tion,' he thought; and the idea vaguely annoyed him. 'How on earth could she have married Tintagel? That girl! . . . One would think from the wording of her note that she'd never seen me before . . . She might at least have reminded me that she'd been here. But perhaps she'd forgotten – as I had!' he ended with a laugh and a shrug. And he turned back slowly to the house, where the estate agent was awaiting him with bills and estimates, and long lists of repairs. Already Sir Helmsley had slipped that burden from his shoulders.

# TWENTY-TWO

WHEN THEIR GRACES WERE IN RESIDENCE AT LONGLANDS THE Dowager did not often come up from the dower-house by the gate. But she had the awful gift of omnipresence, of exercising her influence from a distance; so that while the old family friends and visitors at Longlands said: 'It's wonderful, how tactful Blanche is – how she keeps out of the young people's way,' every member of the household, from its master to the last boots and scullion and gardener's boy, knew that her Grace's eye was on them all, and the machinery of the tremendous establishment still moving in obedience to the pace and pattern she had set.

But at Christmas the Dowager naturally could not remain aloof. If she had not participated in the Christmas festivities the county would have wondered, the servants gossiped, the tradesmen have thought the end of the world had come.

'I hope you'll do your best to persuade my mother to come next week. You know she thinks you don't like her,' Tintagel had said to his wife, a few days before Christmas.

'Oh, why?' Nan protested, blushing guiltily; and of course she had obediently persuaded, and the Duchess had responded by her usual dry jerk of acquiescence.

For the same reason, the new Duchess's family, and her American friends, had also to be invited; or at least so the

Duke thought. The Dowager was not of the same mind; but thirty years of dealings with her son ('from his birth the most obstinate baby in the world') had taught her when to give way; and she did so now.

'It does seem odd, though, Ushant's wanting all those strange people here for Christmas,' she confided to her friend Miss March, who had come up with her from the dower-house, 'for I understand the Americans make nothing of any of our religious festivals – do they?'

Miss March, who could not forget that she was the daughter of a clergyman of the Episcopal Church of America, protested gently, as she so often had before: 'Oh, but, Duchess, that depends, you know; in our church the feasts and observances are exactly the same as in yours . . .' But what, she reflected, have such people as the St Georges to do with the Episcopal Church? They might be Seventh Day Baptists, or even Mormons, for all she knew.

'Well, it's very odd,' murmured the Dowager, who was no longer listening to her.

The two ladies had seated themselves after dinner on a wide Jacobean settee at one end of the 'double-cube' saloon, the great room with the Thornhill ceiling and the Mortlake tapestries. The floor had been cleared of rugs and furniture – another shock this to the Dowager, but also accepted with her small stiff smile – and down the middle of the polished parquet spun a long line of young (and some more than middle-aged) dancers, led of course, by Lady Dick Marable and her odd Brazilian brother, whose name the Dowager could never remember, but who looked so dreadfully like an Italian hairdresser. (A girl who had been a close friend of the Dowager's youth had rent society asunder by breaking her engagement to a young officer in the Blues, and running away with her Italian hairdresser; and when the Dowager's eyes had first rested on Teddy de Santos-Dios she had thought with a shudder: '*Poor Florrie's man must have looked like that.*')

Close in Lady Dick's wake (and obviously more interested in her than in his partner) came Miles Dawnly, piloting a bewildered Brightlingsea girl. It was the custom to invite Dawnly wherever Conchita was invited; and even strait-laced hostesses, who had to have Lady Dick because she 'amused the men', were so thankful not to be obliged to invite her husband that they were glad enough to let Dawnly replace him. Everyone knew that he was Lady Dick's chosen attendant, but everyone found it convenient to ignore the fact, especially as Dawnly's own standing, and his fame as a dancer and a shot, had long since made him a welcome guest.

The Dowager had always thought it a pity that a man with such charming manners, and an assured political future, should seem in no hurry to choose a wife; but when she saw that he had taken for his partner a Marable rather than a Folyat, she observed tartly to Miss March that she did not suppose Mr Dawnly would ever marry, and hoped Selina Brightlingsea had no illusions on that point.

At the farther end of the great saloon, the odd little Italian governess who used to be at Longlands with the Duchess's younger daughters, and was now 'finishing' the Glenloe girls, sat at the piano rattling off a noisy reel which she was said to have learnt in the States; and down the floor whirled the dancers, in pursuit of Lady Richard and the Brazilian.

'Virginia reel, you say they call it? It's all so unusual,' repeated the Dowager, lifting her long-handled eye-glass to study the gyrations of the troop.

Yes; it certainly was unusual to see old Lord Brightlingsea pirouetting heavily in the wake of his beautiful daughter-in-law Lady Seadown, and Sir Helmsley Thwarte, incapacitated for pirouetting since his hunting accident, standing near the piano, clapping his hands and stamping his sound foot in time with Lady Dick's Negro chant – they said it was Negro. All so very unusual, especially when associated with Christmas ... Usually that noisy sort of singing was left to the waits, wasn't it? But under this new rule the Dowager's enquiring eye-glass was really a window opening into an unknown world – a world in whose reality she could not bring herself to believe. 'Ushant might better have left me down at the dower-house,' she murmured with a strained smile to Miss March.

'Oh, Duchess, don't say that! See how they're all enjoying themselves,' replied her friend, wondering, deep down under the old Mechlin which draped her bosom, whether Lord Brightlingsea, when the dance swept him close to her sofa, might not pause before her with his inimitable majesty, lift her to her feet, and carry her off into the reel whose familiar rhythm she felt even now running up from her trim ankles . . . But Lord Brightlingsea pounded past her unseeingly . . . Certainly, as men grew older, mere youth seemed to cast a stronger spell over them; the fact had not escaped Miss March.

Lady Brightlingsea was approaching the Dowager's sofa, bearing down on her obliquely and hesitatingly, like a sailing-vessel trying to make a harbour-mouth on a windless day.

'Do come and sit with us, Selina dear,' the Dowager welcomed her. 'No, no, don't run away, Jacky . . . Jacky,' she explained, 'has been telling me about this odd American dance, which seems to amuse them all so much.'

'Oh, yes, do tell us,' exclaimed Lady Brightlingsea, coming to anchor between the two. 'It's called the Virginia reel, isn't it? I thought it was named after my daughter-in-law – Seadown's wife is called Virginia, you know. But she says no: she used to dance it as a child. It's an odd coincidence, isn't it?'

The Dowager was always irritated by Lady Brightlingsea's vagueness. She said, in her precise tone: 'Oh, no, it's a very old dance. The Wild Indians taught it to the Americans, didn't they, Jacky?'

'Well, I'm sure it's wild enough,' Lady Brightlingsea murmured, remembering the scantily clad savages in the great tapestry at Allfriars, and thankful that the dancers had not so completely unclothed themselves – though the *décolletage* of the young American ladies went some way in that direction.

Miss March roused herself to reply, with a certain impatience. 'But no, Duchess; this dance is not Indian. The early English colonists brought it with them from England to Virginia – Virginia was one of the earliest English colonies (called after the Virgin Queen, you know), and the Virginia reel is just an old English or Scottish dance.'

The Dowager never greatly cared to have her statements corrected; and she particularly disliked its being done before Selina Brightlingsea, whose perpetual misapprehensions were a standing joke with everybody.

'I daresay there are two theories. I was certainly told it was a Wild Indian war-dance.'

'It seems much more likely; such a very odd performance,' Lady Brightlingsea acquiesced; but neither lady cared to hazard herself farther on the unknown ground of American customs.

'It's like their *valse* – that's very odd too,' the Dowager continued, after a silence during which she had tried in vain to think up a new topic.

'The *valse*? Oh, but surely the *valse* is familiar enough. My girls were all taught it as a matter of course – weren't yours? I can't think why it shocked our grandparents, can you?'

The Dowager narrowed her lips. 'Not *our* version, certainly. But this American *valse* – "waltz" I think they call it there –'

'Oh, is it different? I hadn't noticed, except that I don't think the young ladies carry themselves with quite as much dignity as ours.'

'I should say not! How can they, when every two minutes they have to be prepared to be turned upside down by their partners?'

'*Upside down?*' echoed Lady Brightlingsea, in startled italics. 'What in the world, Blanche, do you mean by *upside down?*'

'Well, I mean – not exactly, of course. But turned round. Surely you must have noticed? Suddenly whizzed around and made to dance backwards. Jacky, what is it they call it in the States?'

'Reversing,' said Miss March, between dry lips. She felt suddenly weary of hearing her compatriots discussed and criticized and having to explain them; perhaps because she had had to do it too often.

'Ah – "reversing". Such a strange word too. I don't think it's English. But the thing itself is so strange – suddenly pushing your partner backwards. I can't help thinking it's a little indelicate.'

The dowager, with reviving interest, rejoined: 'Don't you think these new fashions make all the dances seem – er – rather indelicate? When crinolines were worn the movements were not as – as visible as now. These tight skirts, with the gathers up the middle of the front – of course one can't contend against the fashion. But one can at least not exaggerate it, as they appear to do in America.'

'Yes – I'm afraid they exaggerate everything in America . . . My dear,' Lady Brightlingsea suddenly interrupted herself, 'what in the world can they be going to do next?'

The two long rows facing each other (ladies on one side of the room, gentlemen opposite) had now broken up, and two by two, in dancing pairs, forming a sort of giant caterpillar, were spinning off down the double-cube saloon and all the length of the Waterloo room adjoining it, and the Raphael drawing-room beyond, in the direction of the Classical Sculpture gallery.

'Oh, my dear, where *can* they be going?' Lady Brightlingsea cried.

The three ladies, irresistibly drawn by the unusual sight,

rose together and advanced to the middle of the Raphael drawing-room. From there they could see the wild train, headed by Lady Dick's rhythmic chant, sweeping ahead of them down the length of the Sculpture gallery, back again to the domed marble hall which formed the axis of the house, and up the state staircase to the floor above.

'My dear – my dear Jacky,' gasped Lady Brightlingsea.

'They'll be going into the bedrooms next, I suppose,' said the Dowager with a dry laugh.

But Miss March was beyond speech. She had remembered that the fear of being late for dinner, and the agitation she always felt on great occasions, had caused her to leave on her dressing-table the duplicate set of fluffy curls which should have been locked up with her modest cosmetics. And in the course of this mad flight Lord Brightlingsea might penetrate to her bedroom, and one of those impious girls might cry out: 'Oh, look at Jacky March's curls on her dressing-table!' She felt too faint to speak . . .

Down the upper gallery spun the accelerated reel, song and laughter growing louder to the accompaniment of hurrying feet. Teddy de Santos-Dios had started 'John Peel', and one hunting song followed on another in rollicking chorus. Door after door was flung open, whirled through, and passed out of again, as the train pursued its turbulent way. Now and then a couple fell out, panting and laughing, to rejoin the line again when it coiled back upon itself – but the Duchess and Guy Thwarte did not rejoin it.

Annabel had sunk down on a bench at the door of the Correggio room. Guy Thwarte stood at her side, leaning against the wall and looking down at her. He thought how becomingly the dance had flushed her cheeks and tossed her hair. 'Poor little thing! Fun and laughter are all she needs to make her lovely – but how is she ever to get them, at Longlands and Tintagel?' he thought.

The door of the Correggio room stood wide as the dance swept on, and he glanced in, and saw the candle-lit walls, and the sunset glow of the pictures. 'By Jove! There are the Correggios!'

Annabel stood up. 'You know them, I suppose?'

'Well, rather – but I'd forgotten they were in here.'

'In my sitting-room. Come and look. They're so mysterious in this faint light.'

He followed her, and stood before the pictures, his blood beating high, as it always did at the sight of beauty.

'It sounds funny,' he murmured, 'to call the Earthly Paradise a sitting-room.'

'I thought so too. But it's always been the Duchess's sitting-room.'

'Ah, yes. And that "always been" –.' He smiled and broke off, turning away from her to move slowly about from picture to picture. In the pale amber candle-glow they seemed full of mystery, as though withdrawn into their own native world of sylvan loves and revels; and for a while he too was absorbed into that world, and almost unconscious of his companion's presence. When at last he turned he saw that her face had lost the glow of the dance, and become small and wistful, as he had seen it on the day of his arrival at Longlands.

'You're right. They're even more magical than by daylight.'

'Yes. I often come here when it's getting dark, and sit among them without making a sound. Perhaps some day, if I'm very patient, I'll tame them, and they'll come down to me . . .'

Guy Thwarte stood looking at her. 'Now what on earth', he thought, 'does Tintagel do when she says a thing like that to him?'

'They must make up to you for a great deal,' he began imprudently, heedless of what he was saying.

'For a good deal – yes. But it's rather lonely sometimes, when the only things that seem real are one's dreams.'

The young man flushed up, and made a movement towards

her. Then he paused, and looked at the pictures with a vague laugh. She was only a child, he reminded himself – she didn't measure what she was saying.

'Oh, well, you'll go to *them*, some day, in their Italian palaces.'

'I don't think so. Ushant doesn't care for travelling.'

'How does he know? He's never been out of England,' broke from Guy impatiently.

'That doesn't matter. He says all the other places are foreign. And he hates anything foreign. There are lots of things he's never done that he feels quite sure he'd hate.'

Guy was silent. Again he seemed to himself to be eavesdropping – unintentionally leading her on to say more than she meant; and the idea troubled him.

He turned back to his study of the pictures. 'Has it ever occurred to you,' he began again after a pause, 'that to enjoy them in their real beauty –'

'I ought to persuade Ushant to send them back where they belong?'

'I didn't mean anything so drastic. But did it never occur to you that if you had the courage to sweep away all those . . . those touching little – er . . . family mementoes –' His gesture ranged across the closely covered walls, from illuminated views of Vesuvius in action to landscapes by the Dowager Duchess's great-aunts, funereal monuments worked in hair on faded silk, and photographs in heavy oak frames of ducal relatives, famous race-horses, bishops in lawn sleeves, and undergraduates grouped about sporting trophies.

Annabel coloured, but with amusement, not annoyance. 'Yes; it did occur to me; and one day I smuggled in a ladder and took them all down – every one.'

'By jove, you did? It must have been glorious.'

'Yes; that was the trouble. The Duchess –'

She broke off, and he interposed, with an ironic lift to the brows, 'But you're the Duchess.'

'Not the real one. You must have seen that already. I don't know my part yet, and I don't believe I ever shall. And my mother-in-law was so shocked that every single picture I'd taken down had to be put back the same day.'

'Ah, that's natural too. We're built like that in this tight little island. We fight like tigers against change, and then one fine day accept it without arguing. You'll see: Ushant will come round, and then his mother will because he has. It's only a question of time – and luckily you've plenty of that ahead of you.' He looked at her as he spoke, conscious that he was not keeping the admiration out of his eyes, or the pity either, as he had meant to.

Her own eyes darkened, and she glanced away. 'Yes; there's plenty of time. Years and years of it.' Her voice dragged on the word, as if in imagination she were struggling through the long desert reaches of her own future.

'You don't complain of that, do you?'

'I don't know; I can't tell. I'm not as sure as Ushant how I shall feel about things I've never tried. But I've tried this – and I sometimes think I wasn't meant for it . . .' She broke off, and he saw the tears in her eyes.

'My dear child –' he began; and then, half-embarrassed: 'For you *are* a child still, you know. Have you any idea how awfully young you are?'

As soon as he had spoken he reflected that she was too young not to resent any allusion to her inexperience. She laughed. 'Please don't send me back to the nursery! "Little girls shouldn't ask questions. You'll understand better when you're grown up" . . . How much longer am I to be talked to like that?'

'I'm afraid that's the most troublesome question of all. The truth is –' He hesitated. 'I rather think growing up's largely a question of climate – of sunshine . . . Perhaps our moral climate's too chilly for you young creatures from across the globe. After all, New York's in the latitude of Naples.'

She gave him a perplexed look, and then smiled. 'Oh, I know – those burning hot summers . . .'

'You want so much to go back to them?'

'Do I? I can't tell . . . I don't believe so . . . But somehow it seems as if this were wrong – my being here . . . If you knew what I'd give to be able to try again . . . somewhere where I could be myself, you understand, not just an unsuccessful Duchess . . .'

'Yes; I do understand –'

'Annabel!' a voice called from the threshold, and Miss Testvalley stood before them, her small brown face full of discernment and resolution.

'My dear, the Duke's asking for you. Your guests are beginning to leave, and I must be off with Lady Glenloe and my girls.' Miss Testvalley, with a nod and a smile at young Thwarte, had linked her arm through Annabel's. She paused a moment on the threshold. 'Wasn't I right, Mr Thwarte, to insist on your coming up with us to see the Correggios? I told the Duke it was my doing. They're wonderful by candlelight. But I'm afraid we ought not to have carried off our hostess from her duties.'

Laughing and talking, the three descended together to the great hall, where the departing guests were assembled.

# TWENTY-THREE

THE HOUSE-PARTY AT LONGLANDS WAS NOT TO BREAK UP FOR another week; but the morning after the Christmas festivities such general lassitude prevailed that the long galleries and great drawing-rooms remained deserted till luncheon.

The Dowager Duchess had promised her son not to return to the dower-house until the day after Boxing Day. By that time, it was presumed, the new Duchess would be sufficiently familiar with the part she had to play; but meanwhile a vigilant eye was certainly needed, if only to regulate the disorganized household service.

'These Americans appear to keep such strange hours; and they ask for such odd things to be sent to their rooms – such odd things to eat and drink. Things that Boulamine has never even heard of. It's just as well, I suppose, that I should be here to keep him and Mrs Gillings and Manning from losing their heads,' said the Dowager to her son, who had come to her sitting-room before joining the guns, who were setting out late on the morning after the dance (thereby again painfully dislocating the domestic routine).

The Duke made no direct answer to his mother's comment. 'Of course you must stay,' he said, in a sullen tone, and without looking at her.

The Duchess pursed up her lips. 'There's nothing I

wouldn't do to oblige you, Ushant; but last night I really felt for a moment – well, rather out of place; and so, I think, did Selina Brightlingsea.'

The Duke was gazing steadily at a spot on the wall above his mother's head. 'We must move with the times,' he remarked sententiously.

'Well – we were certainly doing that last night. Moving faster than the times, I should have thought. At least almost all of us. I believe you didn't participate. But Annabel –'

'Annabel is very young,' her son interrupted.

'Don't think that I forget that. It's quite natural that she should join in one of her native dances ... I understand they're very much given to these peculiar dances in the States.'

'I don't know,' said the Duke coldly.

'Only I should have preferred that, having once joined the dancers, she should have remained with them, instead of obliging people to go hunting all over the house for her and her partner – Guy Thwarte, wasn't it? I admit that hearing her name screamed up and down the passages, and in and out of the bedrooms ... when she ought naturally to have been at her post in the Raphael room ... where I have always stood when a party was breaking up ...'

The Duke twisted his fingers nervously about his watch-chain. 'Perhaps you could tell her,' he suggested.

The Dowager's little eyes narrowed doubtfully. 'Don't you think, Ushant, a word from *you* –?'

He glanced at his watch. 'I must be off to join the guns ... No, decidedly – I'd rather you explained ... make her under-stand ...'

His hand on the door, he turned back. 'I want, just at present, to say nothing that could ... could in any way put her off ...' The door closed, and his mother stood staring blankly after him. That chit – and he was afraid of – what did he call it? 'Putting her off'? Was it possible that he did not know his rights? In the Dowager's day, the obligations of a wife – more especially the wife of a Duke – had been as clear as the Ten Commandments. She must give her husband at least two sons, and if in fulfilment of this duty a dozen daughters came uninvited, must receive them with suitably maternal sentiments, and see that they were properly clothed and educated. The Duchess of Tintagel had considered herself lucky in having only eight daughters, but had grieved over Nature's inexorable resolve to grant her no second son.

'Ushant must have two sons – three, if possible. But his wife doesn't seem to understand her duties. Yet she has only to look into the prayer-book . . . but I've never been able to find out to what denomination her family belong. Not Church people, evidently, or these tiresome explanations would be unnecessary . . .'

After an interval of uneasy cogitation the Dowager rang, and sent to enquire if her daughter-in-law could receive her. The reply was that the Duchess was still asleep (at midday – the Dowager, all her life, had been called at a quarter to seven!), but that as soon as she rang she should be given her Grace's message.

The Dowager, with a sigh, turned back to her desk, which was piled, as usual, with a heavy correspondence. If only Ushant had listened to her, had chosen an English wife in his own class, there would probably have been two babies in the nursery by this time, and a third on the way. And none of the rowdy galloping in and out of people's bedrooms at two in the morning. Ah, if sons ever listened to their mothers . . .

The luncheon hour was approaching when there was a knock on the Dowager's door and Annabel entered. The older woman scrutinized her attentively. No – it was past understanding! If the girl had been a beauty one could, with a great effort of the imagination, have pictured Ushant's infatuation, his subjection; but this pale creature with brown hair and insignificant features, without height, or carriage, or

that look of authority given by inherited dignities even to
the squat and the round – what right had she to such consideration? Yet it was clear that she was already getting the
upper hand of her husband.

'My dear – do come in. Sit here; you'll be more comfortable. I hope,' continued the Dowager with a significant smile,
as she pushed forwards a deep easy-chair, 'that we shall soon
have to be asking you to take care of yourself . . . not to com-
mit any fresh imprudence –'

Annabel, ignoring the suggestion, pulled up a straight-
backed chair, and seated herself opposite her mother-in-law.
'I'm not at all tired,' she declared.

'Not consciously, perhaps . . . But all that wild dancing last
night – and in fact into the small hours . . . must have been
very exhausting . . .'

'Oh, I've had a good sleep since. It's nearly luncheon-time,
isn't it?'

'Not quite. And I so seldom have a chance of saying a
word to you alone that I . . . I want to tell you how much I
hope, and Ushant hopes, that you won't run any more risks. I
know it's not always easy to remember; but last night, for
instance, from every point of view, it might have been better
if you had remained at your post.' The Dowager forced a stiff
smile. 'Duchesses, you know, are like soldiers; they must
often be under arms while others are amusing themselves.
And when your guests were leaving, Ushant was naturally –
er – surprised at having to hunt over the house for you . . .'

Annabel looked at her thoughtfully. 'Did he ask you to tell
me so?'

'No; but he thinks you don't realize how odd it must have
seemed to your guests that, in the middle of a party, you should
have taken Mr Thwarte upstairs to your sitting-room –'

'But we didn't go on purpose. We were following the reel,
and I dropped out because I was tired; and as Mr Thwarte
wanted to see the Correggios I took him in.'

'That's the point, my dear. Guy Thwarte ought to have known better than to take you away from your guests and go up to your sitting-room with you after midnight. His doing so was – er – tactless, to say the least. I don't know what your customs are in the States, but in England –' the Dowager broke off, as if waiting for an interruption which did not come.

Annabel remained silent, and her mother-in-law continued with gathering firmness: 'In England such behaviour might be rather severely judged.'

Annabel's eyes widened, and she stood up with a slight smile. 'I think I'm tired of trying to be English,' she pronounced.

The Dowager rose also, drawing herself up to her full height. 'Trying to be? But you *are* English. When you became my son's wife you acquired his nationality. Nothing can change that now.'

'Nothing?'

'Nothing. Remember what you promised in the marriage service. 'To love and to obey – till death us do part.' Those are words not to be lightly spoken.'

'No; but I think I did speak them lightly. I made a mistake.'

'A mistake, my dear? What mistake?'

Annabel drew a quick breath. 'Marrying Ushant,' she said.

The Dowager received this with a gasp. 'My dear Annabel –'

'I think it might be better if I left him; then he could marry somebody else, and have a lot of children. Wouldn't that be best?' Annabel continued hurriedly.

The Dowager, rigid with dismay, stood erect, her strong plump hands grasping the rim of her writing-table. Words of wrath and indignation, scornful annihilating phrases, rushed to her lips, but were checked by her son's warning. 'I want to do nothing to put her off.' If Ushant said that, he meant it; meant, poor misguided fellow, that he was still in love with this thankless girl, this chit, this barren upstart, and that his mother, though authorized to coax her back into the right path, was on no account to drive her there by threats or reproaches.

But the mother's heart spoke louder than she meant it to. 'If you can talk of your own feelings in that way, even in jest, do you take no account of Ushant's?'

Annabel looked at her musingly. 'I don't think Ushant has very strong feelings – about me, I mean.'

The Dowager rejoined with some bitterness: 'You have hardly encouraged him to, have you?'

'I don't know – I can't explain . . . I've told Ushant that I don't think I want to be a mother of dukes.'

'You should have thought of that before becoming the wife of one. According to English law you are bound to obey your husband implicitly in . . . er . . . all such matters . . . But, Annabel, we mustn't let our talk end in a dispute. My son would be very grieved if he thought I'd said anything to offend you – and I've not meant to. All I want is your happiness and his. In the first years of marriage things don't always go as smoothly as they might, and the advice of an older woman may be helpful. Marriage may not be all roses – especially at first; but I know Ushant's great wish is to see you happy and contented in the lot he has offered you – a lot, my dear, that most young women would envy,' the Dowager concluded, lifting her head with an air of wounded majesty.

'Oh, I know; that's why I'm so sorry for my mistake.'

'Your mistake? But there's been no mistake. Your taking Guy Thwarte up to your sitting-room was quite as much his fault as yours; and you need only show him, by a slightly more distant manner, that he is not to misinterpret it. I daresay less importance is attached to such things in your country – where there are no dukes, of course . . .'

'No! That's why I'd better go back there,' burst from Annabel.

The Dowager stared at her in incredulous wrath. Really, it was beyond her powers of self-control to listen smilingly to such impertinence – such blasphemy, she had almost called it. Ushant himself must stamp out this senseless rebellion . . .

At that moment the luncheon-gong sent its pompous call down the corridors, and at the sound the Dowager, hurriedly composing her countenance, passed a shaking hand over her neatly waved bandeaux. 'The gong, my dear! You must not keep your guests waiting . . . I'll follow you at once . . .'

Annabel turned obediently to the door, and went down to join the assembled ladies, and the few men who were not out with the guns.

Her heart was beating high after the agitation of her talk with her mother-in-law, but as she descended the wide shallow steps of the great staircase (up and down which it would have been a profanation to gallop, as one used to up and down the steep narrow stairs at home) she reflected that the Dowager, though extremely angry, and even scandalized, had instantly put an end to their discussion when she heard the summons to luncheon. Annabel remembered the endless wordy wrangles between her mother, her sister and herself, and thought how little heed they would have paid to a luncheon-gong in the thick of one of their daily disputes. Here it was different: everything was done by rule, and according to tradition, and for the Duchess of Tintagel to keep her guests waiting for luncheon would have been an offence against the conventions almost as great as that of not being at her post when the company were leaving the night before. A year ago Annabel would have laughed at these rules and observances: now, though they chafed her no less, she was beginning to see the use of having one's whims and one's rages submitted to some kind of control. 'It did no good to anybody to have us come down with red noses to a stone-cold lunch, and go upstairs afterwards to sulk in our bedrooms,' she thought, and she recalled how her father, when regaled with the history of these domestic disagreements, used to say with a laugh: 'What a lot of nonsense it would knock out of you women to have to hoe a potato-field, or spend a week in Wall Street.'

Yes; in spite of her anger, in spite of her desperate sense of being trapped, Annabel felt in a confused way that the business of living was perhaps conducted more wisely at Longlands – even though Longlands was the potato-field she was destined to hoe for life.

## ∾ CHAPTER ଔ

# TWENTY-FOUR

THAT EVENING BEFORE DINNER, AS ANNABEL SAT OVER HER dressing-room fire, she heard a low knock. She had half expected to see her husband appear, after a talk with his mother, and had steeled herself to a repetition of the morning's scene. But she had an idea that the Dowager might have taken her to task only because the Duke was reluctant to do so; she had already discovered that one of her mother-in-law's duties was the shouldering of any job her son wished to be rid of.

The knock, moreover, was too light to be a man's, and Annabel was not surprised to have it followed by a soft hesitating turn of the door-handle.

'Nan dear – not dressing yet, I hope?' It was Conchita Marable, her tawny hair loosely tossed back, her plump shoulders draped in a rosy dressing-gown festooned with swansdown. It was a long way from Conchita's quarters to the Duchess's, and Annabel was amused at the thought of the Dowager's dismay had she encountered, in the stately corridors of Longlands, a lady with tumbled auburn curls, red-heeled slippers, and a pink deshabille with a marked tendency to drop off the shoulders. A headless ghost would have been much less out of keeping with the traditions of the place.

Annabel greeted her visitor with a smile. Ever since

Conchita's first appearance on the verandah of the Grand Union Annabel's admiration for her had been based on a secret sympathy. Even then the dreamy indolent girl had been enveloped in a sort of warm haze unlike the cool dry light in which Nan's sister and the Elmsworths moved. And Lady Dick, if she had lost something of that early magic, and no longer seemed to Nan to be made of rarer stuff, had yet ripened into something more richly human than the others. A warm fruity fragrance, as of peaches in golden sawdust, breathed from her soft plumpness, the tawny spirals of her hair, the smile which had a way of flickering between her lashes without descending to her lips.

'Darling – you're all alone? Ushant's not lurking anywhere?' she questioned, peering about the room with an air of mystery.

Annabel shook her head. 'No. He doesn't often come here before dinner.'

'Then he's a very stupid man, my dear,' Lady Dick rejoined, her smile resting approvingly on her hostess. 'Nan, do you know how awfully lovely you're growing? I always used to tell Jinny and the Elmsworths that one of these days you'd beat us all; and I see the day's approaching . . .'

Annabel laughed, and her friend drew back to inspect her critically. 'If you'd only burn that almshouse dressing-gown, with the horrid row of horn buttons down the front, which looks as if your mother-in-law had chosen it – ah, she *did*? To discourage midnight escapades, I suppose? Darling, why don't you strike, and let me order your clothes for you – and especially your underclothes? It would be a lovely excuse for running over to Paris, and with your order in my pocket I could get the dress-makers to pay all my expenses, and could bring you back a French maid who'd do your hair so that it wouldn't look like a bun just out of the baking-pan. Oh, Nan – fancy having all you've got – the hair and the eyes, and the rank, and the power, and the money . . .'

Annabel interrupted her. 'Oh, but, Conchie, I haven't got much money.'

Lady Dick's smiling face clouded, and her clear grey eyes grew dark. 'Now why do you say that? Are you afraid of being asked to help an old friend in a tight place, and do you want to warn me off in advance?'

Annabel looked at her in surprise. 'Oh, Conchita, what a beastly question! It doesn't sound a bit like you ... Do sit down by the fire. You're shaking all over – why, I believe you're crying!'

Annabel put an arm around her friend's shoulder, and drew her down into an armchair near the hearth, pulling up a low stool for herself, and leaning against Lady Dick's knee with low sounds of sympathy. 'Tell me, Conchie darling – what's wrong?'

'Oh, my child, pretty nearly everything.' Drawing out a scrap of lace and cambric, Lady Dick applied it to her beautiful eyes; but the tears continued to flow, and Annabel had to wait till they had ceased. Then Lady Dick, tossing back her tumbled curls, continued with a rainbow smile: 'But what's the use? They're all things you wouldn't understand. What do you know about being head over ears in debt, and in love with one man while you're tied to another – tied tight in one of these awful English marriages, that strangle you in a noose when you try to pull away from them?'

A little shiver ran over Annabel. What indeed did she know of these things? And how much could she admit to Conchita – or for that matter to anyone – that she did know? Something sealed her lips, made it, for the moment, impossible even to murmur the sympathy she longed to speak out. She was benumbed, and could only remain silent, pressing Conchita's hands, and deafened by the reverberation of Conchita's last words: 'These awful English marriages, that strangle you in a noose when you try to pull away from them.' If only Conchita had not put that into words!

'Well, Nan – I suppose now I've horrified you past forgiveness,' Lady Dick continued, breaking into a nervous laugh. 'You never imagined things of that sort could happen to anybody you knew, did you? I suppose Miss Testvalley told you that only wicked Queens in history books had lovers. That's what they taught us at school … In real life everything ended at the church door, and you just went on having babies and being happy ever after – eh?'

'Oh, Conchie, Conchie,' Nan murmured, flinging her arms about her friend's neck. She felt suddenly years older than Conchita, and mistress of the bitter lore the latter fancied she was revealing to her. Since the tragic incident of the Linfry child's death, Annabel had never asked her husband for money, and he had never informed himself if her requirements exceeded the modest allowance traditionally allotted to Tintagel Duchesses. It had always sufficed for his mother, and why suggest to his wife that her needs might be greater? The Duke had never departed from the rule inculcated by the Dowager on his coming of age: 'In dealing with tenants and dependents, always avoid putting ideas into their heads' – which meant, in the Dowager's vocabulary, giving them a chance to state their needs or ventilate their grievances; and he had instinctively adopted the same system with his wife. 'People will always think they want whatever you suggest they might want,' his mother had often reminded him; an axiom which had not only saved him thousands of pounds, but protected him from the personal importunities which he disliked even more than the spending of money. He was always reluctant to be drawn into unforeseen expenditure, but he shrank still more from any emotional outlay, and was not sorry to be known (as he soon was) as a landlord who referred all letters to his agents, and resolutely declined personal interviews.

All this flashed through Annabel, but was swept away by Conchita's next words: 'In love with one man and married to another . . .' Yes; that was a terrible fate indeed . . . and yet, and yet . . . might one perhaps not feel less lonely with such a sin on one's conscience than in the blameless isolation of an uninhabited heart?

'Darling, can you tell me . . . anything more? Of course I want to help you; but I must find out ways. I'm almost as much of a prisoner as you are, I fancy; perhaps more. Because Dick's away a good deal, isn't he?'

'Oh, yes, almost always; but his duns are not. The bills keep pouring in. What little money there is is mine, and of course those people know it . . . But I'm stone-broke at present, and I don't know what I shall do if you can't help me out with a loan.' She drew back, and looked at Nan beseechingly. 'You don't know how I hate talking to you about such sordid things . . . You seem so high above it all, so untouched by anything bad.'

'But, Conchie, it's not being bad to be unhappy –'

'No, darling; and goodness knows I'm unhappy enough. But I suppose it's wrong to try to console myself – in the way I have. You must think so, I know; but I can't live without affection, and Miles is so understanding, so tender . . .'

Miles Dawnly, then – Two or three times Nan had wondered – had noticed things which seemed to bespeak a tender intimacy; but she had never been sure . . . The blood rushed to her forehead. As she listened to Conchita she was secretly transposing her friend's words to her own use. 'Oh, I know, I know, Conchie –'

Lady Dick lifted her head quickly, and looked straight into her friend's eyes. 'You know –?'

'I mean, I can imagine . . . how hard it must be not to . . .'

There was a long silence. Annabel was conscious that Conchita was waiting for some word of solace – material or sentimental, or if possible both; but again a paralysing constraint descended on her. In her girlhood no one had ever spoken to her of events or emotions below the surface of life, and she had not yet acquired words to express them. At last she broke out with sudden passion: 'Conchie – it's all turned out a dreadful mistake, hasn't it?'

'A dreadful mistake – you mean my marriage?'

'I mean all our marriages. I don't believe we're any of us really made for this English life. At least I suppose not, for they seem to take so many things for granted here that shock us and make us miserable; and then they're horrified by things we do quite innocently – like that silly reel last night.'

'Oh – you've been hearing about the reel, have you? I saw the old ladies putting their heads together on the sofa.'

'If it's not that it's something else. I sometimes wonder –' She paused again, struggling for words. 'Conchie, if we just packed up and went home to live, would they really be able to make us come back here, as my mother-in-law says? Perhaps I could cable to father for our passage-money –'

She broke off, perceiving that her suggestion had aroused no response. Conchita threw herself back in her armchair, her eyes wide with an unfeigned astonishment. Suddenly she burst out laughing.

'You little darling! Is that your panacea? Go back to Saratoga and New York – to the Assemblies and the Charity balls? Do you really imagine you'd like that better?'

'I don't know . . . Don't you, sometimes?'

'Never! Not for a single minute!' Lady Dick continued to gaze up laughingly at her friend. She seemed to have forgotten her personal troubles in the vision of this grotesque possibility. 'Why, Nan, have you forgotten those dreary endless summers at the Grand Union, and the Opera boxes sent on off-nights by your father's business friends, and the hanging round, fishing for invitations to the Assemblies and knowing we'd never have a look-in at the Thursday Evening dances? . . . Oh, if we were to go over on a visit, just a few weeks' splash in New York or Newport, then every door would fly open, and the Eglintons and Van der Luydens, and all the other old toadies, would be fighting for us, and fawning at our feet; and I don't say I shouldn't like that – for a while. But to be returned to our families as if we'd been sent to England on "appro", and hadn't suited – no, thank you! And I wouldn't go for good and all on any terms – not for all the Astor diamonds! Why, you dear little goose, I'd rather starve and freeze here than go back to all the warm houses and the hot baths, and the emptiness of everything – people and places. And as for you, an English Duchess, with everything the world can give heaped up at your feet – you may not know it now, you innocent infant, but you'd have enough of Madison Avenue and Seventh Regiment balls inside of a week – and of the best of New York and Newport before your first season was over. There, does the truth frighten you? If you don't believe me, ask Jacky March, or any of the poor little American old maids, or wives or widows, who've had a nibble at it, and have hung on at any price, because London's London, and London life the most exciting and interesting in the world, and once you've got the soot and the fog in your veins you simply can't live without them; and all the poor hangers-on and left-overs know it as well as we do.'

Annabel received this in silence. Lady Dick's tirade filled her with a momentary scorn, followed by a prolonged searching of the heart. Her values, of course, were not Conchita's values; that she had always known. London society, of which she knew so little, had never had any attraction for her save as a splendid spectacle; and the part she was expected to play in that spectacle was a burden and not a delight. It was not the atmosphere of London but of England which had gradually filled her veins and penetrated to her heart. She thought of the thinness of the mental and moral air in her own home; the noisy quarrels about nothing, the paltry preoccupations, her mother's feverish interest in the fashions and follies of a society which had always ignored her. At least life in England had a background, layers and layers of rich deep background, of history, poetry, old traditional observances, beautiful houses, beautiful landscapes, beautiful ancient buildings, palaces, churches, cathedrals. Would it not be possible, in some mysterious way, to create for one's self a life out of all this richness, a life which should somehow make up for the poverty of one's personal lot? If only she could have talked of it all with a friend . . . Laura Testvalley, for instance, of whom her need was so much greater now than it had ever been in the school-room. Could she not perhaps persuade Ushant to let her old governess come back to her –?

Her thoughts had wandered so far from Lady Dick and her troubles that she was almost startled to hear her friend speak.

'Well, my dear, which do you think worse – having a lover, or owing a few hundred pounds? Between the two I've shocked you hopelessly, haven't I? As much as even your mother-in-law could wish. The Dowager doesn't like me, you know. I'm afraid I'll never be asked to Longlands again.' Lady Dick stood up with a laugh, pushing her curls back into their loosened coil. Her face looked pale and heavy.

'You haven't shocked me – only made me dreadfully sorry, because I don't know what I can do . . .'

'Oh, well; don't lie awake over it, my dear,' Lady Dick retorted with a touch of bitterness. 'But wasn't that the dressing-bell? I must hurry off and be laced into my dinner-gown. They don't like unpunctuality here, do they? And tea-gowns wouldn't be tolerated at dinner.'

'Conchie – wait!' Annabel was trembling with the sense of having failed her friend, and been unable to make her understand why. 'Don't think I don't care – Oh, please don't think that! The way we live makes it look as if there wasn't a whim I couldn't gratify; but Ushant doesn't give me much money, and I don't know how to ask for it.'

Conchita turned back and gave her a long look. 'The skinflint! No, I suppose he wouldn't; and I suppose you haven't learnt yet how to manage him.'

Annabel blushed more deeply: 'I'm not clever at managing, I'm afraid. You must give me time to look about, to find out –' It had suddenly occurred to her, she hardly knew why, that Guy Thwarte was the one person she could take into her confidence in such a matter. Perhaps he would be able to tell her how to raise the money for her friend. She would pluck up her courage, and ask him the next day.

'Conchie, dear, by tomorrow evening I promise you ...' she began; and found herself instantly gathered to her friend's bosom.

'Two hundred pounds would save my life, you darling – and five hundred make me a free woman ...'

Conchita loosened her embrace. The velvet glow suffused her face again, and she turned joyfully towards the door. But on the threshold she paused, and coming back laid her hands on Annabel's shoulders.

'Nan,' she said, almost solemnly, 'don't judge me, will you, till you find out for yourself what it's like.'

'What what is like? What do you mean, Conchita?'

'Happiness, darling,' Lady Dick whispered. She pressed a quick kiss on her friend's cheek; then, as the dressing-bell crashed out its final call, she picked up her rosy draperies and fled down the corridor.

# TWENTY-FIVE

THE NEXT MORNING ANNABEL, AFTER A RESTLESS NIGHT, stood at her window watching the dark return of day. Dawn was trying to force a way through leaden mist; every detail, every connecting link, was muffled in folds of rain-cloud. That was England, she thought; not only the English scene but the English life was perpetually muffled. The links between these people and their actions were mostly hidden from Annabel; their looks, their customs, their language, had implications beyond her understanding.

Sometimes fleeting lights, remote and tender, shot through the fog; then the blanket of incomprehension closed in again. It was like that day in the ruins of Tintagel, the day when she and Ushant had met . . . As she looked back on it, the scene of their meeting seemed symbolic: in a ruin and a fog . . . Lovers ought to meet under limpid skies and branches dripping with sunlight, like the nymphs and heroes of Correggio.

The thought that she had even imagined Ushant as a lover made her smile, and she turned away from the window . . . Those were dreams, and the reality was: what? First that she must manage to get five hundred pounds for Conchita; and after that, must think about her own future. She was glad she had something active and helpful to do before reverting once more to that dreary problem.

Through her restless night she had gone over and over
every possible plan for getting the five hundred pounds. The
idea of consulting Guy Thwarte had faded before the first
hint of daylight. Of course he would offer to lend her the
sum; and how could she borrow from a friend money she saw
no possibility of repaying? And yet, to whom else could she
apply? The Dowager? Her mind brushed past the absurd idea
... and past that of her sisters-in-law. How bewildered, how
scandalized the poor things would be! Annabel herself, she
knew, was bewilderment enough to them: a wife who bore no
children, a Duchess who did not yet clearly understand the
duties of a groom-of-the-chambers, or know what the
Chiltern Hundreds were! To all his people it was as if Ushant
had married a savage ...

There was her own family, of course; her sister, her friends
the Elmsworths. Annabel knew that in the dizzy up-and-
down of Wall Street, which ladies were not expected to
understand, Mr Elmsworth was now 'on top', as they called
it. The cornering of a heavy block of railway shares, though
apparently necessary to the development of another line, had
temporarily hampered her father and Mr Closson, and
Annabel was aware that Virginia had already addressed several unavailing appeals to Colonel St George. Certainly, if he
had cut down the girls' allowances it was because the poor
Colonel could not help himself; and it seemed only fair that
his first aid, whenever it came, should go to Virginia, whose
husband's income had to be extracted from the heavily burdened Brightlingsea estate, rather than to the wife of one of
England's wealthiest dukes.

One of England's wealthiest dukes! That was what Ushant
was; and it was naturally to him that his wife should turn in any
financial difficulty. But Annabel had never done so since the
Linfry incident, and though she knew the sum she wanted was
nothing to a man with Ushant's income, she was as frightened
as though she had been going to beg for the half of his fortune.

The others, of course – Virginia, the Elmsworths and poor Conchita – had long since become trained borrowers and beggars. Money – or rather the want of it – loomed before them at every turn, and they had mastered most of the arts of extracting it from reluctant husbands or parents. This London life necessitated so many expenditures unknown to the humdrum existence of Madison Avenue and the Grand Union Hotel: Court functions, Royal Ascot, the Cowes season, the entertaining of royalties, the heavy cost of pheasant-shooting, deer-stalking and hunting, above all (it was whispered) the high play and extravagant luxury prevailing in the inner set to which the lovely newcomers had been so warmly welcomed. You couldn't, Virginia had over and over again explained to Annabel, expect to keep your place in that jealously guarded set if you didn't dress up, live up, play up, to its princely standards. But Annabel had lent an inattentive ear to these hints. She wanted nothing of what her sister and her sister's friends were fighting for; their needs did not stir her imagination, and they soon learned that, beyond occasionally letting them charge a dress, or a few yards of lace, to her account, she could give them little aid.

It was Conchita's appeal which first roused her sympathy. 'You don't know what it is,' Lady Dick had said, 'to be in love with one man and tied to another'; and instantly the barriers of Nan's indifference had broken down. It was wrong – it was no doubt dreadfully wrong – but it was human, it was understandable, it made her frozen heart thaw in soft participation. 'It must be less wicked to love the wrong person than not to love anybody at all,' she thought, considering her own desolate plight . . .

But such thoughts were pure self-indulgence; her immediate business was the finding of the five hundred pounds to lift Conchita's weight of debt.

When there was a big shooting-party at Longlands every hour of the Duke's day was disposed of in advance, and Nan had begun to regard this as a compensation for the boredom associated with such occasions. She was resolved never again to expose herself to the risks of those solitary months at Tintagel, with an Ushant at leisure to dissect his grievances as he did his clocks . . . After much reflexion she scribbled a note to him: 'Please let me know after breakfast when I can see you –' and to her surprise, when the party rose from the sumptuous repast which always fortified the guns at Longlands, the Duke followed her into the east drawing-room, where the ladies were accustomed to assemble in the mornings, with their needle-work and correspondence.

'If you'll come to my study for a moment, Annabel.'

'Now –?' she stammered, not expecting so prompt a response.

The Duke consulted his watch. 'I have a quarter of an hour before we start.' She hesitated, and then, reflecting that she might have a better chance of success if there were no time to prolong the discussion, she rose and followed him.

The Duke's study at Longlands had been created by a predecessor imbued with loftier ideas of his station, and the glories befitting it, than the present Duke could muster. In size, and splendour of ornament, it seemed singularly out of scale with the nervous little man pacing its stately floor; but it had always been 'the Duke's study', and must therefore go on being so to the end of time.

Ushant had seated himself behind his monumental desk, as if to borrow from it the authority he did not always know how to assert unaided. His wife stood before him without speaking. He lifted his head, and forced one of the difficult smiles he had inherited from his mother. 'Yes –?'

'Oh, Ushant – I don't know how to begin; and this room always frightens me. It looks as if people came here only when you send for them to be sentenced.'

The Duke met this with a look of genuine bewilderment. Could it be, the look implied, that his wife imagined there

was some link between the peerage and the magistracy?
'Well, my dear –?'

'Oh, you wouldn't understand ... But what I've actually come for is to ask you to let me have five hundred pounds.'

There, it was out – about as lightly as if she had hurled a rock at him through one of the tall windows! He frowned and looked down, picking up an emblazoned paper-cutter to examine it.

'Five hundred pounds?' he repeated slowly.

'Yes.'

'Do I understand that you are asking me for that sum?'

'Yes.'

There was another heavy silence, during which she strained her eyes to detect any change in his guarded face. There was none.

'Five hundred pounds?'

'Oh, please, Ushant – yes!'

'Now – at once?'

'At once,' she faltered, feeling that each syllable of his slow interrogatory was draining away a drop of her courage.

The Duke again attempted a smile. 'It's a large sum – a very large sum. Has your dress-maker led you on rather farther than your means would justify?'

Nan reddened. Her dress-maker! She wondered if Ushant had ever noticed her clothes? But might he not be offering her the very pretext she needed? She hated having to use one, but since she could think of no other way of getting what she wanted, she resolved to surmount her scruples.

'Well, you see, I've never known exactly what my means were ... but I do want this money ...'

'Never known what your means were? Surely it's all clearly enough written down in your marriage settlements.'

'Yes; but sometimes one is tempted to spend a trifle more ...'

'You must have been taught very little about the value of money to call five hundred pounds a trifle.'

Annabel broke into a laugh. 'You're teaching me a lot about it now.'

The Duke's temples grew red under his straw-coloured hair, and she saw that her stroke had gone home.

'It's my duty to do so,' he remarked drily. Then his tone altered, and he added, on a conciliatory note: 'I hope you'll bear the lesson in mind; but of course if you've incurred this debt it must be paid.'

'Oh, Ushant –'

He raised his hand to check her gratitude. 'Naturally . . . If you'll please tell these people to send me their bill.' He rose stiffly, with another glance at his watch. 'I said a quarter of an hour – and I'm afraid it's nearly up.'

Nan stood crestfallen between her husband and the door. 'But you don't understand . . .' (She wondered whether it was not a mistake to say that to him so often?) 'I mean', she hurriedly corrected herself, 'it's really no use your bothering . . . If you'll just make out the cheque to me I'll –'

The Duke stopped short. 'Ah –' he said slowly. 'Then it's *not* to pay your dress-maker that you want it?'

Nan's quick colour flew to her forehead. 'Well, no – it's not. I – I want it for . . . my private charities . . .'

'Your private charities? Is your allowance not paid regularly? All your private expenditures are supposed to be included in it. My mother was always satisfied with that arrangement.'

'Yes; but did your mother never have unexpected calls –? Sometimes one has to help in an emergency . . .'

The two faced each other in a difficult silence. At length the Duke straightened himself, and said with an attempt at ease: 'I'm willing to admit that emergencies may arise; but if you ask me to advance five hundred pounds at a moment's notice it's only fair that I should be told why you need it.'

Their eyes met, and a flame of resistance leapt into Nan's. 'I've told you it's for a *private* charity.'

'My dear, there should be nothing private between husband and wife.'

She laughed impatiently. 'Are you trying to say you won't give me the money?'

'I'm saying quite the contrary. I'm ready to give it if you'll tell me what you want it for.'

'Ushant – it's a long time since I've asked you a favour, and you can't go on forever ordering me about like a child.'

The Duke took a few steps across the room; then he turned back. His complexion had faded to its usual sandy pallor, and his lips twitched a little. 'Perhaps, my dear, you forget how long it is since *I* have asked for a favour. I'm afraid you must make your choice. If I'm not, as you call it, to order you about like a child, you may force me to order you about as a wife.' The words came out slowly, haltingly, as if they had cost him a struggle. Nan had noticed before now that anger was too big a garment for him: it always hung on him in uneasy folds. 'And now my time is up. I can't keep the guns waiting any longer,' he concluded abruptly, turning towards the door.

Annabel stood silent; she could find nothing else to say. She had failed, as she had foreseen she would, for lack of the arts by which cleverer women gain their ends. 'You can't force me . . . no one can force me . . .' she cried out suddenly, hardly knowing what she said; but her husband had already crossed the threshold, and she wondered whether the closing of the door had not drowned her words.

The big house was full of the rumour of the departing sportsmen. Gradually the sounds died out, and the hush of boredom and inactivity fell from the carved and gilded walls. Annabel stood where the Duke left her. Now she went out into the long vaulted passage on which the study opened. The passage was empty, and so was the great domed and pillared hall beyond. Under such lowering skies the ladies would remain grouped about the fire in the east drawing-room, trying to cheat the empty hours with gossip and embroidery and letter-writing. It was not a day for them to join the sportsmen, even had their host encouraged this new-fangled habit; but it was well known that the Duke, who had no great taste for sport, and practised it only as one of the duties of his station, did not find the task lightened by feminine companionship.

In the lobby of one of the side entrances Annabel found an old garden hat and cloak. She put them on and went out. It would have been impossible for her, just then, to join the bored but placid group in the east drawing-room. The great house had become like a sepulchre to her; under its ponderous cornices and cupolas she felt herself reduced to a corpse-like immobility. It was only in the open that she became herself again – a stormy self, reckless and rebellious. 'Perhaps,' she thought, 'if Ushant had ever lived in smaller houses he would have understood me better.' Was it because all the great people secretly felt as Ushant did – oppressed, weighed down under a dead burden of pomp and precedent – that they built these gigantic palaces to give themselves the illusion of being giants?

Now, out of doors, under the lowering skies, she could breathe and even begin to think. But for the moment all her straining thoughts were arrested by the same insurmountable barrier: she was the Duchess of Tintagel, and knew no way of becoming anyone else . . .

She walked across the gardens opening out from the west wing, and slowly mounted the wooded hillside beyond. It was beginning to rain, and she must find a refuge somewhere – a solitude in which she could fight out this battle between herself and her fate. The slope she was climbing was somewhat derisively crowned by an octagonal temple of Love, with rain-streaked walls of peeling stucco. On the summit of the dome the neglected god spanned his bow unheeded, and underneath it a door swinging loose on broken hinges gave admittance to a room stored with the remnants of derelict croquet-sets and disabled shuttlecocks and grace-rings. It was evidently many a day since the lords of Longlands had visited the divinity who is supposed to rule the world.

Nan, certain of being undisturbed in this retreat, often came there with a book or writing-materials; but she had not intruded on its mouldy solitude since the beginning of winter.

As she entered, a chill fell on her; but she sat down at the stone table in the centre of the dilapidated mosaic floor, and rested her chin on her hands. 'I must think it all out,' she said aloud, and closing her eyes she tried to lose herself in an inner world of self-examination.

But think out what? Does a life-prisoner behind iron bars take the trouble to think out his future? What a waste of time, what a cruel expenditure of hope ... Once more she felt herself sinking into depths of childish despair – one of those old benumbing despairs without past or future which used to blot out the skies when her father scolded her or Miss Testvalley looked disapproving. Her face dropped into her hands, and she broke into sobs of misery.

The sobs murmured themselves out; but for a long time she continued to sit motionless, her face hidden, with a child's reluctance to look out again on a world which has wounded it. Her back was turned to the door, and she was so sunk in her distress that she was unconscious of not being alone until she felt a touch on her shoulder, and heard a man's voice: 'Duchess – are you ill? What's happened?'

She turned, and saw Guy Thwarte bending over her. 'What is it – what has made you cry?' he continued, in the compassionate tone of a grown person speaking to a frightened child.

Nan jumped up, her wet handkerchief crumpled against her eyes. She felt a sudden anger at this intrusion. 'Where did you come from? Why aren't you out with the guns?' she stammered.

'I was to have been; but a message came from Lowdon to say that Sir Hercules is worse, and Ushant has asked me to prepare some notes in case the election comes on sooner than we expected. So I wandered up the hill to clear my ideas a little.'

Nan stood looking at him with a growing sense of resentment. Hitherto his presence had roused only friendly emotions; his nearness had even seemed a vague protection against the unknown and the inimical. But in her present mood that nearness seemed a deliberate intrusion – as though he had forced himself upon her out of some unworthy curiosity, had seized the chance to come upon her unawares.

'Won't you tell me why you are crying?' he insisted gently.

Her childish anger flamed. 'I'm not crying,' she retorted, hurriedly pushing her handkerchief into her pocket. 'And I don't know why you should follow me here. You must see that I want to be alone.'

The young man drew back, surprised. He too, since the distant day of their first talk at Honourslove, had felt between them the existence of a mysterious understanding which every subsequent meeting had renewed, though in actual words so little had passed between them. He had imagined that Annabel was glad he should feel this, and her sudden rebuff was like a blow. But her distress was so evident that he did not feel obliged to take her words literally.

'I had no idea of following you,' he answered. 'I didn't even know you were here; but since I find you in such distress, how can I help asking if there's nothing I can do?'

'No, no, there's nothing!' she cried, humiliated that this man of all others should surprise her in her childish wretchedness. 'Well, yes – I *am* crying . . . now . . . You can see I am, I suppose?' She groped for the handkerchief. 'But if anybody could do anything for me, do you suppose I'd be sitting here and just bearing it? It's because there's nothing . . . nothing . . . anyone can do, that I've come here to get away from people, to get away from everything ... Can't you understand that?' she ended passionately.

'I can understand your feeling so – yes. I've often thought you must.' She gave him a startled look, and her face crimsoned. 'But can't you see,' he pursued, 'that it's hard on a friend – a man who's ventured to think himself your friend – to be told, when he sees you in trouble, that he's not wanted, that he can be of no use, that even his sympathy's unwelcome?'

Annabel continued to look at him with resentful eyes. But already the mere sound of his voice was lessening the weight of her loneliness, and she answered more gently: 'You're very kind –'

'Oh, *kind!*' he echoed impatiently.

'You've always been kind to me. I wish you hadn't been away for so many years. I used to think sometimes that if only I could have asked you about things ...'

'But – but if you've really thought that, why do you want to drive me away now that I *am* here?' He went up to her with outstretched hands; but she shook her head.

'Because I'm not the Annabel you used to know. I'm a strange woman, strange even to myself, who goes by my name. I suppose in time I'll get to know her, and learn how to live with her.'

The angry child had been replaced by a sad but self-controlled woman, who appeared to Guy infinitely farther away and more inaccessible than the other. He had wanted to take the child in his arms and comfort her with kisses; but this newcomer seemed to warn him to be circumspect, and after a pause he rejoined, with a smile: 'And can't I be of any use, even to the strange woman?'

Her voice softened. 'Well, yes; you can. You are of use ... Thinking of you as a friend does help me ... it often has ...' She went up to him and put her hand in his. 'Please believe that. But don't ask me anything more; don't even say anything more now, if you really want to help me.'

He held her hand without attempting to disregard either her look or her words. Through the loud beat of his blood a whisper warned him that the delicate balance of their friendship hung on his obedience.

'I want it above all things, but I'll wait,' he said, and lifted the hand to his lips.

# TWENTY-SIX

AS LONG AS THE DOWAGER RULED AT LONGLANDS SHE HAD found her chief relaxation from ducal drudgery in visiting the immense collection of rare and costly exotic plants in the Duke's famous conservatories. But when she retired to the dower-house, and the sole command of the one small glasshouse attached to her new dwelling, she realized the insipidity of inspecting plants in the company of a severe and suspicious head gardener compared with the joys of planting, transplanting, pruning, fertilizing, writing out labels, pressing down the earth about outspread roots, and compelling an obedient underling to do in her own way what she could not manage alone. The Dowager, to whom life had always presented itself in terms of duty, to whom even the closest human relations had come draped in that pale garb, had found her only liberation in gardening; and since amateur horticulture was beginning to be regarded in the highest circles not only as an elegant distraction but almost as one of a great lady's tasks, she had immersed herself in it with a guilty fervour, still doubting if anything so delightful could be quite blameless.

Her son, aware of this passion, which equalled his own for dismembering clocks, was in the habit of going straight to the conservatory when he visited her; and there he found her on the morning after his strange conversation with his wife.

The Dowager was always gratified by his visits, which were necessarily rare during the shooting-parties; but it would have pleased her better had he not come at the exact moment when, gauntleted and aproned, she was transferring some new gloxinia seedlings from one pan to another.

She laid down her implements, scratched a few words in a notebook at her elbow, and dusted the soil from her big gloves.

'Ah, Ushant –.' She broke off, struck by his unusual pallor, and the state of his hair. 'My dear, you don't look well. Is anything wrong?' she asked, in the tone of one long accustomed to being told every morning of some new wrongness in the course of things.

The Duke stood looking down at the long shelf, the heaps of upturned soil and the scattered labels. It occurred to him that, for ladies, horticulture might prove a safe and agreeable pastime.

'Have you ever tried to interest Annabel in this kind of thing?' he asked abruptly. 'I'm afraid I'm too ignorant to do it myself – but I sometimes think she would be happier if she had some innocent amusement like gardening. Needlework doesn't seem to appeal to her.'

The Dowager's upper lip lengthened. 'I've not had much chance of discussing her tastes with her; but of course, if you wish me to . . . Do you think, for instance, she might learn to care for grafting?'

It was inconceivable to the Duke that anyone should care for grafting; but not wishing to betray his complete ignorance of the subject, he effected a diversion by proposing a change of scene. 'Perhaps we could talk more comfortably in the drawing-room,' he suggested.

His mother laid down her tools. She was used to interruptions, and did not dare to confess how trying it was to be asked to abandon her seedlings at that critical stage. She also weakly regretted having to leave the pleasant temperature of the conservatory for an icy drawing-room in which the fire was never lit till the lamps were brought. Such economies were necessary to a Dowager with several daughters whose meagre allowances were always having to be supplemented; but the Duchess, who was almost as hardened to cold as her son, led the way to the drawing-room without apology.

'I'm sorry', she said, as she seated herself near the lifeless hearth, 'that you think dear Annabel lacks amusements.'

The Duke stood before the chimney, his hands thrust despondently in his pockets. 'Oh – I don't say that. But I suppose she's been used to other kinds of amusement in the States; skating, you know, and dancing – they seem to do a lot of dancing over there; and even in England I suppose young ladies expect more variety and excitement nowadays than they had in your time.'

The Dowager, who had taken up her almshouse knitting, dropped a sigh into its harsh folds.

'Certainly in my time they didn't expect much – luckily, for they wouldn't have got it.'

The Duke made no reply, but moved uneasily back and forth across the room, as his way was when his mind was troubled.

'Won't you sit down, Ushant?'

'Thanks. No.' He returned to his station on the hearth-rug.

'You're not joining the guns?' his mother asked.

'No. Seadown will replace me. The fact is,' the Duke continued in an embarrassed tone, 'I wanted a few minutes of quiet talk with you.'

He paused again, and his mother sat silent, automatically counting her stitches, though her whole mind was centred on his words. She was sure some pressing difficulty had brought him to her, but she knew that any visible sign of curiosity, or even sympathy, might check his confidence.

'I – I have had a very – er – embarrassing experience with Annabel,' he began; and the Dowager lifted her head quickly, but without interrupting the movement of her needles.

The Duke coughed and cleared his throat. ('At the last minute,' his mother thought, 'he's wondering whether he might not better have held his tongue.' She knitted on.)

'A – a really incomprehensible experience.' He threw himself into the chair opposite hers. 'And completely unexpected. Yesterday morning, just as I was leaving the house, Annabel asked me for a large sum of money – a very large sum. For five hundred pounds.'

'Five hundred pounds?' The needles dropped from the Dowager's petrified fingers.

Her son gave a dry laugh. 'It seems to me a considerable amount.'

The Dowager was thinking hurriedly: 'That chit! I shouldn't have dared to ask him for a quarter of that amount – much less his father . . .' Aloud she said: 'But what does she want it for?'

'That's the point. She refuses to tell me.'

'Refuses –?' the Dowager gasped.

'Er – yes. First she hinted it was for her dress-maker; but on being pressed she owned it was not.'

'Ah – and then?'

'Well – then . . . I told her I'd pay the debt if she'd incurred it; but only if she would tell me to whom the money was owing.'

'Of course. Very proper.'

'So I thought; but she said I'd no right to cross-examine her –'

'Ushant! She called it that?'

'Something of the sort. And as the guns were waiting, I said that was my final answer – and there the matter ended.'

The Dowager's face quivered with an excitement she had

no means of expressing. This woman – he'd offered her five hundred pounds! And she'd refused it . . .

'It could hardly have ended otherwise,' she approved, thinking of the many occasions when a gift of five hundred pounds from the late Duke would have eased her daily load of maternal anxieties.

Her son made no reply, and as he began to move uneasily about the room, it occurred to her that what he wanted was not her approval but her dissent. Yet how could she appear to encourage such open rebellion? 'You certainly did right,' she repeated.

'Ah, there I'm not sure,' the Duke muttered.

'Not sure –?'

'Nothing's gained, I'm afraid, by taking that tone with Annabel.' He reddened uncomfortably, and turned his head away from his mother's scrutiny.

'You mean you think you were too lenient?'

'Lord, no – just the contrary. I . . . oh, well, you wouldn't understand. These American girls are brought up differently from our young women. You'd probably say they were spoilt . . .'

'I should,' the Dowager assented drily.

'Well – perhaps. Though in a country where there's no primogeniture I suppose it's natural that daughters should be more indulged. At any rate, I . . . I thought it all over during the day – I thought of nothing else, in fact; and after she'd gone down to dinner yesterday evening I slipped into her room and put an envelope with the money on her dressing-table.'

'Oh, Ushant – how generous, how noble!'

The Duchess's hard little eyes filled with sudden tears. Her mind was torn between wrath at her daughter-in-law's incredible exactions, and the thought of what such generosity on her own husband's part might have meant to her, with those eight girls to provide for. But Annabel had no daughters – and no sons – and the Dowager's heart had hardened again before her eyes were dry. Would there be no limit to Ushant's weakness, she wondered?

'You're the best judge, of course, in any question between your wife and yourself; but I hope Annabel will never forget what she owes you.'

The Duke gave a short laugh. 'She's forgotten it already.'

'Ushant –!'

He crimsoned unhappily and again averted his face from his mother's eyes. He felt a nervous impulse to possess himself of the clock on the mantel-shelf and take it to pieces; but he turned his back on the temptation. 'I'm sorry to bother you with these wretched details . . . but . . . perhaps one woman can understand another where a man would fail . . .'

'Yes –?'

'Well, you see, Annabel has been rather nervous and uncertain lately; I've had to be patient. But I thought – I thought when she found she'd gained her point about the money . . . she . . . er . . . would wish to show her gratitude . . .'

'Naturally.'

'So, when the men left the smoking-room last night, I went up to her room. It was not particularly late, and she had not undressed. I went in, and she did thank me . . . well, very prettily . . . But when I . . . when I proposed to stay, she refused, refused absolutely –'

The Dowager's lips twitched. 'Refused? On what ground?'

'That she hadn't understood I'd been driving a bargain with her. The scene was extremely painful,' the Duke stammered.

'Yes; I understand.' The Dowager paused, and then added abruptly: 'So she handed back the envelope –?'

Her son hung his head. 'No; there was no question of that.'

'Ah. – her pride didn't prevent her accepting the bribe, though she refused to stick to the bargain?'

'I can't say there was an actual bargain; but – well, it was something like that . . .'

The Dowager sat silent, her needles motionless in her hands. This, she thought, was one of the strangest hours of her life, and not the least strange part of it was the light reflected back on her own past, and on the weary nights when she had not dared to lock her door . . .

'And then –?'

'Then – well, the end of it was that she said she wanted to go away.'

'Go away?'

'She wants to go off somewhere – she doesn't care where – alone with her old governess. You know; the little Italian woman who's with Augusta Glenloe and came over the other night with the party from Champions. She seems to be the only person Annabel cares for, or who, at any rate, has any influence over her.'

The Dowager meditated. Again the memory of her own past thrust itself between her and her wrath against her daughter-in-law. Ah, if she had ever dared to ask the late Duke to let her off – to let her go away for a few days, she didn't care where! Even now, she trembled inwardly at the thought of what his answer would have been . . .

'Do you think this governess's influence is good?' she asked at length.

'I've always supposed it was. She's very much attached to Annabel. But how can I ask Augusta Glenloe to lend me her girls' governess to go – I don't know where – with my wife?'

'It's out of the question, of course. Besides, a Duchess of Tintagel can hardly wander about the world in that way. But perhaps – if you're sure it's wise to yield to this . . . this fancy of Annabel's . . .'

'Yes, I am,' the Duke interrupted uncomfortably.

'Then why not ask Augusta Glenloe to invite her to Champions for a few weeks? I could easily explain . . . putting it on the ground of Annabel's health. Augusta will be glad to do what she can . . .'

The Duke heaved a deep sigh, at once of depression and relief. It was clear that he wished to put an end to the talk, and escape as quickly as possible from the questions in his mother's eyes.

'It might be a good idea.'

'Very well. Shall I write?'

The Duke agreed that she might – but of course without giving the least hint . . .

Oh, of course; naturally the Dowager understood that. Augusta would accept her explanation without seeing anything unusual in it . . . It wasn't easy to surprise Augusta.

The Duke, with a vague mutter of thanks, turned to the door; and his mother, following him, laid her hand on his arm. 'You've been very long-suffering, Ushant; I hope you'll have your reward.'

He stammered something inaudible, and went out of the room. The Dowager, left alone, sat down by the hearth and bent over her scattered knitting. She had forgotten even her haste to get back to the gloxinias. Her son's halting confidences had stirred in her a storm of unaccustomed emotion, and memories of her own past crowded about her like mocking ghosts. But the Dowager did not believe in ghosts, and her grim realism made short work of the phantoms. 'There's only one way for an English duchess to behave – and the wretched girl has never learnt it . . .' Smoothing out her knitting, she restored it to the basket reserved for pauper industries; then she stood up, and tied on her gardening apron. There were still a great many seedlings to transplant, and after that the new curate was coming to discuss arrangements for the next Mothers' Meeting . . . and then –

'There's always something to be done next . . . I daresay that's the trouble with Annabel – she's never assumed her responsibilities. Once one does, there's no time left for trifles.' The Dowager, half-way across the room, stopped abruptly. 'But what in the world can she want with those five hundred pounds? Certainly not to pay her dress-maker – that was a stupid excuse,' she reflected; for even to her untrained eye it was evident that Annabel, unlike her sister and her American friends, had never dressed with the elegance her rank demanded. Yet for what else could she need this money – unless indeed (the Dowager shuddered at the thought) to help some young man out of a scrape? The idea was horrible; but the Dowager had heard it whispered that such cases had been known, even in their own circle; and suddenly she remembered the unaccountable incident of her daughter-in-law's taking Guy Thwarte upstairs to her sitting-room in the course of that crazy reel . . .

# TWENTY-SEVEN

AT CHAMPIONS, THE GLENLOE PLACE IN GLOUCESTERSHIRE, A broad-faced amiable brick house with regular windows and a pillared porch replaced the ancestral towers which had been destroyed by fire some thirty years earlier, and now, in ivy-draped ruin, invited the young and romantic to mourn with them by moonlight.

The family did not mourn; least of all Lady Glenloe, to whom airy passages and plain square rooms seemed infinitely preferable to rat-infested moats and turrets, a troublesome over-crowded muniment room, and the famous family portraits that were continually having to be cleaned and re-backed; and who, in rehearsing the saga of the fire, always concluded with a sigh of satisfaction: 'Luckily they saved the stuffed birds'.

It was doubtful if the other members of the family had ever noticed anything about the house but the temperature of the rooms, and the relative comfort of the armchairs. Certainly Lady Glenloe had done nothing to extend their observations. She herself had accomplished the unusual feat of having only two daughters and four sons: and this achievement, and the fact that Lord Glenloe had lived for years on a ranch in Canada, and came to England but briefly and rarely, had obliged his wife to be a frequent traveller, going from the sol-

dier sons in Canada and India to the gold-miner in South
Africa and the Embassy attaché at St Petersburg, and returning home via the North-west and the marital ranch.

Such travels, infrequent in Lady Glenloe's day, had opened
her eyes to matters undreamed-of by most ladies of the aristocracy, and she had brought back from her wanderings a
mind tanned and toughened like her complexion by the
healthy hardships of the road. Her two daughters, though left
at home, and kept in due subordination, had caught a whiff
of the gales that whistled through her mental rigging, and
the talk at Champions was full of easy allusions to Thibet,
Salt Lake City, Tsarskoë or Delhi, as to all of which Lady
Glenloe could furnish statistical items, and facts on plant
and bird distribution. In this atmosphere Miss Testvalley
breathed more freely than in her other educational prisons,
and when she appeared on the station platform to welcome
the young Duchess, the latter, though absorbed in her own
troubles, instantly noticed the change in her governess. At
Longlands, during the Christmas revels, there had been no
time or opportunity for observation, much less for private
talk; but now Miss Testvalley took possession of Annabel as a
matter of course.

'My dear, you won't mind there being no one but me to
meet you? The girls and their brothers from Petersburg and
Ottawa are out with the guns, and Lady Glenloe sent you all
sorts of excuses, but she had an important parish meeting –
something to do with almshouse sanitation; and she thought
you'd probably be tired by the journey, and rather glad to rest
quietly till dinner.'

Yes – Annabel was very glad. She suspected that the infor-
mal arrival had been planned with Lady Glenloe's connivance, and it made her feel like a girl again to be springing
up the stairs on Miss Testvalley's arm, with no groom-of-the-
chambers bowing her onward, or housekeeper curtseying in
advance. 'Everything's pot-luck at Champions.' Lady

Glenloe had a way of saying it that made pot-luck sound far more appetizing than elaborate preparations; and Annabel's spirits rose with every step.

She had left Longlands with a heavy mind. After a scene of tearful gratitude, Lady Dick, her money in her pocket, had fled to London by the first train, ostensibly to deal with her more pressing creditors; and for another week Annabel had continued to fulfil her duties as hostess to the shooting-party. She had wanted to say a word in private to Guy Thwarte, to excuse herself for her childish outbreak when he had surprised her in the temple; but the day after Conchita's departure he too had gone, called to Honourslove on some local business, and leaving with a promise to the Duke that he would return for the Lowdon election.

Without her two friends, Annabel felt herself more than ever alone. She knew that the Duke, according to his lights, had behaved generously to her; and she would have liked to feel properly grateful. But she was conscious only of a bewildered resentment. She was sure she had done right in helping Conchita Marable, and she could not understand why an act of friendship should have to be expiated like a crime, and in a way so painful to her pride. She felt that she and her husband would never be able to reach an understanding, and this being so it did not greatly matter which of the two was at fault. 'I guess it was our parents, really, for making us so different,' was her final summing up to Laura Testvalley, in the course of that first unbosoming.

The astringent quality of Miss Testvalley's sympathy had always acted on Annabel like a tonic. Miss Testvalley was not one to weep with you, but to show you briskly why there was no cause for weeping. Now, however, she remained silent for a long while after listening to her pupil's story; and when she spoke, it was with a new softness. 'My poor Nan, life makes ugly faces at us sometimes, I know.'

Annabel threw herself on the brown cashmere bosom

which had so often been her refuge. 'Of course you know, you darling old Val. I think there's nothing in the world you don't know.' And her tears broke out in a releasing shower.

Miss Testvalley let them flow; apparently she had no bracing epigram at hand. But when Nan had dried her eyes, and tossed back her hair, the governess remarked quietly: 'I'd like you to try a change of air first; then we'll talk this all over. There's a good deal of fresh air in this house, and I want you to ventilate your bewildered little head.'

Annabel looked at her with a certain surprise. Though Miss Testvalley was often kind, she was seldom tender; and Nan had a sudden intuition of new forces stirring under the breast-plate of brown cashmere. She looked again, more attentively, and then said: 'Val, your hair's grown ever so much thicker; and you do it in a new way.'

'I – do I?' For the first time since Annabel had known her, Miss Testvalley's brown complexion turned to a rich crimson. The colour darted up, flamed and faded, all in a second or two; but it left the governess's keen little face suffused with a soft inner light like – why, yes, Nan perceived with a start, like that velvety glow on Conchita's delicate cheek. For a moment, neither of the women spoke; but some quick current of understanding seemed to flash between them.

Miss Testvalley laughed. 'Oh, my hair . . . you think? Yes; I have been trying a new hair-lotion – one of those wonderful French things. You didn't know I was such a vain old goose? Well, the truth is, Lady Churt was staying here (you know she's a cousin); and after she left, one of the girls found a bottle of this stuff in her room, and just for fun we – that is, I . . . well, there's my silly secret . . .' She laughed again, and tried to flatten her upstanding ripples with a pedantic hand. But the ripples sprang up defiantly, and so did her colour. Nan kept an intent gaze on her.

'You look ten years younger, you look *young*, I mean, Val dear,' she corrected herself with a smile.

'Well, that's the way I want you to look, my child –. No; don't ring for your maid – not yet! First let me look through your dresses, and tell you what to wear this evening. You know, dear, you've never thought enough about the little things; and one fine day, if one doesn't, they may suddenly grow into tremendously big ones.' She lowered her fine lids. 'That's the reason I'm letting my hair wave a little more. Not *too* much, you think? . . . Tell me, Nan, is your maid clever about hair?'

Nan shook her head, 'I don't believe she is. My mother-in-law found her for me,' she confessed, remembering Conchita's ironic comment on the horn buttons of her dressing-gown.

PRESENTLY Lady Glenloe appeared, brisk and brown, in rough tweed and shabby furs. She was as insensible to heat and cold as she was to most of the finer shades of sensation, and her dress always conformed to the calendar without taking account of such unimportant trifles as latitudes.

'Ah, I'm glad you've got a good fire. They tell me it's very cold this evening. So delighted you've come, my dear; you must need a change and a rest after a series of those big Longlands parties. I've always wondered how your mother-in-law stood the strain . . . Here you'll find only the family; we don't go in for any ceremony at Champions – but I hope you'll like being with my girls . . . By the way, dinner may be a trifle late; you won't mind? The fact is, Sir Helmsley Thwarte sent a note this morning to ask if he might come and dine, and bring his son, who's at Honourslove. You know Sir Helmsley, of course? And Guy – he's been with you at Longlands, hasn't he? We must all drive over to Honourslove . . . Sir Helmsley's a most friendly neighbour; we see him here very often, don't we, Miss Testvalley?'

The governess's head was bent to the grate, from which a coal had fallen. 'When Mr Thwarte's there, Sir Helmsley naturally likes to take him about, I suppose,' she murmured to the tongs.

'Ah, just so! – Guy ought to marry,' Lady Glenloe announced. 'I must get some young people to meet him the next time he comes ... You know there was an unfortunate marriage at Rio – but luckily the young woman died ... leaving him a fortune, I believe. Ah, I must send word at once to the cook that Sir Helmsley likes his beef rather underdone ... Sir Helmsley's very particular about his food ... But now I'll leave you to rest, my dear. And don't make yourself too fine. We're used to pot-luck at Champions.'

ANNABEL, left alone, stood pondering before her glass. She was to see Guy Thwarte that evening – and Miss Testvalley had reproached her for not thinking enough about the details of her dress and hair. Hairdressing had always been a much-discussed affair among the St George ladies, but something winged and impatient in Nan resisted the slow torture of adjusting puffs and curls. Regarding herself as the least noticeable in a group where youthful beauty carried its torch so high, and convinced that, wherever they went, the other girls would always be the centre of attention, Nan had never thought it worth while to waste much time on her inconspicuous person. The Duke had not married her for her beauty – how could she imagine it, when he might have chosen Virginia? Indeed, he had mentioned, in the course of his odd wooing, that beautiful women always frightened him, and that the qualities he especially valued in Nan were her gentleness and her inexperience – 'And certainly I was inexperienced enough,' she meditated, as she stood before the mirror; 'but I'm afraid he hasn't found me particularly gentle.'

She continued to study her reflection critically, wondering whether Miss Testvalley was right, and she owed it to herself to dress her hair more becomingly, and wear her jewels as if she hadn't merely hired them for a fancy-ball. (The comparison was Miss Testvalley's.) She could imagine taking an interest in her hair, even studying the effect of a flower or a ribbon skilfully placed; but she knew she could never feel at ease under the weight of the Tintagel heirlooms. Luckily the principal pieces, ponderous coronets and tiaras, massive necklaces and bracelets hung with stones like rocs' eggs, were locked up in a London bank, and would probably not be imposed upon her except at Drawing-rooms or receptions for foreign sovereigns; yet even the less ceremonious ornaments, which Virginia or Conchita would have carried off with such an air, seemed too imposing for her slight presence.

But now, for the first time, she felt a desire to assert herself, to live up to her opportunities. 'After all, I'm Annabel Tintagel, and as I can't help myself I might as well try to make the best of it.' Perhaps Miss Testvalley was right. Already she seemed to breathe more freely, to feel a new air in her lungs. It was her first escape from the long oppression of Tintagel and Longlands, and the solemn London house; and freed from the restrictions they imposed, and under the same roof with her only two friends in the great lonely English world, she felt her spirits rising. 'I know I'm always too glad or too sad – like that girl in the German play that Miss Testvalley read to me,' she said to herself; and wondered whether Guy Thwarte knew Clärchen's song, and would think her conceited if she told him she had always felt that a little bit of herself was Clärchen. 'There are so many people in me,' she thought; but tonight the puzzling idea of her multiplicity cheered instead of bewildering her ... 'There can't be too many happy Nans,' she thought with a smile, as she drew on her long gloves.

That evening her maid had had to take her hair down twice before each coil and ripple was placed to the best advantage of her small head, and in proper relation to the diamond briar-rose on the shoulder of her coral pink *poult-de-soie*.

When she entered the drawing-room she found it empty;

but the next moment Guy Thwarte appeared, and she went up to him impulsively.

'Oh, I'm so glad you're here. I've been wanting to tell you how sorry I am to have behaved so stupidly the day you found me in the temple –' 'of Love,' she had been about to add; but the absurdity of the designation checked her. She reddened and went on: 'I wanted to write and tell you; but I couldn't. I'm not good at letters.'

Guy was looking at her, visibly surprised at the change in her appearance, and the warm animation of her voice. 'This is better than writing,' he rejoined, with a smile. 'I'm glad to see you so changed – looking so . . . so much happier . . .'

('Already?' she reflected guiltily, remembering that she had been away from Longlands only a few hours!)

'Yes; I am happier. Miss Testvalley says I'm always going up and down . . . And I wanted to tell you – do you remember Clärchen's song?' she began in an eager voice, feeling her tongue loosened and her heart at ease with him again.

Lady Glenloe's ringing accents interrupted them. 'My dear Duchess! You've been looking for us? I'm so sorry. I had carried everybody off to my son's study to see this extraordinary new thing – this telephone, as they call it. I brought it back with me the other day from the States. It's a curious toy; but to you, of course, it's no novelty. In America they're already talking from one town to another – yes actually! Mine goes only as far as the lodge, but I'm urging Sir Helmsley Thwarte to put one in at Honourslove, so that we can have a good gossip together over the crops and the weather . . . But he says he's afraid it will unchain all the bores in the county . . . Sir Helmsley, I think you know the Duchess? I'm going to persuade her to put in a telephone at Longlands . . . We English are so backward. They have them in all the principal hotels in New York; and when I was in St Petersburg last winter they were actually talking of having one between the Imperial Palace and Tsarskoë –'

The old butler appeared to announce dinner, and the procession formed itself, headed by Annabel on the arm of the son from the Petersburg Embassy.

'Yes, at Tsarskoë I've seen the Empress talking over it herself. She uses it to communicate with the nurseries,' the diplomatist explained impressively; and Nan wondered why they were all so worked up over an object already regarded as a domestic utensil in America. But it was all a part of the novelty and excitement of being at Champions, and she thought with a smile how much less exhilarating the subjects of conversation at a Longlands dinner would have been.

# TWENTY-EIGHT

THE CHAMPIONS PARTY CHOSE A MILD DAY OF FEBRUARY FOR the drive to Honourslove. The diplomatic son conducted the Duchess, his mother and Miss Testvalley in the wagonette, and the others followed in various vehicles piloted by sons and daughters of the house. For two hours they drove through the tawny winter landscape bounded by hills veiled in blue mist, traversing villages clustered about silver-grey manor-houses, and a little market town with a high street bordered by the wool-merchants' stately dwellings, and guarded by a sturdy church-tower. The dark green of rhododendron plantations made autumn linger under the bare woods; on house fronts sheltered from the wind the naked jasmine was already starred with gold. This merging of the seasons, so unlike the harsh break between summer and winter in America, had often touched Nan's imagination; but she had never felt as now the mild loveliness of certain winter days in England. It all seemed part of the unreality of her sensations, and as the carriage turned in at the gates of Honourslove, she recalled her only other visit there, when she and Guy Thwarte had stood alone on the terrace before the house, and found not a word to say. Poor Nan St George – so tongue-tied and bewildered by the surge of her feelings; why had no one taught her the words for them? As the car-

riage drew up before the door she seemed to see her own pitiful figure of four years ago flit by like a ghost; but in a
moment it vanished in the warm air of the present.

The day was so soft that Lady Glenloe insisted on a turn
through the gardens before luncheon; and, as usual when a
famous country house is visited, the guests found themselves
following the prescribed itinerary – saying the proper things
about the view from the terrace, descending the steep path to
the mossy glen of the Love, and returning by the walled gardens and the chapel.

Their host, heading the party with the Duchess and Lady
Glenloe, had begun his habitual and slightly ironic summary
of the family history. Lady Glenloe lent it an inattentive ear;
but Annabel hung on his words, and always quick to discover
an appreciative listener, he soon dropped his bantering note
to unfold the romantic tale of the old house. Annabel felt
that he understood her questions, and sympathized with her
curiosity, and as they turned away from the chapel he said,
with his quick smile: 'I see Miss Testvalley was right, Duchess
– she always is. She told me you were the only foreigner she'd
ever known who cared for the real deep-down England,
rather than the sham one of the London drawing-rooms.'

Nan flushed with pride; it still made her as happy to be
praised by Miss Testvalley as when the little brown governess
had sniffed appreciatively at the posy her pupil had brought
her on her first evening at Saratoga.

'I'm afraid I shall always feel strange in London drawing-
rooms,' Nan answered; 'but that hidden-away life of England,
the old houses and their histories, and all the far-back things
the old people hand on to their grandchildren – they seem so
natural and home-like. And Miss Testvalley, who's a foreigner too, has shown me better than anybody how to appreciate them.'

'Ah – that's it. We English are spoilt; we've ceased to feel
the beauty, to listen to the voices. But you and she come to it

with fresh eyes and fresh imaginations – you happen to be blessed with both. I wish more of our Englishwomen felt it all as you do. After luncheon you must go through the old house, and let it talk to you ... My son, who knows it all even better than I do, will show it to you ...'

'You spoke the other day about Clärchen's song; the evening my father and I drove over to dine at Champions,' Guy Thwarte said suddenly.

He and Annabel, at the day's end, had drifted out again to the wide terrace. They had visited the old house, room by room, lingering long over each picture, each piece of rare old furniture or tapestry, and already the winter afternoon was fading out in crimson distances overhung by twilight. In the hall Lady Glenloe had collected her party for departure.

'Oh, Clärchen? Yes – when my spirits were always jumping up and down Miss Testvalley used to call me Clärchen, just to tease me.'

'And doesn't she, any longer? I mean, don't your spirits jump up and down any more?'

'Well, I'm afraid they do sometimes. Miss Testvalley says things are never as bad as I think, or as good as I expect – but I'd rather have the bad hours than not believe in the good ones, wouldn't you? What really frightens me is not caring for anything any more. Don't you think that's worse?'

'That's the worst, certainly. But it's never going to happen to you, Duchess.'

Her face lit up. 'Oh, do you think so? I'm not sure. Things seem to last so long – as if in the end they were bound to wear people out. Sometimes life seems like a match between one's self and one's gaolers. The gaolers, of course, are one's mistakes; and the question is, who'll hold out longest? When I think of that, life, instead of being too long, seems as short as a winter day ... Oh, look, the lights already, over there in the valley . . . this day's over. And suddenly you find you've missed your chance. You've been beaten . . .'

'No, no; for there'll be other days soon. And other chances. Goethe was a very young man when he wrote Clärchen's song. The next time I come to Champions I'll bring *Faust* with me, and show you some of the things life taught him.'

'Oh, are you coming back to Champions? When? Before I leave?' she asked eagerly; and he answered:

'I'll come whenever Lady Glenloe asks me.'

Again he saw her face suffused with one of its Clärchen-like illuminations, and added, rather hastily: 'The fact is, I've got to hang about here on account of the possible by-election at Lowdon. Ushant may have told you –'

The illumination faded. 'He never tells me anything about politics. He thinks women oughtn't to meddle with such things.'

Guy laughed. 'Well, I rather believe he's right. But meanwhile, here I am, waiting rather aimlessly until I'm called upon to meddle . . . And as soon as Champions wants me I'll come.'

'In Sir Helmsley's study he and Miss Testvalley were standing together before Sir Helmsley's copy of the little Rossetti Madonna. The ladies of the party had been carried off to collect their wraps, and their host had seized the opportunity to present his watercolour to Miss Testvalley. 'If you think it's not too bad –'

Miss Testvalley's colour rose becomingly. 'It's perfect, Sir Helmsley. If you'll allow me, I'll show it to Dante Gabriel the next time I go to see the poor fellow.' She bent appreciatively over the sketch. 'And you'll let me take it off now?'

'No. I want to have it framed first. But Guy will bring it to you. I understand he's going to Champions in a day or two for a longish visit.'

Miss Testvalley made no reply, and her host, who was beginning to know her face well, saw that she was keeping back many comments.

'You're not surprised?' he suggested.

'I – I don't know.'

Sir Helmsley laughed. 'Perhaps we shall all know soon. But meanwhile let's be a little indiscreet. Which of the daughters do you put your money on?'

Miss Testvalley carefully replaced the watercolour on its easel. 'The . . . the daughters?'

'Corisande or Kitty . . . Why, you must have noticed. The better pleased Lady Glenloe is, the more off-hand her manner becomes. And just now I heard her suggesting to my son to come back to Champions as soon as he could, if he thought he could stand a boring family party.'

'Ah – yes.' Miss Testvalley remained lost in contemplation of her watercolour. 'And you think Lady Glenloe approves?'

'Intensely, judging from her indifferent manner.' Sir Helmsley stroked his short beard reflectively. 'And I do too. Whichever of the young ladies it is, *cela sera de tout repos.* Cora's eyes are very small; but her nose is straighter than Kitty's. And that's the kind of thing I want for Guy: something safe and unexciting. Now that he's managed to scrape together a little money – the first time a Thwarte has ever done it by the work of his hands or his brain – I dread his falling a victim to some unscrupulous woman.'

'Yes,' Miss Testvalley acquiesced, a faint glint of irony in her fine eyes. 'I can imagine how anxious you must be.'

'Oh, desperately; as anxious as the mother of a flirtatious daughter –'

'I understand that.'

'And you make no comment?'

'I make no comment.'

'Because you think in this particular case I'm mistaken?'

'I don't know.'

Sir Helmsley glanced through the window at the darkening terrace. 'Well, here he is now. And a lady with him. Shall we toss a penny on which it is – Corisande or Kitty? Oh – no! Why, it's the little Duchess, I believe . . .'

Miss Testvalley still remained silent.

'Another of your pupils!' Sir Helmsley continued, with a teasing laugh. He paused, and added tentatively: 'And perhaps the most interesting – eh?'

'Perhaps.'

'Because she's the most intelligent – or the most unhappy?'

Miss Testvalley looked up quickly. 'Why do you suggest that she's unhappy?'

'Oh,' he rejoined, with a slight shrug, 'because you're so incurably philanthropic that I should say your swans would often turn out to be lame ducks.'

'Perhaps they do. At any rate, she's the pupil I was fondest of and should most wish to guard against unhappiness.'

'Ah –' murmured Sir Helmsley, on a half-questioning note.

'But Lady Glenloe must be ready to start; I'd better go and call the Duchess,' Miss Testvalley added, moving towards the door. There was a sound of voices in the hall, and among them Lady Glenloe's, calling out: 'Cora, Kitty – has anyone seen the Duchess? Oh, Mr Thwarte, we're looking for the Duchess, and I see you've been giving her a last glimpse of your wonderful view . . .'

'Not the last, I hope,' said Guy smiling, as he came forward with Annabel.

'The last for today, at any rate; we must be off at once on our long drive. Mr Thwarte, I count on you for next Saturday. Sir Helmsley, can't we persuade you to come too?'

THE drive back to Champions passed like a dream. To secure herself against disturbance, Nan had slipped her hand into Miss Testvalley's, and let her head droop on the governess's shoulder. She heard one of the Glenloe girls whisper: 'The

Duchess is asleep,' and a conniving silence seemed to enfold her. But she had no wish to sleep: her wide-open eyes looked out into the falling night, caught the glint of lights flashing past in the High Street, lost themselves in the long intervals of dusk between the villages, and plunged into deepening night as the low glimmer of the west went out. In her heart was a deep delicious peace such as she had never known before. In this great lonely desert of life stretching out before her she had a friend – a friend who understood not only all she said, but everything she could not say. At the end of the long road on which the regular rap of the horses' feet was beating out the hours, she saw him standing, waiting for her, watching for her through the night.

# TWENTY-NINE

'DO YOU KNOW, I THINK NAN'S COMING TO STAY NEXT WEEK!'

Mrs Hector Robinson laid down the letter she had been perusing and glanced across the funereal architecture of the British breakfast-table at her husband, who, plunged in *The Times*, sat in the armchair facing her. He looked up with the natural resentment of the male Briton disturbed by an untutored female in his morning encounter with the news. 'Nan –?' he echoed interrogatively.

Lizzy Robinson laughed – and her laugh was a brilliant affair, which lit up the midwinter darkness of the solemn pseudo-gothic breakfast-room at Belfield.

'Well, Annabel, then; Annabel Duchess –'

'The – not the Duchess of Tintagel?'

Mr Robinson had instantly discarded *The Times*. He sat gazing incredulously at the face of his wife, on which the afterglow of her laugh still enchantingly lingered. Certainly, he thought, he had married one of the most beautiful women in England. And now his father was dead, and Belfield and the big London house, and the Scottish shooting-lodge, and the Lancashire mills which fed them – all for the last year had been his. Everything he had put his hand to had succeeded. But he had never pictured the Duchess of Tintagel at a Belfield house-party, and the vision made him a little dizzy.

The afterglow of his wife's amusement still lingered. 'The –
Duchess – of – Tintagel,' she mimicked him. 'Has there never
been a Duchess at Belfield before?'

Mr Robinson stiffened slightly. 'Not *this* Duchess. I understood the Tintagels paid no visits.'

'Ushant doesn't, certainly – luckily for us! But I suppose he
can't keep his wife actually chained up, can he, with all these
new laws, and the police prying in everywhere? At any rate,
she's been at Lady Glenloe's for the last month; and now she
wants to know if she can come here.'

Mr Robinson's stare had the fixity of a muscular contrac-
tion. 'She's written to ask –?'

His wife tossed the letter across the monuments in
Sheffield plate. 'There – if you don't believe me.'

He read the short note with a hurriedly assumed air of
detachment. 'Dear me – who else is coming? Shall you be
able to fit her in, do you think?' The detachment was
almost too perfect, and Lizzy felt like exclaiming: 'Oh,
come, my dear – don't overdo it!' But she never gave her
husband such hints except when it was absolutely necessary.

'Shall I write that she may come?' she asked, with an air of
wifely compliance.

Mr Robinson coughed – in order that his response should
not be too eager. 'That's for you to decide, my dear. I don't
see why not; if she can put up with a rather dull hunting
crowd,' he said, suddenly viewing his other guests from a new
angle. 'Let me see – there's old Dashleigh – I'm afraid he is a
bore – and Hubert Clyde, and Colonel Beagles, and of course
Sir Blasker Tripp for Lady Dick Marable – eh?' He smiled
suggestively. 'And Guy Thwarte; is the Duchess likely to
object to Guy Thwarte?'

Lizzy Robinson's smile deepened. 'Oh, no; I gather she
won't in the least object to him.'

'Why – what do you mean? You don't –'

In his surprise and agitation Mr Robinson abandoned all further thought of *The Times*.

'Well – it occurs to me that she may conceivably have known he was coming here next week. I know he's been at Champions a good deal during the month she's been spending there. And I – well, I should certainly have risked asking him to meet her, if he hadn't already been on your list.'

Mr Robinson looked at his wife's smile, and slowly responded to it. He had always thought he had a prompt mind, as quick as any at the uptake; but there were times when this American girl left him breathless, and even a little frightened. Her social intuitions were uncannily swift; and in his rare moments of leisure from politics and the mills he sometimes asked himself if, with such gifts of divination, she might not some day be building a new future for herself. But there was a stolid British baby upstairs in the nursery, and Mr Robinson was richer than anybody she was likely to come across, except old Blasker Tripp, who of course belonged to Conchita Marable. And she certainly seemed happy, and absorbed in furthering their joint career . . . But his chief reason for feeling safe was the fact that her standard of values was identical with his own. Strangely enough, this lovely alien who had been swept into his life on a brief gust of passion, proved to have a respect as profound as his for the concrete realities, and his sturdy unawareness of everything which could not be expressed in terms of bank accounts or political and social expediency. It was as if he had married Titania, and she had brought with her a vanload of ponderous mahogany furniture exactly matching what he had grown up with at Belfield. And he knew she had her eye on a peerage . . .

Yes; but meanwhile –. He picked up *The Times*, and began to smooth it out with deliberation, as though seeking a pretext for not carrying on the conversation.

'Well, Hector –?' his wife began impatiently. 'I suppose I

shall have to answer this.' She had recovered Annabel's letter.

Her husband still hesitated. 'My dear – I should be only too happy to see the Duchess here . . . But . . .' The more he reflected, the bigger grew the But suddenly looming before him. 'Have you any way of knowing if – er – the Duke approves?'

Lizzy again sounded her gay laugh. 'Approves of Nan's coming here?'

Her husband nodded gravely, and as she watched him her own face grew attentive. She had learned that Hector's ideas were almost always worth considering.

'You mean . . . he may not like her inviting herself here?'

'Her doing so is certainly unconventional.'

'But she's been staying alone at Champions for a month.'

Mr Robinson was still dubious. 'Lady Glenloe's a relative. And besides, her visit to Champions is none of our business. But if you have any reason to think –'

His wife interrupted him. 'What I think is that Nan's dying of boredom, and longing for a change; and if the Duke let her go to Champions, where she was among strangers, I don't see how he can object to her coming here, to an old friend from her own country. I'd like to see him refuse to let her stay with me,' cried Lizzy in what her husband called her 'Hail Columbia voice'.

Mr Robinson's frown relaxed. Lizzy so often found the right note. This was probably another instance of the advantage, for an ambitious man, of marrying someone by nationality and upbringing entirely detached from his own social problems. He now regarded as a valuable asset the breezy independence of his wife's attitude, which at first had alarmed him. 'It's one of the reasons of their popularity,' he reflected. There was no doubt that London society was getting tired of pretences and compliances, of conformity and uniformity. The free and easy Americanism of this little band of invaders had taken the world of fashion by storm, and Hector Robinson was too alert not to have noted the renovation of the social atmosphere. 'Wherever the men are amused, fashion is bound to follow,' was one of Lizzy's axioms; and certainly, from their future sovereign to his most newly knighted subject, the men *were* amused in Mayfair's American drawing-rooms.

*[At this point the manuscript breaks off. What follows is a new ending by Angela Mackworth-Young based on Edith Wharton's synopsis (see page 412), and on the screenplays for the television series by Maggie Wadey.]*

BOOK

# IV

# THIRTY

In the course of her lengthy unburdenings to Miss Testvalley at Champions, Nan steadfastly refused to speak ill of Ushant; she merely recounted the events at Longlands and her own feelings in the face of them, but Miss Testvalley's heart grew heavy as she listened. The comfort she drew from Nan's steady return to health was mingled with a sense of her own complicity in the sad affair that was Nan's marriage.

Miss Testvalley tried to console herself. The five American girls had so successfully stormed the bastions of English society that Miss March had dubbed them 'The Buccaneers'. They were the envy of Old New York, but that was cold comfort to Laura Testvalley. She tried once more: Conchita Marable had landed on her feet and would remain on them, so long as she contrived to find the necessary money; and the Elmsworth girls' marriages were fashioned from sturdy stuff. Mab Elmsworth had refused the hand of the Duke of Falmenneth and accepted instead a dashing, intelligent young captain in the Guards. But still Miss Testvalley would not be consoled. She blamed herself for the fate of the St George girls, particularly that of Nan St George. They would have fared far better, she told herself, if they had never come to England. Why had she uprooted them so thoughtlessly? Why hadn't she properly considered the likely consequences?

Jacky March informed Miss Testvalley that Seadown still visited Idina Churt when it suited him, and yet he considered it his divine right to plunder Virginia's fortune to support himself (and Lady Churt); and as for Ushant, why, oh why, hadn't she caught Nan fast and kept her from him when he had made it plain that he meant to marry her? She had been such a child then . . . .

But to Nan, it was the sweetest relief to confide in her beloved Val. There was no one so patient in all the world and no one more understanding. At first she had been reluctant to tell Miss Testvalley everything, thinking it disloyal and believing it her duty to shoulder her burden alone; but as Miss Testvalley coaxed the causes of her obvious unhappiness from her, Nan's burden grew lighter and she opened her heart to Miss Testvalley.

'Oh Val,' Nan said, one cold bright morning, 'I've made such a dreadful mistake. I loved Tintagel – the place I mean – and I thought, because I loved the place, that I loved the man. But I did not love the man . . . I know that now.' Nan's tears dampened Miss Testvalley's brown cashmere. 'I've tried and tried to be a good duchess . . . and a good wife – they're not the same thing you know – but each time I think I understand what they want of me I . . . Oh Val . . . darling Val . . . please help me become more like them.'

Miss Testvalley began, automatically, to explain a duchess's duties and public obligations, but Nan's sudden burst of laughter interrupted her flow. 'Oh dearest Val,' she laughed, and she wiped at her tears with the back of her hand, 'I *know* by now what's expected of a duchess, but what's so dreadful is there's no room for *me*, for Nan St George, inside the kind of duchess they want.' Nan sat up. 'Ushant and the Dowager want something . . . someone . . . utterly without ideas of her own . . . they want . . . Oh Val, they don't want me, they want someone who will drudge about performing the necessary duties without changing a thing; they don't want a person at all. They want a tradition.'

Miss Testvalley's eyes filled with tears as she thought how easily she could have discouraged the stammering young Duke when he came to Runnymede . . . if only she had. She asked herself over and over again why she had not. Had she become so engaged in the social success of the American heiresses, and her own part in their success, that she had deliberately shut her eyes to the nature of those upon whom such 'success' depended? Why hadn't she stopped to consider the price that might have to be paid for such a 'success'? Why hadn't she acknowledged what she knew . . . that Nan's wit and originality, her sensitivity and her intelligence, would never flourish in the arid Longlands climate? And was it 'success' to capture one of England's most illustrious dukes for a husband, only to have one's very self dismissed? The mediocrity of the Duke's behaviour towards Nan disgusted Miss Testvalley, but her own part in condemning Nan to such a life disgusted her even more.

Miss Testvalley's heart was full of remorse. 'My silence and my failure to act have made me an accomplice. I have colluded in this unhappy marriage,' she told herself when she was alone. 'Nan St George's spirit has been buried alive, and I have stood by . . . no, far worse, I have helped to dig the grave. But I cannot,' she vowed to her reflection in the dressing-table glass, 'and I shall not, ever, be party to a second burial.'

Miss Testvalley advised Nan to take long walks, 'to strengthen the body and to clear the mind,' and Nan had found the bracing winter winds agreeably invigorating. Her colour returned and her mind was cleared of its confusion as she leaned into the wind and drank in the sharp sparkling air. She strode out over the hills that surrounded Champions and she felt the blood surging in her veins. And if, at times, she paused to find her bearings, it was so that she might look back towards the house that had become her refuge; so that she might think, once more, of her governess and of their long restorative conversations together. The stark winter beauty of the Cotswold hills formed the backdrop against which familiar Nan St George regained her footing. And this Nan St George absorbed the beauty of the countryside and saw everything with reawakened intensity.

She thought about the conversation she had had with Miss Testvalley that very morning. She had told Miss Testvalley that she had resolved to make peace with her gaolers, 'my past mistakes', and by this means, she was certain, her gaolers would cease to imprison her and she would regain her freedom.

But Nan had been surprised to detect a certain resistance to this idea in Miss Testvalley's response; she had believed that her governess would approve. 'I do not doubt that you should take responsibility for your past mistakes Annabel, indeed it is right that you should . . . but only for those mistakes that were made when you knew precisely what you were doing,' said Miss Testvalley with a curious expression in her burning black eyes. 'It is admirable, Annabel, that you have decided to live with the consequences of those mistakes, but there are some mistakes that are never entirely of our own making . . . mistakes that, with the benefit of another's experience, would probably never have been made.' Nan's eyes had widened and Miss Testvalley's tone had softened. 'I have no desire, my dearest Nan, to watch you pay the price for making other people's mistakes.'

'Val?' said Nan incredulously, 'Val . . . whatever can you mean?' but Miss Testvalley would not be drawn further on the subject except to murmur that Nan bear this in mind when she made her peace with her 'gaolers'.

In the long journey of their conversations together Nan had the sense that after this last one she had arrived, if not at a destination, then at least at a clearing . . . at a place where the undergrowth was thinner and did not catch so often at her ankles. It was after this conversation that, as she examined her conscience on the subject of her past mistakes, she began to find it easier to believe in a place of her own in the world, in a place where what she thought and felt was acceptable and not mistaken, even if what she thought and felt was not always what the world about her thought or felt. And as this sense of her self grew and flourished, so too did the love she felt for her governess who had shone the warm light of her own love into Nan's lonely life.

Nan often stayed out until it began to grow dark and, returning to Champions at dusk, she sat by the fire and watched the darkness gather outside. As the glow of the fire brightened, Nan St George – she was less and less able to think of herself as Annabel Tintagel – gazed at the dancing flames while the darkness gathered about her like an old friend. The darkness comforted her, soothed her and calmed her; this was the time of day when she thought her thoughts and dreamed her dreams, and this was the time of day when a gentle calm descended upon her and cocooned her.

'My goodness it's gloomy in here,' Lady Glenloe's ringing tones filled the room. 'I wonder that you can see anything.' Nan smiled and stood to light the lamps. Cora Glenloe started up from the windowseat and suddenly the room was full of sound and light. Lady Glenloe waved a letter over her head and announced triumphantly, 'Guy Thwarte has accepted my invitation,' she glanced down at the letter. 'He says that he would be delighted to stay with us at Champions until the Lowdon by-election is called.'

Lady Glenloe held the letter at arm's length and narrowed her eyes. 'Apparently it all depends upon the health of the present incumbent, Sir Hercules Loft. However,' said Lady Glenloe with a flourish, 'Mr Thwarte arrives at Champions tomorrow afternoon.' Lady Glenloe looked at her daughter and then she hesitated, suddenly at sea in the face of a subject quite alien to her, 'I'm sure, Cora,' she said, 'er . . . that it is time you and I examined your wardrobe.'

This was so unexpected from the sartorially insensible Lady Glenloe that Cora burst out, 'Mama,' while she tried unsuccessfully to suppress a giggle, 'you've never shown the slightest interest in my wardrobe. Can you mean the furniture? Or can you truly mean my clothes?' But Lady Glenloe had already left the room – quite obviously expecting Cora to follow her – and Cora, with a quizzical glance at Nan and a burst of laughter at this unexpected development, ran from the room. Nan returned to her fireside contemplation and smiled. Then she closed her eyes and wondered whether Guy would bring the books he had promised.

In the days that lay ahead, days whose difficulties were still unimagined, Nan St George was to draw upon the memory of these quiet times at Champions as she might draw upon water from some heavenly oasis. It was by this fire that she unearthed a strong new sense of herself, and it was in this room, during the weeks when Guy was at Champions, that she and he talked of all that was most dear to them; this room witnessed the dawn of a deep understanding between them.

For her part, Miss Testvalley had tried to dislike Guy Thwarte from the start. She had tried to dislike him when Nan told her that she and Guy had discussed the sonnets in *The House of Life*. She had thought it quite unsuitable (Annabel hardly knew the young man) but she could not, even then, find it in her heart to dislike him. She tried to dislike him while he stayed at Champions, but again she could not. How could she dislike a man who played so great a part in the restoration of a sense of self to Nan St George? And how could she dislike a man to whom his father was so clearly devoted? She could not.

Sir Helmsley told Miss Testvalley, in staccato bursts of admiration, so much of his son's achievements and of his character that Miss Testvalley was left in little doubt that Guy Thwarte was the physical embodiment of Sir Helmsley's own hopes and dreams. 'I'll lay a wager, Miss Testvalley,' said Sir Helmsley with a chuckle as they took a brisk walk up the drive, 'that there'll soon be a Thwarte once more in the House of Commons.'

'HE *knew* it wasn't an ordinary dog,' Nan said, 'he knew it in his heart.' Guy looked at her and found himself learning towards her. 'He saw the trail of fire that followed at the dog's heels and he knew.'

True to his word, Guy Thwarte had brought Goethe's *Faust* to Champions, and he and Nan had read it together. Now they sat on the windowseat in the morning-room, deep in discussion. 'But even though he saw what his heart showed him . . . he allowed the other man to explain it all away. Faust let the other man –'

'– Wagner,' said Guy.

'– Faust let Wagner convince him that he'd seen nothing but a plain old black poodle.' Nan leaned earnestly towards Guy, so close now that he could feel her warmth and he drew back to save himself from gathering her into his arms. 'I was willing him, *willing* him,' she said, 'not to take the poodle home with him. I knew he'd seen something dreadful . . . something beyond –'

A log tumbled in the grate and broke into a hissing shower. Nan started to her feet, and then she laughed at herself. She glanced over her shoulder at the gathering dusk and she lit the lamp on the table at Guy's elbow. She watched the warm light spread slowly across his features and she was suddenly unaccountably sad. 'We have to believe in what our hearts show us,' she said, and something in her tone touched Guy to his very core, 'and we must act accordingly . . . mustn't we? Even if the rest of the world says that what we see isn't there . . . isn't there at all.'

She turned quickly from his gaze and lit the lamps one by one. They hissed and flickered beneath her busy hands, and then, when the room was filled with a steady yellow glow, she turned back to Guy, who had not answered her. 'Don't you agree?' she said, in a tone that caught once more at his heart. 'Oh, Guy, do please tell me that you agree.'

Guy Thwarte agreed with his whole heart and he marvelled, not for the first time, at the spirit of this warm, intelligent young woman with whom he felt the existence of a mysterious understanding that, each time they met, grew ever stronger. And she seemed to have grown, to have flourished; she was so much more of a woman. And all this, it seemed to Guy Thwarte, had happened in the space of a few weeks at Champions. She spoke with a fluency, an openness, that he was certain she had not possessed before, and he found himself wondering, hoping, that perhaps her transformation owed something to his presence. Perhaps she had stayed away from Longlands in order to gather her strength for . . . for . . . but Guy's train of thought was interrupted by the irrepressible Cora Glenloe who burst into the room insisting that he play a game of cards with her before they changed for dinner. Guy accepted Cora's invitation with a mingled sense of relief and regret. He was beginning to feel that he should not spend too much time alone with Annabel Tintagel; he was no longer certain that he could trust himself not to declare something more, something much more, than friendship for her.

LADY Glenloe strode into the breakfast-room and took her place at the head of the table. Nan smiled a greeting to her and offered to fill her cup. It was a constant source of delight to Nan that Lady Glenloe's 'pot-luck' at Champions meant that there were no servants present in the breakfast-room – such a contrast to the liveried footmen who perpetually lined the walls at Longlands.

Lady Glenloe nodded pleasantly to Nan. 'I'm so glad Sir Helmsley's joined our party,' she said. 'I'm certain he shares my hopes.'

'What hopes, Lady Glenloe?' said Nan, smiling at her and idly wondering what new scheme Lady Glenloe might be getting up.

'Why my dear, my hopes for Cora and Mr Thwarte,' said Lady Glenloe, and Nan's blood froze. 'I saw them ride out early this morning – from my window –' continued Lady Glenloe cheerfully, sublimely unaware of Nan's agonized expression, 'they look so well together.' Lady Glenloe paused, but only to breathe. 'I really believe that Mr Thwarte is in love with my Cora – or about to be in love with my Cora – and I think that she, young as she is, could well be of the same mind . . . well . . . of the same heart. I'm certain that's why he accepted my invitation,' she said conspiratorially, although this was quite wasted on the paralysed Nan, 'and naturally I made it clear that he should stay for just as long as he wished.' Lady Glenloe sighed and smiled happily and then she looked closely at Nan for the first time since she had entered the room. 'But my dear, I do apologize . . . this can be of no interest to you whatsoever . . . the romantic ravings of a doting mother –'

The door opened and Miss Testvalley's entrance distracted Lady Glenloe. Nan was grateful to Miss Testvalley for her timely entrance, for she could not have replied to Lady Glenloe without betraying herself utterly. She felt as if she had been dealt a mortal blow and her body was suddenly heavier than she'd thought possible. Her mind was quite numb and she stared blankly across the table until Lady Glenloe's ringing tones eventually penetrated her stupor. Miss Testvalley was seated beside Lady Glenloe and the two were engaged in conversation and as her own agitated feelings quietened, Nan was conscious that Lady Glenloe's enthusiasm for her subject had made her quite insensible to her own uncharacteristic silence.

'So I thought a small celebration would be in order,' Lady Glenloe was saying.

'Is it wise to plan such a celebration just yet?' replied Miss Testvalley, her black eyes bright as she glanced at Nan.

'Why no . . .' said Lady Glenloe, the flood of her enthusiasm dammed for a moment, 'not just yet. How thoughtful you are Miss Testvalley . . . how thoughtful you are. Naturally I shall wait for Cora to give me a sign.' Lady Glenloe smiled and stood up, the subject closed for the moment. 'And now I must find Kitty. She's taken it into her head that she will become a writer, and – as you've no doubt noticed – she hardly leaves her room. She reads and writes all day with the windows tightly closed. I try to see to it that she breathes some fresh air every day . . .'

Lady Glenloe left the room and Miss Testvalley said, 'Perhaps it's time for you to be going on to Belfield . . . Annabel?'

Miss Testvalley rose and stood behind Nan, her hands on the latter's shoulders. 'I understand that Mr Thwarte has been invited . . . and I expect that it is still a little too soon to return to Longlands.' Miss Testvalley bent to look into Nan's face and, with a faint inclination of her head, she led Nan from the room.

THAT night, after supper, Guy Thwarte stood at the far end of Lady Glenloe's long drawing-room, beneath one of several maps of the Americas. His dark head was bent close to Nan's and he held a lamp to light the southern half of the map. Miss Testvalley watched them apprehensively – Nan's face was pale – but when the light from the lamp momentarily caught the expression on Guy Thwarte's face as he looked down at Nan, something deep within Miss Testvalley stirred.

'You've the necessary skill, I'm sure,' barked Sir Helmsley, startling Miss Testvalley to her feet. 'You know just how to attract the little Duchess's attention . . . don't you?' Miss

Testvalley smoothed her plum-coloured silk. 'My son has failed to engage anyone else in conversation since supper and,' he nodded energetically in the direction of Cora Glenloe who sat with Kitty by the fire, 'it's high time he did so.' Sir Helmsley's cheeks flamed above his auburn beard and he spun on his heel towards Nan and Guy, but Miss Testvalley laid a gently restraining hand on his arm. 'Annabel,' she called softly, and instantly Nan turned towards her, 'it's been a long day. I think I shall go upstairs.'

Nan gathered up her skirts and hurried across the room. 'Darling Val,' she said breathlessly, 'I've hardly spoken to you all evening. Do stay just a little longer.'

Miss Testvalley was troubled by Sir Helmsley's outburst and she did not sleep until dawn. And when at last she did sleep, she was disturbed by a strange dream. She saw Ushant and Guy, poised back to back, with pistols raised. When they paced away from each other Miss Testvalley tried to shout to them to stop, but, as in the manner of dreams, no sound came from between her frantically moving lips. She watched helplessly as the two turned to face each other, and then she saw a thick drifting mist swirl up behind the Duke and slowly, stealthily, the mist enveloped him. Guy's outline was clear against the morning sky, but his adversary could no longer be seen. Guy walked determinedly towards the place where he knew Ushant must be, pushing at the gathering mist with his hand.

Miss Testvalley woke with the words of a shouted warning to Guy Thwarte dying on her lips; she was covered with a fine film of sweat.

Miss Testvalley stood as still as the pillars of the porch that flanked her, heedless of the cold March wind that whipped the loose ends of her hair and tugged at the edges of her brown cashmere. She could still see Nan's sweet face through the carriage window and she could still hear the sound of the horses' hooves and the carriage wheels on the drive. She felt as if she was travelling from Champions to Belfield, and beyond, with Nan.

A warm hand touched Miss Testvalley's cold one. 'Miss Testvalley,' said Cora Glenloe, 'you've been standing out here for simply ages . . . I'm quite sure I heard the carriage leave centuries ago . . . and your hand is as cold as ice.' Cora tugged at Miss Testvalley's hand. 'Do please come inside Miss Testvalley,' she said, 'there's a blazing fire in the morning-room.'

# THIRTY-ONE

SIR HELMSLEY SLAPPED GUY HEARTILY ON THE BACK. 'AT last,' he said, 'at long long last, a Thwarte returns to take his rightful place in the House of Commons . . . now there's a thing. Delighted with you my boy, absolutely delighted.' Sir Helmsley turned away to hide the extent of his delight from his son, but Guy saw his father's tears.

'It wasn't an easy battle,' he began, to give Sir Helmsley time to recover himself, 'at least not at the beginning.'

Sir Helmsley turned back to his son. 'Should think not,' he said, 'nothing worth the candle ever is. But you beat that jumped-up Glaswegian well enough in the end.' Sir Helmsley's expression became grave, 'Though you'll have to drop those radical Liberal ideas of yours – if you're not to have considerably tougher battles ahead.'

'Sir?' said Guy, surprised.

'You know very well what I mean,' said Sir Helmsley, but in his present euphoric state he did not pursue the subject. Instead he said simply, 'I shall go in now,' and Guy watched his father cross the terrace. 'Oh, by the by,' said Sir Helmsley, turning back to Guy, 'I've invited Lady Glenloe and her girls to celebrate your good fortune . . . I . . . er . . . I do believe young Cora has taken quite a fancy to you.' Sir Helmsley turned abruptly and disappeared into the house.

Guy remained outside, although it was a cold evening, because he knew that sleep would not come for some time. He walked down the steep path to the Love which glinted coldly at him in the moonlight, and sat on the cold ground with his head in his hands, trying to decide what to do, trying to expunge Annabel Tintagel's face from his mind and her being from his heart. Each time Sir Helmsley made reference to the Glenloes, and especially to Cora, Guy was immediately transported back to Champions but it was never Cora he saw, it was always Annabel. Annabel laughing, Annabel serious, Annabel's intelligent eyes smiling up at him, surely with something much more than friendship in them. And now that she was gone he felt empty, he felt as if she had taken a part of him with her to Belfield.

Guy stood up and shook his head vigorously. He walked briskly back up the path in the moonlight and through the walled gardens. The pale silver-grey stone of the chapel was almost white in the moonlight, and Guy, suddenly visited by yet another image of Annabel, pushed the door open and went inside. He sat down heavily and leaned his forehead against the hard wooden pew in front of him, breathing in its familiar smell. He closed his eyes.

Lizzy Robinson laughed. 'Why, my darling Nan,' she said, embracing her friend, 'you look better than I have ever seen you look . . . there's something altogether different about you . . . something more . . . you're not in love are you?' Lizzy's keen eyes searched Nan's but she didn't wait for an answer and Nan was glad of that. The two friends sat in Nan's bedroom at Belfield and Lizzy told Nan about herself and about Hector; about the new wing they planned to build at Belfield; about their son, Thomas, now almost one year old, and Lizzy told Nan that she was expecting another child. 'Might as well populate this gigantic old house as quickly as possible,' said Lizzy, her dark eyebrows arching. 'But tell me

Nan, how are you? And where did this elegantly dressed young duchess come from? And who is she dressing for? But – oh my – is that the time?' said Lizzy, glancing at the clock on the mantelpiece, 'I must hurry . . . we'll talk again later . . . there are so many things to do, to think about, with my house full of guests.' And Lizzy blew Nan a kiss and flew from the room.

Nan wondered whether she would tell Lizzy . . . perhaps she would tell Conchie . . . Conchie would understand completely and she would not give Nan away. Conchita knew just what it was like to be 'in love with one man and married to another', she had said so at Longlands, and now Nan saw that her own predicament precisely echoed Conchita's. She had not, until that moment, put it into words, but there it was staring her in the face, 'I am in love with one man and married to another'. Nan St George was in love with Guy Thwarte, and she missed him dreadfully. Her mind was never free of him . . . he was all she wished to talk about and all she knew she must not talk about. She longed to see his face, to hear his voice, to watch him move . . . and she dreaded her return to Longlands and to Ushant. She wanted to put it off for as long as possible; she didn't know what else to do.

Nan could no longer pretend to be Annabel Tintagel. She had never known who Annabel Tintagel was anyway and now, thanks in no small part to Guy Thwarte, she was able, truly and freely, to be herself. She felt strong . . . and she felt that, at last, she had found a long-lost, and yet utterly familiar, self. A self whom Guy Thwarte understood, without explanation, a self whom Ushant did not understand and never would.

Nan felt the strong current of communication that flowed between herself and Guy . . . and she felt as if she had been waiting for him all her life. Lady Glenloe's confidences – on that fateful morning at Champions – had shown Nan, with brutal clarity, just how strong were her own feelings for Guy

Thwarte. And never before had she felt such pleasure, such pain, nor such utter helplessness.

Miss Testvalley had made Nan's excuses for her, she had packed for her, and Nan had left Champions in a state of dreadful paralysis. After a month at Belfield her equilibrium had returned somewhat, but she could not help hoping, against hope, that Guy would come to her there. She saw him wherever she went, but still he did not come. Nan tormented herself with imaginings . . . of all manner of terrible things that had befallen Guy, and every evening in the drawing-room before dinner, she told herself that he would be the next person to walk through the door. But he never was.

Nan shook herself. She must gather her wits, she must think what to do, she must act sensibly. But she longed to see his face, to talk to him, to be near him. She had not known that it was possible to miss one person so very much.

NAN was the first down for dinner that evening and, as Lizzy and Hector's guests entered the room one by one, or in pairs, Nan played the same fateful game with herself. Each time the drawing-room door opened she half-closed her eyes, but each time she opened them the result was just as it had been on every other night at Belfield. Guy Thwarte did not enter the drawing-room and Nan knew, somewhere deep in her heart, that he would not.

The sound of the dinner gong echoed down the hall and Hector, wondering why Nan's luminous beauty had escaped his notice until now, proffered his arm. As they walked in to dinner Nan, in her best imitation of an inconsequential enquiry, said, 'I suppose Mr Thwarte will be here soon?'

'Oh,' said Hector, looking down into her shining eyes, 'surely Lizzy's told you?' Nan shook her head dumbly and Hector was surprised by the sudden disappointment he saw in her face. 'It must have slipped her mind,' he said, 'there's so much to do here . . . but Guy Thwarte won't be joining our party.' Nan watched her feet moving mechanically, one in front of the other, towards the dining-room. 'Sir Hercules Loft,' continued Hector, 'finally gave up the ghost . . . the by-election's been and gone, and Guy Thwarte is the new Liberal Member for Lowdon. I'm looking forward to hearing him speak from the Opposition benches . . . he'll make a fine opponent.'

When they entered the dining-room Nan was glad of Lizzy's murmured, 'Sir Blasker, would you take your place beside me,' and 'Why Nan, you're on Hector's right, of course,' and 'Mr Clyde would you sit between Lady Dick and Lady Tripp,' because she had, momentarily, lost her bearings. She made mechanical conversation and she caught Hector looking at her oddly and Conchita looking at her sympathetically (perhaps she had already guessed?), but she survived dinner without incident and afterwards she excused herself early.

LIZZY stood in the cavernous stone hall at Belfield and held out both hands for the telephone. 'Mr Robinson, Ma'am,' said the manservant. 'Thank you Steele,' said Lizzy as she grasped both halves of the instrument, 'thank you.' And then Lizzy shouted into the telephone as if she was shouting into Lady Brightlingsea's speaking trumpet. 'What darling? . . . Guy's maiden speech? . . . I'm so glad it went well . . . yes, yes we travel to London next week.'

Lizzy glanced up and saw Nan coming down the stairs. She looked dejected and pale and she was too thin, thought Lizzy, but she still had what Lizzy called her 'new look' about her, she had become the best-looking woman of them all. Lizzy took a deep breath and said, in what Hector called her 'Hail Columbia' voice, 'Darling, I shall bring Nan with us . . . yes . . . to London. It'll do her good . . . she needs . . . what? . . .

Because I've already invited the St Georges to stay for a few days . . . it's the least we can do while they're in London. Yes, she's right beside me and she's smiling. See you next week . . . 'bye darling, 'bye.'

# THIRTY-TWO

CONCHITA MARABLE STOOD IN THE DRAWING-ROOM OF HER London house in front of a dying fire. She stretched her arms up over her head and looked at herself in the glass above the mantelpiece. Her sallow skin glowed warmly in the candle-light and her red hair shone. Conchita smiled at her reflection and opened her enamelled cigarette case. The front door closed violently and Conchita slowly put down the cigarette case. Dick Marable appeared on the threshold, 'clinging on to the side of the door,' thought Conchita 'like a drowning man.'

Conchita fixed her husband with her pale aquamarine eyes. 'I thought I asked you not to come to the house without telling me first,' she said coldly.

Dick Marable stumbled into the room. 'I wanted to see you and . . . if I tell you I'm coming . . . you only make sure that you're not here.'

'I'm tired, Dickie, and you're drunk.'

'It's all part of the cure, Conchie darling, you know it is,' said Dick Marable, his words slurring into each other.

Conchita stood very still. 'What cure Dickie?'

'Alder says mercury's the thing, but I say whisky does the trick.'

Conchita sank into the chair behind her and put out a

hand to ward off her husband as he stumbled towards her.
'Don't worry Conchie,' he mumbled, 'he says you'll be all
right. It's been too long since you and I . . . he's sure you'll be
all right.' He crumpled to the floor at Conchita's feet, as if his
body had no substance, as if he were nothing more than his
clothes, and Conchita covered her beautiful mouth with her
hand, her pale eyes wide and frightened. Richard looked up
and nodded vigorously, drunkenly, three or four times, and
then he stretched out his arm towards Conchita. 'Conchie, I
must know,' he said, through lips that suddenly seemed
unable to form the words he strove for, 'Conchie . . . I know
Edward is mine,' and Conchita's big heart softened for she
knew what was coming, 'but Sophie . . . Sophie is mine too
. . . isn't she?' Conchita knelt on the floor beside the frail
form that was her husband. 'I mean to say,' he managed to
continue, 'there wasn't anyone else then, was there?'

'No,' said Conchita, 'there wasn't anyone else then,' and
she turned away to hide the tears of pity while her husband
let out an anguished cry and then sobbed in uncontrollable,
shuddering waves of relief.

Conchita stood up. 'I think you'd better stay the night,'
she said. 'I'll ask Mrs Flowers to prepare a bed for you. But
Dickie . . . please be gone in the morning . . . before the children wake.'

NAN St George sat beneath a tree in the park on a mild May
day. She had thrilled at the prospect of staying in London
because London was where Guy was . . . but she had been
hurt by Hector Robinson's insistence (she had finally confided in Lizzy and Conchita – they were too observant and
she could not keep it from them) that under the circumstances he could not allow Guy Thwarte to be a guest in his
house, not while Nan was under his roof. 'What you do with
your life Annabel,' he had said on her first morning in
London, 'is entirely your affair. But I do not intend to incur

the Duke's disapproval – or worse – for any reason, and there-fore, while you stay with us, Guy Thwarte shall not be our guest.'

It seemed to Nan that the whole world was conspiring to keep them apart and in her misery she took the only medi-cine she had ever known to work – long walks alone. But however she planned her walks, wherever else she intended to walk, she found herself drawn again and again to one place. Nan St George found herself outside the Palace of Westminster hoping for, longing for, a glimpse of Guy. And after a time, a time when she never once saw him outside the gates, she began to attend the debates.

She had just come from a debate that afternoon and, as always when she heard Guy speak, she was filled with pride and with a deep sympathy for the causes he espoused and the people he championed. He spoke so well, so eloquently, and so passionately. Watching from inside the extraordinary cage that was known – she laughed softly to herself – as the 'Ladies' Gallery', Nan longed to tell him how she felt.

Nan thought herself safe enough behind the brass grilles and metal latticework of the Ladies' Gallery; she knew she would not attract attention because the Members could not see into the Gallery from the floor of the House to identify their female visitors. 'Ridiculous,' Lizzy had said, 'Hector can't even see me when I come to hear him. What could they possibly be afraid of, those old fuddy-duddies . . . are they afraid that the mere sight of a woman might distract them from their arguments?'

The only people who saw Nan on her frequent visits were the other occupants of the Ladies' Gallery, and they seemed friendly enough. And it was such sweet pleasure to Nan to attend the debates. The sound of Guy's voice and the sight of his face drew her back to Champions time and time again, and as she watched him she remembered Miss Testvalley's parting words on the day she left Champions, 'The right

words will come when the time is right for them to be spoken,' she had said enigmatically. 'And you will know that
time, should it come.' Miss Testvalley had embraced Nan
and said, 'Now don't forget my promise . . . I shall come
straight to you if ever you should need me,' and she had
kissed Nan quickly and turned away. When Nan had looked
back through the carriage window she had seen Miss
Testvalley's slight figure dwarfed by the Champions' porch,
and she had watched Cora Glenloe come out to claim her.

'THE life of a duchess seems to be suiting you admirably well
. . . Duchess,' said Colonel St George affably, his eyes twin-
kling at Nan. 'You're looking as pretty as a peach.' Nan bit
her lip and looked down. 'Now, now Duchess,' said the
Colonel, lifting Nan's chin with his forefinger, 'I was paying
you a compliment.' Nan managed a wavering smile for her
father but, for the most part, she sat distractedly between her
parents in the dining-room at Claridges. 'Perhaps it's time
you paid a visit to the old folks, eh?' said the Colonel.

'My dear,' he addressed the silent Mrs St George across the
table, 'ain't that an idea? And bring that young duke of yours
along too. Might do him good to have a change of scenery.'

The Colonel patted Nan's hand affectionately but Nan
heard his voice as though it were travelling towards her from
the far end of a long dark tunnel that connected her with her
childhood. She remembered what he used to say to her all
those years ago: 'You just call on me child, when things want
straightening out.' Nan bit her lip again and, concentrating
hard on the ornate plasterwork above her head, she said, 'I
don't think I could persuade him to travel that far . . . he
doesn't think America is worthy of . . .' and here Nan broke
off helplessly and had to bite her trembling lip once more
before she managed, 'He doesn't think America is worthy of
his patronage.'

Colonel St George put his large hand on his daughter's

forearm and looked at her. Something akin to pain registered on his customarily benign features and later, when Mrs St George had retired, the Colonel found that he could not sleep. He went into the next room and lit a cigar and he paced about the room until dawn.

# THIRTY-THREE

'THIS WAY YOUR GRACE,' SAID THE USHER WITH A NOD OF recognition to Nan, 'Mrs Robinson.' The usher opened the door to the metal latticework enclosure and the two women passed him with a faint rustle of silk. Lizzy acknowledged the nods and smiles of the women who sat on the wooden seats inside the enclosure, and she and Nan took their places at the front.

Lizzy stretched her arm protectively along Nan's shoulders as the House debated noisily below them. Nan's dilemma touched Lizzy's heart and she wished there was something she could do for her. She smiled as Nan's face glowed. 'She must have seen him,' thought Lizzy and her heart bled for her friend as she watched her lean forward eagerly. Lizzy turned away from Nan and saw the familiar flurry of waving white papers below her as the Members attempted to catch the Speaker's eye.

'Mr Hector Robinson,' said the Speaker and Hector Robinson, the Conservative Member for Burton, remained standing on the Government benches, while the other Members settled down. 'I agree with my Right Honourable friend, the Member for Waredale,' said Hector, 'in every particular, and may I respectfully suggest to my Right Honourable friend the Prime Minister that urgent steps be taken to warn the Russians, in the strongest possible terms, against any attempt to blockade the Suez Canal.'

Lizzy lifted her hand from Nan's shoulders to the nape of her own neck. It suddenly seemed to her that the women ranged behind them on the wooden benches were much closer than usual, and that they radiated a searing heat. 'But, of course,' she smiled to herself, 'I am behaving ridiculously! It's merely my condition . . .' Lizzy's doctor had told her, only that morning, that he suspected she was carrying twins. Lizzy glanced sideways at Nan and thought how delighted she would be when she learned the news, and then she returned her attention to the debate. Below them, on the floor of the House, Guy Thwarte was on his feet waving his order paper from the Opposition benches, determined to catch the Speaker's eye.

'Mr Guy Thwarte,' said the Speaker.

'I would like to thank the Right Honourable Member for Burton for his concerns which is, rightly, the concern of the whole House. But I must say this. While we, on this side of the House, wholeheartedly support his sentiment, we must insist that an outright declaration of war against Russia be resisted. Russia has not yet occupied Constantinople, and still she may not, and we must, first and foremost, ensure the safety of the young men of these islands. It is our duty to remember that the lives of our young men are too precious by far to be squandered in unnecessary battle.'

A chorus of gruff male voices rang out 'Hear hear! Hear hear!' and then Hector Robinson was on his feet again. 'As the Right Honourable Member for Lowdon knows only too well . . .' but Hector's voice faded from Nan's ears as Guy's voice filled her head: '. . . that the lives of our young men are too precious by far to be squandered in unnecessary battle.' She was delighted with him.

\* \* \*

Nan looked about the oak-panelled room which was crowded with Members of Parliament murmuring congratulations or commiserations to each other.

'There they are,' said Lizzy, at Nan's elbow, and she quickened her step.

Guy Thwarte and Hector Robinson stood at the far end of the room and as Nan and Lizzy walked towards them, Nan was struck by their affability, their friendliness towards each other, the way Hector slapped Guy amiably on the back, despite their opposing political views, despite Hector's refusal to have Guy under his roof while she stayed with them. And she trembled at the sight of Guy and at the thought of speaking to him . . . she must behave naturally, she must not give herself away.

'You made your point well,' Hector was saying, 'but don't you think –?' Hector stopped, realizing that Guy was not listening. He watched as Guy attempted, unsuccessfully, to contain his surprise and delight at the sight of Nan St George.

'Congratulations, my Hector,' said Lizzy, her dark eyes burning with admiration for her husband, and then, turning to Guy, 'you both spoke well.' Lizzy held out her hand to Guy and several Members crowded around their little group, congratulating Hector or Guy, depending upon their political persuasion. Nan's eyes shone as she watched Guy, her head still full of the words of his speech, and he smiled back at her.

Hector and Guy introduced several Members to Lizzy and to Nan, but one fresh-faced young man, the Member for Waredale and a friend of Hector's, addressed Nan with something approaching hostility. 'So how does your Grace find our House?' he said, and seeing Nan's puzzled look he continued, 'when compared with the Other Place?' When Nan still hesitated, the young man's smile became a sneer. 'I refer, of course, to their Lordships' House.'

'Fascinating,' replied Nan, at length, belatedly saving herself (she had never set foot inside the House of Lords), 'quite fascinating . . . despite the curious cage you consider necessary to conceal us from you. I believe that the Peeresses' Gallery,' Nan rushed on with rising panic as the expression on the face of the young Member for Waredale grew sardonic, 'is quite open . . . is quite open to their Lordships' view.'

The young Member for Waredale was triumphant. 'Your Grace *believes*?' He paused for effect. 'But surely your Grace *knows* the precise situation of the Peeresses' Gallery.'

'His Grace has only made rare appearances in their Lordships' House since his marriage,' said Guy curtly, miraculously at Nan's side, and then, bending towards Nan he said, 'I'd like your opinion, your Grace,' and he took Nan's elbow and steered her away from the Member for Waredale across the crowded room. Nan turned her anxious eyes towards Guy.

'What do you want to ask me?' she faltered.

Guy smiled down at her. 'I wanted the opportunity to talk to you alone,' he said, and he inclined his head towards an empty corner of the room.

'Guy,' said Nan, 'Guy . . . I've been coming to see you . . . I couldn't stay away.'

'What do you mean?' said Guy, so anxiously that Nan wanted to touch him, to reassure him, but she knew that she could not, not in front of all these people. 'I've been coming to hear you . . . to see you . . . almost every day since I've been in London,' she said, at length.

'And the Member for Waredale's wife comes to hear him almost as often,' thought Guy with a shudder, but he only said, 'You've been coming to the House of Commons without telling me? . . . Were you never going to let me know you were here?'

'I was afraid,' replied Nan, and seeing the concern in Guy's eyes, she suddenly said, mock-seriously, in an attempt to tease him and to break the almost unbearable tension between them, 'I was afraid that it might ruin your career to be seen with a married woman.' Guy laughed despite himself and stepped away from Nan with an exaggerated movement. 'So long as we stay in public sight and keep, what? –' he stepped deliberately further away, '– eighteen inches between us? I'm sure my reputation will survive.'

They stood in silence for a few moments but, despite their apparent light-heartedness, they were uneasy. Eventually Guy said, 'Why did you come to London, Annabel?' and over her shoulder he caught Hector's disapproving glance from across the room.

'Because,' said Nan, suddenly miserable, 'I couldn't bear to go back home. Not yet. Because I suppose I knew we would meet again . . . eventually.' She looked up at him. 'Can I count on you as a friend?'

Guy raised his hand to touch Nan's arm and then quickly lowered it. Like Nan he was acutely aware of the circumstances in which they found themselves, and he felt that every pair of eyes in the room was directed towards them. 'I could hardly call myself anything less than a friend, but can I say "yes" without misleading you?'

Nan looked up and smiled a radiant smile; as always he understood her and she felt a surge of confidence. 'I can't think any further ahead,' she said, 'at least not yet.'

Guy smiled down at Nan and thought how beautiful she was at that moment and how vibrantly alive. Without another word she turned and together they walked back across the room towards the crowd of Members who surrounded Lizzy and Hector, the required eighteen inches separating them for all the world to see.

Miss Testvalley's position as governess to Cora and Kitty Glenloe at Champions afforded her a freedom that she had not known for many years. Lady Glenloe's unusually open and educated mind teemed with ideas for the edification of her daughters and she herself would, on occasion, tutor her daughters in certain subjects. This left Miss Testvalley with time on her hands, time that, she smiled at the thought, was spent pleasantly enough in the company of Sir Helmsley Thwarte. And Sir Helmsley served as a welcome diversion from her preoccupation with Nan.

They drove, at Sir Helmsley's customary breakneck speed, along a sloping open road between green fields. 'It is, as always, a delight to drive out with you, Miss Testvalley,' said Sir Helmsley, 'particularly when you are not surrounded by a flock of girls.' He urged the pony on.

Miss Testvalley smiled. 'Thank you,' she said.

'By the by,' he said, turning to her abruptly, 'what in God's name is the Duchess up to?'

Miss Testvalley was considerably taken aback, but she replied calmly enough, 'I'm sure she's not up to anything.'

'Then,' said Sir Helmsley looking directly into Miss Testvalley's eyes, 'what is my son up to, eh? You must have heard the rumours. The whole place is alive with the rumours.'

Laura Testvalley knew that Sir Helmsley would not believe her if she gave what she called a governess's answer (that she heard so much less than the servants), so she merely echoed him. 'Rumours?' she said.

'Goddammit woman,' said Sir Helmsley, 'I'm not deaf or blind. Nor, unfortunately are Ushant and his mother. I gather from the Dowager that Annabel is to be seen daily at the House of Commons. I repeat, what is my son up to? You know that I was laying odds on his growing interest in Cora Glenloe . . . only a month or two ago. Makes me feel a bit of a fool, but that's hardly the point. What I say is, if my son's chasing after our little American Duchess, he's playing with fire.'

Miss Testvalley, who had attempted to interrupt Sir

Helmsley's flow more than once, now said firmly, 'I'm sure he's doing no such thing.'

'No?' said Sir Helmsley. 'I'm not sure that I entirely trust you when it comes to young Annabel Tintagel. After all you are very fond of her, and she claims you for her favourite person in the whole world.'

The pony and trap moved quickly along the sloping open road. 'As you well know I have the highest hopes of my boy,' continued Sir Helmsley, 'and if he loses Ushant's patronage –'

'But surely Guy is independent now?' said Miss Testvalley.

'Country people vote with their landlord, Miss Testvalley. Guy can do nothing without Ushant's backing.' Sir Helmsley urged the pony on angrily and Miss Testvalley put up a hand to hold onto her hat, but her face showed no sign of fear or apprehension.

'Things may have changed,' shouted Sir Helmsley above the noise of the pony and trap, 'but they haven't changed that much. Men haven't changed that much.' He looked sideways at Miss Testvalley. 'Nor have women, come to that.'

'You should know,' said Miss Testvalley, well aware that she was being provocative and suddenly enjoying herself because the danger had passed, at least for the moment.

Sir Helmsley turned to Miss Testvalley and his smile spread upwards from his lips to his eyes, 'And may I know just what that remark is supposed to mean?' he said.

Miss Testvalley looked directly at Sir Helmsley who reined the pony in to an abrupt halt and waited for her reply. 'You are a man,' said Miss Testvalley, 'and I hear that you have considerable experience of women.'

'Oh, I see,' said Sir Helmsley. 'You are selective with your rumours. Some you hear and some you do not. Does this mean, Miss Testvalley, that there might be a possibility of negotiations . . . between us?'

'Negotiations?' echoed Miss Testvalley innocently.

Sir Helmsley's smile deepened but he looked away. 'Negotiations, my dear Miss Testvalley, between you and me,' he said, 'are long overdue. We cannot expect people of our age to have no past. But my past is past. Over. Done with.'

Miss Testvalley moved imperceptibly along the wooden seat. 'Sir Helmsley,' she said, 'I think, when you say such things, you should look me in the eye, so that I may judge whether I may believe you.'

Sir Helmsley looked into Miss Testvalley's burning black eyes and she inclined her head. Sir Helmsley's eyes told Miss Testvalley that he spoke the truth, at least truth enough for the present purpose, and she smiled at him and then nodded faintly. Sir Helmsley leaned forward and touched the curving lines beside Miss Testvalley's mouth with the tips of his fingers. Miss Testvalley did not resist his touch.

LAURA Testvalley stood in the middle of her room at Champions. It resembled all the rooms she had occupied in the great English houses of her former employers. It was large, the floorboards creaked beneath a worn carpet and the dark furniture was old, worn out, and badly upholstered. Her own few modest possessions were like points of light in the room, but tonight Laura Testvalley was less conscious of the gloom and general shabbiness of the room. She sat at her dressing-table looking at the packet that Sir Helmsley had pressed into her hand that afternoon. She had waited until now, until she was alone and certain that she would not be disturbed, before unwrapping it.

Laura took the card from its square white envelope and read, 'With sincere admiration, Helmsley.' Laura smiled and undid the tissue wrapping. Her hands flew to her face and she gasped as she gazed at a gloriously coloured, expensive silk shawl. Laura Testvalley picked up the shawl and held it to her cheek. She looked at herself in her glass and the colours of the shawl transformed her already happy face. She wrapped the shawl around her shoulders and stood up. She gave a soft cry of delight and then she twirled round and round so that the shawl flew about her, radiating its brilliant colours into the farthest corners of her gloomy room.

# THIRTY-FOUR

NAN LOOKED UP AT THE GREY SKY AND SHIVERED. THIS MILD season that the English called summer and that, in other cir-cumstances, she would have welcomed, suddenly irritated her and made her long for the harsh heat of a Saratoga sum-mer. She walked quickly with her head down and the soles of her boots rattled over the cobblestones as she tried to avoid the puddles. Rose, the faithful maid who had travelled with her since she had left Longlands, walked a little way behind her but Nan's heart was so heavy that she had forgotten Rose. The words of Ushant's message whirled about in Nan's mind; he had summoned her the way a master might sum-mon a servant and Nan's hands twisted and tore at the mes-sage they held beneath her wrap.

*Annabel. Understand Colonel and Mrs St George departed. Return Longlands. Or explain. If latter meet St Mary's Marylebone half-past ten Friday. Ushant.*

Nan became fearful when she thought of what she planned to say to Ushant because she knew this was not yet the right time, but something in her rose up and refused meekly to obey Ushant. She would explain.

She was walking – the forgotten Rose a few paces behind her – to avoid the inevitable attention that her ducal car-

riage would draw, but what she had to say would . . . would
. . . Nan pulled at her cloak and hurried on. Thunder rolled
overhead but a sudden flash of lightning made her lift her
chin defiantly.

When Nan reached the church, the heavens opened.
Suddenly remembering Rose in the downpour Nan ushered
her inside – despite Rose's protestations that she remain outside – and signed to her to wait on the bench in the porch.
Nan closed the heavy wooden door and the sound echoed
throughout the cold empty church. She walked into the
church and waited, for a moment, while her eyes adjusted to
the dim light. It was eerily quiet and for the first time it
struck Nan as a very strange place for Ushant to choose for
their meeting. Nan took a deep breath and walked up the
aisle, looking about her as she went. She stopped abruptly as
a man – Ushant – stood, suddenly beside her, his arm
restraining her.

'I agreed to let you stay on in London to see your parents,'
he said, omitting all the customary preliminaries and barely
managing to conceal his anger, 'but now that they have
returned to America, it is time for you to come home. And
still you refuse.' Nan opened her mouth to speak but Ushant
held up the palm of his hand to silence her. He turned and
began to pace uneasily up and down the cramped space
between the pews, staring at his feet. 'I do not wish to discuss
our situation, or your feelings, Annabel. I only insist that you
play by the rules.'

This was so unexpected that Nan could only say, 'What
are the rules?'

She had imagined him angry, shouting, stammering,
accusing her of all manner of things, demanding to know
what she intended to do, but he merely said that he had no
wish to know how she felt and that she must follow the
'rules'.

Ushant looked at Nan for the first time. 'Must I really spell them out?' he said disdainfully, as though he was addressing a capricious child, 'Have you learned nothing in your years in England?' He moved his right hand to silence her again and then curled it into a fist. Nan took a step backwards but Ushant did not touch her. He raised his forefinger. 'You must spend at least a third of the year at Longlands.' He raised his second finger. 'You must perform your duties there, as you have done until now,' he stammered, 'perfectly satisfactorily.' Ushant took a deep breath, 'And as long as you continue in this way . . . as long as,' he raised his third finger, 'whenever you are in London you are at least formally in residence at Folyat House and not camping out like a gypsy, then I shall turn a blind eye to . . . to whatever you may choose to do.' Ushant stared coldly at Nan and his look sent a shudder through her. 'In these matters,' he said, raising his little finger, 'discretion is everything. Should you create a public scandal, I shall divorce you.' Nan steadily held her husband's gaze.

'I shall, of course,' stammered Ushant, 'name your lover and cite him as co-respondent, which would naturally ruin any chance he may have of political success.' Ushant's raised hand trembled and, in an attempt to control it, he pressed his outstretched fingers across his damp upper lip.

Everything Nan had planned to say, to explain, to blame herself for and so save her husband's dignity and his feelings, vanished from her mind. She stepped up into the pew where Ushant stood and looked directly into his eyes. 'So anything is permissible as long as one is not discovered?' she said contemptuously.

Ushant gripped Nan's arm, but she sensed that it was more to keep himself upright than to intimidate her. His anger was beginning to overwhelm him . . . just as Nan had witnessed so many times as Longlands. 'Can't you see that to make love to another man's wife is merely an error of taste? But to make a husband look ridiculous – in public – is criminal,' stammered Ushant.

Nan snatched her arm away and turned on her heel, clapping her hands over her ears. Ushant's crumpled message fell to the floor and he shouted after her, but it was a shout of desperation. 'You – you don't seem to realize what generous terms these are. You have not yet produced an heir! Mother recommends I return you to Longlands by force.'

Nan stopped in her tracks and turned in the aisle, her hands hanging by her sides. 'So why don't you?' she said coldly.

Ushant stepped out from the pew and, despite the gloom in the church, Nan could see how her husband's face worked with a dreadful mixture of pain, anger and impotent helplessness. He walked towards her and she thought he would force her to go with him, but he did not. He walked past her quickly with his head bowed. When he reached the heavy wooden door he gripped the iron handle and wrenched the door open, then he flung back over his shoulder at Nan, 'I shall not force you, Annabel because I . . . I am not a monster, do you understand? I am not a monster!'

The astonished Rose cowered in a corner of the porch while Ushant pushed the church door wide open and marched stiffly down the stone steps. Nan stood quite still until she could no longer hear her husband's footsteps, and then she too walked down the stone steps, gesturing to Rose to follow her. The air was fresh and rain-washed and Nan breathed deeply as if to expel every particle of the stifling air in the church from her lungs.

Nᴀɴ stood in the nursery doorway watching Lizzy play with Thomas. A nurse sat on a chair in a corner under the high windows, thoroughly absorbed in the child and his devoted mother. The nursery windows were spattered with raindrops and a shaft of pale sunlight fell onto Lizzy and her son. Nan leaned against the door, exhausted and cold, and it seemed to her that of all of them, it was Lizzy with her quick wit and her natural intelligence who had understood England and the English better than any of them. It was Lizzy who had bided her time when Hector pestered and pestered her to marry him and it was Lizzy who had decided, with her head *and* with her heart, to marry Hector when she felt the time was right. Lizzy and Hector understood each other perfectly and Lizzy was happy. Nan on the other hand, with her belief in the romantic, and her loving poetic heart, had seen nothing as it truly was.

Lizzy and Hector had no 'rules'. Lizzy had married a man with whom she was at ease and with whom she could be herself. The only Englishman Nan was at ease with and could be herself with, was Guy and . . . Nan shuddered . . . she had failed Guy, failed him utterly. She had not spoken a word in Guy's defence to Ushant, and she had not spoken a word of how she, Nan, felt. Ushant's cold calculating approach had horrified her and she felt the iron cage of his 'rules' clang shut about her. Perhaps . . . perhaps she could stay with Lizzy . . . just until she had decided what to do.

But as Nan St George thought about what she must do she felt her strength evaporate. The strength that had grown so wonderfully over these past few months ebbed away. Nan St George found it difficult to breathe; the air around her held the image of another self, Annabel Tintagel sidled around her, subtly altering her vision and breathing her air. Nan St George knew that Ushant had it in his power to ruin Guy Thwarte's career, and that he would not hesitate to do so. She could not allow that to happen, but neither could she live according to Ushant's loathsome 'rules'.

Annabel Tintagel smiled slyly from the shadows and said, 'But I can live according to his rules. I know how to make life bearable with him. I can be as predictable as one of his,' she moved her head jerkily from side to side, 'clocks. And if I play my cards right I can still see Guy Thwarte,' (his name sounded oddly on her lips), 'at certain times of the year and

according to my husband's prescribed rules. It's all quite possible you know, quite quite possible.' But the broken-hearted
Nan St George replied, 'I can't live like that. And neither
could you if you had ever loved . . . if you had ever truly been
loved,' and a dreadful moan escaped her.

Lizzy started and turned towards the door. 'Why, Nan,' she
said, 'I didn't hear you. You've been out so long I was beginning to think you'd been kidnapped!' Nan walked into the
nursery, distracted and pale. She knelt on the floor beside
Lizzy and Thomas. She was near to tears but she struggled to
hold them in. 'I – I spent the afternoon shopping. I'm
exhausted. I'm sorry I frightened you.' Nan held out a small
packet. 'I – I bought something silly to wear to Conchie's
party. Look!' Nan lifted an aigrette from its tissue wrapping
and held it out for Lizzy to inspect. Lizzy smiled, but her heart
was heavy: she knew Nan had not been shopping, at least
not all afternoon, and Hector had made her promise, only
that morning . . .

'There's something I must say to you,' said Lizzy, motioning
for the nurse to look after Thomas and ushering Nan from
the nursery. 'I won't beat about the bush, darling, but the fact
is you've been away from your husband for four months now.
And people are beginning to talk.' Nan stared dumbly at
Lizzy as they walked down the stairs. 'Hector has heard mali-
cious gossip about you and Guy in the House.'

'I don't see what business it is of theirs,' said Nan, but it
was a half-hearted defence.

'It's hardly surprising,' Lizzy continued. 'It's not as if you
were some little Miss Nobody.'

'What about Lady Nye?' said Nan desperately, 'Isn't she
funding Tommy Tennant as MP for somewhere or other? No
one raises a peep –'

'Nan,' interrupted the keen-eyed Lizzy, 'that doesn't sound
a bit like you. And you're not funding Guy anyway.'

Nan continued valiantly. 'And you know Richard doesn't

care what Conchie does so long as her lovers are rich enough to pay off his debts.' But Nan's strength failed her and she could not go on with her charade. She stopped on the stairs as the tears welled in her eyes and her throat tightened.

'Nan darling,' said Lizzy, 'you must know that Hector and I would love to have you here with us for ever . . . but honestly Nan, I do think –'

'That I should leave,' said Nan for her friend. 'I know. I must leave for both your sakes,' and she gestured at Lizzy's growing roundness, 'and for your children and . . . and,' said Annabel Tintagel, 'I must return to Longlands. I know.' But Nan St George hung her head and then she looked up at Lizzy and her eyes shone with her tears. 'But . . . oh Lizzy . . . where shall I ever find the strength? How shall I say goodbye . . . to him . . . how shall I ever say goodbye?'

Lizzy Robinson opened her arms and the weak, exhausted Nan St George fell into them, sobbing as though her heart would break.

# THIRTY-FIVE

GUY THWARTE PACED UP AND DOWN HIS ROOM. IT WAS A warm night and the sounds from the street below floated up to him through the open window. He gazed out at the familiar turrets and pinnacles of the Palace of Westminster and then he turned away. He sat down and picked up his book, but he could not concentrate. The surprise – and delight – of seeing Nan, and the knowledge that she had been coming to the House almost daily to see him and to hear him had touched him deeply. He sat at his desk and drew a sheet of paper towards him. He picked up his pen . . . he wanted to tell Nan that he loved her – that he had fallen deeply in love with her – and yet he knew he must tell her that they should never see each other again. He tried to imagine a world without Nan and he despaired at the thought. He had returned to England with high hopes for his future and he had achieved much already . . . but all this seemed as nothing in a world without Nan. He wrote a few words but he could not write, 'We must never see each other again.' He stopped writing and then he crumpled the sheet of paper between his hands and hurled it across the room.

THERE was a hesitant knock at the door and Guy, wondering who would call at this late hour, opened the door to Rose,

Nan's faithful maid. She stood shyly on the threshold, her head bowed.

'What is it?' said Guy anxiously. 'What's happened?'

'The Duchess of Tintagel asks to see you,' said Rose softly.

'The Duchess is here? Why send her up!' said Guy, turning back into the room to find his jacket, but Rose's voice behind him continued, 'She won't come up sir. She says, please, for you to come down.' Guy shrugged on his jacket, blew out the lamp and hurried after Rose along the passage.

Nan waited in the shadows while Rose returned to the carriage which stood under some trees on the other side of the road, and then emerged from the shadows for a moment, so that Guy should see her. He hurried across the street towards her, his arms outstretched, but when he was close enough to see her face he stopped abruptly. 'You're going back,' he said. 'You've come to tell me you're going back.'

'Forgive me,' were the only words Nan could find.

'You feel more for Ushant than you . . . than you . . .'

'No!' said Nan, 'no. This has nothing to do with what I feel for Ushant. I'm not going back to Ushant.'

'What then?' said Guy, hardly able to say the words.

'Oh Guy,' she said, 'it's as if I've woken from a childish dream. I suddenly see everything with a dreadful clarity.' Nan clasped Guy's hands in hers where they remained, heavy and motionless. 'I don't want . . . I cannot live a life of lies and hypocrisy. I could never live like that. You must understand that, don't you?' Guy nodded dumbly. 'I chose this life . . . I chose to marry Ushant . . . I chose to become his duchess . . . and there is much to do at Longlands, and at Tintagel, and Folyat House needs –'

'– What are you talking about?' Guy interrupted. 'Are you trying to tell me that you enjoy being a duchess too much to sacrifice a duchess's life . . . I thought you were braver than that, Nan.'

Nan dropped Guy's hands. 'Do you imagine', she said, 'that

it is easier to go back than it is to stay here? Is that what you think? That I don't need all the courage I possess to go back? Don't you see? It has all been a dream . . . our time at Champions was a wonderful, beautiful dream, but it was a dream. I must take up my courage and face what I have done . . . and live with it . . .' Her voice trailed away as she looked into his eyes.

'Nan,' he said, 'my darling Nan, this is not like you . . . this is self-defeating . . . this is –'

'Please don't,' interrupted Nan. 'Please don't say harsh things that I shall remember when I'm alone.' Nan turned away from Guy and she wept. He stood quite still for a long moment, and then he drew her backwards into his arms.

'I can't let you go. I can't,' he faltered, 'I won't let you go unless you tell me you don't love me.' Nan wiped her tears away with her hand and Guy rested his chin on her shoulder, his cheek against hers. 'Say it,' said Guy, 'Look at me and say you don't care for me.'

'You know I can't do that,' said Nan softly, turning towards him inside the circle of his arms, 'but life requires more of us . . . much more of us . . . than merely to give in to our passions. I will never forget the wonderful dream that was Champions . . . but we live in a world that does not tolerate such dreams. I must return to my real life and you must . . .' she faltered, 'I must go home,' said Nan with such finality that Guy's arms dropped like dead weights to his sides.

Nan's eyes filled with tears once more as she gazed hopelessly at Guy and, for a moment, he thought that if he held onto her tightly and refused to let her go, she would stay. But his arms remained at his sides and she ran from the shadows and across the street to her carriage. Nan ran without looking back, but she felt as though she was running up an impossibly steep hill, and that her carriage would always remain the same distance from her, no matter how fast she ran.

Nan stumbled blindly into the back of the carriage and sank onto the seat opposite Rose. She heard Rose tap on the glass for the driver to move on, and she was dimly aware of the carriage lurching forwards, and rumbling away along the cobbled street.

# THIRTY-SIX

LADY SEADOWN SAT IN HER BOUDOIR IN THE WEST WING AT Allfriars and she shivered. A heavy publication lay open on her knee but she was not reading it; she gazed through the window at the drifting snowflakes. After a while she turned back to the fire and stretched her hands towards its flames (Lady Brightlingsea had conceded that she might request her fire before the lamps were lit), but her expression grew irritable as she observed another patch of peeling plaster on the wall beside the mantelpiece (she had elicited no concessions in that regard).

When her hands were warmed Virginia Seadown returned her attention to the publication on her knee. She smiled a cold little smile of satisfaction as she traced the Brightlingsea coat of arms with her finger and read: 'Marquess of Brightlingsea, [Marquess E. 1579]', and then on the next line '[Name pronounced Brittlesey].' Virginia knew the entry by heart and she drew her finger down the page until she reached: 'Grandchildren living', and here her smile deepened as she read: 'Frederick Henry St George Seadown, Viscount Brancaster, b. 4th January, 1875'; and 'Lady Flora Honoria Virginia Seadown, b. 8th September, 1877.'

Virginia shut the publication and said, brightly, 'At least the children's names appear in all the right places even if,' her bright tone faltered, 'even if their father would scarcely know their faces.' Miss March, who sat opposite Virginia, fidgeted uncomfortably but Virginia continued, 'And Frederick . . . my little Frederick will be the next Lord Seadown.' Miss March remained silent, prompting Virginia to add anxiously, 'Won't he?' and Miss March, who had been momentarily inattentive – Virginia's remarks were so predictably similar on this subject – was startled, but she checked her 'You know perfectly well that he will,' when she saw Virginia's lip tremble.

Instead she said, in the tones of a nurse comforting a child, 'Why of course he will Jinny dear, of course he will.'

The few books that graced Virginia's boudoir were all of the kind she had just closed, and the fewer paintings (in front of which she spent many hours emulating attitudes and postures) might be termed cousins to her books. But Virginia's tableaux vivants before her husband's ancestors, although remarkably accurate in demeanour, were unmistakably different in aspect: her beauty exceeded anything that the Brightlingseas, or the painters of their portraits, could muster and it was, at least at first, on account of her looks that Lord Brightlingsea had paid her particular attention. But as the years passed Lord Brightlingsea had shown Virginia in his gruffly absent-minded way that he was genuinely fond of her and this had, at times, compensated for her husband's prolonged absences.

Virginia, her mood shifting once more, clapped her slim white hands together and cried, 'Oh Jacky, just *think* how Mrs Parmore and Mrs Eglinton must *wish* I was *their* daughter . . . the only reason I *ever* want to go back to New York,' she breathed, 'is to have the exquisite pleasure of receiving . . . and declining . . . their invitations to dine. They simply wouldn't dare to cut me now.' And then, as if something had cast a shadow over this glorious image she said, frowning slightly, 'I can't think why Lady Brightlingsea insists on going about in those sagging tweeds . . . in all weathers. And as for her shoes . . .' Virginia sank back into her chair in disgust, while Miss March, safely back on familiar territory, smilingly surveyed Virginia's collection of family photographs (framed so very like her own), until she found the one of herself nestling beside the ceremonial portrait of Lord Brightlingsea, which all but hid a small photograph of Colonel and Mrs St George.

Miss March had been a frequent visitor at Allfriars since Virginia's marriage. Lady Brightlingsea had summoned her in the vague hope that she might have a restraining effect on what she called Virginia's more 'American' habits (she pronounced the word as she might pronounce 'outlandish'). 'I tell myself that it is of little consequence what Conchita and Dickie do any more . . . they are quite beyond the pale,' Lady Brightlingsea had confided to Miss March, 'but Seadown is the heir . . . and his wife must understand what's expected of her . . . in all things.'

Miss March had accepted the invitation with some trepidation, but she had found Virginia surprisingly accommodating, and it was delightful to Miss March to stay *en famille* at Allfriars – quite delightful – even if Lady Brightlingsea had entirely forgotten that Miss March was herself an American, and Lord Brightlingsea had relegated the memory of their brief engagement to the farthest recesses of his mind, never to be retrieved.

And so it was that under Miss March's watchful eye Virginia willingly acquired the customs and habits of her adopted country until she was indistinguishable from her adopted countrywomen. 'Miss Testvalley would be horrified,' thought Miss March with her nervous little laugh. Indeed Virginia Seadown became such a passable imitation of a female of the Brightlingsea line that she was, on occasion, mistaken for one born to it.

But Virginia did not remain entirely insensible to the price she paid for her new identity. She had discarded her origins as carelessly as she might discard her outmoded fashions at the end of the season, but the lining of her newly acquired clothes frequently felt as if it were fashioned from the coarsest homespun. It chafed against her smooth pale skin until she was forced to recall that this new identity of hers was wholly dependent upon her marriage to a husband who was a husband in name only.

'But that doesn't signify,' she told herself with her cold little laugh, 'after all it is precisely because his name is of such consequence that I am who I am.'

Miss March looked up. 'I am much relieved to hear that your sister has returned to Longlands,' she observed, and she smiled as the rounded vowels of Virginia's perfectly accented English replied, 'Yes . . . I can't think what can have possessed her.'

At that moment the door flew open and Seadown burst in. This was so unexpected to both women (they had no idea that he was at Allfriars) that Miss March's small wrinkled hands fluttered about her face, while Virginia stood, regally commanding her husband with her glinting sapphire eyes to stop this unwelcome advance into her private apartments. But Seadown appeared not to notice. 'Please leave us Miss March,' he said abruptly, and he continued his advance, unchecked, towards his wife.

'To what do I owe the honour?' said Virginia icily, when Miss March had closed the door behind her. Her husband's presence only served to remind her of his frequent absences – and of his chief reason for them – and beneath her glacial composure Virginia was bewildered and unprepared.

'I –' Seadown sat down heavily in the chair so recently vacated by Miss March. 'It's . . .' he took a deep breath and Virginia was horrified to see tears in his eyes, 'it's Idina,' he blurted out and he held his head in his hands. Virginia's blood froze. They never discussed Lady Churt and Virginia had no wish to discuss her now . . . but her husband was determined.

'She's taken her life,' said Seadown plainly. 'She's taken her own life.' Virginia stared at her husband, at first confused and then fearful. Seadown lifted his head wearily. 'She has drowned herself.'

'Oh, how horrible,' wailed Virginia, 'how utterly, utterly horrible,' and she began to sob.

'They found her last night,' continued Seadown mechanically, 'at Runnymede. Her body –' Seadown stopped and swallowed hard, 'her body was caught under the jetty.'

For a moment Virginia hid her face in her hands and then she began to pace about her boudoir. 'Oh poor poor Idina . . . it's dreadful . . . quite dreadful.'

Seadown watched Virginia and a stray thought floated above the mire of his confusion and unhappiness. 'My wife must be the only woman in the world,' the thought fluttered aimlessly, 'who can retain her beauty in the face of impossible odds . . . her face is daubed with patches of red, her eyes are bloodshot, and yet she is magnificent.'

'I'm so so sorry,' said Virginia regaining her composure, 'I never meant it to lead to this – I –' she stopped as a look of horror spread across her husband's features.

'You never meant? –' He stared dumbly at his wife.

'I have a dreadful confession to make,' she said, and Seadown suddenly longed to stop his ears and refuse to hear her. 'When I was in London last summer,' Virginia's voice was insistent, 'when Papa and Mama were in London I didn't stay in London all the time . . . I went to Runnymede. I told my parents that I was coming back here to Allfriars but I went to see Idina.' Seadown stared at his wife. 'I – I had to find out if you and she were still . . . I had to know.'

Seadown, already drained by the events of the last twenty-four hours, looked at his wife with a resigned expression. He had suffered more than he had thought possible, and yet, plainly, there was more to come. 'What happened?' he said, 'what did you say to her?'

'I only meant – I never meant her any harm – not that sort of harm anyway . . .' Virginia dabbed at her tears with a white cambric handkerchief. She walked to the window and looked out over the snow-covered parkland; she did not once look back at her husband as she spoke. 'I told Idina that we were expecting our second child . . . I wanted her to stop seeing you. I knew you'd never stopped . . . seeing her . . . and I wanted to make sure that she knew that you and I were still . . . still . . . I told her that if she ever bore your children they wouldn't be . . . I told her that my children, not her children, would hold positions of rank and title. I told her to remember that. I said that her children would always be little,' Virginia faltered, 'little bastards. I wanted to say it over and over again. Little bastards . . . little bastards. I told her that she was nothing compared with me. Nothing.'

Virginia's back trembled visibly and she covered her face with her hands. Her voice became so soft that Seadown had to strain every nerve to hear her until, at length, he went to stand beside her at the window. 'But she really had everything . . . didn't she?' whispered Virginia, 'Everything. And I had nothing. She had your love, didn't she? And that counts for more than all this.' Virginia spread her arms wide and then let them drop back down to her sides. 'It is my fault that Idina took her life.'

Seadown slipped his arm about Virginia's waist (she made no move to prevent him) and gently turned her towards him. 'It is not your fault, Virginia,' he said at length, 'and it never was your fault. Everything is my fault. If I had stopped . . . seeing Idina there would have been no need for you to go to Runnymede last summer. It is I, not you, who have ruined everything. I have caused so much stupid suffering,' Seadown faltered, and then continued. 'I kept Idina, Jinny. She was always in need of money . . . even the meagre sums that I succeeded in persuading Papa to part with, and it seems that she allowed a certain Lord Percy to invest her money for her. Although he scarcely managed to provide her with a living, he caused her no financial hardship either . . . but lately this . . . this Lord Percy has taken several ill-advised decisions and the result is that Idina is . . . was in debt to the extent of several hundred pounds.'

Seadown took a deep breath and tightened his grip on Virginia's waist. She stiffened, but she did not attempt to remove his hand. 'Last week Idina asked me for the sum she owed and I told her that I could not provide her with it all at once. She had no one else to turn to . . . she faces . . . she faced bankruptcy.' Seadown swallowed hard. 'I meant her to understand that I should give her what I could and that I should raise the rest just as soon as . . . as . . . She must have believed that I did not intend to help her . . . at all.'

Virginia looked up into her husband's tear-filled eyes and a spark of anger ignited her cold heart. Doubtless it was her own money – the money from her marriage settlement – that Seadown had persuaded his father to part with so frequently, and Virginia wondered whether he had contemplated asking her directly for the money Idina needed this time? The money that would have saved her life. Her calculating heart told her that he would have asked her, but that he had failed to find the necessary courage, or a sufficiently plausible reason, in time. And now it was too late.

Seadown put his hands on his wife's shoulders. You see I am to blame for everything,' he said, 'and you are blameless.' Virginia assented to this with the faintest inclination of her beautiful head, while her eyes steadily held her husband's gaze. At length Seadown tore his eyes from his wife's and continued. 'I am dreadfully sorry for what I have done, for causing you, and all those I love, so much stupid, unnecessary suffering. And I wish,' he faltered once more, 'I wish that I had had the sense to love you . . . to honour you . . . from the beginning, as you deserve.'

Virginia looked at her husband's pale freckled face and resisted a momentary impulse to touch his cheek. Her heart, the heart that had been hardened by his frequent visits to Runnymede, whispered that she could ask whatever she wanted of him now, and in the future, and he would acquiesce. Virginia drew herself away from her husband's grasp. She would make no demands upon him now, but soon she would . . . perhaps tomorrow. She would make him earn his right to his place beside her, and beside their children. And all the while she thought these things she watched her husband's face and, as he began to speak once more, Virginia glowed triumphantly: he was irrevocably hers.

'I scarcely have the right to ask you this,' Seadown was saying, 'and it is an ill-timed request but . . .' Seadown bent his face to his wife's and she did not move away, 'Virginia, dearest Jinny, I want to return . . . to Allfriars. I want to be with you . . . and with our children.' He paused and then, encouraged by another infinitesimal inclination of his wife's head, he continued, 'Will you have me, Virginia? Have I your permission . . . your blessing . . . to come home?'

# THIRTY-SEVEN

LORD BRIGHTLINGSEA WAS IN JOVIAL MOOD AS HE STRODE
out onto the gallery at Allfriars, his gun tucked under his
arm. The house was alive with children (not, by his lights, a
natural cause for celebration, but some of these children
guaranteed the Brightlingsea succession) and it was
Seadown's boy's birthday. And besides, Seadown had been at
Allfriars for more than four weeks together and had not once
asked for money (there'd been some kind of sea change in
the boy). And as for the beautiful Lady Seadown, she was
enough to brighten the dullest day and today, on her son's
third birthday, she positively glowed.

Lord Brightlingsea leaned over the gallery and the assembled company in the great hall below him fell silent. Frederick
hid amongst the folds of his mother's skirts and a nurse held the
baby Flora. His eldest grandson, Edward Marable, looked –
Lord Brightlingsea scratched his head – just like . . . just like . . .
and as for young Sophie Marable, there was a lot to be said for
an injection of Spanish blood to boost the flagging Marable
looks (Selina said the blood was Spanish at any rate): Sophie
was the prettiest little girl in the hall. And even if his daughters, save Camilla, hadn't yet hunted down husbands, Lord
Brightlingsea was not inclined to lament the fact. 'All in good
time . . . all in good time,' he told himself.

Lord Brightlingsea straightened his tall frame. 'Well now,' he boomed, and an excited shout went up from the children, 'are you ready?'

'YES,' they cried together.

'Are you incomparably,' Lord Brightlingsea spoke deliberately slowly, 'incontrovertibly ready?'

'Y-E-E-E-E-S,' shouted the children, verging on the hysterical.

'Do you all like cream cakes?'

'Y-E-E-E-E-E-E-E-S,' shrieked the children, and their mothers and their nurses covered their ears.

'Then by Jove we'll sound the salute,' said Lord Brightlingsea and he fired two shots into the ceiling, reloaded, and fired once more.

The children, by now utterly hysterical, were caught and calmed by numerous nurses and mothers, all except Thomas Robinson who was so over-excited that Lizzy caught him and with the help of two footmen she hauled his struggling, giggling, reddened form outside into the raw January air where she forced him to walk up and down in front of the house several times. Thomas Robinson complained vociferously that she wouldn't like it if he did that to her, but Lizzy resolutely walked him up and down, up and down, until his hysteria subsided and his naturally pale colour returned.

Already old enough to know when he was beaten, the two-and-a-half-year-old Thomas Robinson walked sedately ahead of his mother across the great hall towards the dining-room, whose double doors had been flung open to reveal a long table laden with treats for the birthday tea. But when he saw that his mother was temporarily occupied with his twin baby brothers and their nurses in a corner of the great hall, he broke into a run.

The children and the adults took their places at the table in the dining-room, while Lizzy waited in the great hall for

Lord Brightlingsea to descend the stairs. He came down slowly, leaning on a silver-topped cane, the butt of his gun slung over his free forearm. When Lord Brightlingsea reached the great hall he handed his gun absent-mindedly to the housekeeper – who stood at the bottom of the stairs – and watched, puzzled, as she disappeared down a stone passage, holding the gun at arm's length and shaking her head.

'Thank you m'dear, thank you,' said Lord Brightlingsea, acknowledging Lizzy and walking stiffly across the great hall. 'Can't arrive at my grandson's party without a pretty woman on my arm, eh?' Lizzy smiled and took Lord Brightlingsea's arm and Nan ushered them to their places between herself and Virginia. Lord Brightlingsea beamed at Virginia, but since he could not very well lean across the charming woman who'd just brought him into the dining-room (darned good-looking . . . who on earth was she?) to talk to his daughter-in-law, he turned his attention to Nan who sat on his left. 'Glad to see you m'dear. Glad to see you. No children of yours here . . . what? How old are you?'

Nan smiled and said 'I'm twenty-one, Lord Brightlingsea . . . there's plenty of time.'

Selina Brightlingsea shouted across the table. 'Don't listen to him Annabel, whatever he's saying. It's invariably something ill-considered,' and she lifted her ear-trumpet to ensure that she should hear her husband.

'You'd better get a move on m'dear . . . must have children you know. The race is disappearing fast. Soon there'll be none of us left.'

'You have several grandchildren already, Lord Brightlingsea,' said Nan affectionately, 'and at least two of them are boys. Besides my children wouldn't be direct descendants of yours . . . and that's what you want, isn't it?'

'Yes, yes, yes,' mumbled Lord Brightlingsea, 'but there's always room for more, that's what I say. Eh?' And he looked

vacantly at Annabel who suddenly slipped her arm round his neck and kissed him swiftly on his veined cheek.

WHEN the happy birthday song had been sung and the tea had been eaten, Lord and Lady Brightlingsea left the party. The children played games organized by their nurses and watched over by their parents, and then the children called for Nan, who had been sitting against a wall deep in conversation with Conchita.

The children sat in giggling lines on the floor and pleaded with Nan to do what Frederick called her 'meetayshuns' and, at length, she was prevailed upon by both children and adults alike, and she began.

'Who's this?' she said, holding an imaginary ear-trumpet to her ear and assuming a bad-smell-under-her-nose expression.

'Grandma, Grandma,' shouted Frederick, giggling.

'And this?' Nan stood stock still, her arms outstretched, her face averted, a picture of disgust.

'Aunt Honoria,' shouted Sophie, 'when she doesn't want to go riding and Grandma says what does she think all these acres are for?'

The children shrieked with laughter and the adults attempted, unsuccessfully, to contain theirs. 'And this?' said Nan, grinding her teeth furiously, stamping her foot and handing something behind her without turning round.

'Uncle John,' cried Edward, 'when he's missed his twelve-teenth pheasant.'

While Nan continued with her parodies of the Brightlingsea family and the children wriggled and giggled, Lizzy Robinson murmured to Conchita, 'I think Annabel's back . . . don't you? For a while I thought she was heading in your direction . . . but the danger seems to be over.'

Conchita's pale eyes darkened. 'It's not quite that simple, Lizzy,' she said, 'I think she's putting up a very good show. But we shall see.'

DESPITE Jinny's protestations, Nan had left Allfriars the next day. 'I promised Ushant I would join him in London,' she had said, 'we return to Longlands at the end of the month.' And when Jinny had looked disappointed, Nan had added, 'I would love to stay Jinny darling, but you must see that I can't.'

'Of course I see, Nan,' said Jinny, 'but that doesn't mean that I can't hope you might change your mind . . . or your plans.'

Nan could think of nothing more pleasant nor more peaceful than to linger at Allfriars with her sister (she thought she had detected a warmer, less aloof, softer-edged Virginia on this birthday visit), but she had promised Ushant that she would return to London, and so she had. Now she sat at her dressing-table in her bedroom at Folyat House and she was glad to be there, she was glad to be alone. Only when she was alone could she relinquish the pretence; and only when she was alone could she allow her thoughts to stray to Guy Thwarte. But she mustn't think of him; she had promised herself that she would not think of him; she must concentrate on the task in hand . . . she must ring for Rose and change for dinner.

Annabel Tintagel had discovered that when she bent her mind to the details of her daily life and when she concentrated sedulously upon the routine minutiae of her tasks at Longlands, or at Folyat House (they never went to Tintagel now, they never even mentioned the place), several days would pass quite uneventfully. But she had to apply herself constantly, she had to keep busy, she must, at all costs, remain occupied, otherwise . . . otherwise she might forget who she was.

It was the Dowager's greatest delight to see Annabel throw herself bodily into the duties and the daily routine of her position. 'You have become the valued soldier I so hoped for in my only daughter-in-law,' she had observed to Annabel after they had spent a particularly gruelling month in London performing their public duties, 'and all the more welcome a recruit to the Tintagel ranks for being – at first – such an unpromising one.' Blanche Tintagel had given Annabel one of her difficult smiles and Annabel knew that she had been received back into the fold.

But now . . . now she must ring for Rose and change for dinner and tomorrow there was the new housekeeper to interview and Ermie . . . hadn't she promised to do something with Ermie tomorrow? Nan sighed with relief when she thought of her sister-in-law. Although they were not particularly close, while Ermie stayed at Folyat House Nan did not have to dine alone with Ushant. Conversing with Ushant lightly, inconsequentially, in front of the ever-present servants made Nan feel at her most vulnerable. Those were the times when she dreaded what she might do; the times when she was overwhelmed with the desire to scream, or to burst into tears. But with other people present at the table she felt safer from herself; it was easier to be Annabel Tintagel when other people were present because they knew just how Annabel Tintagel should behave, even if she sometimes forgot.

There was a knock at Nan's door and without waiting for an answer Lady Ermyntrude Folyat flew into the room. 'Oh Annabel,' she said breathlessly, 'thank heavens you're here. Ushant promised he'd return to chaperon me . . . us . . . and now he's sent a message to say that he's dining at his club – with Lord Percy. He promised he'd be here . . . he promised.' Lady Ermyntrude fell onto Annabel's bed and leaned against the wooden post, her green eyes wide and pleading. 'Annabel, would you come to the opera with Mr Wallace and me? Ushant won't allow me to go without a chaperon and he – Mr Wallace – will be here any minute and I do so want to go with him. I think – I think Ushant's done it on purpose . . . Oh Annabel, do you think he disapproves of Mr Wallace?'

Nan stood up and smoothed her dress. 'Of course he doesn't, Ermie darling,' she said with an unaccustomed rush of sympathy for her sister-in-law, 'I expect he just couldn't get rid of Lord Percy – you know what he's like – and anyway,' she put her arm round Ermie's sadly drooping shoulders, 'Ushant knew I'd be here, so naturally he knew there'd be someone to accompany you to the opera.'

'Oh Annabel,' said Lady Ermyntrude throwing her arms around Nan with an uncharacteristic show of emotion, 'I shall wait for you in the drawing-room. He'll be here any minute,' she cried and ran from the bedroom.

Mʀ Wallace sat between Annabel Tintagel and the Lady Ermyntrude Folyat in the Tintagel box at Drury Lane. He thought the Duchess very beautiful, but he found her manner quite distant. She seemed not to hear his polite enquiries during the intervals – perhaps she thought him beneath her – and so, eventually, he turned his broad pale face to the Lady Ermyntrude – or Ermie – as she had just given him permission to call her. He reflected that, for a large girl, she was exceptionally gentle and for a girl at the wrong end of her twenties, she was surprisingly youthful. She blushed at his reference to the harmony created by the green of her dress and the green of her eyes, and he smiled indulgently upon her blushes.

For her part, Ermie thought Mr Wallace's curling black hair and his bushy black eyebrows the handsomest she had ever seen, and she fairly blossomed in his company. She was grateful for her sister-in-law's tactful withdrawal from their conversation so that she could converse with Mr Wallace without interruption (a far pleasanter chaperon than Ushant would have been), and the drama being played out on the stage below her almost entirely escaped her notice.

Not so Nan. She was entranced and saddened and transported by turns as wave upon wave of glorious music soared

and surged and swelled about her. Ushant hated the opera
and consequently attended as few performances as possible,
but Nan longed to attend, and by the end of this performance she thought she would die of heartbreak. Her throat
ached and her handkerchief had become a crumpled wet rag
in her hand; she thought she had never been so moved by a
drama nor heard such music.

'It's only a story, Annabel,' said Ermie, leaning towards her
as their carriage clattered through the wet London streets.
'Don't be so sad.' Ermie laid her hand on Nan's arm. 'I asked
Mr Wallace if he thought people really felt like that . . . like
Tristan and Isolde I mean . . . and he said that if we did we
should all die of our emotions and then where should we be?'
Ermie giggled nervously but Nan's eyes darkened as a long
line of ghostly figures, their mouths red and gaping and their
voices echoing Mr Wallace's unconsciously murderous words,
filled her head. 'And then where should we be? And then
where should we be?' She twisted the gold signet ring that
Ushant had given her for their anniversary present (the first
anniversary he had remembered) until it bit into the skin of
her finger and drew blood.

'Annabel . . . Annabel,' came Ermie's voice from a great
distance, 'Annabel are you all right?' With a tremendous
effort Annabel recovered herself and said, 'Don't mind me,
Ermie, I'm all tired out from the journey . . . from Allfriars . . .
that's all. I shall be quite all right tomorrow, you'll see.' Nan
closed her eyes and Ermyntrude gazed through the carriage
window at the shining wet streets. She wondered how soon
she dared ask Mama if Mr Wallace might come to stay at
Longlands.

'You should have consulted me first,' said Ushant, his colour
rising, 'and in future, before you chaperon any of my sisters,
you shall consult me.' He sank back into the leather seat
opposite Annabel and looked through the window.

'But she so wanted to go to the opera,' said Nan, 'and I really don't see the harm.'

'Of course you don't see the harm, as you put it. You wouldn't because you weren't brought up to it. But I have yet to meet this Mr Wallace,' he uttered the name with distaste, 'and for all I know he could be the most disreputable, unsuitable –'

'– Ushant,' said Nan leaning forwards and resting her hand on her husband's knee, 'she'd been looking forward to going to the opera with Mr Wallace and you let her down at the last minute. But she obeyed your instructions in every regard.' Nan paused and Ushant shuffled uncomfortably in his seat. 'Does it so offend you to see Ermyntrude happy?' said Nan.

At this Ushant glared at Annabel but resisted his desire to voice the words that leapt to his lips. He turned his face back to the window and stared out at the sodden countryside. Neither spoke to the other for the remainder of the journey, but Ushant's mind teemed.

'I suggest that you allow her at least some of her own ideas,' the Dowager Duchess had said to Ushant when Annabel had returned to Longlands after that . . . that ridiculous episode . . . 'after all, I'm sure that we cannot lay all the blame for the failure of your marriage at Annabel's door, and it is time that we Tintagels tried,' – she had held up her hand to silence his protest – 'tried to live in the nineteenth century before it becomes the twentieth.' Ushant had paced his mother's room furiously, but he had listened. 'One further word and then you may go,' the Dowager Duchess had said, fixing him with her piercing black eyes, 'Leave her in peace for six months. We must be quite certain that she is not carrying another man's child.'

Ushant had protested his certainty that even Annabel wouldn't have taken her . . . her liaison to such extremes, but the Dowager Duchess had raised her hand and continued implacably, 'And during that six months Ushant, you shall have the opportunity to court your wife, to pay her the kind of attention she quite naturally expects . . . the absence of which, I suspect, drove her to this unseemly episode in the first place.'

The troublesome business of providing heirs for the Tintagel line was never far from Ushant's mind and the loss of his son (for Ushant was sure it had been a son), was, he reflected, due entirely to Annabel's naïve notions about the treatment of tenants. But now his mother was taking Annabel's part, despite her unreasonable behaviour, and it dawned upon him that she meant to ensure the Tintagel succession by so doing, and that he would be wise to do the same. His mother would make a formidable enemy, and he felt beleaguered enough as it was. Reluctantly he owned that his mother had the measure of Annabel and it would be for the best to treat his wife as she suggested.

However he still had to contend with his renegade Liberal MP who had recently informed him that he intended to move a motion on the reform of the House of Lords – the very institution that guaranteed him his seat in Parliament – the imbecile! How dare he? Especially since . . . especially since . . . Ushant resolved to use every means at his disposal to prevent Guy Thwarte from moving such a motion, and for the remainder of the journey to Longlands he concentrated his anger in that quarter.

# THIRTY-EIGHT

GUY THWARTE STRODE CONFIDENTLY INTO THE HOUSE OF Commons and took his place on the Opposition back benches. It was warm in the House and he was reminded of a warm day more than a year since. He glanced up, he could not help himself, at the Ladies' Gallery, and thought about how frequently Nan had watched him and listened to him from that Gallery, without his knowledge. Would she ever sit there again? He smiled inwardly as he saw her face, her sweet eager intelligent face, as she told him how eloquently, how passionately he spoke, and he longed for the support of her presence today, he ached for it, but he knew in his heart that she would probably never hear him again.

The speaker called the House to order and Guy inwardly rehearsed his argument, ready for the fray. The debate began and Guy listened keenly, carefully noting his opponents' arguments.

The Conservative Member for Lincoln was on his feet, and Guy watched Hector Robinson turn and smile approvingly at his ally on the Government benches. 'I beg to remind this House,' said the Member for Lincoln, 'that it is not for nothing that the power of the State has been kept in the hands of those who have property.' Guy leaned forward and his colour rose. 'If we destroy that system we give over power into the hands of the irresponsible multitude, and we should have to take the consequences!' The Member for Lincoln sat down and the House was filled with cries of 'Well said, sir' and 'Hear Hear'; and from Guy's side of the House, 'A fallacious argument,' and 'Not so, not so.' As the commotion subsided, Guy Thwarte stood to speak and with an upward glance at the Ladies' Gallery ('For luck,' he told himself), he began.

'The Honourable Member for Lincoln is, of course, perfectly correct: political power in this country is bestowed by mere accident of birth. More than four million acres of England are in the hands of just twelve individuals and those twelve individuals are all members of the Upper House. Is it surprising that the Lords deny justice and delay reform?' Guy, warming to his theme, continued, raising his voice above the angry murmurs of dissent on the Government benches opposite him. 'I call upon this House to introduce, as soon as practicable during the present Parliament, a measure to abolish the House of Lords as an hereditary Upper Chamber.'

Guy Thwarte's voice was momentarily drowned by cries of outrage from the Government benches and by noisy cheers at his elbow, but amongst the noise Guy's keen ears caught (or did he imagine it?) a sly voice saying 'We already have considerable evidence that the Honourable Gentleman has little need of legislation in his attempts to undermine the Peerage.'

When the House was once more called to order Guy, fired by this last remark whether imagined or real, continued angrily, 'The Lords may keep their rank and their titles, their stars and their garters –' ('You are too lenient!' rang out from his own benches.) '– Indeed,' Guy continued, 'they may keep anything and everything that is rightfully theirs . . . and that includes all their inherited privileges. But I say to this House, most sincerely, that the time has come to challenge their Lordships' presumed right to control the way in which we govern ourselves.' Guy Thwarte sat down with a flourish and looked about him. The House was once more in uproar, and then, at last, Hector Robinson's voice carried clear across the Chamber.

'The Honourable Member for Lowdon has spoken with passion on a subject close to his heart,' said Hector, 'but it is a subject upon which, I beg to suggest, passion has clouded his understanding. The House of Lords is not a bastion of privilege, it is the people's last line of defence against the tyranny of the single chamber.'

'MY dear boy,' said Sir Helmsley holding his son at arm's length, 'let's have a look at you. Hmmm . . . I see London has painted you the usual disagreeable shade of grey . . . but we'll soon have some colour back in you . . . and clear your head of that radical London fug, eh?'

'Father, my head has never been clearer, and my feelings about the role of the House of Lords in the government of this country are –'

'– Never mind that now,' interrupted Sir Helmsley, to Guy's astonishment (he had expected a difficult, if not an explosive exchange with his father on the subject), 'Miss Testvalley is here and she's looking forward to seeing you.' Sir Helmsley put his hand affectionately on Guy's shoulder, and together they walked across the hall.

Miss Testvalley rose when the two men entered the draw-ing-room, dropping a book onto the chair behind her, and as Guy crossed the room to take her hand he was struck by how unlike herself she looked, or, at least, how unlike his memory of her. Something about her had softened, her edges were less sharp, and her thick dark curling hair was loosely braided so that it curved gently about her face. She looked almost beau-tiful as he took her hand and smiled down at her.

'Will you be here long, Guy?' she said, and the intensity of her gaze momentarily distracted him.

'No . . . no,' he replied at length. 'I am summoned to Longlands tomorrow.' Miss Testvalley looked at him, her attention heightened. 'The Duke has something of a quarrel with me . . . over my advocacy of the reform of the House of Lords.'

Miss Testvalley smiled a brilliant smile, but Sir Helmsley suddenly snorted in disgust. Guy turned to him, 'So now it comes,' he thought.

'I should think he has a quarrel with you my boy,' said Sir Helmsley, his colour rising dangerously. 'What do you intend by this latest piece of radical political nonsense, eh? You'll lose Ushant's patronage if you're not careful. I really do think –'

But his rising anger suddenly dissolved into a smile as Miss Testvalley, miraculously beside him, took his arm and without raising her voice, said, 'We agreed, Helmsley, didn't we? You solemnly promised me that you would not raise the subject tonight,' she said and Guy marvelled at her steadying influence upon his volatile father. 'And now,' she continued softly, as Sir Helmsley's reddened face gradually resumed its customary colour, 'I think you wanted Guy's opinion on your new rose . . . shouldn't you show it him now, before it is too dark?' Miss Testvalley smiled up at Sir Helmsley and Guy saw his father give the little brown woman at his side an affectionate glance.

That night, over dinner, despite his father's excellent spirits and Miss Testvalley's stimulating company, Guy Thwarte felt utterly alone. The warm summer air blew in from the terrace, heavy with the scent of his father's new roses, and Guy tried to unravel his conflicting feelings. He was, he realized, anxious about his imminent visit to Longlands, but it was not merely on account of his expected confrontation with Ushant.

As he watched the easy way his father and Miss Testvalley conversed, his only desire was to escape them. He could not bear to watch their intimacy and his head was full of the idea that he might (and that he might not) see Nan tomorrow. But surely Ushant would keep her from him? Surely he would not even tell her that he was coming? And yet his lonely heart leapt at the thought that he might catch a glimpse of her.

'When you return from Longlands my boy,' his father was saying, 'we'll drive over to Champions, you and I. It's time to put that young Cora Glenloe's mind at rest, don't you think? Miss Testvalley tells me she's been pining for you.'

'I have said nothing of the kind,' said Miss Testvalley severely, turning the full force of her burning black eyes on Sir Helmsley, 'positively nothing of the kind.'

BOOK

# THIRTY-NINE

THE DOWAGER DUCHESS LAID HER HAND ON ANNABEL'S arm and her mouth puckered into its pinched smile. 'We English are not as forthright as your countrymen,' she said, 'but I would like you to know that you have made remarkable progress, Annabel, in the face of . . . difficult circumstances. I understand – perhaps more than you might imagine – that it is not an easy task to remain wedded to the Tintagel ideals and I want to thank you for your renewed devotion to your duties.'

They stood outside Annabel's bedroom door, and the Dowager's small, hard eyes flickered away from Annabel's face and became fixed upon something of evident fascination just above Annabel's head. 'However,' she said, and her lips formed a determined line, 'you have yet to bear Ushant an heir . . . and that is, after all, the principal reason for this marriage.' The Dowager looked at Annabel once more and with an awkward grimace that passed for a smile, she walked quickly away down the long passage.

Nan slowly opened the door to her bedroom. The warm summer air was oppressively still, and the murmuring drone of voices from the east drawing-room hung in the air below her window, punctuated by an occasional staccato burst of laughter. Nan readied herself for bed – she had dismissed

Rose – and the droning voices gradually quietened to the soft murmur of two or three voices. Annabel glanced at herself in her tall cheval glass, and then crossed the room to her door. She turned the key in the lock as she had done for as long as she could remember and then, slowly, she turned it back. She took a lamp from her dressing-table and put it beside her bed . . . she resolved to read for a while. She knew that her husband and Lord Percy (a frequent visitor to Longlands) would be among the last to bed.

ANNABEL must have fallen asleep, for when she next looked at the lamp beside her bed it was low and guttering and the great house was quiet. She adjusted the regulator on the lamp until it burned true once more and then, grasping the lamp firmly, she walked along the passage towards her husband's bedroom. Annabel tried to picture Ushant's face when he saw her on the threshold; she tried to imagine his expression. Would he smile one of his difficult smiles (inherited from his mother), or would he merely nod and remain impassive? But Nan could not picture her husband's face at all. She stopped and closed her eyes, the tips of her fingers resting on a small table in the passage, and still she could not summon her husband's face.

She thought of Jinny and her beautiful face came easily; she thought of all those children at Allfriars on Frederick's birthday and she saw them clearly, one by one; she thought of her dearest Val and instantly her neat brown face presented itself; and she tried, once more, to picture the face of her husband. But his face would not come. And then, quite unbidden, Guy's face, the face that she had banished from her mind, smiled sadly at her, just as he had smiled at her the last time she had seen him. Nan shuddered and opened her eyes. 'Soon,' she whispered to herself, 'soon I will go to him . . . but not yet,' and she turned and walked disconsolately back the way she had come.

A floorboard creaked under Nan's foot and she stood still – she had no desire to be discovered – and then she heard another softer sound, a muffled crying. She turned down a narrow passage that led off the main passage and hurried towards the sound; it was coming from Ermie's room and it was heart-rending.

Nan knocked softly on Ermie's door but there was no answer. She knocked again, louder this time, and she tried the door handle but the door was locked against her. 'Ermie,' she whispered, 'Ermie, it's Annabel. What's the matter?'

'Go away,' came Ermie's harsh whisper.

'Ermie,' whispered Nan. 'Don't be so sad . . . tell me what's wrong.'

'I never want to talk to anyone . . . ever ever again,' came Ermie's desolate wail. 'Please go away.'

Nan stood in the passage for some time but Ermyntrude did not open her door, and at length Nan turned and hurried back along the narrow passage. When she reached the main passage she hesitated for a moment and then she turned and ran towards her husband's bedroom. She knocked and without waiting for an answer she opened the door and flew into the room, her lamp flickering in her hand.

Nan stopped dead at the end of her husband's bed and the light from her lamp flickered across the peaceful sleeping scene before her. Her hand flew to her mouth to stifle a gasp of astonishment, and then softly, very softly, so as not to disturb the tranquillity in the room, Nan turned and left Ushant's bedroom, closing the door quietly behind her.

GUY Thwarte looked about him in the soft dawn light. He watched the sun's first rays suffuse the silver-grey stone of his beloved Honourslove with a 0rose-pink glow, and then he set his face to the south and urged his horse forwards.

NAN sat up in bed hugging her knees. The morning light flooded her room and she felt strangely peaceful. She felt a sudden sympathy for her husband that, she owned, she had never felt before . . . and in such unexpected circumstances. She sighed and wondered how many generations of this great house – this great dynasty that was Tintagel – had been sad lonely people weighed down by the burden of duty, forbidden to love where their hearts led them. She wondered how much longer the Tintagel dynasty could survive under such conditions.

Nan shivered as she heard footsteps hurrying past her door. She thought of Ermie and she half-guessed at her trouble. 'But at least I can do something for Ermie,' she thought. 'I shall speak to Ushant about her just as soon as I can.' Nan's opportunity to do so came sooner than she could have hoped.

ANNABEL closed the door of her husband's study and leaned against it while Ushant looked at her from behind his monumental desk. He stood, awkwardly. 'I sent for you to tell you that I shall be occupied with estate matters for most of the day,' he said. 'I am sorry to leave you alone with our guests, but mother will help . . . and I shall join you in the evening.'

Annabel smiled at him. 'Of course you must attend to your affairs,' she said, 'but there's something I'd like to ask you,' and seeing his irritable expression she said quickly, 'it won't take a minute.'

'All right,' said Ushant, glancing at the clock on the mantelpiece (it was one of his favourites), 'if it won't take long.'

'I heard Ermie crying last night,' said Annabel, 'and I know that Mr Wallace left, unexpectedly, this morning. Ermie was weeping as if her heart would break. I wondered if you –'

'– Wallace came to me yesterday and asked for her hand,' said Ushant abruptly. 'I should never have allowed mother to invite him here so frequently . . . then this . . . this ridiculous relationship would not have developed.'

'I believe Ermyntrude is in love with Mr Wallace,' said Nan, seriously. 'I hope you gave them your blessing.'

'Typical of the man to approach me when I was occupied with other things,' said Ushant irritably and he began to pace about the study that always seemed so much too large for him. 'Anyway I sent him packing. The man is universally known to be a bad lot.'

'Ushant,' gasped Nan, 'you know perfectly well that's not true. How could you?' and she dropped into one of her husband's uncomfortable chairs beneath the imposing mantelpiece.

'Ermyntrude has a title. She has money in her own right. Her place is here. With our mother.'

'Oh Ushant,' said Nan, 'this is indescribably cruel. There are plenty of people to look after your mother. I can look after your mother. Why should your sister have to forsake her future happiness to . . . to look after your mother?'

'It's too late for Ermyntrude to marry,' stammered Ushant. 'It smacks of desperation.'

This was too much for Annabel. She stood and faced her husband, her voice heavy with a harsh bitterness that he had not heard before. 'Ermyntrude is twenty-nine years old . . . that is neither too old nor is it too late. Ermie loves Mr Wallace and for all I know, he loves her. Why else would he ask for her hand in marriage?'

Ushant looked at Nan with an expression of amazed exasperation on his reddening features, but Nan rushed on, 'Why should she be condemned to a life without a husband . . . a life without children? Why? Just because you can't bear to see anyone else happy. Is that it?' And something wild and furious rose within her that, she dimly recognized, was now quite beyond her control. 'You will not admit that you know what it's like to be in love, will you? You press any feeling that threatens to show its face into service, or you dismiss it utterly. You think only of duty and . . . and . . . what is correct . . . You'd prefer it if all human beings tick-tocked mechanically . . . just like all your horrible clocks . . . wouldn't you? Wouldn't you?'

The Duke's features were dangerously florid and for a moment he saw nothing but blackness before him. Then a swift movement penetrated his blackened vision and he caught the swirl of his wife's skirts as she turned and left his study.

USHANT had given Guy Thwarte precise instructions upon how to reach the Longlands estate office – avoiding the house – and Guy had arrived at the appointed time, in the middle of the afternoon. When Guy held out his hand which Ushant shook perfunctorily, he felt his patron's anger like a tangible magnetic field about him, and he was suddenly drained of his customary strength in the face of an argument.

'I warned you six months ago,' said Ushant, 'but it appears that you have deliberately,' he emphasized the word, 'deliberately gone against my express wishes.' Ushant's pale eyes were like steel and his reddened jaw twitched.

'If I may not speak for the people whom I represent –'

'– You represent me,' said Ushant, pacing the room and rubbing his jaw with his forefinger and thumb as if to still its insistent twitching, 'and you represent families you've known since you were a boy . . . not a few of whom are members of the Upper House.'

'When I stood for election you knew my views, your Grace,' said Guy flatly. 'They have not changed.'

'But when you won the by-election you became my . . . my,' Ushant faltered, searching for the right word, 'spokesman,' he stammered.

Guy stared at Ushant. 'You expect me to speak in the House as you direct me to speak. But, unless I agree with you *and* I think that the views of the people I represent have been taken into account, I cannot. It is my duty to listen to the people whom I represent and to speak for them.'

'You were not elected to "speak for them,"' said Ushant. 'You were elected to speak for me. A man who bows to the masses has no mind of his own, no freedom to act on principle. Such behaviour heralds the end of politics as an honourable profession. But,' said Ushant looking at Guy sideways, 'honour may not, of course, be your first concern.'

Guy's eyes darkened. 'Very few of the "masses" yet have the vote. But when the right to vote extends to all, and I believe that day is not far off –'

'If you wanted to find a dull-witted, violent drunkard in this constituency,' interrupted Ushant, 'where would you look?'

Guy Thwarte, bewildered by Ushant's sudden change of tack, momentarily lost the thread of his argument and Ushant seized his opportunity. 'You're an ambitious man Mr Thwarte, but you only have one foot in the stirrup. You depend upon me, utterly, to provide you with everything you need to get on. You are mistaken if you think you can progress or even proceed on your own. I have it in my power to block your path, to knock your foot out of that stirrup, any time I damned well please. And I will, make no mistake Mr Thwarte, I will use my power without hesitation . . . without hesitation. And as for your arguments, they're . . . they're third rate. They're the arguments of a political adventurer . . . or should I merely say . . . an adventurer? I will not tolerate such behaviour where I preside.'

Guy Thwarte gave up his argument altogether. What had begun as an attack upon his political behaviour had descended into an attack upon his personal behaviour, and on that subject he would not be drawn. It was a matter of honour to him that he endure whatever personal insults Ushant should choose to rain down upon him, and that he should not attempt to defend himself on that subject.

'I cannot continue this conversation, your Grace,' said Guy. 'If what you wish for is my resignation, then you may have it. I –'

'– No, no my dear chap,' said Ushant with another sudden change of tack and tone. 'No, no . . . not at all. Just as long as this little matter is behind us . . . forever.'

Guy could not answer Ushant. He was unable to fathom where his opponent's true argument with him lay, but he suspected that his speech in the House of Commons had provided Ushant with the chance to vent his fury over a quite separate subject, and thus he had rendered Guy powerless to answer the charges laid against him.

'Make sure you leave by the same way you came,' Ushant was saying, 'kick over the traces, eh?'

As Guy Thwarte left Longlands, riding slowly along a winding, neglected back drive, the sound of girlish laughter rose from the house below him on the still evening air. And then he heard Annabel's laughter, but it was a shrill unnatural laugh and Guy's back stiffened as he urged his horse away from the sound.

# FORTY

G̲UY THWARTE COULD NOT RID HIMSELF OF THE SOUND OF Annabel's unnatural laughter. It echoed in his head for days after his unpleasant encounter with Ushant, and he found that she was constantly in his thoughts and he feared for her. It was she who had said that she could not live a life of lies and hypocrisy, and that was why she had left London. But what was she living now? And what of his life now? Weren't their lives just as false as one another's, feeling as they did for each other (she had not denied it) and yet failing to allow their feelings to have their true expression?

Guy's own feelings for Nan had grown stronger since she had left London, no matter how hard he tried to deny them. The more he tried to stifle his emotions, the stronger they grew. He thought about her everywhere he went and he saw her everywhere he went. He thought about their days together, those glorious days at Champions, and he believed that he now knew what it would be like to die of love. He would leave the country, that was it, that was what he would do. But then again he would not. How could he leave the country when his reason for living moved and breathed upon English soil?

Guy Thwarte did not frequent the places Annabel frequented because he did not trust himself. He knew that if he saw her he would betray himself, if not by what he said, then

by a look, or a touch. Truly he did not think he could bear to
be in the same room without showing her how he felt. It was
better by far to stay away. So he divided his time without
enthusiasm between Honourslove, Champions and the
Palace of Westminster and his sense of honour had more
than once forced him to cut short a visit to Champions, as
Cora Glenloe's trusting glances pierced through the dark wall
of his own unhappiness. Every time Cora Glenloe smiled at
him Guy could only think of Nan, and he felt keenly the
unkindness of placing Cora in the very predicament in
which he found himself. He must free her from the hopeless-
ness of falling in love with someone who could never be hers.

Guy stood up from his desk. He would tell Cora now . . .
he would drive over to Champions directly.

'Miss Testvalley – Laura – and I have some important news
to communicate to you,' said Sir Helmsley, detaining his son
with his arm as he strode across the hall. Guy turned and
guessed from his father's hesitant use of Miss Testvalley's first
name, and from the high colour of his face, precisely what his
father had to 'communicate' to him and he held out his
hand. He was delighted for his father and, for a moment, forgot his own unhappiness.

'My congratulations to you father,' he said, 'I hope you will
both be very happy. But where is the lady in question?'

'In the drawing-room,' said Sir Helmsley, with a sideways
jerk of his head. 'She said I should tell you myself . . . something about not wanting to be in the way when I told you.
Between father and son, she said,' said Sir Helmsley, and Guy
thought, not for the first time, what a remarkable woman
Miss Laura Testvalley was and how well she understood the
workings of the human heart.

Sir Helmsley put his arm about Guy's shoulders and as
they walked towards the drawing-room Guy looked about
him and wondered how Miss Testvalley felt about the house
that he and his father loved so much. And his heart told

him that the new mistress of Honourslove would love and cherish the house just as he would, when his turn came.

Nan St George paced the floor of the Correggio room in a state of extreme agitation. She had tried to contain her outburst against Ushant but she could not. She had tried to quell her feelings the way Annabel Tintagel would, but Nan St George had burst forth and overpowered Annabel Tintagel. Nan St George felt passionately on behalf of her sister-in-law Ermyntrude, but that passion had overflowed into accusations against her husband which she had not intended. Her anger would not be checked; she had been consumed by the desire to denounce Ushant's self-satisfied world, a world where women were not permitted feelings or desires. She realized now that she had wanted him to roar and rage at her, but, as usual, his anger had emerged in short stammered sentences which showed Nan that his defence against passion was instinctive, inarticulate and yet far stronger than any words. His ancestors had behaved thus for almost four hundred years and Nan realized that Ushant would never alter the pattern.

Nan knew that her outburst had been a shriek of despair, a cry for her own freedom, and she saw that her husband intended to kill her passion, if he could, with his disdain. She had vowed that she would not be governed by her passions, but she could not live a dispassionate life. Ushant had been trained to do so from the moment he was born, but Nan's heartfelt plea for Ermie (and for herself) came from the very depths of her being and could not be stifled any longer. She knew now that she could never live according to Ushant's rules, nor within his walls, no matter how hard she tried.

She turned to the chair in front of her desk which was covered with sheets of writing paper – evidence of her many attempts to communicate something of what she felt to Miss Testvalley – she would make one last effort to write a letter.

My dearest Val (she wrote),
I have failed yet again in my miserable attempts to recon-
cile myself with my gaolers.

She sucked the end of her pen and stared through the window.

I never was any good at letters, so please be patient with
me and I will try to explain. You are the only person in the
world I can tell and the only person in the world (apart
from Guy . . .) who will at least try to understand.

I have been reckless and impulsive and didn't think
before I spoke and . . . and I have hurt Ushant very much
without meaning to, but he won't discuss it. Something
inside me refused to be silent any longer, and before I
knew it I'd said what I felt – what Nan St George really
feels – and now we just don't speak about it. In fact we
don't speak at all. I am living – if you can call it living –
inside an iron cage and the bars are fashioned from his
silence. I've tried to break out but he simply dismisses me
. . . you know what he's like. But I can't go on living like
this, Val. And when I feel like this, I think of Guy, and
that makes it even worse. I think of what he would have
done if I'd said such awful things to him . . . but then I'd
never have had to say such awful things to him.

What am I saying Val? Perhaps I should tear this up.
Perhaps what I am telling you is too dangerous to write.
But I must tell you . . . I don't know who else to tell and I
can't remain silent any longer. I can't trust anyone else . . .
and I can't keep it all locked up inside me or I'll burst.

Nan pushed her chair back and began to pace about her
room once more. She stopped beneath one of the Correggios
and then she hurried back to her desk.

Ushant cares for appearances and precedence and rank
and order, and these things do have their place, I know,
but he seems to care nothing for beauty, nor for the thrill

of a glorious day, nor has he any sympathy for his fellow human beings (because, I believe, he has none for himself). We two are utterly different, and although I have tried as hard as I know to adopt the attitudes and the duties and all the paraphernalia that go with being his wife, and I have honestly tried to discover what it is that would make our lives bearable together, he seems quite unable – or quite unwilling – to understand the slightest thing about me.

I suppose I sensed it from the very beginning and that's why I never talked to him of the things that have meaning for me. But since my return I have tried, and he looks at me blankly, as if poetry and painting and ideas and beauty were as alien to him as the mistakes I still make over who should sit where when all his dreary titled family come to stay. I have sincerely tried to live his life, Val, but it seems that I cannot do it any longer, even when I intend to. I cannot keep myself down . . . I thought I could bury the self, the me who came back at Champions, when I returned here. But she keeps coming back, quite without my intending her to, and this time I don't want to let her go, I want to hold on to her. She's the true Nan St George and I know her . . . she is mine, she is me.

But if I am not to bury her, then I cannot remain Ushant's wife because Nan St George cannot live like this. And isn't it wrong to live a lie anyway? Surely it is crueller to Ushant to remain here and pretend that I am someone I am not, than it is to leave him. Or am I merely giving myself the perfect excuse?

Nan rang for a servant and requested a fire. The day was unseasonably dark and cold and when the fire was lit she sat beside it, continuing her letter on her knee.

Surely my past mistakes should not condemn me to lead the life of someone who is not, and never will be, truly me.

Especially not since I have learned so much from them . . .
my mistakes, I mean. I have learned that I cannot live a lie
and that I do not wish to hurt anyone but, more than anything, that I am not afraid to be on my own, nor to speak up
for myself. I have learned that I would prefer to live alone
than to go on with this twilit half-life here with Ushant . . .

Perhaps I should become a governess like you, dearest
Val. You have taught me enough so that I should be able
to earn my living, haven't you?

But then – and I must be truthful to myself and to you –
my thoughts turn often to Guy Thwarte. When I left
London I told him that our time together at Champions
was a dream – a wonderful dream – but a dream. Now I
believe that it was the only true and real thing I have ever
known. When I am with Guy there is a perfect understanding between us that I have known with no other –
save with you. With him my confidence never falters and
the words do not hang back . . . I am never at a loss. I am
myself and sometimes, oddly, I feel as though I were him.

But, dearest Val, what I really mean to ask you is this. If I
believe that I can see something, even if the rest of the
world cannot see it, have I the right to reach for it? May I
not be my truest self while I live? And if I must leave Ushant
to become that self, then shouldn't I do so? And if a part of
that self resides in Guy Thwarte, is it so terribly wrong to
want to unite those two selves?

Dearest, wisest, most patient-hearted Val, please advise
me. Could you . . . would you come to stay at Longlands
for a few days, if Lady Glenloe can spare you? I need, desperately, to talk this over with you before I make my final
decision . . . because whatever I decide will be final, I
know that now. I shall await your answer impatiently.

With my very best love, Nan.

PS: If I don't hear from you I shall know that you feel unable to advise me and that I must decide for myself . . . and I shall understand.

As always, your Nan.

Nan folded her letter and addressed it to Miss Testvalley, in care of Lady Glenloe at Champions. She sealed the letter and then, impulsively, she kissed it before she rang for a servant and instructed him to ensure that the letter caught the very next post. When the servant left her room Nan gathered up all the sheets of writing paper from her desk, all her unsuccessful attempts to explain to Miss Testvalley how she felt, and she fed them, one by one, to her fire, making them catch and flare brightly and burn. She watched them until the last one wavered weightless and grey above the flames, until it turned a wild somersault on an updraught and was drawn aloft and out of her sight.

# FORTY-ONE

THE ANNUAL OCTOBER FÊTE AT CHAMPIONS WAS UNDER WAY and the rain had held off. The sun shone patchily and Lady Glenloe bustled about issuing orders in her ringing tones (particularly to those whom she suspected of neglecting their duties) while the thronging children contrived to undo the adults' careful preparations at every turn.

'Ah, Miss Testvalley,' said Lady Glenloe breathlessly as Miss Testvalley crossed the lawn that ran the length of the south side of the house, 'the very person. Would you please instil some manners, some sense of propriety, into the children. They've just undone the ribbon that marks the end of the egg-and-spoon race, and my patience has deserted me. I'm certain you'll do better.' Laura Testvalley smiled and sped across the lawn in the direction indicated by Lady Glenloe's wildly waving arm.

'That's a pretty shawl, Miss Testvalley,' said Sophie Marable, 'you don't usually wear things like that.'

The colour rose momentarily in Miss Testvalley's cheeks. 'Thank you, Lady Sophia,' said Miss Testvalley, but she was not to be distracted from her purpose. 'Now,' she said, 'who can explain why this ribbon is lying on the grass when it should be fixed between the winning posts?' There was a loud and confused chorus of: 'He did it!' and 'She made me!' and

'Thomas, you promised not to tell,' but Miss Testvalley's calm influence soon had the ribbon fixed between the posts and the children playing amicably together . . . at least until the next time.

Miss Testvalley left the children and, seeing Sir Helmsley signalling to her from the other side of the lawn, quickened her step towards him. She passed the high yew hedge that bordered an arbour on her left and, from the corner of her eye, she caught a quick movement and at the same time heard: 'Val,' urgently whispered. Miss Testvalley glanced in Sir Helmsley's direction and seeing him occupied with Guy Thwarte, who had just arrived, and with the Glenloe girls, she hastened into the arbour to be confronted by an agitated Nan.

'Didn't you get my letter?' said Nan, her face a flurry of worried frowns.

'What letter?' said Miss Testvalley.

'The letter I sent you . . . ages ago.'

They sat on a wooden bench, hidden from view by the high yew hedge. 'Why Nan, no one has told you have they? I was sure Ushant would tell you. I was with my family in Denmark Hill, and I have only just returned. I thought I should tell them in person . . .' Miss Testvalley paused. 'Sir Helmsley and I are to be married. I came with him from Honourslove today. I have not been at Champions for –'

But Miss Testvalley could not continue for she found herself enfolded in Nan's arms and Nan, half-way between laughter and tears, said, 'How wonderful. Oh Val, how delightful. Let me look at you. Tell me everything. I want you to tell me everything. Where will you live? Will you live –' she faltered, 'at Honourslove? And,' she rushed on, 'when are you to marry? How long have you been engaged? You've never looked so beautiful . . . and wherever did you find this magnificent shawl?' said Nan holding out one end of Sir Helmsley's present.

Miss Testvalley laughingly answered Nan's questions one by one, but she soon saw that Nan was barely able to concentrate on her answers and she hastened to her conclusion. 'Now,' she said, wrapping her shawl closer about her shoulders and glancing up at the sky, 'what was it that you wrote to me . . . you who so rarely write letters?' But Nan's answer was to burst into tears of such anguish that Miss Testvalley held her close and rocked her back and forth as if she had been a small child.

Eventually Nan said, 'I wrote for your advice. I didn't know what to do. I have been unhappy at Longlands ever since I returned, although I've tried so hard not to be. And I have been miserable without Guy Thwarte, despite trying my hardest not to think of him. I have failed on both counts and oh, Val, dearest Val, I've let you down so badly.'

Miss Testvalley shook her head and smiled at Nan. 'I promised you that I would be at your side should you need me, should the time come, and here I am . . . belatedly.'

'I thought you hadn't replied because you wanted me to decide for myself, to make up my own mind . . . that's what I said I should understand if you decided not to reply . . .'

Miss Testvalley gathered Nan into her arms and shook her head once more. 'If you only knew the number of times I've rewritten the past, putting in all the things I might have said and done to prevent your marriage. If I had done what I should have done when the Duke came to see me at Runnymede –' Nan stifled a gasp, 'your situation, my dearest Nan, might have been entirely different. And, as I tried to tell you when you stayed here, I think it wrong . . . quite wrong . . . that you should suffer the unhappy consequences of mistakes that were made, as it were, as much for you as by you.'

The two women sat side by side for a long time without speaking, and then Miss Testvalley took Nan's hand into her own. 'I love you, dearest Nan, as I would love a daugh-

ter of my own. And if I were your mother, I would coun-
sel you to follow your heart. I watched you and Guy
Thwarte when you stayed here last summer and I saw
something worthy of the sacrifices you will undoubtedly
have to make. I saw something worth giving up everything
else for; I saw your deep abiding love for one another,' she
paused and her black eyes shone with tears, 'and so I give
you my blessing.'

Nan clung to Miss Testvalley and then pulled away.
'Follow your heart,' said Miss Testvalley, 'because your heart
is true Nan St George. You will find that the words you need
will come soon enough now. The time has come for you to
speak your heart.' Nan hugged Miss Testvalley and kissed her
and thanked her and at last they stood up. 'If anyone should
ask why we were talking for so long,' said Miss Testvalley
with a quick smile, 'I shall say that I was telling you of my
marriage plans.'

'Oh Val, oh dearest, dearest Val,' said Nan as they walked
towards the gap in the tall yew hedge, 'Shall you be as happy
as I know I shall? –' Nan stopped and stared out across the
lawn. Miss Testvalley followed her startled gaze and saw Guy
Thwarte walking with Cora Glenloe towards the white marquee. Nan shrank back between the walls of the high yew
hedge, tugging at Laura Testvalley's sleeve.

'Of course,' she said flatly, 'he's here to see Cora, isn't he?'
and Nan's face expressed such desperation that it was all Miss
Testvalley could do to restrain herself from catching Nan and
holding her fast, in full view of all at the fête on the lawn
before them. 'Of course,' repeated Nan, barely knowing what
she was saying, 'he will marry Cora, won't he? Cora will make
him a perfect wife.' Nan looked about her distractedly.

'He's here because he's the local MP,' said Miss Testvalley,
trying to reassure the desperate Nan, and she looked deep
into Nan's eyes. 'Shall I tell him you're here?' she said and
Nan took a deep breath. 'Yes,' she said, 'Quickly Val. Before I

lose heart.' Nan returned to the wooden bench behind the high yew hedge and Miss Testvalley hurried across the lawn towards the marquee.

LONG trestle tables covered with white cloths and piled high with sandwiches, pies and cakes stood under the canvas. There were two huge tea-urns and numerous jugs of lemonade and there were wooden kegs of beer. Conchita Marable shepherded Edward and Sophie; Virginia Seadown held Frederick by the hand and little Flora, who was taking her first struggling steps; Thomas Robinson careered around the marquee evading his mother and her instructions to him to sit down and behave himself; and the servants handed out the tea, the lemonade and the beer and passed round the plates of sandwiches.

Laura Testvalley stood on the threshold looking for Guy. When she saw him, on the far side of the marquee, she walked directly towards him without pausing to speak to anyone on her way. When she reached Guy he bent his head to hear what she had to say and then he put his cup of tea down and hurried from the marquee. Miss Testvalley watched him go and then, aware that someone was watching her, she turned and saw Sir Helmsley looking at her curiously. She smiled at him and moved towards him.

Cora Glenloe, her eyes never far from the place where Guy Thwarte was, watched him leave and then instinctively she followed him. When she reached the entrance to the marquee she stopped and saw Guy walk towards the high yew hedge. Cora watched the distance between them lengthen and she hesitated, and then she ran across the lawn behind him. Guy disappeared through the gap in the yew hedge and Cora flew in, a moment later, behind him. And then she stopped dead. She saw Guy leaning over the Duchess of Tintagel in a way that he had never leaned over her and, for a moment, she was unable to move. Then, with a cry that made both Nan and Guy look up, she turned and ran from the arbour.

Cora Glenloe ran sightlessly across the lawn and into the marquee. She stopped and looked helplessly about her, and then she turned and fled in to the house. She did not hear her mother call to her, nor did she hear Sir Helmsley push the trestle table angrily from him. She did not see the Duke of Tintagel's startled glance as she ran past him, neither did she see Miss Testvalley stand as if to run after her, and then change her mind.

'A most successful day, Lady Glenloe,' said the Rector, bending over Lady Glenloe's hand, 'and as always we are indebted to you.' Lady Glenloe smiled and murmured her thanks to the Rector and his wife for their support, and then she took Sir Helmsley's hand as he and Miss Testvalley prepared to leave.

The guests were grouped in twos and threes on the terrace, awaiting their turn to thank Lady Glenloe and to say goodbye. Ushant was one of the last to take Lady Glenloe's hand. As he bowed to Lady Glenloe, he said, without looking up, 'Have you seen Annabel, Augusta?' and Lady Glenloe's hand froze in Ushant's. 'I've looked everywhere for her,' he continued, 'and I can't find her. Do you suppose she might be in the house?'

For some reason that Augusta Glenloe could not explain, a vision of her stricken daughter, as she stood on the threshold of the marquee, filled her mind. She replied absently to Ushant, 'Cora may know where she is. I will send for Cora.' At that moment Sir Helmsley Thwarte strode angrily back across the terrace towards Lady Glenloe and the few remaining guests fell silent as he pushed his way through them. Laura Testvalley hung back on the edge of the terrace while the departing guests stopped in their tracks and turned from their carriages to discover the cause of the commotion behind them.

'Have you seen my son?' bellowed Sir Helmsley, his colour rising fast and then, seeing Ushant and Lady Glenloe standing silent and pale and apparently quite unable to answer him, he looked wildly about him and searched the faces of the silent guests as if his life depended upon finding his son's face among them. 'Can't seem to find him anywhere,' said Sir Helmsley, his tone suddenly deathly quiet, 'quite unlike him to leave without saying goodbye.'

'Miss Testvalley,' said Lady Glenloe, and her imperious tones rang the length of the terrace, 'would you find Cora and bring her here . . . at once.' Laura Testvalley nodded and quickly crossed the terrace towards the open French windows. The astonished guests began to murmur to one another as they watched Sir Helmsley stride determinedly across the terrace after Miss Testvalley. Sir Helmsley's eyes were dark and his tone furious as he called after her, 'Laura . . . Laura . . . LAURA,' he commanded, 'WAIT!'

Ushant and Lady Glenloe remained standing together, unable to think of anything to say. Lady Glenloe's guests seemed to have forgotten entirely that they had been in the process of leaving Champions. They talked animatedly in excited buzzing groups as if they had only just called to mind the one subject they had intended to discuss all afternoon.

SIR Helmsley strode behind Laura Testvalley as she hurried across the hall; he caught her arm as she started up the stairs. Only when they were half-way up the stairs and would not be overheard, did he let go of her. Miss Testvalley turned to face him, half-knowing what he would say, half-hoping that he would not say it. She stood two or three steps above Sir Helmsley and waited. Her brilliant shawl slipped from her shoulders onto the stairs.

'You've known all along, haven't you?' said Sir Helmsley, his colour dark above his auburn beard. 'You've been their go-between.'

Laura Testvalley turned from Sir Helmsley, stepped over her shawl and walked up to the landing where the great staircase divided. Then she turned back to face him. 'No,' she said, 'I have not. I knew only that they felt something for each other, but until today I did not know –'

'– That little American upstart and my son,' gasped Sir Helmsley, hardly able to say the words.

Miss Testvalley moved towards him. 'Annabel's marriage was a terrible mistake, a mistake I colluded in –'

'Mistakes have to be lived with,' said Sir Helmsley contemptuously. 'I suppose you mean Annabel was unhappy? Do you think my own marriage was happy? Do you think most marriages are happy? I didn't love my wife, but she brought out the best in me –'

'Did she?' said Miss Testvalley quietly. 'Or did she only ensure that you played safe? At least your son has the courage of his convictions.' Miss Testvalley backed away from Sir Helmsley as he moved towards her. She thought he would strike her, but he lowered his arm.

'I thank God I've been saved from my convictions,' he said. 'What in God's name did you think you were doing? Is self-destruction your idea of courage?'

Laura Testvalley leaned against the wall. She seemed suddenly smaller, frailer, almost helpless and Sir Helmsley, despite his anger, made a move to put his arm around her, and then checked himself. 'Can a woman never be free,' said Laura Testvalley, 'to choose a life? To love, and to have a will of her own?'

'What makes you think you haven't a will of your own, Miss Testvalley?' said Sir Helmsley, his colour rising ever more dangerously. 'Surely you have just exercised it?' and Sir Helmsley turned on his heel, stooping to pick up Laura's shawl as he went. He flung the bright shawl over his shoulder and walked down the stairs without once turning back to Laura and Laura, with a heavy heart, walked on up the stairs

to her room, groping blindly now at the wall, now at the ban-
nister, now tripping on the edge of her skirts, until she
reached her room.

Laura Testvalley opened her door and looked around her
gloomy room and then she flung herself onto her bed and
sobbed, for all the world as if she were a young woman . . . a
young woman who had just lost her first love.

# FORTY-TWO

USHANT AVOIDED THE INEVITABLE INTERVIEW WITH HIS mother for as long as he reasonably could, he would have liked to postpone it indefinitely. But her latest summons had included the threat of an invitation to Jean Hopeleigh (still unmarried, still hunting a title) and her mother, and Ushant acknowledged his mother's tactic by agreeing to a meeting. He planned to extract a promise from his mother to cancel the invitation to the Hopeleighs in exchange for his agreement upon the other subject.

On his way to the dower-house on a bleak winter morning, Ushant wondered, not for the first time, why he had not stopped Annabel, why he had not commanded her to return to his side, but he sensed, dimly, that he was incapable of such a display. He was inordinately nervous of women, of what they might do or say, particularly in public, and he could not have taken the risk . . . heaven only knows what she might have done if he had . . . . But he raged inwardly at Annabel for her public humiliation of him and for forcing his present difficulties upon him. He had always felt that the behaviour of women was incomprehensible and, but for his duty to provide an heir for the Tintagel line, he would have preferred to avoid them altogether.

Ushant entered his mother's cold drawing-room, prepared to do battle.

'Sometimes, Ushant, your obstinacy frightens me,' said the Dowager. 'If you do not divorce her you cannot remarry. And it is your duty to remarry.'

Ushant paced the room nervously.

'You cannot expect me to accept that the Tintagel line ends with you,' the Dowager said bitterly. 'Not when I think of everything I went through to preserve it. I could never escape my duty.' She glanced up at her son and her small black eyes glittered. 'And even if *she*,' she laid especial emphasis upon the word, 'came crawling back on her knees, I should insist you divorce her.' The Dowager's lips were pressed into a thin line and her voice was constrained. 'I should insist. Oh . . .' the Dowager wrung her hands, 'it is quite dreadful what young women think they can get away with nowadays. I shall never forgive her. Never. And after all my kindnesses to her.' The tears formed on her short lashes and spilled over onto her pinched cheeks. 'Our generation is dying out,' she said. 'I had a letter from Selina Brightlingsea yesterday –'

'– I know,' said Ushant, turning to face his mother. 'I had a letter from Seadown. Old Lord Brightlingsea is dead.' He stared at his mother's lifeless hearth.

'Well at least he's well provided for,' said the Dowager, 'at least he has heirs for his line.' Ushant saw his mother's tears and was seized by a desperate urge to leave her room. 'I am the only male heir to the Tintagel line,' said the Duke mechanically, 'and I shall do my duty, I promise.' Ushant moved towards his mother, 'But please mother, let me go about it in my own way.' The Duke stooped and touched his mother briefly on the shoulder, stammered something inaudible, and left her freezing drawing-room.

USHANT wandered the passages at Longlands. He opened the door to Annabel's bedroom and let himself in. He walked around her room touching the brushes on her dressing-table, the clothes in her wardrobe. Nothing there had changed and it seemed to Ushant that at any moment Annabel would run into the room laughing, or serious, or full of one of her new ideas . . . ideas that he had held in such contempt and that now, inexplicably, he would have welcomed.

Ushant dined alone and he read while he dined. He stared at one of his favourite clocks until its sound filled his head and he could not stand it. He left the dining-room and the servant returned yet another plate of uneaten food to the cook.

Ushant opened the door to Annabel's boudoir and stood before the paintings that she had loved. He made a vain attempt to recall what she had said about them, but he could only remember his own irritation when she had removed all the family paintings and photographs that had looked so well in the spaces between the Correggios.

'I took them down to give these magnificent paintings the setting they deserve,' she had said. She didn't understand anything; how could she have removed his great-aunts' illuminations of Vesuvius? And as for taking down the sporting photographs of his father and of himself . . . the woman had not the slightest respect for family traditions. 'But, naturally,' he reassured himself, 'hers were *American* ideas. My future wife,' his anger rose as he stalked from the room, 'shall be English and she shall share my views in all things.' Ushant slammed the door behind him and turned the key in the lock. He dropped the key into a porcelain vase on a table in the passage and walked quickly away from his wife's boudoir.

LAURA Testvalley smoothed her hair and stood up. The Glenloes had left unexpectedly for Scotland and the great house was empty. Laura's modest horse-hair box and her trunk lay open on the floor, her few possessions barely filling them. She gathered up her books, the most precious of her possessions, from her writing-table and carried them across the large room. She laid them carefully in her trunk and returned to the writing-table. She opened a small black note-book and slipped a letter between two pages, then she wrapped the notebook, wrote an address on the outside and slipped the packet into the pocket of her black merino.

Miss Testvalley rang for the servant and instructed him to take her box and her trunk downstairs and then, pausing for one last look around the room where her happiest memories would forever remain, she turned and closed the door behind her.

The hall echoed with Miss Testvalley's footsteps and she looked neither to right nor to left. The servant held the door open for her and Miss Testvalley walked between the great stone pillars of the Champions porch and climbed into the waiting carriage. The wheels of her carriage ground their way slowly up the drive and the rain that drove against the car-riage window transformed Miss Testvalley's last view of Champions into a wavering watery image.

Guy Thwarte walked across the drawing-room at Honours-love towards his father. Sir Helmsley sat at the piano and he did not hear his son's approach. He stopped playing and looked through the window at the hard ground and the bare trees outside, and then he looked up sharply as he heard a footstep. He stood to face his son.

'Well I have to hand it to you,' he said bitterly, 'you're either a brave man or a fool to turn up here.'

Guy held out his hand to his father who ignored the ges-ture. 'There are things I must say to you, father,' he said, his voice constrained by his attempt to keep his feelings in check, 'I believe you have not read my letters, or you have decided not to reply to me . . . but I could hardly go away without say-ing goodbye. I am going to South Africa. I've secured a posi-tion as an engineer. The South Africa Company is building a railway link between the Cape and Durban.'

Sir Helmsley was taken aback, this was news indeed. It was one thing to behave with the expected degree of hostility towards the offending member of society – even one's own son, until sufficient time had elapsed – but it was quite another to have one's initiative stolen and one's equilibrium upset by the announcement of . . . of such unexpected plans.

'Best place for you under the circumstances,' Sir Helmsley ventured at length.

Guy took a deep breath. His father had made no indication that they should sit down, so they remained standing. 'I have handed in my official resignation –'

'To Ushant?' interrupted Sir Helmsley.

'No,' said Guy, 'I went to the constituency office at Lowdon.' There was a pause and the two men looked at each other. Sir Helmsley was the first to look away. 'I'm desperately sorry for the pain I have caused,' said Guy, 'and I am especially sorry father, to have caused you such distress. But there was no other way.'

Sir Helmsley began to walk about the room and his conflicting emotions battled for supremacy. At length he turned back to his son. 'Guy,' he said, 'Guy I beg you . . . go to Africa if you must, but go alone. Break off this insane liaison.'

'That's something I'm not prepared to discuss,' said Guy firmly.

'Then, by God,' said Sir Helmsley, his anger successfully over-riding all other emotions, 'you'll lose Honourslove, I can promise you that. I shall redraft my Will. You . . .' he jabbed his finger at Guy and his cheeks flamed above his auburn beard, 'you've destroyed – in one suicidal move – everything I ever hoped for . . . for you. You are no longer my son.'

Guy waited for his father's hectic pacing about the room to subside and then he said, gently, 'Father, you hoped that I would live in a certain way and achieve certain things . . . but you hoped that I would be . . . and do . . . these things for you, not for me. You hoped to see me follow in your footsteps and I believe, sir, that I love this house every bit as much as you do, but I have always lived my life in a different manner and, I think, with different principles. And it may even be,' said Guy, his voice breaking, 'that the time for such houses, even houses as beautiful and graceful as our own dear Honourslove, is over.'

Sir Helmsley dropped into a chair. 'Laura should never have behaved as she did,' he said. 'If it hadn't been for her –' he broke off. '– I haven't seen her since the fête at Champions, and I shall not see her again.'

Guy crossed the drawing-room and stood looking down at his father. 'If you choose to see nothing but dishonour in my behaviour, so be it. But it is shabby of you, father, to blame Miss Testvalley . . . and it makes me inexpressibly sad that you should not see her. She would have made you a good wife.'

Sir Helmsley's head sank onto his chest and Guy pulled up a chair, close to his father's. 'Sir,' he said, 'Annabel is to come with me to Africa. We shall be married in Cape Town . . . your grandchild . . . your grandchildren . . . will be born in Cape Town . . . and we intend to make a success of our new lives.' Guy paused and laid his hand on his father's arm. 'But, sir, let us not part without –'

Sir Helmsley turned his auburn head towards his son and Guy was moved to see his father's eyes shining with tears. Briefly the two men embraced and then Sir Helmsley pushed Guy away roughly. 'Now leave, Guy,' he said and his son stood up, pressed his hand against his father's shoulder and walked away down the length of the drawing-room.

Guy's departing footsteps echoed inside Sir Helmsley's head long after they were gone.

HECTOR and Lizzy Robinson sat in bed, reading the morning newspapers. A pale wintry sunlight filled the bedroom and the partially open window let in the sounds of early morning London. A bright fire burned in the grate and the remains of their breakfast was strewn over trays on their bedside tables, and, as was the Robinson custom, their children were with them. Thomas knelt on the floor piling wooden blocks one on top of the other, and the twin boys scrambled about on their parents' large bed.

Suddenly Hector folded his newspaper back with a crackle. 'Oh I say, Lizzy,' he said, 'here it is.' Lizzy Robinson turned towards her husband. '"The twelfth Duke of Tintagel is suing his wife, the American heiress Annabel St George,"' read Hector, '"for divorce on the grounds of her adultery". Oh my Lord!' Hector glanced at his wife, 'listen to this . . . "with Mr Guy Thwarte, Liberal MP for Lowdon . . ."'

'Sssh . . .' said Lizzy, 'the children.'

Hector glanced at the boys, reassured himself that they were preoccupied, and continued. 'Well there's one blessing . . . at least he's not a Tory.'

Lizzy's dark brows arched. 'Really Hector,' she said, but then she relented, 'Do go on,' she said, 'what else does it say?'

'"This is the first time scandal has rocked this illustrious family since Henry VII created the first Duke of Tintagel in 1505 . . . the Duchess's sister is Lady Seadown, who recently became the eleventh Marchioness Brightlingsea following the death of her father-in-law, the tenth Marquess."'

'Dear Heaven,' said Lizzy, her eyes alight, 'they don't mention us, do they?'

'It doesn't look like it,' said Hector scanning the page, 'it doesn't look like it.'

There was a knock at the bedroom door and two smiling nurses gathered up the twin boys and called to Thomas to accompany them.

Lizzy kissed her husband and then, pushing back the bed-clothes with her feet, she stood, stretched luxuriously and walked to her dressing-table. She watched her husband in her glass as she brushed her long dark hair. 'I hope Nan will find happiness,' she said wistfully, 'I truly hope she will. Because if she doesn't, she's burned her boats and she won't get another chance.' She turned to her husband. 'At least,' she said smiling at him, her keen eyes on his face, 'it'll never happen to us. We'll never have to go through all that agony and', she narrowed her bright eyes, 'all that public scrutiny and censure.'

Hector Robinson put down his newspaper and climbed out of bed. He walked across the pretty room towards his wife and when he reached her he stood behind her and placed his hands proprietorially on her shoulders. Their eyes met in the glass.

'That we will not, my Lizzy,' he said, his syllables precise and his tone assured, 'that we will not.'

# FORTY-THREE

LADY BRIGHTLINGSEA WORE HER CRÊPE WITH DIGNITY. SHE sat erect and alone in the carriage that followed Lord Brightlingsea's hearse through the bleak flat landscape towards the Brightlingsea burial ground. She wore two veils so that it was difficult to distinguish her features and, from her point of view, lent the air of a gently fading photograph to all that she surveyed.

'Thank heaven Virginia has not turned out like that other woman,' she thought, 'I don't know where I should be if she had. If Brightlingsea had known about it, it might have killed him . . . and poor dear Blanche, whatever will she do? Of course Virginia is the very model of an Englishwoman,' her thoughts roamed imaginatively, 'and an Englishwoman does not behave like that. She's even settled Seadown . . . quite extraordinary . . . she's succeeded with him where many would have failed. So exactly the sort Blanche should have chosen for her own dear Ushant.' Lady Brightlingsea's thoughts continued in this reassuring vein until her carriage stopped and the servant opened the door and pulled down the steps.

The eleventh Marchioness Brightlingsea handed her mother-in-law from her carriage and stood by her as she adjusted her veils, smoothed her black bombazine, lifted her chin and prepared to face her world. 'Thank you my dear,' she said to Virginia and then her eyes rested upon the horse-drawn hearse. The four black horses stood motionless but the black crêpe on the tall hats of the four men who stood before and behind the hearse fluttered in a cold gust of wind, and the black shroud on the coffin fluttered as Selina Brightlingsea clutched at her daughter-in-law's arm.

'It's all right, Mama,' said Virginia soothingly, 'we're all here.' Lady Brightlingsea steadied herself against Virginia and lifted her chin once more. She watched as Seadown and Ushant, Dickie and that agreeable young friend of Ushant's, Lord Percy, lifted the shrouded coffin onto their shoulders and Lord Brightlingsea's final journey began.

The procession formed a tightly knit group that moved as one up the incline. No one, not even a child, strayed from the group and no one spoke, except to murmur an appropriate word of solace. No one mentioned those who were absent from the procession, indeed most in the procession did not consider anyone to be absent. They had closed ranks and consigned to oblivion those who did not observe their customs. Thus they lived and thus they died. And so, although they all heard the unexpected sound of a carriage arriving below them, not one of them turned to look.

A veiled woman stepped from the carriage. She held a wreath and she looked up at the steadily progressing little group above her. The stark countryside glinted beneath a pale wintry sun and the woman took a step forwards, hesitated and hung back.

Conchita Marable, on the pretext of straightening Edward's shirt-collar, looked sideways at the veiled woman and her hand flew to her mouth over her own veil. Her swift movement did not go unnoticed and the other mourners warned her with their glances. Lizzy Robinson took an involuntary step sideways but Hector restrained her with a fierce, 'Lizzy!'

But Conchita signalled to a nurse to watch her children and she turned and walked down the incline towards the veiled woman. Instantly the procession closed the gap that Conchita left, as though nothing had happened. The service began and the Rector's voice carried from the graveside down to the two women.

'Darling Nan,' said Conchita embracing the veiled woman, 'darling, darling Nan.'

'I had to say goodbye,' said Nan. 'Would you put this on his grave for me?' Conchita's aquamarine eyes, now filled with tears behind her veil, glanced up the hill and then back down at Nan. She took the wreath from Nan and gave her hand a squeeze and then, impulsively, she embraced her friend once more.

'It would be you, wouldn't it, dearest Nan,' she said, 'you who, in the end, had more courage than the rest of us put together.'

'And it would be you,' whispered Nan into her friend's ear, 'who had the courage not to cut me.'

'I never desert a friend,' said Conchita, 'never. Be happy, darling Nan, won't you?' and with one last glance into Nan's veiled eyes Conchita turned and walked back up the incline. Nan watched Conchita place her wreath beside the coffin, and then she turned and climbed into her carriage. She tapped on the wall for the driver to move on and her carriage rattled its lonely way over the frozen rutted track. Nan shivered inside the carriage and pulled her black wrap tightly around her shoulders.

# FORTY-FOUR

THE DAY WAS BRIGHT AND CLEAR, THE GROUND SPARKLED with frost and when Nan caught her first glimpse of the sea it glittered its greeting to her. Their carriage was travelling along the tops of the South Downs and the sun flashed palely through the trees.

'When I set sail from New York,' said Nan, turning to Guy and blowing on her cold fingers, 'I dreamed of falling in love with an Englishman . . . but I never guessed that I should be divorced first.'

Guy took Nan's cold hands in his and rubbed them. 'Do you mind so very much?' he said.

'Oh no, not at all. I didn't mean that . . . I just meant how strangely things turn out . . . how they never happen the way you expect.'

Guy smiled and tucked Nan's hands into the pocket of his coat. She leaned her head against his shoulder and closed her eyes. Nan's fingers, warmed once more, felt a parcel, or a packet, in the depths of Guy's pocket. Nan pulled the packet from his pocket. 'What's this?' she said.

Guy was momentarily confused, and then he remembered. 'Oh goodness Nan,' he said, shocked that he should have forgotten, 'it arrived for you this morning and in the rush to leave I put it in my pocket and forgot all about it.'

Nan turned the packet over. 'This is Val's handwriting,' she said and she tore at the outer wrapping of the packet, suddenly apprehensive, until she saw that she held a familiar black notebook in her hand. She pressed it to her bosom. 'Oh Guy,' she said, her eyes shining, 'this was Val's most trea-sured possession,' and then, seeing Guy's troubled expression, she said, 'Has anything happened to her?'

Guy rapped on the carriage wall and the carriage stopped. 'Oh Guy,' said Nan desperately, 'what is it? What's happened to Val?'

'It's my father,' said Guy, unable to stop himself. 'He has bro-ken their engagement.'

'– Oh, no,' broke from Nan, 'oh no no no,' and her eyes filled with tears. She looked up at Guy. 'Why didn't you tell me?'

'Because I knew that, somehow, she would tell you herself, and I thought it better to come from her.'

Nan gripped the black notebook and she felt something pressing against her palm. She opened the notebook and she saw a letter addressed simply to 'Nan St George'. Nan handed the open notebook and the letter to Guy.

'You open it,' she said disconsolately, 'I can't bear to.'

Guy put the black notebook on his knee, open at the page, and picked up the letter. 'Are you sure you want me to read it?' he said and when Nan merely nodded, he opened the let-ter and began to read.

'My dearest Nan,

By the time you read this you will, I believe, be on your way to South Africa, but I could not bear that you should leave without a word from me. The right time came and the right words have been spoken and I wish you and Guy every hap-piness . . . the happiness that I believe you truly deserve, because it is a happiness born of difficulty and sacrifice.

'I shall have left these shores by the time you read this. I shall go to Italy for a time, until those concerned have had time to forget and, perhaps, to forgive.

'Sir Helmsley saw fit to break our engagement and I suppose,' Guy faltered, 'I suppose, by his lights, he did the right thing. He desperately needed someone upon whom to vent his fury for what he saw as Guy's unforgivable behaviour . . . and I was that someone. No doubt it is for the best. I should always have had a quarrel with him over the two of you.'

Guy turned the page. 'I send you Blake's Notebook which, as you know, Dante Gabriel gave to me. Treasure it Nan, as I have treasured it, for it is full of wisdom.' Guy looked up and saw the tears silently and freely flowing down Nan's cheeks. She did nothing to stop them. He continued, 'You are wise to leave these islands . . . England is no friend to passion, particularly when it bursts forth and overthrows her deeply entrenched traditions. You shall live and breathe more freely away from her constraints.'

Guy had almost reached the end of Miss Testvalley's letter. He put his arm about Nan's shoulders before reading the final words. 'I shall never forget you Nan St George,' he read, 'and I shall think of you often. I salute you both and I send you both my love, Laura.'

'Oh Val,' groaned Nan, 'what have you suffered . . . because of us?' Guy drew Nan to him and as he did so the notebook slipped from his knee. Nan caught it and her fingers held the page.

'Oh look,' said Nan, 'look where she put her letter. She chose this page on purpose, I know she did. She often read this to me. It was her very favourite.' Nan held the notebook up for Guy and he read:

*He who binds himself to a joy*
*Does the winged life destroy;*
*But he who kisses the joy as it flies*
*Lives in eternity's sun rise.*

Nan wiped at her tears with the back of her hand and they

sat for a long time in silence, and then Guy folded the letter and Nan slipped it back inside the black notebook. As she closed the notebook something caught her eye – a flash of bright colour. Between the back cover and the end pages was a bright red pressed flower, and Nan was suddenly transported to a hotel where a border bloomed with red geraniums and white mignonette. She closed her eyes and she saw herself gather a handful of the bright flowers and run with them to the kitchens where she requested a vase and some water and, ignoring the servant's offer to put the flowers in the lady's room herself, she ran up the stairs. She entered a bare narrow room and she placed the posy on her new governess's chest of drawers and then, breathless and excited, she flew from the room.

Nan closed the notebook and put it carefully on the seat beside her. She turned to Guy. 'What kind of life will she have now?' she said. 'What kind of life will she lead?' Guy opened the carriage door and they stepped out into the bright winter's day. 'I think she will do well enough in Italy,' said Guy, 'after all she is Italian, and the Italians are quite different from the English.'

Nan gripped Guy's arm. 'I shall write to her,' she said, 'just as soon as I can discover where she is. I shall tell her that she shall always be the most welcome guest in our house . . . wherever we are. Oh Guy,' said Nan, 'if only she was still in England I should insist we return, this minute, to fetch her . . . to take her away from all those disapproving faces.'

'She has already taken herself from them,' said Guy, and he gathered Nan into his arms and kissed her and they stood for a long time, lost in each other and oblivious to the world.

Miss Laura Testvalley and Miss Jacky March sat by Miss March's tiny hearth in the heart of Mayfair. Miss Testvalley

coaxed the fire to life and then she turned to Miss March.
'Every decent family in the land now knows me as the governess who facilitates elopements, don't they?' she said. Miss
March smiled her nervous little smile and her small hands
fluttered above her bosom.

'Not quite the danger I had anticipated for you Laura,' she
said. 'When I christened our girls "The Buccaneers" I didn't
imagine piracy on quite such a scale.'

Laura Testvalley smiled at Miss March. 'Nor I, Jacky,' she
said. 'Nor I.'

Laura Testvalley walked to the window and then she
turned back to Miss March. 'Thank you for taking me in,
Jacky,' she said. 'I shan't embarrass you by staying on.'

'What shall you do, my dear?' said Miss March. 'Shall you
go to Italy?'

'No,' said Miss Testvalley, 'I shall remain here. I shall not
give anyone the satisfaction of banishing me. And as for
what I shall do . . . I have always found something. I have
supported myself – and others – since I was seventeen, and I
shall continue to do so.' Laura turned her head quickly away
from Miss March who made an involuntary movement
towards her, but Laura was soon composed once more. 'And I
have managed without love – that kind of love – for forty
years. I shall manage another forty on the same terms,' she
said. 'But oh Jacky, when I realized that Nan and Guy had
run away together, I could have shouted aloud.' Laura
Testvalley pressed the back of her hand to her mouth and her
black eyes shone like torches.

Miss March stood beside Miss Testvalley and looked at
her. 'But I shall survive,' said Laura Testvalley, tilting her
head backwards, 'We Testavaglias have always been sur-
vivors.'

NAN and Guy stood on the crest of a hill. The sea glinted
below them in the winter sunlight and the wind tugged and

pulled at their travelling clothes. They turned and stood looking back at the frosty countryside of their beloved England and then Guy took Nan's hand. Slowly, looking about them as if to stamp each image firmly upon their minds forever, Guy Thwarte and Nan St George walked back to their carriage.

# EDITH WHARTON'S SYNOPSIS FOR *THE BUCCANEERS*

THIS novel deals with the adventures of three American families with beautiful daughters who attempt the London social adventure in the 'seventies – the first time the social invasion had ever been tried in England on such a scale.

The three mothers – Mrs St George, Mrs Elmsworth, and Mrs Closson – have all made an attempt to launch their daughters in New York, where their husbands are in business, but have no social standing (the families, all of very ordinary origin, being from the south-west, or from the northern part of the state of New York). The New York experiment is only partly successful, for though the girls attract attention by their beauty they are viewed distrustfully by the New York hostesses whose verdict counts, their origin being hazy and their appearance what was then called 'loud'. So, though admired at Saratoga, Long Branch and the White Sulphur Springs, they fail at Newport and in New York, and the young men flirt with them but do not offer marriage.

Mrs St George has a governess for her youngest daughter, Nan, who is not yet out. She knows that governesses are fashionable, and is determined that Nan shall have the same advantages as the daughters of the New York aristocracy, for she suspects that her daughter Virginia's lack of success, and the failure of Lizzy and Mabel Elmsworth, may have been due to lack of social training. Mrs St George therefore engages a governess who has been in the best houses in New York and

London, and a highly competent middle-aged woman named Laura Testvalley (she is of Italian origin – the name is corrupted from Testavaglia) arrives in the family. Laura Testvalley has been in several aristocratic families in England, but after a run of bad luck has come to the States on account of the great demand for superior 'finishing' governesses, and the higher salaries offered. Miss Testvalley is an adventuress, but a great-souled one. She has been a year with the fashionable Mrs Parmore of New York, who belongs to one of the oldest Knickerbocker families, but she finds the place dull, and is anxious for higher pay and a more lavish household. She recognizes the immense social gifts of the St George girls, and becomes in particular passionately attached to Nan.

She says to Mrs St George: 'Why try Newport again? Go straight to England first, and come back to America with the prestige of a brilliant London season.'

Mrs St George is dazzled, and persuades her husband to let her go. The Closson and Elmsworth girls are friends of the oldest St George girl, and they too persuade their parents to let them try London.

The three families embark together on the adventure, and though furiously jealous of each other, are clever enough to see the advantage of backing each other up; and Miss Testvalley leads them all like a general.

In each particular family the sense of solidarity is of course even stronger than it is between members of the group, and as soon as Virginia St George has made a brilliant English marriage she devotes all her energies to finding a husband for Nan.

But Nan rebels – or at least is not content with the prizes offered. She is, or thinks she is, as ambitious as the others, but it is for more interesting reasons; intellectual, political and artistic. She is the least beautiful but by far the most brilliant and seductive of them all; and to the amazement of the others (and adroitly steered by Miss Testvalley) she suddenly captures the greatest match in England, the young Duke of Tintagel.

But though she is dazzled for the moment, her heart is not satisfied. The Duke is kindly but dull and arrogant, and the man she really loves is young Guy Thwarte, a poor officer in the Guards, the son of Sir Helmsley Thwarte, whose old and wonderfully beautiful place in Gloucestershire, Honourslove, is the scene of a part of the story.

Sir Helmsley Thwarte, the widowed father of Guy, a clever, broken-down and bitter old worldling, is captivated by Miss Testvalley, and wants to marry her; but meanwhile the young Duchess of Tintagel has suddenly decided to leave her husband and go off with Guy, and it turns out that Laura Testvalley, moved by the youth and passion of the lovers, and disgusted by the mediocre Duke of Tintagel, has secretly lent a hand in the planning of the elopement, the scandal of which is to ring through England for years.

Sir Helmsley Thwarte discovers what is going on, and is so furious at his only son's being involved in such an adventure that, suspecting Miss Testvalley's complicity, he breaks with her, and the great old adventuress, seeing love, deep and abiding love, triumph for the first time in her career, helps Nan to join her lover, who has been ordered to South Africa, and then goes back alone to old age and poverty.

The Elmsworth and Closson adventures will be interwoven with Nan's, and the setting will be aristocratic London in the season, and life in the great English country-houses as they were sixty years ago.

Edith Wharton (née Newbold Jones) was born in New York in 1862 into a wealthy and well-established family. She was educated at home by governesses but spent a significant part of her childhood travelling with her parents in Europe. She lived in New York as a teenager and it was there that she made her début into society and met and married her husband, the Bostonian, Edward Wharton. The marriage, however, was not happy and ended in divorce in 1913 by which time Edith Wharton had established a permanent residence in France.

Although writing was always an important part of Edith Wharton's life and she wrote her first novel, *Fast and Loose*, when she was fourteen, she did not publish a novel until she was forty. Her first, *The Valley of Decision*, a historical romance set in eighteenth century Italy, came out in 1902, and she then went on to produce more than forty volumes of short stories, novels, travel writing, autobiography and criticism. Amongst her best-known works are *The House of Mirth* (1905), *Ethan Frome* (1911), *The Custom of the Country* (1913) and *The Age of Innocence* (1920). Wharton was made a Fellow of the American Academy of Letters in 1930 and received the Pulitzer Prize for fiction for *The Age of Innocence*.

Edith Wharton was very cosmopolitan; she travelled widely and had many friends who were influential in art and letters at the turn of the century. She was proficient in French, German and Italian and wrote books about France, Italy and Morocco. She lived in Paris throughout the First World War and made an enormous contribution to the war effort, fund raising, organizing hostels, providing jobs and clothing for refugees. She was made a Chevalier of the Legion of Honour by the French government in recognition of her great work.

Edith Wharton was born a wealthy woman and her earnings from her fiction, including the sale of film rights, ensured that she remained one. She was successful with the critics as well as with the reading public and her reputation today stands as high as in her lifetime. She died in 1937 in France and is buried at Versailles.